She came from the front of the hut, dressed in a white robe fringed in gold, a torque of silver and gold around her slender throat, an enameled brooch set with coral falling to her bosom. Iona had entered.

"There is need for counsel," she said quietly, her eyes brittle, her mouth set. "We are racing toward defeat."

"The Iceni will not be defeated!" Arawn shouted loudly, drawing a cheer from the assemblage.

"That is rhetoric, Arawn," Iona said above the uproar. "It is our hope, our desire, our sworn oath that we not be defeated! Yet slogans will not disperse the Romans. They will drive us into the sea."

She hesitated a moment, taking a slow, deep breath. "There will be no more single combat!"

"Iona!" Dagda stood furiously. "It is our way, it has always brought us victory. Iona, you are about to destroy us."

"Dagda," she answered in a tone the general had never heard before from this girl, "I am your queen, and I am to be addressed as such. You are my general, and as such it is your place to obey. I will be called Boudicca; my orders will not be gainsaid."

Boudicca
Elizabeth Wolfe

POPHAM PRESS

ace books
A Division of Charter Communications Inc.
A GROSSET & DUNLAP COMPANY
51 Madison Avenue
New York, New York 10010

BOUDICCA

Copyright © 1980 by Elizabeth Wolfe

All rights reserved. No part of this book may be reproduced in any form or by any means, except for the inclusion of brief quotations in a review, without permission in writing from the publisher.

All characters in this book are fictitious. Any resemblance to actual persons, living or dead, is purely coincidental.

A Popham Press Book

First Printing: October 1980

Published simultaneously in Canada

2 4 6 8 0 9 7 5 3 1
Manufactured in the United States of America

Boudicca

In the year 60 A.D., Roman London was razed by the last Celtic queen, a woman named Boudicca.

This novel is a reconstruction of her life, a testament to a lost people—the Celts.

Chapter One

The sun flashed in the alder wood. The quick-running rill weaving through the deep forest caught the smooth gray stones of the streambed and misted into the air, painting shifting, prismatic patterns. The shadows crossed and recrossed among the tangle of brambles along the stream as the last hours of sunlight were devoured by the rush of coming dusk. To the south the death roar sounded.

Yet Iona did not hear it. Tawny, long of limb, her flesh smoothed and tempered by the hunts of fifteen summers, she finished her bathing. The coolness of the air raised goosebumps on her flesh; the single drop of water at the base of her throat caught an errant ray of late sunlight and was transformed momentarily into a sparkling, chatoyant jewel. Iona brushed it away as she stepped from the icy stream.

Thramane stood at the water's edge, holding Iona's cloak, and the girl stepped into it, shivering. Thramane rubbed her shoulders through the cloak, then wiped back the girl's dark hair tenderly.

"We should hurry back," Iona's companion said.

"For what? It makes no difference to me," Iona answered haughtily. Thramane turned Iona by the shoulders until they were facing each other.

"Not even Breyton?"

"No," Iona replied, tossing her head. "Not Breyton. Nor Leun nor Arawn. It is their sport—to me it does not matter."

Thramane's mouth tightened, but the older woman did not respond. Together they walked from the forest, pennants of crimson streaking the skies to the west across the grassy plain. Low gray clouds had massed along the horizon. Southward-swarming ducks cut dark silhouettes.

Not yet, Thramane thought, as they walked slowly homeward through golden dusk. *It does not yet concern you, Iona. Your woman's flesh belies a child's heart.*

Yet no Celt can live unconcerned with war, untouched by blood. The fate of the Iceni, all Celtic peoples, was written in blood long ago. And there is no escaping such a heritage.

It was the hour before nightfall that the Iceni army finally came upon the Coritani, preparing a night camp in a shadowed glade beyond the Killdeer Stream.

Athair, massive chest rising and falling with the anticipation of battle, sat his gray horse, steady blue eyes watching the enemy camp.

"There are the ox thieves," Barra grunted. Barra's brutal eyes closed slightly in dark pleasure.

Athair's gaze flickered to his lieutenant, but he did not answer him. Instead he turned to the giant,

Throg, who had stepped from his horse and stood in the slight breeze stroking his beard.

"Take the foot soldiers, Throg," Athair commanded. Throg nodded, leaping into the saddle with amazing agility for a man of his enormous bulk. Silently he slipped away to the men who waited in the deep shadows of the woods.

The sun faded rapidly in the western skies, long, jagged arrows of crimson spilling out on the sun-silvered clouds. Athair's hand went slowly up in signal.

"It's that coward, Kowlter. They'll not take Iceni cattle again," Barra grumbled. He fixed his shield in place and unsheathed his long, slightly curved sword. A fine weapon, rich with blood tradition, it had been forged by a magic smith from across the wide river.

King Athair rode slowly, back erect. The Coritani had not seen them yet. From behind them they could hear the sound of rushing horses. Athair turned in his horse's saddle, a smile forming: the young lions—Breyton and Arawn—charging together down the long, grassy slope, not wanting to miss a moment of it.

Breyton's long blond hair streamed out behind him as the horses of the two Iceni, stride for stride, drove toward the advance party.

As they reached their king's side, the warning cry was raised in the Coritani camp. Athair touched his heels to the gray horse, startling it into a dead run, a savage cry of exultation rising to his lips.

Suddenly they were in the enemy's camp, the horses scattering the campfire, utensils, Coritani soldiers everywhere.

Breyton, swinging his sword in wide loops,

slashed a makeshift shelter to pieces, thatch flying as three Coritani burst naked, weaponless from the hut.

"Come back!" Breyton circled his horse, shouting over his shoulder. "Gather your weapons! Let me see the color of Coritani blood!"

He leaped from his horse then, his naked body glistening in the firelight, his hair in mad profusion, sword gleaming in his strong hand. Breyton threw back his head and laughed, his teeth flashing as an angered Coritani snatched up his sword and shield and rushed toward the young Iceni.

They locked into naked battle, the Coritani swinging his sword with violent hatred. Breyton parried, laughed again and cut with his own sword, drawing blood from his adversary's shoulder.

Athair had not dismounted. He cut about him with his sword like an avenging god. Barra had found two men among the rocks and he was all over them, his blue and gold cloak swirling around his shoulders. To the south there was a sudden, unearthly roar. Throg had crossed the stream with his foot soldiers and engaged the main party of the Coritani.

Breyton saw it all from the corners of his eyes, heard the grunting of the dark, powerful man he faced across his sword, saw a lone horse running free, its master dragging on the ground.

His senses were filled with all of the activity—the deepening shadows, scattered embers from the fire. Yet he fought as if there were nothing in all of the world for him but this dark, skilled Coritani Celt he faced.

The man's sword whirred past his ear, but Breyton was able to step aside, then forward and slash downward with his own sword, throwing the weight of his massive shoulders behind it. There was a muted sound, a split instant when time seemed to freeze into a bloody tapestry; then the Coritani's head rolled free of his body and the man slumped to the dead earth.

Athair was still on his horse, lashing out with his blade. An Iceni, lance protruding from his hip, staggered past, eyes empty. Hands were laid on Athair's bridle. One he severed.

In the midst of a crowd of enemy Coritani, each wanting the head of the Iceni king, Athair felt the press of their bodies, the grunts, the slapping together of flesh, the cries of pain.

Then he saw Breyton. Still laughing, the young lion strode toward his king, striking left and right until the Coritani broke and ran.

The first of Throg's men had broken into the camp. Barra, bloodsoaked, cursing the world, rumbled down from the rocky hill. Athair sat breathing heavily, touching the wound on his thigh gingerly. Breyton rested on his sword, his naked body streaked with sweat and dust.

Arawn, the lover of war, rode through the deserted camp at a mad pace, three heads dangling from his horse's neck. With a whoop he leaped from his horse, embracing Breyton.

"The cowards," Arawn shouted, still holding an arm around Breyton's shoulder. "They'll not be back."

"The cattle?" Athair asked Barra who was still cursing.

"Over the knoll, my king," the dark-eyed general answered.

Throg lumbered up to where they waited. The

giant was not smiling, yet he seldom did. A melancholy man, Throg allowed the others to express their common satisfaction with the result of the battle.

"We found them at the river," Throg reported. "Ten men dead. Two of ours."

Athair nodded thoughtfully. The shadows had bled into one another, the sky retaining only the barest fragments of color and diffused light. A night hawk called in the deep forest.

"And Kowlter? Did anyone see the great Coritani prince?" Athair asked with black sarcasm.

"He got away, the coward," Barra reported. "Dagda went after him with six men. They'll not find him now," he added, peering into the darkening sky. "The Coritani know too well how to hide."

"There will be another time," Athair said. "Another battle. Wait a while for Dagda; perhaps the gods are with him."

But Kowlter was not to be found. It was full dark before the Iceni warriors reached Viron—the great fortified home of the tribe. A wooden stockade a mile in circumference rested at the apex of an astounding series of earthworks and labyrinths built up over the centuries of conflict by the Iceni Celts.

Fires burned brightly on top of the dark hill as Athair triumphantly led his warriors through the high gates of Viron.

A cheer, which had been raised the moment Athair was sighted, rose to a blood-thrilling chorus of acclaim. Men were hugged, welcomed, the gory trophies admired.

Arawn's spindly-legged younger brother, Tylch,

ran off joyously with the head of the Coritani, Othgar. He climbed to the roof of Breyton's hut and impaled the bloody relic on a sharpened stake, waving his hands and jumping up and down until he fell from the roof to an accompanying concert of laughter.

Athair stepped down heavily from his horse, throwing off his stained cloak and pants. Lania stepped slowly to him, her eyes damp.

"What is it, my queen?" Athair bellowed. "Are you not happy to see me return?" He grabbed her in his massive arms and together they walked off, Athair commanding over his shoulder: "Slaughter a boar, Nertomorus!"

Breyton slid from his horse's back, still feeling the savage joy in his breast, aware of the enemy's blood drying on his body, on his horse's neck. Then his eyes caught the slender form of Iona in the shadows near the spring. He raised a hand.

"Iona!"

He stepped toward her, his chest swollen with pride, his eyes glittering with the residual electricity of battle. But the girl was gone. Athair's daughter had simply slipped away, saying nothing, her eyes haughty.

"She's not for you," Arawn said. He laughed as he said it, placing a rough hand on Breyton's shoulder, but Breyton shook it off.

"She's only a girl; she'll learn," Breyton said, almost hopefully.

"It's *me* she'll discover," Arawn joked, but Breyton paid no attention to his friend's jibe, his eyes fixed on the shadows. Then he beamed a smile.

"Or Cymru," Breyton suggested, smiling again.

Cymru was a bitter, crooked little man.

"Or Prasutag—he's womanly enough to please her!"

Breyton smiled yet, but there was no humor in it. "Let's wash, Arawn!" he said, taking his friend's arm. "Then let us share Athair's boar, and drink until we are drowned in good wine."

Together they walked toward the spring, their booming laughter mingling with that of the other Celts, the lowing of the recaptured cattle, the excited chattering of the children.

Away from all the sound, the excitement, Iona wove through the shadows, unnoticed, until she came to that secret place she loved so well. A jumble of white rocks, the largest of which was split by the roots of a gnarled old oak which jutted out against the sky. From there she could see the distant ocean, the ribbon of the moon-glossed river flowing to it. The oak, like twisted wrought iron screened the white, scarred globe of the moon.

An owl perched in the oak, ruffling then settling its feathers, apparently unaware of Iona. The wind was chilly now, the evening growing damp. She shivered and leaned her forehead against the still warm boulder. The empty land took on a deep green hue before the moon; the river glittered with a silver sheen. And beyond it all—the sea.

What serpentine behemoths slept beneath it or gnawed at the bones of dead ships she did not know. Nor did she know anything of those distant lands with odd sounding names which the Druid, Thrueldan, alone of all the Celts could recount.

What drove her thoughts to the sea? The skies. Unhappy with the ways of her people she found solace in deep thought, yet she understood little.

She did not know what lay beyond Viron. Only that there was something. . . . But what?

The stars massed, whitening the skies beyond time. There, too, being found existence. There, too, worlds caught fire, grew, collided in fiery explosions; worlds in collision like thought colliding against thought—so rapidly occurring that it had no meaning through the vastness, the timelessness of things.

All of it, Iona concluded, was without meaning, yet rife with possibilities, with problems to be overcome, with puzzles to be answered as the naked human being alone confronted her own deep legacy, her vast unforeseeable future down the long road. A road which might lead to paths beyond the stars, beyond thought as mankind grew. If they grew.

As one hopes each infant will grow to be a mighty warrior, comely maiden, thoughtful Druid, one wishes for the people, for all of humanity an easy birth, a rapid growing, strong limbs and keen vision, a sense of destiny beyond what has been the destiny of her fathers', her mothers' disappointments.

One wishes, catching glimmerings of knowledge beyond, of destinies beyond time, of truths sublime and distant, not ours to know.

The wheel turns, time inverts upon itself, knowledge flares up and is decimated by its own fragile offspring. People struggle for goals of paramount importance, work lives away, shout to the heavens of this and that belief, truth, object only to find at a single lost deathbed moment . . . that it was not absolute at all, but a bastard remnant of other lives, other suffocated dreams.

Yet roads to wisdom must be open somewhere. Could Thrueldan open them to her?

Somewhere must be ears which heard, eyes which saw beyond the day's light. How else could a great people like the Iceni have risen above those savages Thrueldan spoke of: those people who dressed in skins, ate their own dead, and did not know of fire?

Inspiration must come at times, knowledge. Yet where did it arise? Surely there was a source beyond man's own thoughts.

Surely a purpose, a reason beyond birthing, mating, eating and passing on to forgetful blackness.

Yet of these things Thrueldan would not speak, and none of the others knew what she meant when she broached the subject. They were content with their measure of mead, with beef in their bellies, furs warming them when they slept, with their warring.

So perhaps she was wrong. Perhaps it was only a vague, undirected longing, some womanly seed sprouting mournful buds, hopeless dark flowers within her breast.

But it did not seem so as she watched the never ending stream of silver lights against the dark skies, as the sequence of life flowed over, around and through her very soul. There seemed to be . . . something.

"I want to know it," she whispered. "I want to."

Yet there was no response from the limitless fields of stars, from the immense and quite black caverns of thought. Only ghostly enticements, only secret longing.

Athair was washed and scented with perfumed

oil. He reclined on his massive pile of skins as Lania worked on his wound. Tender woman—his eyes shone with quiet pride as she doctored him, her lips pursed seriously, her fingers deftly attending the lance wound. How many of these had she seen? And some which should have taken his life.

"The boar is roasted," Athair said, sniffing the air with relish.

"It is." Lania stood and bowed to her husband. Outside, the pit roared as the warriors preparing the feast removed the massive boar from the fire. "Keep a firm hand on them this evening, Athair," Lania advised.

"Too firm a hand cannot rule," Athair said, rising to test the leg which had grown stiff. "It was a fine battle," he said reflectively, watching the fire from the doorway, the high-spirited warriors surrounding the pit. "In other times you might have enjoyed entering the fray yourself, Lania. You were a fighter, wife . . . you still are," he added with a faint smile.

"Not I," Lania replied. "For my tribe, for my child I would fight," she said, turning her dark eyes to Athair, "as Celtic women have always fought beside their men. But not for the sport, my king. Not for the sport."

"It is no sport when my cattle are stolen," Athair said, his booming voice more powerful than he had intended. "They would take the food from our stomachs! And I will always fight. While I am able. When I am no longer able, bury me standing with my lance in my hand so that my spirit may continue to war against the enemies of the Iceni."

Athair swept his yellow robe around his shoulders and stood for a moment facing the alcove in which he kept the skulls of his dead adversaries. "These—they would not have quit until the Iceni were ruined. Yet they knew always that Athair would fight. They will not come against my people lightly. This I have sworn to; this a king is obligated to."

He picked up one of the relics, an old skull with a cleft in it. He fingered it for a moment before replacing it. Iona had come in and Athair turned to face her.

"Breyton was very bold today, Iona," Athair said.

"Yes."

"He saved my life, Iona."

Iona could only nod her head. The powerful man before her, beard combed, imperious in manner, seemed a god to her as he had since childhood. A benevolent yet stern god to be obeyed and feared. How many times had he appeared at the threshold, bloodstained, exultant, the wind twisting his lion's mane of hair? Yet she was sure he was quite immortal.

"Can you say nothing?" Athair asked.

"I am happy Breyton was bold. If you wished it."

"And what do you wish of a man?" Athair asked, studying the dark-haired girl before him. She held her hands before her, framing an answer.

"You would not wish to hear it, Father."

"And why not?" he demanded.

"Because I would not wish him to be a warrior."

Athair's face wrinkled into displeasure. He slapped his hands on his thighs angrily. "You get it from your mother," he said, disgust tinting his words. "You do not like our warring! Do you not consider that the Coritani want only our blood? My skull? Do you think Kowlter would treat you, Lania, or our daughter with respect?"

"I did not mean . . ." Iona began, but her father silenced her with an impatient gesture.

"It is in strength that we survive. Weakness would be the death of our people. That is the way the world is hewn."

When the women did not answer as Athair's eyes searched their faces, he made a deep disparaging noise and swept out into the night.

"He is right," Lania sighed as the two women were left alone. "Come to me, girl. Let me look at you."

Iona stood before her mother, head bowed slightly, dark eyes downcast, fine breasts and hips showing through the thin material of her cloak, strong legs, long and straight, slightly full lips petulant at the moment but capable of bursting into smiles which cast rainbows.

Lania lifted the girl's chin with her finger. She smiled, saying nothing for a moment. This girl was the product of her life—the reason she had lived, the reason she might go happily into the darker regions when the night trumpets summoned her. She lifted Iona's hand to her lips and kissed it.

"Your father only wants us to share in his triumphs," Lania suggested.

"He wants me to marry Breyton," Iona answered, her eyes sparking.

"Yes, that too." Breyton carried a warrior's blood in his veins. It was natural for Athair to wish a grandson of such a union. The king was devotedly fond of Breyton. He had trained the blond warrior personally in the arts of arms. "Would that be so bad?" the old woman asked softly.

"He calls me with his manhood," Iona admitted. "Savage, proud thing he is. Yet . . . his life will be short. I will live to see his head on an enemy lance. I will live to see my heart torn out by this fever for war we have."

Lania did not reply. She turned busily to her work. She did not want to support the girl in this. Athair should not be opposed in a matter of marriage. Yet she understood. She understood well.

Lania picked up the bloody dressing she had removed from Athair's leg and threw it into the fire where it hissed for a moment, the flames flaring briefly before the fire settled to a warm golden glow.

Athair brushed past Dwan Karnash as he strode through the cool evening toward the warriors' hut where the celebration had already begun. The voluptuous young woman stepped aside for her king, her lips forming a questioning smile.

"Dwan Karnash," Athair nodded. "If you are looking for Breyton, he is inside," the king told her.

"Then send him out," the blond girl laughed. "I wish to salute our victory as well."

Athair grinned despite himself. If Iona was not careful, this woman would have Breyton. After all, a man only waits so long for what he wants.

The inside of the house was smoky, filled with men. Athair waved a hand and worked through the throng, answering greetings with a laugh, a shake of the hand, a jibe. He sat at the place of honor reserved for him. A quart of mead in a silver cup was thrust into his hand by the giant, Throg, who sagged beside him, sharing the king's throne of furs.

The warriors reclined on piles of skins, drinking wine and mead indiscriminately, throwing down pints at a draught. Werken, the bard, strummed his lyre in the corner, singing an old song praising King Aegnus.

Barra, wearing a shirt of chain-mail, his hair freshly perfumed and tied back, sat to one side, boasting of his day's work.

"I took three men where no other could have scored one kill," he said loudly, his speech slightly slurred. He drank deeply again from his wine cup, purple trickling from the corners of his bearded mouth. "I have their heads to prove it!" he shouted in answer to a chorus of derision. Reaching behind him he grasped a decapitated head which he threw into the center of the circle of warriors.

"And that was Thyragarth," Barra went on. "Tell me it is not! The mightiest of all the Coritani," he belched.

"Among their youth, yes," Throg shouted back.

Athair laughed heartily, slapping the giant on the shoulder. Barra scowled and was ready to respond when Arawn stood.

"You may as well have stayed home, Barra," the young man boasted. "All of you—you have accomplished no deeds to match my own." The young lion tilted back his head and drank a massive quantity of mead as he circled the room, bare chest catching the firelight. "I killed half of them myself. When I am at the point of attack, the enemy must break and run!"

"Yes," old Dagda said, scowling. "It is your bathing habits which repel them."

Arawn's answer could not be heard above the laughter. Breyton came forward, leaping to the center of the room. He wore a scarlet cloak around his shoulders, scarlet and blue trousers, a golden torque around his throat. This sacred collar was of gold, half an inch in diameter, ending in two lion heads with emerald eyes.

"Yet I alone carried the battle to them," Breyton boasted, a half-mocking smile on his lips. "I alone rode among them . . ."

"Before they had their trousers on or their swords in their hands," Barra said sullenly. "And for such courage you claim the hero's portion of the boar, I imagine."

"Athair will allow him the haunch," Dagda said. He was growing methodically drunk. Athair's eyes flashed. For all of the boasting, some of it leading to knives being drawn, and now and then to death, the king was not fair game. Still Dagda went on. "After all—Athair should offer you the loin . . ."

"Be quiet, Dagda," Throg said in throaty warning.

"Ah!" Dagda waved a hand and settled back onto his skins. Athair still glowered at his general. The man drank too much.

"Give to Breyton your daughter, my king," Arawn suggested, "and to Arawn—who truly deserves it—the haunch of boar. But then who is the more honored?" Arawn laughed and took a long drink. "Who the more fortunate?"

"You, Arawn," Nertomorus said. The gray-haired man hoisted a glass to Breyton. "Iona will own you, my boy."

"To be so owned . . ." Breyton said, touching his heart. He sighed and feigned a faint, falling onto a pile of skins, spilling Nertomorus's wine. Hands reached out and punched him in jest.

What Nertomorus had said was true enough. Among the Celts the wife ruled the household if her possessions were greater than her husband's. Yet Breyton was unconcerned with the letter of the law. He was confident in his physical self, confident that Iona could be mastered in that way.

"But I do not joke," Dagda said sourly. He was wobbly on his feet. "Why does this young hulk receive the hero's portion? What is he but muscle and stupid effort, young loins? Who thinks for him?"

Breyton, who had been on the floor, still joking, froze.

His eyes locked with Dagda's. He came to his feet. Barra was beside Dagda, his closest friend, yet now he stepped back, eyes flickering from Dagda to Breyton, to Athair whose face showed nothing.

"What do you mean, Dagda?" Breyton demanded.

"Mean? I mean you are stupid!" Dagda shouted, wine again spilling from his mouth.

Breyton tensed, his hand reflexively going to his knife. No man made a move to interfere. They simply watched, even Athair.

Breyton stepped closer to Dagda who stood twitching, his black beard wet with wine, his own knife under his hand. Astonishingly, Breyton smiled.

"You are correct, my general," Breyton said mildly, blue eyes twinkling. "I am but a stupid soldier, you a clever general. Just look who you have chosen to lead, and who I have chosen to follow."

Dagda blinked dully once and then the house burst into laughter. Breyton shrugged and stepped forward, taking Dagda's hand. Still Dagda did not smile. Sullenly he sat beside Barra, whispering a word into his ear.

"Now!" Athair said, rising heavily on his wounded leg. "The boar is roasted. Let us eat before liquor carries us away."

The king walked to the pit and unsheathed his own knife, removing the hero's portion—the right haunch, which he presented solemnly to Barra. In surprise the general took it and nodded.

"You were the pride of the Iceni this day, Barra. And the scourge of the Coritani. Death to all our enemies!" Athair bellowed.

"Death to those who would come against us," Throg echoed, standing to his full height of six and a half feet. "And," he added in a lowered voice, "praise to a wise king."

The boar was sliced and eaten on knife point, washed down with even greater quantities of mead and wine. Nertomorus already slept in the corner, his gray chin against his chest.

"And these new invaders, Athair?" Arawn asked, sitting next to his chief, arms around his legs.

"These . . . Roman men?"

"Yes. It is said they have come to enslave us. I hear from a man of the Atrebates that they have burned their encampments, taken their women."

"They will die as well," Athair said, wiping his beard with the back of his hand. "Romans—who are they? What are they? They are not even Celts! Let them fight with the cowardly Atrebates. I pledge them blood if they come against our people!"

* * *

Thrueldan, the Druid, sat in the shadow of the ceremonial hut, peering at the stars, arms wrapped around his knobby knees. At his bare feet rested a small golden boar's head with a circle inscribed on it. A semicircle of sticks was thrust into the earth at some distance.

"Thrueldan?"

Iona had slipped up beside him. The night was clear, yet damp. The sounds of roaring laughter rolled through the camp of the Iceni coming from the warriors' house. An owl silhouetted itself briefly against the silver moon, wings beating in fluid motion.

"Iona." Thrueldan drew a line in the dirt from the sticks to his boar's head, then nodded with obscure satisfaction. "Nearly Samhain," Thrueldan said in his strange, raspy voice. "Two weeks."

"Two weeks until Samhain. It hardly seems possible." The cattle would have to be driven home then, the preparations made to appease the dead spirits who wander the earth on that mysterious first evening of winter. A chicken, Iona knew, would be killed in each household, the blood sprinkled on the four corners of the huts, keeping the spirits away.

How did Thrueldan know the time to celebrate feasts, Iona wondered? With his sticks and circles, gazing at the stars, catching the rays of the first winter sun.

Thrueldan collected his sticks and rose, stretching his back. "Two weeks."

"You know much, Thrueldan," Iona said as they walked together toward the priest's house. "Tell me, do you know anything of the Romans?"

"Them!" Thrueldan spat on the earth in contempt. "Too much." He opened the door to his musty hut and went in.

"You have been across the waters, haven't you?" Iona asked, following. Thrueldan put his apparatus away and lit a torch, the eerie glow flickering on the rounded walls, catching the skulls he kept there, some of them with mysterious markings painted on them.

"I have. Many times I have traveled the sea. To the great conclaves of Druids held in Chartres, in the land of the Carnute Gauls."

"Where is that?" Iona asked, seating herself.

"Over the sea," Thrueldan smiled. He sat next to his princess, pouring a small quantity of wine into a skull which was set in beaten gold. "Are you now interested in such things, Iona? Is it time for your education to begin in earnest?"

"Yes, Thrueldan," she said excitedly, her eyes glowing in the firelight. "It is time that I knew more of the world than our camps and our woods, our fields. I have been gazing at the stars, Thrueldan," she went on in a lowered, secretive voice, "asking them things which they do not answer."

"What does Athair say to this?" Thrueldan inquired, raising an eyebrow as he tipped his ivory and gold cup.

"I haven't spoken to my father yet," she admitted. "He still believes I should wage battle, mate, and bear a son."

"I will speak to him," Thrueldan promised. His crooked face watched the girl fondly. "If you believe it is time, then it is. Education must be sought after; it must be the time for it. As there is a time for all things according to the stars." Thrueldan nodded to himself, finishing his drink.

In the odd lighting of the room it almost seemed that the skull-cup leered at Iona. She shivered once, shortly.

"Just now your father is absorbed by things of the sun, Iona. His battles, his races, his struggles to rule. He has forgotten the dark knowledge—softer, more graceful knowledge. When he was a young man . . . well, that doesn't matter now."

"Some day I too will go across the eastern sea," Iona said, not watching the Druid, but the fire which danced in red and gold arabesques.

"Perhaps. But then you would certainly meet the Romans you are curious about. And they are not fond of us, Iona. We are a threat to them and their world."

"But who are they?" she asked, perplexed.

"A southern people. They have come north, called by who knows what demand of their blood. Perhaps, like the Celts, they only love the warring," Thrueldan shrugged.

"They can have no warriors to match Breyton or Arawn," Iona said crisply. "And none who can match me with the javelin!"

"I believe you are right," the Druid said. "Yet there are many of them. Very many. And they have weapons the Celts have no knowledge of. Ways of fighting we do not understand. When they come," Thrueldan said grimly, "it will be very hard. Very hard for our people."

"My father does not believe that!" Iona snapped.

"Oh, but he does," Thrueldan said, his eyes fixing on Iona. "That is why he does not admit it, why he curses them before the warriors. Why he presses for his wishes . . . he knows. He knows."

Outside, the reddening moon was being summoned to its cradle below the forest. The stars glittered through the deep skies; the ground was touched with frost. From the warriors' house roars of riotous celebration still rolled. Iona, arms wrapped around her, walked homeward. Suddenly she noticed the solitary figure near the south gate of the stockade. Curiously, she walked up to the man.

"Prasutag?"

She whispered the question and his head came around. A silent, soft-faced man, Prasutag was apart from the others in many respects. Although he was a feared warrior, he almost never attended the feasts, nor did he boast of his prowess.

"It is Prasutag, Iona," he replied. His eyes gleamed in the starlight. He shrugged as with embarrassment at having her draw nearer.

"You do not join the merrymaking, Prasutag."

He shook his head and sighed, turning a quarter away from Iona.

"Don't you wish to speak to me, Prasutag?" she asked coyly.

"It is not that, Iona," he protested. He ran a hand through his short, curly hair nervously.

"Surely you do not fear Breyton, like some of these others?"

"Fear Breyton?" He turned back to her, genuinely surprised. "No," he went on thoughtfully. "In fact I've never given any thought to fear—of Breyton, of the Coritani. I suppose Breyton could defeat me in a contest of arms—perhaps easily, but I don't fear him. After all, Thrueldan reminds us frequently that life and death are the same. Death the darker side of life. What should I fear?"

"You have the soul of a Druid yourself, Prasutag," Iona said. He was a different sort of man, this shy warrior. Softer? Perhaps. Perhaps only different. She watched him with critical eyes as he strolled away after bidding her good evening.

Inside the warriors' hut someone bellowed a curse. There was a following rumble and Iona turned, walking slowly to her father's house.

As she undressed she hummed a little tune. As she drew the furs over her she pondered a deep symphony. She was awake a while longer, watching the deep, stoic heavens.

Love is a simple thing. A body, a thought, an urge to continue the race's dreams. Yet again longings come which have no biological basis. Wishes to please, to merge with this other in ways unnamed, incredible.

So Breyton came with his unspoken emotions. How could he name them—there were no words he had learned. It appeared to him, in his ignorance, that the way to touch the heart of the problem was to touch Iona with his deepest tool.

Yet he could not know that he had no prayer of reaching her in that way, although she knew and longed for a deeper touching.

A communion. With whom? In what way? To what end?

She had learned no words for it either. It was only a deep, far-reaching, motherly wish to . . . be with . . . someone nameless, faceless, masculine yet tender to the point of femininity; one to whom nothing need be said, who did not have to be touched to be felt.

Hopeless. This simple urge. The urge to love;

how hopeless and pathetic it seemed. Yet pathos could not kill it, nor hopelessness. Nor could wishing fulfill it.

Chapter Two

From the corners of Celtic England the tribes gathered for Samhain. Not only the despised Coritani, but the clever Belgae who were said to have invented enameling and towns; the dark-haired Parisi from the far northlands came as well. The people of Atrebates and those of the Regni, the Cornovii who wore only furs and painted their faces. All bore trade goods and gifts, and rode their finest war horses or racing chariots. The women were in scarlet and yellow and blue cloaks, flowers in their hair, the men in plaid trousers, multi-colored cloaks trimmed with gold, or wearing their finest coats of mail forged by the sorcerer-smith of their tribe.

Boar-headed trumpets blared from the catwalks along the stockade walls of Viron as the representatives of all the Celtic tribes were welcomed and guided through the complex battlements of Viron.

Athair, wearing his gold crown which he generally disdained, smiled with pride as he watched them arrive, being guided through the labyrinths, the fortified earthworks.

"The Coritani know they'll never uproot us from our fortress," he whispered to Nertomorus. "It must be causing Kowlter's blood to surge to see what we have built."

The general smiled in return. Athair's closest friend, Nertomorus had thinning, long hair, a ready wit and hands of iron. It was said Nertomorus could crush a man's throat with the grip of either hand, yet Iona had never seen the man raise a hand in anger.

She took leave of her father and strode happily among the arriving throng. Bloodshed was strictly forbidden at Samhain; even quarreling or excessive boasting could land the offender in a hastily built gaol.

Walking among the gathered peoples, Iona saw enemies of her people, men and women she had been taught to hate. Yet today, on this farewell to summer, no hatred was tolerated.

Kowlter, the despised Coritani chieftain, had kissed Athair's beard and Athair had gripped him tightly by the shoulders as if Kowlter were a lost friend.

A Coritani girl ran past, laughing as she did so, pursued playfully by Leun, the Iceni. That bloodthirsty queen of the Cornovii, Caldera, spoke familiarly with the Belgae king although Iona knew they had met in fierce battle only months earlier.

"We Celts are one," Thrueldan told her. "Despite our wars, our hatreds. We are one people, and it is right that we should mingle from time to time to remember that it is so."

Breyton was sharing a skin of wine with Arawn

and a stranger. He glanced up, wiped his beard and called to Iona, but she did not answer. Arawn nudged the stranger, a Belgae, and he too looked up as Iona walked swiftly away, Arawn's laughter burning her ears.

Already a horse race had been arranged for a small prize, and four riders, two of them women, waited at a starting rope while a final wager was placed before they thundered away to a cacophony of shrieks, curses and laughter. The dust billowed into the clear air and heads turned to watch the riders streak past, the dark-haired girl on the bay stallion momentarily in the lead.

The youth played at curling. Arawn's brother, Tylch, turned to wave to Iona and was tripped and dumped to the earth, rising with a sheepish smile.

Iona laughed, waved and walked on. There was excitement everywhere, and goods of all descriptions—jewelry, cloth from across the sea, delicately engraved bronze mirrors, enameled Belgae goods.

There were statues of the gods and goddesses: Epona riding a horse in furious chase, her hair streaming behind her; several golden statues to Cernunnos and Belenos. There were straw figures meant to be burned in offering to Sequana as the supplicant prayed for bodily health.

Above it all was the roar of contest, the songs of minstrels, the ringing heroic tales of storytellers perched on scaffoldings hypnotizing their audiences.

Oxen were roasting on slowly turning spits; wine was being poured from wooden casks. Children shrieked past Iona, sweet breads clutched in their hands.

Prasutag sat alone, examining a cloak of red and

yellow checks he had purchased from a Cornovii tailor. His head came up when Iona's footsteps approached.

"Do you favor this, Iona?"

"It's handsome," she agreed, turning it over in her hands. "Won't you be in the chariot race, Prasutag?"

"No." Prasutag shrugged as if it were of no importance to him.

"Breyton will win," Iiona said, watching Prasutag's eyes as she did so.

"Probably. His horses are strong and wind-quick."

"There's a beautiful prize, Prasutag. A great bronze cup."

"Yes, I've seen it," the man answered. "Excuse me." Maddeningly Prasutag walked away, new cloak slung over his shoulder. Iona watched, hands on hips.

"Prasutag is quite strange," a voice complained behind her, "not to wish to speak with you."

"Cymru. Are you enjoying yourself?"

"Very much." The hunched little man was drunk already though it had not passed noon; that showed in his bloodshot eyes. Otherwise he seldom had the courage to speak to Iona, though at times he followed her about like a ragged little dog. She despised Cymru, yet tolerated him on this day. Her thoughts were still with Prasutag.

Prasutag was a fine warrior, a sturdily built man, yet quiet to frustration, unconcerned with the rewards of valor, and seemingly untouched by feminine magnetism.

"Will you be in the javelin, Iona?" Cymru asked. She had nearly forgotten his presence. Looking back to Cymru, she found the strangest leer on his lips, his eyes riveted to her breasts.

"Yes, of course," Iona answered with a toss of her head. "And I will win it for the Iceni. Now, Cymru, if you will excuse me..."

"I will be watching you, Iona," the small man said, his pathetic eyes still fixed on her. Suddenly his gaze changed and, nodding, he turned and hobbled rapidly away, stumbling a little.

"So—you hurried from me to be with another man!" Breyton's voice boomed. He strolled toward her, a god among the smaller men he passed, golden hair streaming, broad shoulders glistening in the sunlight, his perfect teeth set in an incorrigible smile.

"And so if I choose to...?"

"Only do not choose," Breyton said. Impulsively he picked her up, and swinging her in a circle as if she weighed nothing, he kissed her mouth with his which tasted of wine and sent an intoxicating thrill through her veins.

"Put me down," she said with forced rigidity.

"Promise to walk with me a while?"

She nodded, flashed a pretty smile, and Breyton lowered her to the ground, planting another kiss on her forehead. Together they strode among the crowds. The blond Iceni lion and the beautiful daughter of King Athair. She laughed with Breyton, chased after him, rested her head on his shoulder.

Yet she wondered—when Breyton had joked about a tryst with Cymru—why had she first thought he was accusing Prasutag?

After a time they stopped to listen to a bard from across the river. He sang stirringly of magic and brave warriors. Arawn had caught up with them and together they drank sweet Atrebates wine.

When the sun was high Arawn and Leun fitted Breyton's chariot, tightening the spokes of the iron wheels, harnessing the gaudily trapped white horses he would drive.

Leun first noticed the sullen Coritani watching them as they worked, braiding the tails of the horses. "Look there," he said in a low voice to Arawn.

Arawn flashed a glance at the broad, toothless Coritani, and his constant smile tightened. "Othgar's brother. The man Breyton defeated at Killdeer Stream."

"What does he want?" Leun grumbled. His hand automatically had gone to the hasp of his dagger. Arawn's hand locked onto his wrist.

"No. Athair would have to punish you, Leun."

The younger man put his knife away reluctantly. The Coritani still watched them, a thin expressionless face set atop muscular shoulders, he had not moved.

"You!" Arawn said loudly. "What do you want?"

"Is that the chariot of Breyton?" he asked.

"It is."

"So." He added nothing more, but slipped out of the stables.

"What was that about?" Leun wondered.

"I think Breyton ought to be told. Something's up."

"You stand about so glumly," Breyton said. He had just come in from the sun, Iona beside him. His massive chest was decorated now with a pendant gold chain; his wrists sported golden bracelets, his hair was combed back, a loincloth wrapped loosely around him completing his attire. "Who was that I saw leaving as we came up?"

When they told him, Breyton laughed it off and went out to try the team and chariot. Iona could not see it so lightly.

"The man wants revenge," she guessed.

"True. But he'll not take his measure of Breyton. Not here at least." Arawn pondered it a moment, his eyebrows thoughtfully knitted. "Yet in a chariot race much can happen."

"I'll have my father stop the race then," Iona said, but even as she spoke she knew Athair could not, would not. Nor would Breyton allow it. The pride of the Iceni was at stake. And they were a prideful race.

From the platform that had been raised near the granary Athair held sway, surrounded by the Coritani king, Kowlter, Queen Caldera of the Cornovii, and the Belgae and Atrebates kings. The trumpets were sounded from below, signaling the beginning of the chariot race, the most prestigious event of the Samhain gathering.

As Iona watched, four chariots were lined side by side at the starting rope, Breyton on the outside, next to him the Belgae with the huge black horses, then the Atrebates woman wearing a flaming red cloak, red ribbons hung on her horses' manes. On the far side was the Coritani representative, the man they had seen at the stables. He pulled on his gloves and glanced at Breyton then to the tower where Kowlter watched back.

Athair stepped solemnly forward, bowed to the

Celtic assemblage, and dropped a yellow scarf. As it hit the earth the charioteers whipped their horses into frantic motion.

The race was to be a mile around the compound of Viron—two laps around a plotted course. Breyton broke into an early lead, a wild laugh coming from his mouth as he circled the first corner post. The Iceni youth cheered wildly, following along until their hero disappeared in a whirlwind of dust.

Just behind Breyton was the woman of the Atrebates, a sallow, muscular girl with the reputation of a valiant soldier. She gripped the reins tenaciously with a single hand while her other flayed at the horses with a cracking whip.

The Belgae was a massive man with black hair and a huge beard. His black horses gained momentum on the quarter-mile straightaway, closing the distance as Breyton and the Atrebates woman rushed for the second pole. The Coritani seemed to be saving his horses, pulling a shoulder length behind the Belgae.

Breyton's horses swung smoothly around the second pole, his chariot nearly on one wheel, the horses' nostrils flaring. He was cheered not only by the Iceni, frantic in their worship of the young lion, but by the women of the Coritani and Belgae tribes.

The blond god of the Iceni swirled his whip, tossed back his head and laughed, turning once to watch the Atrebates woman fall off the pace as he neared the third pole of the first lap.

The demonic Belgae had begun to make his move. He drove his horses furiously onward, letting the urging whip slash against their flanks at the slightest hesitation. He thundered past the woman of the Atrebates, coming within a length of Breyton as they rounded the third pole and rushed headlong past the viewing stand.

"Look at him!" Arawn shouted joyously, gulping a swallow of wine as he leaped in the air.

"Sting them!" Leun called, and as if his voice had carried to Breyton, his whip again stung the horses.

Iona watched silently, her heart beating wildly, the dust rolling over them. Athair sat solemnly above them, but she knew he would soon be on his feet cheering with the rest of them. Breyton's magnificent shoulders bulged as he gripped the reins strongly, his eyes flashed. He looked briefly at Iona before the horses swept past.

The Atrebates woman was nowhere to be seen; perhaps a horse had pulled up lame on her. The Belgae now seemed to be falling back as they rounded the first corner pole for the second time. After a gallant onslaught, his horses seemed tired. It was the Coritani who was gaining ground, passing the faltering, bearded Belgae as they entered the straightaway.

"He means to kill Breyton," Arawn said tightly. He dashed to the stable to catch a better view of the racers as they rounded the second pole.

The Coritani, eyes intent, deadly, drew nearer to Breyton as they came out of the corner, locked wheel to wheel, the Coritani as somber as Breyton was joyous.

With a twist of the reins, the Coritani thudded his chariot against Breyton's and the Iceni had to draw up slightly to avoid being spilled as the chariot careened. The flashing smile vanished instantly from Breyton's mouth. He might have lost control of his horse accidentally; yet the man was a Coritani, and Breyton did not lay the incident to circumstance.

Angrily Breyton whipped his horses forward. He striped them with one lash, two; the third fell on the back of the Coritani charioteer who winced with the pain, cursed in angry retort and lashed back with his own whip.

"They've made a war of it," Leun breathed. They were rushing down the back straight, Breyton slightly behind, his wheels ominously close to those of the Coritani. If the chariots were to lock wheels, it would mean certain injury, perhaps death to both men.

Athair's hands clenched his chair tightly, but he smiled and, turning to Kowlter, said in an undertone, "It's you or us, it seems."

"What?"

"The Iceni will triumph, or the Coritani," Athair clarified. "The others are well off the pace."

Kowlter nodded stiffly, and lounged back as if he had not gotten the other meaning, as if it were of no importance to him; yet his eyes were bolted to the action. These Iceni must be taught a lesson. They were not invincible. If not on the battlefield, then on the field of play the lesson would be driven home.

Side by side the two charioteers raced down the last quarter-mile, past the granary where the youth of the Iceni perched, cheering madly for Breyton. At that moment the wheels of the chariots locked, Breyton lashing out once more with his whip as he drove his chariot deliberately, suicidally into the Coritani's wheels.

The Coritani's toothless mouth opened wide, soundlessly, as his chariot tumbled through the air. Breyton's right wheel spun free, cartwheeling through space as he leaped forward, landing astride the chariot tongue.

In a mad maelstrom of dust the Coritani's chariot collapsed, the driver landing on his neck near the last corner post. Breyton's chariot limped forward, the single intact wheel wobbling precariously.

At the last moment that wheel, too, spun free and Breyton crossed the finish line standing on the dragging tongue of the chariot, his hand stretched victoriously skyward.

He reined up abruptly, the horses in a lather, the tongue of the chariot describing an arc in the earth. He jumped from the broken chariot, arms uplifted. A long red welt ran across his face and shoulder.

"The victory is for my king!" Breyton shouted. Athair lifted a hand from the tower in response as the children and warriors gathered around Breyton. Iona was there, her heart beating wildly. She was in his arms suddenly, feeling the pulse in his chest. "And for my princess," he whispered.

She held him tightly, her face pressed against his chest. "You will be killed," she said so softly that her voice carried to no one else in the clamoring crowd. Breyton lifted her chin with concern. He said nothing, but only held her more tightly.

"You will be killed." She said it only to herself the second time. Breyton accepted the garland from Athair as Iona continued to cling to him.

This man would die. He hurled himself toward death. He chose to follow the beast of night, to open his veins for the spectre of valor. He would be taken one day. Suddenly. Without warning, the gods would call for his blood, his soul.

"Breyton," she said, "you were born to die valiantly. And you pursue your fate religiously."

"It is the Coritani who is dead," he answered as a child might have, unaware of what she meant.

A glorious man-child walked the earth: this Breyton. Haughty, laughing, wearing the boots of giants, with the heart of a child, understanding nothing but games and war. A beautiful beast, certain to be snatched from them.

When she raised her head again, she found they were walking by the river, the sounds of the games, of the carnival far behind them.

"I must wash," Breyton said. Casually he stripped off his loincloth and walked into the river, diving under for a long minute before emerging, laughing, shaking his hair to clear his eyes.

He stood for a moment in the waist-deep, quick-running silver river, beads of water on his chest. His narrow waist and muscled abdomen gleamed with water droplets. Then he raised his hands in beckoning, and Iona found herself stepping from her dress, wading to him in the river where he wrapped his arms around her.

He pulsed with life, this transient creature. He was filled with hot blood, his chest rising spasmodically as he kissed her on the throat, the ears, the breast. Still he lived. The tribe lived. War.

She pulled his head down with her arms, then let him carry her into the deep glade where the sun mottled the fern; the grass beneath her was rich and deep.

Through the canopy of the elms she watched the deep cupola of the sky, watched the white moon slink past, felt life around her and within her. "Iona . . ."

She put her mouth to his, silencing him, her hands stroking his golden mane, his back. She kissed him deeply and let him be a part of her, let the day and night merge, the sky turn round on itself.

Chapter Three

Samhain had come and had passed. Iona awoke to the tinkling of bells, the thundering of drums, the clatter of horses' hooves. Rushing to the door, gathering her cloak about her, she watched the last of a long column of Iceni funnel through the massive gates of Viron.

Lania was just outside, her face lined with concern—the lines of care which Iona had seen so often and recognized instantly.

"They ride to battle," she said, clutching her mother's arm.

"Yes, to battle," Lania answered without turning her face. A small, wretched creature in a worn blue robe, she watched as the last of the force, among them Cymru and Prasutag, cleared the gate, then it was swung tight behind them.

"I was told nothing of this," Iona said, astonished.

"Your father did not wish you to ride, Iona."

"Yet . . . nothing was said. The Coritani are at the herds again, then?"

"No, not the Coritani. It is the Roman men, Iona. They have come across the river. They have come to claim our lands."

"The Roman men." Iona stood a moment with her mother. So at last they had come. The Roman men.

The cold dew glittered in the sunlight as Athair led his armed force through the forest and onto the carpet of long green. Below, the Romans massed, waiting. Athair held his hand up in signal and the men slowed, awaiting his words.

"Let them see what we are made of," Athair said, his voice tight with anger. "No man may cross the Killdeer without my agreement. No army without shedding the blood of its soldiers."

"Drive them back!" Barra chimed.

"Death to the Roman men," Arawn said, tripping his cloak from his muscular torso. Then he leaped onto his horse's back and with Tanbar, Hilden and others, he drove down the slope, his voice raised in fierce war-challenge.

Breyton was not far behind. The young warriors of Viron, eager for their first battle, followed him, their idol.

Throg bellowed a curse against Roman blood and lunged forward with his infantry. Athair waited a moment as the Celts streamed out across the fields, then he hefted his shield from his saddle and walked the great gray stallion forward.

Arawn met them at the point. The Romans had not moved, fleeing or attacking, but held their position behind their man-sized rectangular shields.

Arawn rode in a tight circle, throwing his lance

near the ranks of the men in red. Gaining no response, he leaped from his horse, shield before him, sword in his sturdy hand.

"I am Arawn—the war lover—of the Iceni Celts. I have killed an enemy of the Iceni every day of my life. Today I will kill a dozen of you. Die cowardly, or die bravely, but come forward to die!"

Not a man among the Romans moved. Arawn strode forward, his sword over his head. Behind him rushed Tanbar and Hilden with four other young bucks, eager for their first taste of war. Arawn stepped through the ranks of red-clad, helmeted Romans, shouting curses as he strode.

"Are you men or lumps of clay!" he shouted at the disciplined files of soldiers, jeering them as they remained in ranks.

Finally a Roman soldier, unable to contain himself, broke from the ranks and Arawn parried his first sword thrust, dodged his second and responded to the third with a death stroke. A blood-chilling yell filled the air as Arawn savagely beheaded the legionnaire.

Instantly the Roman ranks came to life. The foot soldiers fell back fifty paces behind the rows of archers who unleashed a deadly barrage of arrows, cutting the Celtic phalanx to ribbons.

Tanbar, in his first action, died with an arrow through the throat. His cousin, Hilden, was gutted by three arrows. Arawn screamed savagely and layed about him with his avenging sword before falling back to his horse which he discovered dead on the grass.

"Arawn!"

It was Breyton. He rode past at full speed, and Arawn took the horse's mane and swung behind his friend as a second wall of arrows filled the sky with singing death.

Throg's battle command was barely audible above the din as he lined his infantry. As he ordered them forward into the fray, another hail of Roman arrows bled the Iceni ranks, and at that moment the Roman infantry rushed forward, closing a pincer.

Throg's men were caught in the middle, the cavalry of Dagda in the path of the onslaught and they withdrew rapidly, leaving shattered bodies behind on the stained earth, horses pawing at the air in a death run, young Celts bleeding, their throats filled with death roars.

"Back!" Throg commanded, but even the order of their commander could not restrain the younger Celtic warriors from trying the Romans in single combat. Yet there was no single combat for the Romans. A Celt was battered by the arms of three Roman warriors, swords puncturing him without skill, without even malice, but with deadly, cold efficiency.

War was no game to this Roman machine, but a challenge to be met and overwhelmed without regard to chivalry. There was no heroic act, no bravery, but the weight of the mass. The victory was won for the generals, for the emperor, not for the individual combatant.

Dagda's cavalry was crushed by the onslaught of Roman horses, Throg's men trapped in the closing vise of the archers. Valiantly they fought back, attempting a charge forward, yet it was futile. Athair watched grimly, his eyes tight slits. When . . . when before had he been forced to call retreat? Yet he did it now, and those who were still able scattered, following Throg and Dagda to the woods where the Iceni reserve pelted the pursuing Romans with lances and slings, driving them backward until at some unseen signal, the Romans withdrew themselves, re-forming their ranks into a boxlike unit.

"We will go in again," Barra gasped. His chariots had been totally ineffective. Athair did not answer. On the field a massive machine was being drawn into place. Athair watched it with curiosity until it became evident it was a war machine.

At a signal the great catapult unleashed a hail of fiery fragments, striking fire in the woods. A man was battered into the earth by a stone. A second catapult came into range and a third. Arawn was beside his king, a bloody trophy hanging from the neck of Breyton's horse, yet there was no savage triumph in this young lion's eyes, only grave concern, anger.

"Give me the word, my king," Breyton said breathlessly. His sword was gripped tenaciously. Beside him Leun, bloodsoaked, badly bruised on chest and thigh, waited.

"No." Athair said it coldly, his eyes hard.

At that moment the second and third catapults were unstrung, and the woods were filled with incendiary particles, deadly bombs. Athair heard the screaming of his men, watched the Romans reload the machines as archers rushed to within range. Slowly, reluctantly, his hand went up again and the Iceni dispersed in the woods, fleeing across the river, some at a dead run, some mortally wounded, the fire of the Roman machines roaring in the burning woods as they retreated.

Athair sagged into his chair, facing the fire. His

arms hung limply, his eyes were blank. Lania scuttled about busily, concern etching her face. Iona sat tensely for a long while, not daring to speak, before she picked up her cloak and went out into the chill air. Beyond the southern woods she could see lines of campfires against the black hillocks beyond.

Prasutag was leaning against the stockade wall, his torso bound. Iona went up to him, but he did not move. His chin rested on his wrist and he seemed absorbed by the fires as well.

"Are there many of them?" she asked.

"Many," he replied without moving. "Very many of them. More than five times our number. And they attack always. They will not take our cattle and return to Rome. They will not steal our maidens away and rush back to the sea. They will not rest," Prasutag went on in a low voice, "until they have killed us, every one, or subjected us to their rule."

"The Iceni will never surrender," Iona said proudly. Yet there was a pained tremor in her voice.

"Then we will have to fight to the last soldier. They have machines. . . . Iona"—Prasutag turned to her suddenly, his thoughtful eyes on hers, his sad, broad mouth moving slowly, as if it pained him to speak—"if they win, our way of life will be no more. Our lands will not be ours, perhaps our language will disappear. They may force us to become slaves, to speak their savage tongue, to live in their way or to die."

Iona drew back, shocked by Prasutag's words. "No! You speak traitorously, Prasutag, with a coward's voice."

"No, Iona." Prasutag's voice was even.

"I do not wish to hear this."

"I say it only because it is the truth. Ask Thrueldan, he knows the ways of the Romans. Ask him what has happened to the Celts of Gaul. As for being traitorous—I shall fight—I shall do whatever my king commands until I can do no more. I shall die, but that will not make my words less true."

"You would not say these things to Athair, to the others." Iona was not only angry now, but frightened. Vivid images of the Iceni camp in ruins, the people in bondage, came to her, streaked with the coloring of blood.

"No, I would not say these things to the others. They, too, might think me cowardly. They know nothing but to fight. To strike back. Assuming victory shall follow on the heels of valor. Yet is is not always so, Iona . . . not always."

Iona's eyes were fixed in horrified fascination on the campfires of the Romans. As many as the stars in the night sky, it seemed. How could it have happened? Athair would not allow this! Angrily she tossed her head and stamped her foot. Prasutag seemed not to notice her, however; instead he turned back to his watching. Watching those damnable fires.

Breyton was near the cattle gates. Iona hesitated, seeing his eyes on her. Then she rushed across the open space between them and fell into his powerful arms. Breyton would not let this happen! Nothing frightened Breyton, man or savage creature, goblin or Roman. . . . He kissed her bare shoulder, her throat, surprised at her sudden ardor.

"Iona . . ."

"Shh. Do not speak, Breyton, my beautiful man. Not on this night."

Together they walked into the fields, and she let him cover her with his assurances that things would be as they always had, that nothing Prasutag had glumly predicted could come to pass, that there would always be Breyton, always the earth beneath them to till, always the Iceni nation.

Chapter Four

The Romans had marched nearer yet. They had camped in Nightstar Meadow the evening before. They dragged their terrible war machines behind them against Viron.

Dawning was only a red promise in the eastern sky as Athair led his men out, moving heavily to his war horse. Leun, silhouetted against the still-dark sky, hobbled after them, unable to join in this combat.

Breyton laughed and joked with Arawn at this early hour, unaware of the eyes of concern which followed them as they mounted their horses.

Iona stood shivering near the wall of her house, Thramane beside her. Lania had not come out of the hut on this morning. That, in itself, was unusual. She never failed to see Athair off.

Prasutag limped past heavily, his shield slung across his shoulder. He glimpsed Iona and started to speak, yet kept his silence, merging with the other shadowy figures near the horses.

It was only a moment before Barra led his charioteers out, followed by Dagda's cavalry. The shaded faces flashed past in the columns of war. Many of them were marked for death—that had never concerned Iona before. Perhaps she had never believed it. Now it weighed heavily on her.

The beautiful Dwan Karnash was going forth to fight, haughtily astride a strapping black gelding. Duelda was there as well, Nertomorus's wife. It revealed how deeply Nertomorus was concerned, to allow the old woman to once again take up arms. There were many women with them and Iona longed to be going, though fear caused her heart to tremble. Athair would not have permitted it.

"One lancer less, one daughter more," he had told her heavily, his mustached lips brushing Iona's cheek. Then, for a single illustrative moment he had embraced his daughter as he had not since she was a child.

Throg's foot soldiers now streamed past in the golden light. Arawn's young, bright-eyed brother, Tylch, was among them. So cheery, these, the youngest of the men. So marked for death. Tylch waved a happy hand at Iona, proudly strutting with his war shield and new sword.

Throg himself lumbered to his chariot, pulled on and strapped his bronze helmet, then whipped his horses forward, the gates of Viron closing behind him.

Iona spun on her heel, walking to Thrueldan's hut. The Druid was resting on his haunches, drawing circles in the colored sand of his floor. Three sticks lay at random angles in the sand beside him.

"It augurs bad," he said without turning to look at Iona. "It augurs bad."

"Then you must call after Athair! Tell him that the stars are against him."

"He knows, Iona. I advised him." Thrueldan rose, dusting his palms. "Yet the Romans advance. They will be at Viron's gates in three days if they are not pushed back. It augurs bad...." Thrueldan sat in his low chair, hand waving helplessly in the air.

From the rear chambers, the tattooed Druidess, Danadil, came forward bearing a skin of wine and a goblet. She said nothing, this priestess, but poured the wine into Thrueldan's cup, sprinkling in a white, powdery substance.

Iona waited as the dark man drank. Then she spoke, hands clenched together on the table top.

"Prasutag has been telling me things..." she began.

"Oh?" Thrueldan lifted his eyebrows curiously, his lips fixed to his cup, his long tattooed fingers encircling the golden goblet. "Prasutag is a wise young man."

"He has been speaking"—Iona laughed unconvincingly—"of defeat."

"It is a possibility a wise man must consider," Thrueldan admitted. "It is wisdom to foresee all events and to be prepared to deal with these alternatives."

"It cannot occur!"

Iona rose and stalked the room, her hands working against one another.

"Because it has not happened in your lifetime? In mine? No, Iona—it can occur. Only blind faith can lead some of our people to believe in their invincibility."

"He said . . . the Romans will not leave us with our cattle, taking their spoils."

"That is not their way." Thrueldan watched the young princess. Her face was a portrait in dismay. To the young the very conception that all of their world might collapse is appalling; yet worlds have always collapsed: civilizations disappear without a trace, tongues are forgotten. Conqueror upon conqueror moves across this earth in man's eternal foray against himself. To believe at any time that it has finally ended is to be subdued by blithe ignorance.

"Yet perhaps it will not happen," Iona said, a hopeful smile parting her full lips. She took Thrueldan's head in her hands and smiled still more fully. "You old pessimist—perhaps it will not happen."

"Perhaps not, Iona. For Athair's sake let us hope they are successful today."

"For my father's sake. . . ." The idea rocked Iona. She had, of course, heard that a king who was no longer capable must be displaced. There were many songs, many legends of kings who had been supplanted following failure in war. Yet Athair had always been her king! There was only Athair. "He cannot be faulted," she objected, dropping her hands.

"The gods fault no one. The fates do not condemn. They simply roll past, their decisions inevitable, Iona."

Nightstar Meadow was empty. Silent in the gray dawn. Frost lay beneath the oaks among the hillocks. A lone rook cocked its head, then took wing, cawing ominously. It flew to a single tree where others of its kind blackened the limbs with shuddering, glossy foliage.

There was nothing there, no one. Then, suddenly, the fields and forests were filled with the blood-red of the Roman uniforms. Marching in lockstep, in exact files, in perfect formation, infantry in the advance, archers just behind, their well-mounted cavalry strung out through the woods, they advanced.

Somewhere beyond them a faceless, nameless general sat atop a gigantic platform constructed for viewing, so that the master might deliberately, with the skills of years of formal training, position the chess pieces on his bloody board.

Athair's chest heaved. His face was drawn taut. He counted the Romans roughly and glanced at Throg on his right hand and at Nertomorus on his left. Then he swiveled in his saddle, looking at the bright, hopeful, combative faces behind him in the deep, shaded glen.

"Today we throw them back," Breyton said softly.

"Then tonight you will marry Iona," Athair answered.

His deep heart, seemingly aged years by the events of a few days, longed only to once see a grandchild of that union. Chubby, with curly blond hair, pudgy child's hands, and a winning smile. . . .

The trumpets roared at his sudden signal, and Dagda's cavalry rumbled forward, thrusting down the slope toward the point of the Roman legion.

"Athair. King." Throg's eyes were heavy,

pouched. For a moment he lay a heavy, gnarled hand on Athair's wrist.

"Tell them it is for their wives, husbands, children."

"I will," Throg promised. He circled back through the woods, haranguing his gathered foot soldiers as the cries of battle reached their ears. Dagda's men had met the Romans.

Athair drew on his helmet and unsheathed his mighty sword. Breyton sat beside him, eyes alert to the clash below. "I will take a dozen of them on my own!" Breyton shouted. "Let every one do the same."

"Take but six and return to Iona," Athair said quietly.

Then the Iceni king's sword was raised, and the main body of warriors moved forward in the rough form of a spearhead. Throg's infantry rushed to encircle the left flank of the Roman legion. Yet many of the youth, unable to control their bloodlust, their rush after glory, had already broken ranks and charged into single combat.

The Romans stood wooden as the trees themselves, in ranks as deep as the winter clouds off the Atlantic.

With a bellow Arawn darted forward, his piercing yell igniting those around him. The mass of the Iceni pitched forward, and again the Roman archers advanced to the forefront, laying down an iron barrage against them. Horses buckled at the knees, rolled and whinnied in frantic pain, their riders crushed beneath them.

Athair waded into the depths of the battle. All around were red-cloaked Romans. Enough to cover the earth, it seemed. For every one struck down, three rose to take his place. With a leap of his heart, Athair realized that again the Romans had somehow closed behind them. Cavalry massed under an oddly inscribed battle flag had come from the woods and waited a signal. There was no way out, no hope of victory. There was only blood. Across the deep blue of the plains, for a single instant, Athair glimpsed remote figures in bronze directing the battle from atop the Roman dais.

Methodically signals were flashed, men dispatched. There was no way to assault this wave of red. There was only agony, the screaming, pain-inspired groans, the weight of the sword in Athair's hand which could not be rested for a single moment. While they watched, sitting in their chairs—these other generals. These chess masters.

Breyton roared loudly, striking all around him. Still joyous in battle, though aware of their immediate danger, the Iceni, towering above the shorter, crimson-clad Romans, struck out.

There was another sort of bellow from Arawn. Cutting forward through the legions of Romans, he had found Tylch dead, before he could have cut his first stroke, a Roman lance through his heart. Arawn held his brother aloft for a moment, his mouth torn with anguish, his eyes streaming tears. Then he lay the youth aside carefully, as if unaware of the combat all around him. He knelt and kissed his dead brother's lips.

In the very shadow of an attacking Roman, Arawn the war-lover clenched his sword tightly and stood, cutting about him, and the Romans went down like wheat before the scythe.

But it was not enough. Nothing was enough.

Barra's charioteers had been cut to ribbons. Throg's infantry had never reached the river crossing at all. The Roman cavalry, attacking from the rear, was able to butcher the trapped Iceni. Still Athair held his ground, fighting beside the madly vengeful Arawn and the now sober, brutal Breyton.

Nertomorus had appeared from nowhere, pushing through the forward throb of the red legions, and he took Athair's arm roughly.

"Call retreat. They'll all die on this spot, Athair!"

Athair nodded, recognizing a fact to which he was reconciled, and he raised his sword once again, trying to fall back. The Roman press was little less to the rear, however, the cavalry still riding among the Iceni, slaughtering the best of their youth.

Athair stepped back, stumbled over a body, and grabbed madly for his horse's reins. He spotted Arawn submerged in a sea of crimson cloaks, and Breyton beside his lifelong friend.

"Breyton!" Their king surged forward, his great horse knocking men aside with its shoulders. He cut to the right, to the left, fighting furiously. The Romans recognized Athair for the Celtic king and they tried frantically for him, each man wanting the blood reward on Athair's head.

"Arawn!"

Athair was beside the two young lions. Arawn's right arm dangled uselessly, his eyes were still glazed with madness, with sorrow for Tylch.

"Get up, Breyton!" Athair shouted. On the rise to the south, he saw the Roman war machines being wheeled forward.

Realizing that now the Roman cavalry behind

them would have to disperse or be shelled by their own catapults, Athair chose this moment for final retreat. "Breyton!"

Struggling free of a Roman hand, flesh torn by combat, Breyton caught the glance of Athair, although above the tumult of voices, steel against steel, the shrieks of death, he could not hear Athair's command. He touched Arawn's shoulder and withdrew, walking backward toward Athair's horse, his sword fending off the approaching Romans.

The Romans were intimidated by this towering, muscular Iceni and they did not press after him eagerly. Arawn, however, had waded still deeper into the scarlet horde, seeming to wish to drown his sorrow in battle death.

"Arawn!" Athair shouted fiercely. Breyton was behind him on the king's faltering gray horse. Athair spurred the animal forward, toward Arawn. Die if they must, lose if they must; but Athair would not see the young lion cut down uselessly before his eyes.

"Arawn!"

Arawn turned momentarily to face his king. Then again he turned to combat, eyes black and fierce.

"Arawn!" Breyton yelled. "It's useless!"

"I command you, Arawn," Athair hollered, and Arawn at last turned to them, his face a stone mask. There was a huge welt across the bridge of his nose, a horrible gash down his cheek from eye to chin. As if not comprehending, he stared at his king.

"Come!" Athair bellowed, waving his arm, and

Arawn nodded, disentangling himself from the bloody rush of combat.

The red damask woven by the dying sun was on the screen of gray clouds strung out across the darkening horizon. A lone owl swooped low across the meadows, clamped talons to a field mouse, and winged homeward toward the deep woods of Fox Throw.

The gates of Viron were fast and guarded. Leun had sat the day long, watching. His injured leg throbbed with fiery pain, yet he would not rest or receive treatment for it.

"Soon," Iona ventured.

"Soon—yet I hear no cries of jubilation," Leun muttered.

Together they watched, and then a shadowy form appeared in the dimly lighted meadows beyond Viron. A second shadow staggered forward, a third and a fourth, dragging a defeated weapon.

One by one the warriors of the Iceni struggled homeward, weaving their ways through the battlements, the labyrinths of Viron. The watchers above were silent; the straggling soldiers as quiet as dismal death.

Athair, who had been the first to depart through the massive gates of the citadel, was the first to return. Iona rushed to embrace him. Her king, her father, had survived a brutal battle. Yet he looked neither to the right nor to the left as he stepped from his exhausted horse.

Instead he moved toward Thrueldan's hut, oblivious to the cries of Iona.

Leun hobbled painfully toward the open gate. Gratefully he saw Breyton returning, head held high, blood staining his garments. Yet Breyton, too, seemed oblivious to all. Arawn walked clumsily homeward, the reason for his staggering gait soon apparent.

In his arms was the limp figure of his brother, Tylch. Battered, appearing much older in death than he had in life, he had been brutally treated by the fortunes of his time.

Iona's head turned this way and that, the wretched, scarred and hopelessly empty faces passing in sorry procession. There was none more pathetic than Nertomorus who walked past Iona without recognizing her. When she took his arm, he said vacantly, "I could not even find Duelda's body."

So that was how it had gone. Tragedy treading on the heels of adversity.

"Leun—" Iona wished to speak with him, with anyone, yet Leun had no stomach for it, no tongue with which to speak after watching the battered ranks. He walked unsteadily away.

She ran toward the river, her eyes streaming tears. Yes! He was there!

Breyton sat heavily on a flat stone at the water's edge, arms leaden, head bowed. There was a deep cut across his shoulder, yet it had stopped bleeding.

"Breyton!" she breathed, then hesitated.

He turned to face her. Then he stood and gathered her in his arms. They stood together, eyes closed tightly, unmoving as the last flaming arrows of the dying sun withdrew into the black mass of all-conquering night.

"I want to marry you," Breyton said quietly. He had not moved. His breath was on her ear. Iona felt a tear race across her cheek and melt against his bare chest. She nodded.

"I want a son," Breyton said, petting her face. "I wish to leave my living blood on the earth."

"Tomorrow," Iona said. She lifted her eyes to Breyton's and he kissed her. Lightly, first on the lips, then on the tip of her nose. They spoke no more of it, but walked arm in arm through the deep forest shadows. Iona's breath was labored, she noticed with surprise. Her heart beat wildly.

She glanced at the man beside her. All right then —he would be her husband. They would begin a new life within Iona. The Celtic people would survive.

Athair was stiff with the rigors of the battle. *An old man,* he told himself. "I am an old man."

Lania, gentle woman, still worked around the hut, cleaning corners Thramane had cleaned hours earlier. There was no point in speaking now. The last hours, those written by the fates the day Athair was born, were approaching. The hour of closing.

Without dressing, pulling only a worn purple cloak across his shoulders and chest, Athair struggled to his feet. A wound in his side tore open as he did so, and he winced with pain. A muffled oath broke his lips.

Lania turned to face him. Their eyes met across the dimly lighted room. A shrunken, hunched woman. A broken, wounded king, her husband. Lost hours filled their common thoughts for a broken fragment of a second. Lania's eyes were filled with sudden tears, her mouth turned down in ill-concealed anguish.

"Woman—" Athair stretched out a massive

hand, dropped it slowly, then turned abruptly and stalked from the house.

The camp was filled with the sounds of mourning. A loud wailing had arisen in Arawn's house when he carried his brother home, and it had not ceased. A faltering horse rested near the well, its haunches against the earth, its front legs fruitlessly pawing at the ground.

Cymru wandered past, still dressed in his blood-soaked garments, a sword still in his hand.

"Cymru!" Athair called, but the crooked little man heard nothing. His mind had never been strong; perhaps Cymru had been broken entirely on the field.

Athair walked more quickly now, watching the red rising moon through a gap in the oak trees on the knolls. Thrueldan's hut was lighted.

"Thrueldan!" Athair cast aside the curtain and entered the empty, sweet-smelling hut. A fire burned in a bronze cup on the empty table, emitting a weaving, bluish flame. The hearth, however, was cold.

"Thrueldan!" Athair called loudly. "Danadil, Shama!"

There was no answer from within. Athair stood in the doorway, arms akimbo, the starlit western sky behind him. His beard was matted, his side throbbed with pain. He watched the flickering, blue flame bend in the slight breeze.

Finally Thrueldan came forward from the deeper recesses of the hut, wearing nothing but a golden necklace. The Druid's body was strangely painted, one-half yellow, one-half red.

"My king." Thrueldan came forward and kissed Athair's beard, bowing deeply as Athair rested a hand on his back. "You have decided?" Thrueldan asked, straightening.

"It has been decided," Athair said after a long pause. He watched the blue flame, still fascinated by its wavering light.

"Tomorrow then," Thrueldan said.

"What do the stars tell you?"

"Tomorrow is a propitious day, my king."

"Then it will be tomorrow."

The house was quiet when Iona came in and slipped into her bed. Athair was not there, which was unusual. She had wished to tell him the news he had waited long to hear. She and Breyton would be married. Married? The thought thrilled, puzzled, amused, and frightened her all at once.

She fell asleep at last. It seemed it had been hours since she closed her weary eyes, but she at last fell asleep to dream. Yet what could it mean to dream such dreams as Iona?

Where crimson, winged goddesses intertwined in battle, and naked, golden-haired men ran after them, their eyes wide, mouths open in nameless horror.

Iona was among them, beyond them, she did not know which. Arms reached out to strangle her, or perhaps to love her and she pulled away from them, her own shrieks filling the caverns of her thoughts.

Then slashing, silvery blades loomed up, cutting the hearts from eagles, filling the empty recesses of timelessness with sticky, flowing blood. Here and there a captive head emerged and the mouths called to her; hands stretched out for her aid; eyes pleaded for mercy, for forgiveness, for death, for food? Who could tell which?

He came. A massive, sunburned stranger with eyes as soft as a doe's, with muscles hard and firm as an oak tree, with a heart which knew her inner heart, knew words she would speak before her lips could frame them.

Words which were beyond man's thought: a subtle yearning—a need to find a unity with another, a place in time, out of time, where all things flowed together, as a single heart became all of eternity. And Iona became a part of it, yielding her own heart, her mind, her body to this man-thing, this eternity which sheltered, warmed, became her.

To dream such dreams!

Chapter Five

They came together on the bald knob beyond the grove of ancient oaks. It was the moment after sundown, the last efforts of the bleeding sun blending with the purple of coming night as a single star hung above the eastern horizon.

The fire crackled and blazed at the center of the ritual circle, spraying golden, short-lived sparks into the air, lighting the faces of the Celts with shifting, demonic shadows.

Hands clasped together; they moved slowly, dancing in a circle, ritually following the death of the sun, the coming of night with the motions of their bodies.

Iona found herself fascinated by the darting, spiraling flames, herself wound up in the spell woven by the fire, by the energy of so many people gathered for one purpose.

A log popped and collapsed in the huge bonfire, and Iona felt her muscles tense involuntarily. Beside her danced Throg, amazingly agile in his movements for a man of such age and bulk. The firelight glittered in his eyes and coated his naked chest with glistening lacquer. The general looked directly into the fire at all times, she noticed.

On Iona's other hand was Lania. Her mother held her gray head proudly, yet her eyes darted here and there about the perimeter of the clearing, searching.

As if by some secret signal, the tempo of the dancers increased suddenly. They whirled and spun faster and faster in a mad circle. Iona's head swam; her hair dropped in damp ringlets across her face. Still the fire ... it burned more brightly with the fierceness of night. It seemed the arms of flame would break free, swimming into the dark womb of night, striving toward a distant, necessary appeasement.

More quickly they whirled. Throg's raspy breathing was in Iona's ear. Lania stumbled, yet kept her footing. The others were little more than a phantom blur across the firelight, though she clearly saw Breyton, his head thrown back in savage exultation. The others may as well have not existed.

Iona swam through a dream as she moved, her head dizzy, her legs growing wobbly, the fire ... there was only the fire and the beating of her heart, the massive hand of Throg and the frail hand of Lania, both of which seemed disembodied as they clenched hers.

It stopped.

The frantic dance ended abruptly, the circle coming to a halt. They stood trembling, like so many reeds in the wind. Iona's face was damp, her feet hot from the dancing. Thróg's massive, whitehaired chest heaved.

Soundlessly the Druid came forward. Soundlessly they received him. No voice uttered a syllable, but a common tremor reached Iona's softer senses.

Lania's hand tightened on hers as Thrueldan crept forward, inching into the warm firelight from the shadows of the night like some cautious insect. He wore a scarlet robe and carried a skull in each hand. Gently he put them down as if sensation still lived within these globes of yellowed ivory.

Iona's eyes flashed to the deeper shadows where a man waited. It was only a moment before Athair came forward, his mouth grim, tired, his shoulders set. He was naked, his scarred torso still firm, his arms hanging loosely at his sides.

Behind him came the Druidesses. They were naked as well, their purple, tattooed bodies lending an underworld color to the firelit ceremony.

Shama had deep black circles painted around her eyes; looking at her face, Iona had the impression of gazing at an empty-eyed skull. Danadil moved in a slow circular dance, her hands weaving and separating in ritual gestures intelligible only to the Druid and herself.

Athair stood near to the fire, so near that it seemed he would be scorched, yet he seemed ready to feel no pain on this evening.

Iona watched this sad-eyed man for a long moment. Her father, the great warrior. He had carried her in his arms to her first horse, steadied her as she took her first steps, walked with her proudly beside him to start the games at the gatherings of the Celts. . . .

Iona watched in fascinated horror as Thrueldan swept back his cloak and removed the razor-edged, slightly curved knife beneath it. He held it aloft, sanctifying it, letting the firelight purify the steel.

Danadil was beside him, on her knees, her breasts nearly touching the earth as she bent far forward. Iona gazed in hypnotic fascination at the Druidess's tattoos. She had seen them dozens of times before, even those of her broad hips, but she had never really perceived their significance until this moment.

Sequana, the mentor of the physically afflicted, rode a great blue bull across Danadil's upper thigh, the bull's head twisted back sharply in eternal surprise. Belenos was tattooed there: a fat, supercilious creature with wide, circular eyes. Epona, the horse goddess, swept up Danadil's spine, two great stallions rearing up beside her. Across the Druidess's breasts, Cernunnos ranged with his minions—all the beasts of field and furze. A jackal suckled at Danadil's teat, a boar supine before Cernunnos frozen just beneath it.

A flashing falling star cometed across the woman's abdomen impacting into frozen, death-inspired signs at her navel. . . .

Shama stood, screamed out pathetically and turned her back to the fire. She stood quivering for a moment, rubbing the insides of her purple, illustrated thighs. Then she fell face first against the hard earth and dragged herself forward, chanting words of no meaning. At the edge of the clearing she recovered a wicker basket. Her hand dipped into it and she returned, dancing in tight circles, her head thrown back, a struggling white cock in her hand.

Shama presented it to Thrueldan and with a single stroke he severed the rooster's head. The body ran off in crazy circles until it toppled over, blood oozing from its neck, feet clawing at the air.

The cock was still twitching, its wings beating in a last futile expression of its existence when Danadil brought forward a black goat. She herself dispatched this creature, sacrificing it to the whims of fate's winds, raising the Druid blade directly over her head. It hung there for an instant, like some sword weighing judgment; then it plunged and as Danadil groaned in ecstasy—or crazed fear —it took the jugular of the goat, spilling blood over the earth and onto Danadil.

"The world ends; the world begins," Thrueldan intoned. The Druid now stood before Athair. The king had not moved, nor flinched, but seemed completely detached from it all. "Your works follow you, Athair," Thrueldan said slowly. Then he turned, waiting.

In a moment it happened. The pale clouds before the eyes of Thrueldan summoned the rising pale moon from behind the dark line of trees.

Thrueldan waited, watching the waxing moon. He waited one moment as the rim of this darker light silhouetted the broken oaks. Then he spun, stepped forward one stride and sunk the blade of the knife into Athair's abdomen, tearing upward with the sharp edge to reach the heart swiftly.

Athair stood stock still, caught the blood of his body in his cupped hands, stumbled, then felt the strings of his legs come undone. He toppled forward, his eyes gazing at Lania, at Iona and Throg.

Iona's throat constricted. Lania's hand tensed and dug at her own with sharp fingernails. Throg's hand was wooden. He did not move as Athair landed on his face, his bloodied hands clawing at the earth. He rolled over, convulsing, and looked at Thrueldan saying something which was only a gurgling, strangled expression.

Thrueldan stood over his king, his eyes intent on the motions of the body, the arabesques painted in the sand by the spurting blood. He read the future there, it was said, read the propitious and the calamitous. It was there that the fingers of the gods sketched the future of the Iceni nation, ominous or joyous, and it was Thrueldan's obligation to interpret correctly or to travel on in the same way as Athair.

Finally Athair was still. Thrueldan stood silently, the bloody sacrificial knife dangling from his hand. Shama had gone into a trance, swaying backward and forward slowly from her kneeling position, her breasts swinging lazily. Danadil stood rigidly before the coming yellow moon, arms outstretched.

The fire had died to a trembling flame.

It had gone to dully glowing golden embers before Thrueldan spoke. The chill wind off the lowlands swept across them; Iona shivered uncontrollably.

"I read the stars," the Druid intoned. He stepped across the body of his dead king and moved toward the ring of onlookers. "I read the coming sun. I tell the springtime."

Thrueldan seemed hardly in control of himself; he held the knife before him in bloody hands. Dagda stared fiercely at the Druid, his black eyes on the blade. Barra was with him. They still stood, hands clasped, as if the dance would begin anew.

"Lead us forward!" Thrueldan shouted loudly, his head flung back. His scarlet robe was stained with the deeper maroon of Athair's blood. Dagda started forward then hesitated. Barra smiled mockingly.

"Lead us." Thrueldan took one step more and bowed to the earth, laying the sacrificial knife at the feet of Iona.

"Lead us," he repeated, his eyes glittering, watching her soft face. "For so it was written in your father's blood, so it is beseeched by the common blood of our tribe."

Chapter Six

Iona walked shakily toward the altar to Cernunnos in the deep woods where the sunlight through the trees mottled the dark earth. There she rested a while, her head thrown back.

She had been born near this sacred oak grove. Here, it was said, her father had been crowned king. Here he would be interred, in a fighting posture as he had wished, lance in hand, facing the southern menace.

Breyton came slowly forward, his feet making hardly a sound on the leaf-covered earth, his shadow flickering across those of the oaks.

"So. It is done," he said. He ran a hand through his hair, hardly knowing what to say next. Iona had not turned to face him. Her eyes seemed remote, her face was expressionless.

"And the sword has passed to you."

"It has passed. The burden of our people," she answered meditatively.

"Iona—I shall stand beside you. Despite Dagda and Barra. Thrueldan's decision will not be challenged. You will be our queen, and I your husband."

Iona's head swiveled slowly toward him; her long neck was the white of alabaster disappearing into her gold-fringed red cloak. Her eyes were larger than ever, at that moment the eyes of a doe.

"No."

Breyton did not react at first. His face collapsed in puzzlement.

"No? What do you mean, Iona?"

"We cannot marry, Breyton. Not now."

"Nothing has changed!"

"Everything has changed. Breyton, I am not responsible now for preserving our race only in a single, tiny form. I am responsible," she said, standing, "for all of the living souls. For all of the Iceni nation. You must see."

"I see nothing but a whimsical woman!" Breyton said angrily.

"You see your queen," Iona replied, her voice brittle. There was a cool fire in her eyes now, and Breyton was aware of it, yet he was not a man to be cowed or to be refused lightly.

"We must marry. Athair willed it. I will it!" He paused and stepped closer to her, intending to take her in his arms, yet he was held at a distance by some power he did not understand. "*You* willed it, Iona . . . you! You willed our union."

"A day can be a lifetime, Breyton. Everything has changed," she said in frustration, with regret.

"I have a great battle ahead of me. How can I lead my people if I must be concerned constantly with you? Or with the life of another within my womb?"

"You are my Iona. . . ." Breyton's mouth pleaded for hers, his eyes flashed with a mingled passion and fear.

"The sword has passed to me, Breyton. I am not your Iona. I am your queen." She took his hand tenderly. "Please, Breyton, understand."

"I understand you will not have my child," he said, tearing his hand from hers. "I understand I have made a fool of myself!"

"Breyton . . ."

"Do not worry, Iona. I will fight for you. I will obey, *my queen*. I will follow your rule. I will kneel. . . ." And he knelt, touching his lips to the hem of her skirt. Then, angrily, Breyton stalked from the clearing, his legs covering ground in great strides.

"Breyton!"

He did not stop, hesitate, nor look back. Iona stepped after him. Then stopped. "Breyton," she said in a muted voice, her hand touching her trembling lips.

Breyton walked without noticing his direction. The sun was cool, the western breezes swift. A jackdaw whirled in the November sky. The willowbrush along the river hummed with the sounds of insects, and once with the motion of a retreating boar.

He walked until his feet burned, until he had left the walls of Viron far behind. The perspiration streamed from his forehead, his hair hung in damp ringlets. He had come to a pond near the rising gray cliffs of Stralp Dunum, a squared hill along the banks of the Ouse—a seaward-flowing river.

There he sat on a flat, yellow rock, sifting dust between his fingers, tossing angry pebbles against the pacific face of the murky Ouse.

"Breyton?"

He turned his eyes to find her there.

A tall, blond woman, naked in the coolness of day, long legs, flashing blue eyes, perfect breasts. Dwan Karnash's clothing lay at her feet.

"Do you need me, Breyton?" she asked. A hand stretched out to him, and he stood, his fury transforming to a passion which demanded release, demanded the forgetfulness of such an encounter. He stepped to her, and she smiled, her sighs in his ears as he embraced her tightly.

"I have waited a long time, Breyton. So long for you."

He said nothing. Gently he laid her down; her eyes were closed, her eyelids fluttering. Her mouth was open to his and he kissed her with savagery.

Thrueldan waited with Lania. With the Druid were Nertomorus, Throg, and the Druidesses, Shama and Danadil. Iona did not come in until the hour before sunset, when the sweet purple of dusk had changed the shadows, and a first halo announced the coming moon.

She came forward regally, her steps measured, her head held high.

"Sit down, Iona," Thrueldan offered.

"I will do as you request, my priest," Iona responded, her voice oddly tight. "Yet I disclaim the name Iona. I will be Iona no longer. For I am no longer a huntress, a daughter, a child, a girl. I will be a queen, and my name shall be changed as the day has changed to night, as the sword has been passed."

"It is right and appropriate," Thrueldan said, bowing. "Have you chosen your name?"

"Boudicca."

"Then you shall be Queen Boudicca." Thrueldan turned to Shama and received the heavy crown. Captured by the Celts of Galatia from a black king to the far south, it had been plundered by the Celts of Gaul and worn by their fiery king, Vercingetorix before his death at the hands of Caesar. It had been bloodstained, twice stolen, and thrice worn as the mark of rule before Athair had demanded it as the price of allegiance from the defeated Belgae thirty years earlier.

Now Thrueldan placed this ancient crown on the head of Iona and bowed deeply to her. Lania kissed her daughter's hand and Nertomorus brought forward Athair's sword, placing it upon her lap as she sat, head erect, eyes flat.

"I vow my loyalty, Queen Boudicca," Throg rumbled. Then the giant bowed also, touching the sword with his hands.

Dagda was late to arrive. He shouldered through the crowd in the warriors' hut to find his place near the fire. He had turned to locate Barra, and before his head had swiveled back, Iona had entered.

She came from the front of the hut, dressed in a white robe fringed in gold, a torque of silver and gold around her slender throat, an enameled brooch set with coral falling to her bosom.

Throg, Dagda could not help but notice, was walking behind her as if pledging allegiance. Nertomorus strode with his new queen as well, wearing a red cloak, sword at his side.

"Please do not drink until we have counseled," Iona said to Cymru who had opened a sack of wine. Cymru stared at her crookedly, but nodded, stopping up the winesack.

"What is the need for counsel?" Barra asked. His eyes were badly swollen; he stood with difficulty. "Strike back! Do you want us to pledge our fealty? We do so, my queen."

Barra delivered this last sentence somewhat sourly, but his words were his pledge.

"Thank you, Barra," Iona replied quietly, her eyes slightly brittle, her mouth set. "But there is need for a counsel. We are racing toward defeat."

"The Iceni will not be defeated!" Arawn shouted loudly, drawing a cheer from the assemblage.

"That is rhetoric, Arawn," Iona said above the uproar. "It is our hope, our desire, our sworn oath that we not be defeated! Yet slogans will not disperse the Romans. We are running!" she went on, her voice rising tremulously. "And we are being beaten. They will drive us into the sea."

"They will not," Arawn responded passionately.

Iona ignored the young man's fervor. Yet when he stood again to repeat his vow, accompanied by many oaths on Belenos and curses against the Romans, Iona interrupted.

"This is a part of the problem," she said, stretching a finger toward Arawn. Arawn shrunk back as if stung, his hands going to his breast.

"My queen . . ." Arawn stammered.

"Not you in particular, Arawn. We all know of your bravery, your stamina, your allegiance to the Iceni crown. But," she continued, facing the general congregation, eyes touching every man there, "this attitude must be defeated before the Romans can be beaten.

"They come in their ranks and files, in precision formations, archers in a line behind shields. They work like a machine which would grind Iceni bones. While our people willingly throw themselves on their lances!"

She hesitated a moment, taking a slow, deep breath. "There will be no more single combat!"

"Iona!" Dagda stood furiously. "It is our way, it has always brought us victory. Iona, you are about to destroy us."

"Dagda," she answered in a tone the general had never heard before from this girl, "I am your queen, and I am to be addressed as such. You are my general, and as such it is your place to obey. I will be called Boudicca; my orders will not be gainsaid."

"Iona!" he said angrily.

"You forget yourself so quickly," she reminded him.

"Queen Boudicca," Dagda said, swallowing hard, his arms stretched out in supplication, "we are not Romans. What would you have us do—line up like wheat to be mown? March forward as the Romans do? Forgetting all our skills? We are not links in a battle chain—we are men! Shall we behave as these foreign dogs do?"

"If it is necessary, Dagda." She let her eyes linger on those of the battle-weary general. Finally, as if collapsing in astonishment, he sat.

"I will command all forces," Iona said sternly. "There will be no forays, no single combat which I have not commanded. Every man, each woman is to be under my will ... until the Romans have been driven from our homeland. Until the earth is soaked with Roman blood."

"Is that all?" Dagda asked, bowing slightly. His puffy eyes held a glare of sheer animosity.

"No. Sit down, Dagda. It is not all."

Iona paced the floor a moment, hands catching for words. "Peace must be made with the Coritani."

"No! The devil, no!" Barra shouted.

Arawn leapt to his feet in disbelief. Cymru opened his wine sack and drank heavily, muttering obscenities. Nertomorus spoke for them all.

"My queen, good Boudicca—" He wiped back his graying hair, moving forward in a gesture of supplication. "As long as there has been time, the Coritani have been our enemies. They are of Celtic blood, yes," he said, shaking his head, "but they are sworn, bitter enemies. Can my elkhound lie down with wolves? Can the sun rise from the western sea? How then can you ask such an unthinkable, no—*unnatural* peace be sued for?"

"And during the meetings of the tribes, Nertomorus ... what is it we have then but an unnatural peace? Enemy beside enemy. Brother beside the man who has laid his brother low; wives near the men who have cleaved their husbands' skulls? It *is* unnatural. I affirm that." Iona stepped nearer to the old soldier, taking his hand gently in her own for the briefest moment.

"Yet we cannot fight on two fronts!" she proclaimed loudly, suddenly filled with fire. "With the Romans at our threshold, the Coritani at our back gate, we are bleeding our people!"

"Then what is it you suggest, Queen Boudicca?" Dagda asked in roughly veiled sarcasm. "That we kiss our enemy on the one hand, and march humbly forward, in well-disciplined ranks on the other to be slaughtered?"

"I do not ask! I command! There will be no more consultation. I thought we could speak as warriors to monarch—now I see that you are more concerned with your pride than with victory. You would follow your ancient, bull-headed notions to the grave rather than accept new conceptions!" Angrily she slashed at them with eyes and words.

"You are traitors—you! You would turn your backs on the Iceni for the sake of your manhood. False pride! If the Iceni are to survive, to prevail," —she went on in a softer, nearly beseeching tone— "we must find a new way to fight. Otherwise they will crush us with their numbers and their artillery and their precision. It will mean the death of the nation to continue in the old fashion," she added, pausing as her eyes closed and her fists clenched. "And as Athair has pledged, so I pledge—the nation must not die! Only the Iceni people is of importance! Hate me, but follow me."

"I follow you," Throg said slowly in a guttural, powerful voice.

"And I follow you, my queen," Breyton said. He had appeared from the shadows of the doorway to add his support. He was astonished at her sudden strength and boldness. Fondly he watched her standing erect before these warriors.

Iona blinked and turned her eyes down, her heart warming.

"I follow, of course," Nertomorus said. "You are my queen, and the descendant of my kings."

One after the other the warriors rose; even a reluctant Dwan Karnash came to her feet. Only Dagda, head bowed, did not pledge his blood.

"Throg is my commander," Iona said shortly. "Breyton his second." Then to the murmur of the crowd, the startled raising of voices, the disbelief on the faces of Dagda and Barra, both of whom were displaced by the command, she strode regally from the hut, leaving the nobles to themselves.

Thrueldan had waited just outside the hut. The sounds of drinking and strident comments from within filled the night air.

"You did well," Thrueldan said. "Most of them understand your point of view. Most will follow. Yet you have made a dangerous enemy. You have injured Dagda's pride. Let us hope, my queen, that this does not come back to haunt our effort."

"Dagda was wrong," Iona insisted.

"Yes. But you will discover that you cannot rule these men with iron will. They must be flattered at times, at times reprimanded like children, yet their pride cannot be taken from them. You will learn, Queen Boudicca, you must learn."

"I will learn," she vowed. "All that you can teach me, all that history has to teach. I will learn to flatter, to persuade, to kill."

Thrueldan watched her for a moment, then walked slowly away leaving her to her thoughts. The gentle girl, this carefree huntress, skilled with arms, yet not at war. She had been thrust into a warrior's stance. She must learn to lead. Quickly. She must learn the arts of war. If not her, then who?

If not Iona, no other would have the opportunity. It would be too late.

Chapter Seven

Massed in the cold light of pre-dawn, the Roman Ninth Legion covered the empty vale like a scarlet-coated horde of invading insects.

Marcus Atreus rested comfortably on the high dais while Catilus, his energetic lieutenant, paced the platform. Marcus Atreus lifted an eyebrow, studying the pinched face of Catilus.

"There's nothing to be done yet," Marcus reminded Catilus.

Catilus turned to his general as if he had not heard him, yet he nodded and sat beside the ruddy Atreus, nervously drumming his fingers on the arm of his chair.

"Damnable country," Catilus muttered. "The sun never shines. Damnable Britain. Fog and damp. One longs for Rome," he sighed. For Rome and the daughters of Catilus who were growing, turning into women as he chased these barbarians across the length of this accursed gray island.

"Perhaps we will be going home soon," Marcus

Atreus suggested. "Another battle like that last and our army of conquest will be replaced by an army of occupation."

"One admires the courage of these barbarians," Catilus said as Marcus, by a hand signal, arranged the phalanx to face the northern forest. "Brave . . . yet stubborn beyond endurance. To the point of suicide."

"They come," Marcus Atreus said softly.

Catilus glanced up to the northern forest perimeter, his hands involuntarily clenching. A group of a hundred or so mounted Celts had appeared, sifting through the shadows noiselessly, spectres moving across the deep green of the grass.

"The same as before," Catilus said. Yet there was no confidence in his voice.

"The same," Marcus said, rubbing his cleanshaven chin thoughtfully. He waved a hand again, and the right wing of the battle formation wheeled to face the Celts. The graybeard, Varius, was scuttling among his foot soldiers on his black charger. Rhoetus sat his horse like a stone soldier; Marcus could imagine the glare in the massive Neapolitan's hard eyes, and it caused the Roman general to smile.

Simonedes had stepped beside Marcus Atreus's chair. Marcus frowned slightly on recognizing the emperor's nephew. The little man was a nuisance, his mannerisms annoying, his arrogance an affront.

"The fields shall be stained scarlet before the morning's done," Simonedes said with smug satisfaction. His hand was on Marcus Atreus's chair. Marcus wondered vaguely how Simonedes himself would fare in battle against an enemy's muscle bunched behind a deadly lance. . . .

"They're attacking!"

Once more led by the mournful, challenging trumpets, four dozen or so wicker-sided chariots of the kind long outmoded on the continent charged down the long slopes. The Romans held their position as Marcus Atreus watched.

Queen Boudicca sat her horse in the alder wood, peering from the deep shadows. Throg led the charioteers on this day, his massive mane stiffened with lime, his armor gleaming bronze in the sunlight which parted the clouds at the hour of battle.

Marcus Atreus signaled to Varius, and the left flank of the Roman pincer wheeled to block the corridor into the broken country to the east.

Throg flailed mercilessly at the horses drawing his chariot. He drove nearly to the commander of this Roman division, eyes wild, massive arms raised in challenge. He buried his lance at the feet of Varius who stared back with curiosity. His soldiers, rigidly disciplined, did not move or reply to the aggression of Throg.

"Roman slugs!" Throg bellowed, holding back his huge, stamping chariot horses. "Cowardly weasels! I challenge any of you. Any two! Five!"

Then, his eyes sweeping the legion for one long moment, finally locking with those of Varius, he spat contemptuously and wheeled his chariot away, long sword describing menacing arcs as it flashed in the sunlight.

"Hold," Marcus Atreus said in a low voice to Catilus. The signal was flashed by mirror to Varius who held his men in check with a raised hand.

The right flank of the Ninth Legion had moved

into position now, under the big, broken-nosed Rhoetus. The Neapolitan felt his facial muscles twitching, his skin growing hot as he wished, as always, for there to be a beginning to battle so that there might more quickly be an end. He was concerned, yet he showed no concern on his dark, chiseled face.

"Hold!" Rhoetus commanded.

On the rise, the infantry of the Celts appeared. Coming forward from the forest depths, beating swords against shields rhythmically, some leaping madly up and down in challenging movements.

Marcus Atreus waited still.

At a signal from Catilus, the ranks of archers moved forward. The horsemen and charioteers were just out of range yet. Simonedes was leaning across the rampart of the dais, his slack mouth trembling in anticipation.

"Now they'll taste it. Now they'll taste it!" he exulted.

Marcus Atreus's cold eyes flickered to the emperor's nephew. Catilus stood, arms twitching. In the ranks Varius and Rhoetus waited.

On the hillrise Queen Boudicca watched, then nodded slightly to Barra who gestured forward with his lance. He scowled heavily, started to say something to his queen whose eyes were intent on the battlefield, then withdrew slightly.

The Celts surged forward, savage shrieks filling the air as steel flashed, and hooves thundered across the dark earth. A chariot broke apart on a stony rut in the midst of the crush forward, and the first of the cavalry were already nearly upon the Romans. A Roman legionnaire tumbled from the ranks, a Celtic lance through his chest; the arm of

Catilus dropped suddenly, powerfully, as if in retaliation.

Varius's hand went up, and a shower of arrows rained on the Celts. Throg flinched as a steel point drove against his shield. Then he laughed and drove his chariot forward into the ranks of archers who were notching fresh arrows. His massive sword sang through the air, taking three Romans before he turned swiftly back, one of his horses streaming blood from the shoulder. Leun had dismounted and he crow-hopped forward, his lance finding a firm target.

On the dais, Catilus again lowered his arm and Rhoetus, cursing violently, ordered his infantry forward, his own sword hot in his massive hand. He saw the man beside him go down, saw a Celt being dragged past by his own horse, then the field blurred into a wash of color, shouting, screams of pain and steel flying through the skies.

Throg watched a man die under his sword, then he circled back slightly. Leun had made it to his horse, an arrow in his thigh. The Roman pincer had begun to close, and close rapidly. Throg glanced toward the forest.

"Now?" Barra demanded.

Queen Boudicca did not move. She watched the battle erupting below them. The Roman grip closed on her soldiers. Dwan Karnash had been thrown from her horse and she had leaped to Cymru's chariot. Throg still waited his queen's signal.

"Now? Surely now!" Barra implored, stepping nearer to her.

"Now," she nodded and Barra's lance was thrust into the skies. Throg saw the signal instantly and he fell back, calling his troops.

"We have them," Simonedes said from the dais. "They're breaking. Running."

Arrows streamed after the Celts who had turned and were now reentering the forest. Only a few remained on the field. A few of the dead.

"Now we've broken them!" Simonedes shouted, his head thrown back, a bit of spittle dribbling from the corner of his mouth.

"Marcus!"

Marcus Atreus turned to Catilus, a question on his lips, yet already he had seen the smoke. "The camp!"

"Damn them!" Catilus was signaling furiously. Yet Varius was far off to the left, his men lost among the hillocks, and Rhoetus was much too far from the camp.

Smoke rose in billowing black clouds. The stores. The tents. Everything needed to last the winter. Marcus Atreus stood, wiped back his hair, and winced. Simonedes was in front of him. The short man was nearly apoplectic.

"What does this mean!" he shrieked.

"It means," Marcus Atreus said simply, "that they have won the battle."

Varius's corps was quick-marching back toward the camp, but it was a half-mile away, and whatever damage could be done would have already been done, the attackers vanished.

Breyton sat watching the camp burn, the tents collapsing like tinder, the corn crib only a pile of smoldering ash; the cattle stampeded toward the marshes.

Arawn drew up beside him breathlessly, his face

smudged with soot. He led a magnificent stallion in gold trappings.

"A present for our queen," Arawn laughed. Breyton's eyes flashed to the far hills where he knew she would be watching the fires burn.

"What a woman that one is," Breyton said softly. "The heart of a queen, the mind of a general."

"The Romans will be through for the winter," Arawn said. He watched the last of the Celts clamber out of the valley where the blackened heap of the Roman camp still smoked. Farther up the vale he could see the Romans coming, yet they had no wish to continue the battle now.

"Come Breyton." Arawn turned his mount, still leading the long-striding stallion.

Breyton sat his battle horse another long moment, watching the camp, the far, forested hills, the empty, smoke-filled skies. Then he turned his horse, angrily, and followed after his friend.

Chapter Eight

Arawn returned at the point of the raiding party, dust billowing and swirling at the feet of the horse he rode. Dismounting with a leap he found himself nearly before Iona. The young man shouted, swung onto the back of the captured white stallion and spurred it forward, riding three times around the compound, circling the great post, weaving among the huts.

"For you, my queen," he shouted finally, dismounting from the quivering white stallion. "A gift from the Romans."

It was a magnificent animal. Iona studied the long haunches, the tremendously muscled chest, and she patted the horse's shoulder with pleasure. "I thank you, Arawn."

"No, we thank you, Queen Boudicca. We will not again have to worry about these jackals taking our cattle, our land, our blood."

Iona did not answer. She instead gave the signal for the victory celebration. Shouting, dancing gleefully, the warriors rode or walked away, some to bandage wounds, some to bathe for the feast. Throg alone stood beside his queen.

"You do not think the Romans will go?" he asked soberly.

"They have so many men. So much machinery. They did not come to stay a season, but an eternity. We have only won our first contest. Let them celebrate," she said, watching Arawn and Leun who had fallen to an impromptu wrestling match. "Let them laugh while they can."

Lania sat in the corner of her home, her old fingers working at some sewing. Iona walked to her mother and kissed her gray hair gently.

"We have won?" Lania asked, her watery eyes downcast.

"Yes." Iona patted her mother's frail shoulder and began undressing, calling for Thramane.

While Thramane brushed her hair, Iona watched her mother, seeing not only a stooped woman, but a young, vigorous, raven-haired huntress she still remembered from her girlhood. How strong Lania had seemed then; how quickly the burdens of war, the weight of rule had aged her.

"We have won," Iona said, rising as Thramane finished dressing her hair and went off to bring the oils and perfumes, "yet I would rather we had lost the battle and had Athair as father and husband."

Slowly, uncontrollably, Iona felt a trembling rack her shoulders, a single hot tear sting her cheek before she could brush it away.

"But Athair would never have wished defeat," Lania reminded her. The old woman put aside her sewing and came to Iona, touching her cheek with the back of her hand. "The tribe must come first.

Our people. That was what Athair believed to the death, and what you must believe. Always."

"Yet—" Iona kissed her mother's hand, her lips lingering, her eyes fixed on the small fire in the hearth.

"It is only that the burdens of leadership are now coming home to you, Iona," her mother said. "Now you understand that your people depend on *you*. You alone. It is a terrible burden! Perhaps you will come to understand your father, his ways, better in the long days to come.

"The stress, the desire to prevent the death of the people. These will be terrible times, Iona, yet you are strong enough for it. Endure! Never show your weaknesses in front of them; never admit fear though it tears at your throat and heart. That is what Athair would have advised you.

"Your life is that of the Iceni nation. A people depends on your strength. You are no longer my Iona, my daughter, but my Queen Boudicca. Do not forget it for a moment."

Arawn was deep in his cups as Boudicca entered the ceremonial hut; shouting and dancing around the room he was savagely exultant. Barra seemed sober, yet his eyes were heavy. Throg brooded on his pile of skins, a heavy arm draped over a cushion.

The others were loudly cheering each other, and nearly in unison they rose in salute as their new queen entered.

"Today we have emptied their stomachs!" Leun shouted, his long hair falling into his face, a new gold medallion shimmering on his smooth chest. "Tomorrow we will crush their spines."

His wounded leg gave out on him and Leun

tumbled merrily into Dagda's arm. Dagda cursed, shoved him aside and drank deeply from his own cup before standing.

"You would perhaps expect it from me least, Boudicca," Dagda said, "yet I raise my cup to you. It was a strong victory, and nearly bloodless for us. Strength to the Iceni; death to the Roman slugs!"

Iona's goblet was filled by the servant boy, and she sat back contentedly, enjoying the low glow of the fire, the smells of meat, the warmth of respect due a leader, a sovereign for the first time.

The thin Werken, the bard, strummed quietly in the corner, breaking at moments into raucous choruses when the warriors scuffled.

Dwan Karnash lounged near Breyton, her eyes glossed with wine, her arm resting languidly on Breyton's thigh. Once, haughtily, she toasted Iona. Iona pretended to take no notice of the gesture which was both mockery and challenge.

When the boar had been roasted, the queen cut the hero's portion and impaled it on her poniard. Her gaze flickered over Throg's face, over Dagda and the sour Cymru, yet she knew to whom she would offer the hero's share.

She strode directly to Dwan Karnash and stood before her, back erect. Dwan Karnash's eyes came up. There was fire in them, and her full mouth trembled slightly before she spoke.

"Give it to another, my queen. For myself—I have already won the hero's portion." Then her hand clenched Breyton's well-muscled thigh, and Dwan Karnash broke into harsh, drunken laughter.

Dagda's mouth turned down in suppressed amusement as Breyton tried unsuccessfully to say something salving. Arawn broke into a grin. Still Iona stood before Dwan Karnash, her gaze steady, face placid.

"As you wish," Iona said finally. Her eyes looked briefly at Breyton's, and she seemed to see in his eyes a swiftly passing succession of moments —clouds shifting in the wind, reflecting in the waters, birds winging through a crimson evening. Finally the young man's eyes turned from her.

"I think it is fitting, in that case," Iona said, "to give our young conqueror the portion. Take it, Breyton. You fought well today."

Breyton accepted the boar's haunch without speaking. Dwan Karnash laughed again, loudly; but the eyes of the warriors were fixed on Iona. She revealed nothing; she had the bearing of a queen, the reserve necessary to rule.

"I thought she would skewer Dwan Karnash with that dagger of hers," Leun whispered. Arawn shook his head. The smile was gone from his face.

"Drink!" Iona had hoisted a glass. In three swallows it was gone, and she threw her goblet into the pit where it drew sparks. "Drink and let us dance. Werken! Play a merry tune!"

The minstrel struck up a tune and Iona pulled Throg to his feet. For a moment they danced, the others joining them in this war celebration. Then Iona let Throg's heavy hand drop, and she slipped from the hut into the black night.

A star died in heaven, flashing toward earth. An omen, a messenger, she did not know which. Slowly she walked from the camp, the sounds of rejoicing falling away to silence. Her mind shut out the night.

She walked a whispered wood. Sunlight cut figures on the earth. Leaves crackled beneath her feet. She was naked, her heart visible to all, her essence begging for another essence to become a unity with hers.

Waters fell from the heavens. Warm, melting rains which decayed the massive trees as flame devours candles.

And she was a part of it. There was no pain to it; it was simply a giving up of Iona, of herself. A renunciation.

Were such thoughts madness?

Dark birds swam past in myriad procession. Bluebirds walked beneath her feet, her bare toes nudging their softness. Carefully she waded through them. They became deeper, their rustling, downy bodies caressing her thighs, her breasts, until only her head protruded above the mass of blue softness.

And their voices sang in her throat until the giant silenced their song. Was this madness?

Thrueldan might know as he knew all; yet in the dream the face of the giant might have been Thrueldan's own dark face, and she vowed not to speak to the Druid of it.

The wind was chill off the eastern sea. Marcus Atreus wrapped his cloak tightly about his shoulders as he viewed the destroyed camp. Soldiers sifted through the ash heap searching for anything of value. A worn sandal, an ounce of beef had suddenly become valuable.

To the south another group of men worked in the woods, chopping boughs to be woven into flimsy shelters. If the winds could be believed, there was rain in the air, and weeks of living in damp, porous shelters ahead.

"I was sorry to hear you lost your horse," Catilus said. The bald man scurried along beside his chief. His narrow face was creased with concern.

"It was a shame. Some Celt is well mounted on Placidus."

"Simonedes sulks still," Catilus remarked. They had stopped to study the remains of their stable.

"Men like him," Marcus said with a sigh, "believe it all comes so easily. Wealth, honor, victory. That is the burden of the high-born. Struggle has no meaning for them. It simply bores them, or infuriates them. They have never suffered failure themselves, and so the blame falls to those who surround them."

"Will he write the emperor of this?" Catilus asked, his legs again straining to keep pace with Marcus Atreus as they continued the survey of the razed campsite. Three wounded men lay under a broken oak, their faces waxen, bruised.

"He will write," Marcus guessed.

"Yet you do not seemed concerned, Marcus."

"Why should I be?" he shrugged. "I am given credit for victories. Why not accept the blame for defeat?"

Yet he was worried. The emperor's nephew wished the battle for Britannia to be ended rapidly, cleanly. He wished to govern the Celts after they had been crushed, in effect giving Simonedes a nation of his own to rule far from Claudius's Rome. Or so Marcus believed. Yes, Simonedes would write to his uncle.

Simonedes was more dour than ever at the evening meal in Marcus Atreus's patched tent. The short man tried to cover his bitterness, his disgust with this cold, damp northern land and all of its inhabitants. He was bathed, oiled, wearing a clean scarlet robe. Yet the wine on the table was the last of his stores—the filthy Iceni had taken the rest— and the wind twisted through the jagged gash in Marcus Atreus's tent.

Varius seemed much older, yet his eyes were alert; he drank his wine slowly, wiping at his gray beard. He glanced at Marcus Atreus.

"Will there be time for another offensive, Marcus?"

"There is time. Yet we lack the supporting stores. Our men are cold, ragged, and ill-equipped. Besides," he shrugged, "one never knows these days where the Celts will make a stand. We certainly cannot afford to pursue them inland without provisions."

"We cannot withdraw for the winter," Simonedes said, waving a ringed hand. He said it quietly, but it seemed in the nature of a command.

"Simonedes," Varius said, "if the rains come we will be at the mercy of the Celts. Perhaps we should consider withdrawing to Verulamium." The old general fingered his cup.

"No," Simonedes insisted. He stood and walked to the tent flap, the wind catching his cloak, lifting his dark hair. "By spring I wish this situation to be settled, Britannia secured."

"Simonedes!" Marcus Atreus stood, his ruddy face flushed with anger and wine. "To do so would be to surrender half our forces to the whims of a hard winter."

"Victory costs blood," the aristocrat shrugged.

"Whose? Not yours!" Varius said, suddenly inflamed.

"You will be silent, Julius Varius!" Simonedes exploded. "Perhaps you do not remember to whom you speak."

"I recall," the old general said, angrily slapping his wine cup down before stalking from the tent. Marcus Atreus sat staring at his goblet, turning the stem between his palms.

"And you, my commander?"

"I agree with Varius," Marcus said softly. "Yet I support the emperor's representative in whatever decision he finds compelling."

"Good." He fixed his haughty gaze on Marcus. "Then that is settled. As for Julius Varius . . . perhaps senility excuses his behavior. Perhaps he has been in the field too long."

"If you are determined that we must try to dispose of the Iceni before spring, Simonedes, then we must attempt to provision ourselves. We must reinforce our line soldiers!"

"You have a thought?" Simonedes asked excitedly.

"It can be done. Possibly. By transferring the Londinium guard. But if we sent word this very moment. . . ." Marcus Atreus shrugged and fell silent.

It was possible that the Londinium troops might arrive early enough to be of help. If the Celts did not choose to mount a total assault. If the rains did not come soon and hard, washing the roads away.

Marcus himself thought little of the idea; yet if Simonedes was determined to fight through the winter, there was no other way to avoid disaster.

"Summon a rider," Simonedes ordered the centurion at the door. "And see that he has three good horses."

Simonedes smiled to himself. By spring then. By spring! "Have another glass of wine with me, Marcus," he said warmly, rubbing his hands together. His eyes glittered with excitement. His own empire!

"Let us drink, Marcus Atreus. Let us drink to final victory!"

The position of Marcus Atreus steadily worsened as he complained in his letters to Rome. The rains had come and lingered for fifteen days before breaking to a damp cloudiness, leaving the earth a sodden, impassable bog.

> *The Celts continue to display unusual, novel tactics, Claudius. Now they have fallen to firing arrows from the woods. Lances appear out of nowhere, guided by no hand, thrust out of the concealing low fog to claim our lives.*
>
> *Whereas formerly the Celts were eager to rush headlong against our massed formations, they now strike and wisp away. Two men were found dead within our camp perimeter this very morning—of Iceni lances.*

The men were nearly rebellious. Sour, gray faces peered up at Marcus Atreus and Rhoetus as they toured the camp, arranging still more sentries.

"It wears against the soldiers," Rhoetus said in that low, rumbling voice, "and erodes their confidence in their leaders."

"Yet it costs us few lives," Marcus commented.

"If the reserves from Londinium can arrive soon enough—if they *do* arrive—we will be at a far greater strength than before. If only we can last until spring."

"The dysentery, the foul spirits, may cost us a greater loss than Celtic weapons," Rhoetus suggested.

They had stopped on a low knoll overlooking the camp. Far to the north, through the shifting fog, they saw what possibly was a Celtic campfire.

"What is it they feast upon so often? Boar?" Rhoetus asked. "Let us send out men to hunt this boar."

"I have sent out parties," Marcus advised him. "They have not come back from the hunt."

"Devils!" Rhoetus growled.

"The same as we, Rhoetus. They fight, we fight. Survival and conquest . . . eternally man's lot."

"What do you make of these new tactics they employ?" Rhoetus asked, squatting on the grass. He toyed with a leaf.

"They have found a tactician," Marcus answered simply. "A general who employs the weapons he has and does not throw flesh upon our lances."

"I have considered," Rhoetus said thoughtfully, "that the Celts are employing these guerrilla tactics because they are weakening. Perhaps they are too weak to mount a full attack. If we were to make a final thrust . . ."

"No. I will not chance it. I favor attack always, as you know; but not with my men in this condition. Besides, Rhoetus, has it occurred to you that the Iceni might be buying time not because they are weakening, but because they are growing stronger, gaining support?"

"The same as we are? But from where, Marcus? These Celtic tribes have limited reserves. They cannot draw from Gaul and Iberia, Thrace and Syria, Egypt as we can."

"From where . . . it was an idle supposition," Marcus said. "Still, they seem to be waiting for the right moment, and I have no idea it will grow easier for us from this time on, Rhoetus. We have hardened their will, not broken it."

Iona, the Queen Boudicca, was dressed in a sheer white robe without ornamentation. On her knees in the willow glade she waited while Thrueldan spoke to the waters, to the stag-god, Cernunnos, to the heart of life which originated in the forest shrine.

There was a small stone altar there, with a top of clear alabaster. In the altar also was a nook where rested the skull of a man killed by Cernunnos himself on a summer's day when fire spit out of an empty sky following a false swearing.

Thrueldan's back was rigid, yet the muscles in his face swam and twisted like the surface of the flowing stream. His eyes showed nothing but white as he rested on his knees, a slaughtered boar under his knife.

Then his voice began in words which were not Celtic, and his hand, still holding the sacrificial knife, twitched.

Shadows wove together forming patterns; the sun glowed in the high reaches, clouds closing the eastern sky. Still Thrueldan spoke to the gods, to the protectors of the Iceni.

When he finally rose, wearily, limply, Iona herself staggered as she took her feet. They had arrived at the shrine just before dawn; now the western sun was a reddish memory on the high silver clouds.

Slowly the Druid came to her, his mouth open, his eyes deep. The knife fell from his hand without Thrueldan's awareness. He came to Iona, fingers still bloodied.

"Yes," he nodded. "The gods will it. Yes!" Thrueldan shouted.

"Then let it be so," Iona said. "I will send a messenger tonight."

So Thrueldan agreed.

The gods had spoken.

There could be no argument with her plan now from the generals. The Iceni were battered, crippled. The Coritani would be summoned. The Regni from the south coast. The Atrebates from the western lands. There would be a Celtic League. A massing of the Celtic people. Enough to meet the Romans, enough to drive them back into the sea!

Chapter Nine

Iona, the Queen Boudicca, sat her bench regally, the finest furs draped over her arms, skins across the floor of the large hut. Throg, arms crossed, lips tight, stood behind her, Nertomorus beside her.

Kowlter and the others of the Coritani delegation had arrived first, wearing chain-mail and bearing arms. The Belgae king, silent, seemed nervous. Tambil of the Regni was rigid, jaw set. Queen Caldera of the Cornovii sat woodenly near the door, awaiting the words of the young Iceni queen. Representatives of the Parisi and Brigantii tribes were there from the far north countries. Curious men in furs and braided hair, they watched the young Queen Boudicca with the curiosity of predators.

"The Romans are at our gates," Iona began, rising. Her bearing was strong, her arms, braceleted in gold, tensed as she spoke.

"So we recognize," Tambil of the Regni said sourly. "They have trampled our crops and stolen our women. Yet the Iceni have never offered us succor."

"Was it ever sued for?" Iona demanded.

"Would it have made a difference?" King Tambil asked. A red-bearded man with pale blue eyes, he stood only three feet from Iona.

"Perhaps not," she admitted. "Yet it took a time before the Iceni—or any of us—recognized the Roman plot for what it is."

"And what do you mean by that, girl?" Queen Caldera asked harshly.

"I mean that the Roman war is not a war of appropriation, but a war of domination. They mean with all of their strength to destroy the very memory of the Celtic nations."

"It cannot be done," the Belgae King, Lambar, laughed.

"Who says that this is their aim?" Kowlter demanded savagely. "The Iceni? The Iceni who mean to trap us with their own lies, drawing us into a snare?"

"No, Kowlter," Iona said patiently. "The Romans themselves admit this is the point of their war. Thrueldan, the Druid, has knowledge of Roman words, of Roman boasts. And it is their aim to own the world."

"Zarkdan, our own Druid, has said the same," the king of the Parisi said thoughtfully.

"I have heard nothing of it," Kowlter said. Turning imperiously to Iona, he demanded, "What else has your Druid told you, child-queen?" Mockingly, he awaited an answer, hands spread out before him.

"What else does Thrueldan tell me?" Iona mused thoughtfully. It was important that she ig-

nore Kowlter's baiting, and she did so. "What else
... that there was a Roman called Julius Caesar
who went into Gaul and massacred two hundred
thousand Helvetii who wished only to flee the Roman war machine. Men, women, children.

"What else has my Druid told me? That near
Avaricum forty thousand Gallic Celts under Vercingetorix were slaughtered.

"You know of Vercingetorix—all of you, at least
by reputation—a great warrior. Yet his people
would not join in common cause. Factions argued,
splintered, debated, warred and surrendered without solidity of mind."

"That was fifty years ago," Kowlter commented.
"In your father's time and across the sea."

"And the Romans have only grown stronger.
And we weaker. They have advanced across that
sea. Our island is the last refuge of free Celtdom.
We are the last of our race. Are we to be obliterated for the same reason Gaul was smothered
by Roman red? Can we not learn from history?
Must we bleed to learn? Must we be defeated
before we understand the strength of a united nation as Rome is, the inherent weakness of our
loosely confederated tribes?" Then she paused a
moment, catching each sovereign's eyes.

"Must we suffer defeat to learn what victory's
price was?"

"It has gone badly to the south," the man of the
Atrebates said, stroking a thinning gray beard.
"When the ships landed we thought to fend them
off. Yet more ships came, lining our coasts with
forests of masts. Then we tried to beat them back,
to make treaties. Yet they continued to advance, to
break their word. Finally we withdrew into the fens

where we hide like cowardly dogs."

"No Celtic king should admit to this!" Kowlter shouted. "To hide, to run! The shame of the gods on you!"

"Yes, you can say that, Kowlter. Wait until they cross the Ouse into the northlands. Then you will see. Then you will know," the gray-bearded king said solemnly. "They were five to our one. What could we do but bleed?"

"Now Viron is threatened," Iona said, stepping forward with great animation. "Since the Romans crossed the Tamesis and took Londinium we have waged our war. Yet we lose. Slowly. Ever so slowly we lose ground, lose our people's blood."

"Yes. So we know. What is it you propose?" Kowlter demanded impatiently.

"We Celts are one," Iona said. "Yet we have divided. Still we fight among ourselves while our enemies, in lesser numbers, overwhelm us individually. Let us join together. Let us put down the attacking wolf one final time. Let us take him by the jugular until he can no longer dare to assault our islands."

"It cannot be done," Queen Caldera said throatily. "It has been tried before. A League Britannia. To no avail."

"The necessity was not there at that time. Now it is our survival in the balance."

"And who would provide the leadership for this grand league?" Kowlter shouted. "The Iceni child-queen?"

"I would," Iona answered. "Yes, Kowlter, wipe that look from your face. I would because it is *here* the Romans are massed. Fresh troops are en route even now from Londinium, my eyes in the forests tell me. It is Viron the Romans will attack. And Viron alone is capable of withstanding the Roman war machinery—you above all others should know that, Kowlter. I recall that you have attempted Viron's fortifications in the past."

"I refuse," Kowlter snapped, waving a disgusted hand.

"I cannot refuse," the Belgae, Lambar, said, "yet I must discuss this matter with my generals. Our plight has been severe."

"We would fight under any command if the force were large enough to ensure victory," the Regni king commented. "We have a blood grudge against these butchers. We hide, but we are waiting, in those lowland fens. Waiting for children to be born, to take arms. Yes, by the gods! We will join you, Queen Boudicca, if there are numbers of Celts."

"As Lambar said, we must consider it," the queen of the Atrebates said.

"Consider then," Iona said. "But consider this: a great battle is building here, in the Iceni homeland. We are the strongest nation of all Celtic Britannia, by far. If we are defeated here, all of the islands will fall. All of Celtic Europe will be but a vague, forlorn memory.

"Our children will be born in slavery, bred to serfdom, abused, belittled, neglected—our proud children. Our noble blood, warriors' blood, shall be plowed into the earth or bled on the rack, or watered with Roman blood. Consider it! But consider it fully."

"And if the decision is affirmative, Queen Boudicca," Kowlter asked bitterly, "what then shall we do?"

"We will mass at Viron," she answered. "Every man, woman, child, from fen and forest; the battlements will be refined still more. Still greater traps and walls will be built. Then we will fight from the woods, from the fens, tearing at them as daws can tear the falcon."

"And *our* homelands? Our crops? Our cattle?"

"What you can bring, bring," she said slowly, her eyes resting briefly on every representative. "What you cannot transport, burn until it is only ashes. I will not have Celtic houses shelter them, Celtic crops feed them. Poison the waters! Trample the corn. Slaughter the cattle."

"Do you have any idea what you demand?" Queen Caldera asked slowly. "Do you know what you ask of us?"

"I know. I do know, Caldera." Iona took half a step nearer the older woman. "I am asking what is necessary."

"It did not go badly," Nertomorus said as the last of the foreign delegates passed through Viron's fortifications, heading their separate directions as they emerged onto the meadows.

"No, not badly, yet not well enough," Iona answered. "Now they will confer, bicker, debate . . . perhaps until it is too late."

"Much has been asked of them," Nertomorus observed as they walked from the conference hut. "To destroy all they possess, putting all faith in a traditional enemy. I imagine we should hesitate as well, had they come to us with such a suggestion."

"We must gain time," Iona said. They had entered her home. Thramane had placed food and wine on the table. Iona sat across from Nertomorus and explained, "The Romans have called reinforcements from Londinium. I believe they will be here within the week."

"How many?"

"Perhaps a hundred thousand," she answered heavily.

"Far too many," Nertomorus agreed. "What can we do?"

"Until . . . unless, the other tribes can be convinced to join us, we will be greatly outnumbered. We must therefore mount our own offensive and keep the Roman wolf at bay, off balance, unable to poise for a strong attack."

"More raids? Burning?"

"Yes—but more still, Nertomorus."

Iona stood, moving about the room, her young face prematurely lined with worry. "We must deal the Roman a heavy blow before he is reinforced. Perhaps we will need subterfuge to offset his machinery and knowledge of tactics."

"You have something in mind, I assume?"

"I do, Nertomorus. Yet," she said, sitting to face him once again, her head bent forward, dark eyes serious, liquid, "I believe it is best if no one in the camp knows of it yet."

Nertomorus felt his mouth tighten. "You fear treachery?" he asked in disbelief.

"I think it is best to exercise caution," Iona said simply. Yet Nertomorus would not be put off.

"If you think we may have an informer in our midst . . ."

"Leave this to me, Nertomorus. Please. Think no more about it, but make certain our forces are provisioned, ready to march at a moment's notice. Bring the cattle from the northern woods closer to

Viron. There may be no time to gather them when we need meat."

"Yes, my queen," Nertomorus replied, bowing severely.

"And, Nertomorus, speak none of this to any man or woman."

Iona's eyes were hard now, the tendons in her throat taut. Nertomorus nodded again, somewhat stiffly. Scratching his chin thoughtfully he went out into the grounds. Throg was waiting to meet him, yet Nertomorus said nothing.

Together the two old soldiers walked to the warriors' hut. Smoke rose into the dark skies, the pale moon hung pendant among the wispy, silver clouds. Throg threw a heavy arm around Nertomorus's shoulder as they made their silent way.

Just before they turned the corner near the granary, Nertomorus caught a glimpse of a slippery, crooked figure in the shadows near Iona's hut.

Cymru! And what business could that half-wit have there?

"Why did you stop?" Throg asked. "Did you see something?"

"No. Nothing," Nertomorus shrugged. Yet he marked it strongly in his memory.

Chapter Ten

Julius, the centurion, dragged the man forward. The Celt's eyes were both blackened, his nose broken, his lips split.

The Celt was thrown down roughly and shackled outside the tent, his chains rooted to a post. The Roman soldiers examined him curiously. Inside the tent a small fire blossomed. Simonedes nodded to the reporting centurion.

"Well?"

"He has said nothing. These Celts are stubborn, sir."

"So is the lash strong," Simonedes answered sharply. Without information the Roman Ninth might be broken utterly, good men dying, reputations shattered, his own neck thrust into the noose of disgrace.

"What is it you wish, then?" the centurion asked finally. A burly man with a scarred nose, his face showed no emotion.

"What I wish," Simonedes exploded, slamming

his fist against the camp table, "is information!"

"He will not speak."

"Then find a method no tongue can resist," Simonedes said softly, impatiently. Damn these centurions, these commoners who believed torture beneath them. They had no imagination and little intelligence. They must be continually guided, constantly prodded.

Marcus Atreus appeared suddenly in the doorway, his hair windblown. Outside a gray wind twisted in the oaks. Leaves scattered across the dark earth. "We have a prisoner?" Marcus asked.

"Yes. An Iceni warrior," Simonedes responded.

"I was not told of it."

"There was nothing to be told," Simonedes said haughtily, leaning back in his chair. His foot had begun to ache. He was subject to spells of the gout, and with the cold weather it seemed to have settled in once again.

The emperor's nephew smiled. "When we have information of a tactical nature, my dear Marcus Atreus, it shall be passed on to our generals."

Marcus bowed slightly, quickly, from the neck and swept from the tent. The crooked little Celt chained to the post caught his eye for a moment. There was no ignoring the signs of physical abuse. Marcus felt his jaw twitch. Torture was not among his weapons of war. It was not the way of a soldier, but of an inquisitor.

"Sir?"

Simonedes glanced up at the centurion who still waited rigidly at attention. The firelight caught the bronze of his embellished breastplate.

"What is it?" he snapped.

"You wish..."

"I wish information to be obtained from the prisoner! I demand it! Must I guide you, take you by the hand, centurion?"

Julius bowed deeply and backed from the doorway, his cheeks burning. Two soldiers stood beside the chained Iceni. Without glancing at them, Julius waved a hand. "Continue."

It was then four in the afternoon; at ten o'clock a rap on the tent frame, a calling voice awakened Simonedes. With a start he sat up in bed. Shivering in the cold, he walked to the doorway. Julius was there, his face oddly ashen.

"Sir," the centurion reported, "we have information."

As Simonedes stepped back, his eyebrows arched in anticipation, the Iceni was shoved through the opening. He fell against the dust of the floor. There were red welts on Cymru's back from hip to neck. One eye had been damaged. His hands were black, broken. He stood, staggering forward clumsily, battered internally by the blows of many fists, by the strokes of many kicks.

Simonedes smiled faintly as the Celt stumbled and collapsed on his face once again. The Roman took his wine cup, filling it.

"So," Simonedes said, "we have broken one of these famed Iceni warriors!"

He yanked Cymru's head roughly around by the beard, a smile still playing on his narrow mouth. "So you wish to speak, barbarian. And what have you to say?"

"I . . ." Cymru hesitated. The interpreter had come in, standing meekly by the table where a candle glowed dimly.

"Tell him to speak or receive double what he has

already taken," Simonedes ordered, his hand describing a threat before Cymru's eyes.

"Tell him to go to hell," Cymru said. He watched as the words were translated by the nervous interpreter. Then Simonedes's foot met his throat and Cymru rolled over, choking on his own blood.

"Take him away," Simonedes said indifferently. "If he will not speak, beat him until he cannot!"

Cymru had rolled to his knees, blood dripping from lips and nose. He began trembling as the words were translated. Slavering, he crawled forward on hands and knees, dragging himself toward the Roman nobleman.

"No more, my lord. No more, my liege. My god!"

"Flay him alive," Simonedes said turning his back.

"I will speak. I will speak!" Cymru cried, lowering his face to the floor, the dirt mingling with the blood on his lips. "I will speak."

"Then do so! I lose patience."

"It will be on the morning of the third day from today. The Iceni will mass at Viron. They will divide into a double force. . . ." Cymru's eyes were showing only white; he sagged forward and coughed heavily.

"Go on! There will be gold in this for you, Celt. Rest. Food . . . are you hungry, thirsty? We will give you a warm bed to sleep away the pain in."

"They will split into a double force," Cymru went on. His head reeled with pain, his limbs trembled. "And come upon the Roman legion from the west. Yet this will be only a feint. They wish the Romans to fall back and be engulfed by the main force which shall approach from the east and block off all retreat."

"Is there more?" Simonedes demanded, lifting Cymru's blackened face.

"There is no more. Roman retreat ... the massed Celtic forces behind the legions. Iceni victory...." Cymru raised his face, a hopeful smile on his battered features. "Lord! You spoke of gold. You may keep it. Yet warmth ... food ... I have had no food in three days. I beg you, my lord!"

"Take him away," Simonedes ordered them, loathing burning his mind. "Take this filth from here."

"And feed him?" Julius asked.

"And kill him. Break his bones and kill him."

Cymru was dragged from the tent, his eyes wild, his legs kicking out viciously, his screams filling the tent of Simonedes with echoing horror.

"Heroic barbarians!" Simonedes spat. He drank again, deeply, and motioned to his servant. "Summon Marcus Atreus. Tell him that I have won his final victory for him."

Iona was just outside the gates of Viron, alone beneath the stars. All of nature, aloof and stoic, watched back as she smiled against the night. From afar a strange howling cry filled the air. A wolf? A man in extreme pain? An omen sent by Cernunnos? She could not be sure.

But it was cold, and she shivered in the night. It was damp, the coming northern clouds promising rain. Nertomorus seemed to materialize from nowhere, his loyal gray head nodding to his young queen.

"The world awaits," Nertomorus said in an oddly muffled voice.

"It awaits."

"Do the stars spell doom, Queen Boudicca, my dear Iona? Or is victory etched upon the sky flag?"

Iona, shuddering in the cold night, said nothing for a time. "Thrueldan would say that the gods do not reveal these answers to his pleas; I reply that our hearts dictate the omens."

"And what shall I reply to that?" Nertomorus asked quietly.

"That you shall obey."

"I shall. As I always obeyed Athair, my queen."

"Ready the troops, Nertomorus. Tonight! Tomorrow we strike."

"Tomorrow! Without the gathered Celts? Without the Belgae and Regni?"

"Without them. A summons has reached my ears. A cry for action, from the night. Ready the men. We leave the hour before dawn."

Day broke cold, gray. Marcus Atreus drew his cloak around him more tightly, cursing the cold day, the Celts, and Simonedes in particular.

Rhoetus walked beside his general, breath issuing in steamy clouds from the Neapolitan's lips.

"So, the politician has taken the reins," Rhoetus grunted.

"Yes," Marcus said shortly.

"It is bad when civilians dictate the course of combat. No matter how accurate his information, it leaves us with an inflexible posture."

"And what is there to do about it?" Marcus Atreus demanded hotly, his eyes softening as Rhoetus drew back. "The emperor's nephew! One can hardly dispute his orders. He is hungry for a rapid resolution, hungry for recognition, it seems."

"As you say, Marcus, there is nothing to be done. Look at Varius—the old man will end his days in disgrace now. Demoted at his age for insubordination!" Rhoetus spat in disgust. "For speaking the truth."

Together from a grassy knoll they watched the ragged corps of the Ninth Legion fall into battle ranks. "We should have waited," Marcus agreed. "The Londinium reserves will be here soon. Simonedes has no idea how many Celts we might be facing today . . . I don't think he recognizes their rough skills."

"Caesar would have mocked this expedition," Rhoetus complained. The massive Neapolitan observed the coming horseman and touched Marcus Atreus's shoulder.

Marcus turned to see Simonedes arriving, his helmet gaily plumed, his shield shining.

"Simonedes—you wear battle dress," Marcus Atreus commented, assisting the emperor's nephew from the gaudily caparisoned black horse. "Surely you do not mean to test your skill at arms?"

"No, Marcus. I find your concealed humor offensive. I do not find it incongruous to wear my own armor. It is your custom." Simonedes stepped from his saddle awkwardly.

"Yes, Simonedes. I meant no offense. It was a pleasantry perhaps not fitting to the grave occasion."

Rhoetus kept a wooden face. He had fought under Marcus Atreus for fifteen years. The Roman general wore armor out of habit. There were battle scars on his breastplate, well earned. If the enemy forces were to break through, they would find their match in Marcus Atreus. As for this prancing little politician, Simonedes, Rhoetus doubted he knew which end of a halberd did the damage.

Together the three Romans strode through the scattered, sunlit oaks, Rhoetus leading Simonedes's horse as they reached the command point. The sky had broken momentarily, a brilliant, flat ray of golden sunlight piercing the deep, rolling gray above the long meadows. The birds perched in the trees, sensing more rain.

"You have extracted the Celtic battle plan from the traitor?" Marcus asked as if it were of no importance. He surveyed the broad, bluish-green meadows.

"Yes. His words were informative."

"Good. I will trust in your leadership, Simonedes. The glory of the day shall be yours." Marcus nodded, strapped on his helmet and stepped heavily into the saddle of his own horse. "And what of the Celt, Simonedes?" he asked without turning his face back. "Has he been bound and jailed?"

"Bound with a certainty, jailed in the strongest of cells, Marcus," Simonedes replied.

The Roman Ninth Legion forded Killdeer at Larkspur where the low, sandy bluffs break off to merge with the high forested country. Below that, the broad open country of Troth, ten miles south of Viron, fanned out in level plains.

Celtic runners had been spotted throughout the early morning, darting shadows in the woods, sometimes in plain view of the advancing Roman troops. What intelligence the runners might be carrying, they could not guess.

Rhoetus left his flanking column to ride to where

Marcus Atreus was. They conferred quietly.

"Look at our troops, Marcus. Are we expected to break through the Celtic front and assault their fortress? They drag, many are walking wounded, our horses weary."

"Simonedes expects us to break through." Atreus was not confident in his words. "We may face a great number, Rhoetus. More than we have seen before."

"What makes you think that?"

"A logical surmise. Their tactics have changed—improved. I sense a difference in their thinking somehow. I would even venture to suggest they may have finally formed a defensive league among themselves."

The impact of his last words was great on Rhoetus who realized the seriousness of it, the implications. "If this has been achieved, they may actually outnumber us."

"The prospect is unnerving," Marcus replied hollowly. "With our men in this condition. Yet Simonedes is certain this is not the case. He is also certain that his informant told the truth when he revealed the Celtic battle plan."

"How can he be so sure? These Iceni are fiercely loyal."

"Yes. Loyalty does wilt, however, when hot irons are applied, when fingers are broken one by one." Marcus Atreus smiled, yet there was no humor in the expression, only bitterness. Rhoetus nodded silently and drew back toward his position.

The main Celtic force came upon them suddenly, rising from the grass, a rumbling shaking the silent earth. A massing of fifty thousand warriors. As the Romans watched, frozen, the Iceni branched into a double force, forming an inverted *V*.

Simonedes, frothing with exultation, rushed to the forefront, whipping his horse until blood appeared on its flanks. He halted with a wrenching jerk of the reins beside Marcus Atreus, his eyes wild as he studied the deployment of the Celtic army.

"I told you!" he said triumphantly. "It is exactly as I was informed. The force splits into a prong. Yet the main force is even now massing to our rear. Can't you see it, Marcus?"

"I can see that there are fifty thousand warriors before us, Simonedes," Marcus replied woodenly.

"Yet we can break through. We must! It is the rear that we must fear and avoid. The wedge of Celts can be broken, and once through their ranks we are in a dominating position, at the very gates of their capital."

"Give the command," Marcus said. Simonedes's bloodied horse danced in tight pirouettes. Rhoetus flashed a sparking glance at Marcus Atreus. Catilus had arrived, and he glanced hesitantly from Simonedes to Marcus.

"Do as Simonedes commands," Marcus Atreus instructed him. With an air of disdain he turned his horse and withdrew slightly to the rear.

"Forward!" Simonedes shouted and Catilus signaled the phalanx.

The Roman Ninth poured across the plain, rushing willingly into the teeth of the Iceni pincer. Simonedes urged them forward with tiny violent motions of his fists. Catilus glanced at Marcus Atreus, but said nothing.

Three hours of battle on the sultry meadows scattered the dead of both sides against the grass.

The Ninth Legion was being beaten and badly, yet Simonedes was sure the Iceni would soon fall back. Anxiously he dispatched runners to the rear to bring first word of the Iceni thrust he expected there.

As Cymru had predicted, the Iceni at last sagged and fell back, chariots dispersing first, the foot soldiers covering the weakened Roman attack.

"Back. We must fall back," Marcus Atreus said in exasperation, no longer able to control his instincts. The Iceni had withdrawn, yet still obviously held the advantage. Simonedes smiled smugly and refused to issue the command.

Catilus looked frantically from his general to the emperor's nephew. "Do you wish to re-form?" Catilus asked.

"No! Signal advance," Simonedes said. His arms were crossed on his chest. A mild breeze swept the low knoll. He was experiencing his first chess game where the figures were of flesh and blood, and relishing it.

Catilus nodded and signaled reluctantly. The Roman forces moved still farther into the collapsing pincer of the Iceni.

"Retreat!" Marcus muttered in pained exasperation. "We must."

The last of his forces were nearly inside the jaws of the Celtic *V*, a disastrous tactical position on any battlefield at any time, superior forces or not.

"Forward, Catilus," Simonedes shouted again. Rhoetus had hesitated, his division holding its place as if hoping for a correction of the signals from Catilus.

"You will see," Simonedes said. "Then you shall see the advantage of intelligence in war. Your textbook strategy is all very fine, Marcus—" Simonedes's voice broke off in horror.

Behind the first ranks of Iceni a fresh party had appeared, advancing to the relief. Nearly double the original force, the new Celtic divisions closed the pincer jaws with deadly efficiency. The Ninth Legion was being decimated before their eyes.

Catilus, without awaiting an order from anyone, signaled retreat, yet it was already too late. The Iceni trap had tripped shut on the legion.

"They're being butchered." Simonedes walked aimlessly forward, removing his helmet. He turned helplessly back toward Marcus Atreus. "Yet my informant . . . under torture—"

"Managed to give you exactly the information the Iceni war leader wished you to have, Simonedes. He was very strong, wasn't he? This weakling of a Celt!"

Chapter Eleven

The short days of winter had begun. Long gloomy nights when the rains fell in silver ribbons, endlessly it seemed, drumming against the fortress Viron. Iona had ordered still more buttresses and earthworks thrown up, and the people labored through the cold hours, day upon day until the extreme defenses reached far onto the plains. In circumference the defenses measured some five miles.

Of the Romans they had heard nothing, yet eyes in the forest reported that the Ninth Legion had fallen back toward the sea. The Londinium divisions had arrived, yet—weakened as the original force was—the Romans felt disinclined to attempt a winter offensive.

What the Iceni could not know was that Marcus Atreus had written to Rome and had been promised three hundred thousand fresh troops for the planned spring assault on Viron.

Of the League Britannia, nothing further had been accomplished. Iona's proposals went unanswered although the Belgae twice sent runners to inquire into particulars. Kowlter adamantly refused to reply to messengers sent to the Coritani. The others replied, yet noncommittally.

Dwan Karnash still hunted, even though she wore the fourth-month roundness of her maternity. She and Breyton had been married the day after the Ninth Legion had withdrawn.

Dagda sat darkly in his hut day after day, his drinking becoming obsessive and extreme. The general seemed barely in his senses half the time. One late night he had leaped up, running naked into the compound, sword in hand, exclaiming that he saw the Romans advancing.

Throg and Prasutag had barely been able to restrain him and drag him home. Throg's thumb was accidentally cut off in the struggle and the giant spent hours cursing the fate of a soldier who had survived a hundred battles intact only to be maimed by a man of his own general staff.

Iona alone seemed not to mind the winter, the weeks of sunless days and eternal dampness, the mud which oozed into every building. She dreaded only that first sunlight of vigorous spring, knowing what would come.

She urged the workers on. They slaved through the rain with heavy barrows of muddy earth. Others sharpened stakes and buried them in the ground or dug carefully concealed pits. The outer earthworks were raised to a height of thirty feet, fifty feet through at the base. The inner walls were even more impressive, some sixty feet tall, laced with honeycomb labyrinths. Above it all Viron cut against the somber skies, a massive fortress, a fierce redoubt.

The rain was a steely-meshed curtain, the clouds clinging close to the earth. Occasional great eruptions of thunder split open the skies, fantastic bridges of bone-white lightning arced over.

Prasutag found Iona standing on the rampart, her hair washed across her face, her clothing soaked. Below her men still labored across the sodden earth, sliding in the ooze of red mud. Yet they moved, like demons in some watery, gray Hades, their faces waxen as great chains of lightning illuminated their features.

"Iona!" Prasutag shouted above the roar of the falling waters. "It is enough!"

"It is not enough," she replied, still looking ahead, rain streaming from her face, arms crossed. "It cannot be enough!"

"It is too much, Iona!" He took her shoulder gently. "It is enough . . . for now. Nothing can be accomplished. The men are weary, soaked; the earth cannot be packed under these conditions."

"The Romans will be working tonight," she replied, still without emotion. A brilliant filament of white lightning darted earthward, showing her features clearly. Her full lips were slightly parted. They trembled as she watched Prasutag.

"Not unless they are also mad," Prasutag said. "Iona—you are straining yourself, straining our people. It is not right. We will need all of our strength in the days to come. Come in now, you will take a fever yourself."

"All right," she responded as a child might. Her

words were oddly weak; her command to the workers was barely audible and had to be relayed to those farther away. She turned stiffly, arms still crossed, holding her cloak. Head slightly bowed, she walked with Prasutag back toward her hut.

Lania's head came up as they entered, concern flashing immediately in her eyes. Thramane clucked like a hen as she rushed around, finding dry clothing, stoking the fire.

Prasutag spoke with Lania of trifles as Iona was undressed, rubbed briskly and dressed in dry clothing in the other chamber. Iona's mother did not broach her concern, nor did Prasutag speak of it. The young queen was tired, tense. Prasutag told himself it was concern for the nation that had worn Iona down. He did not allow himself to believe that it was Dwan Karnash's joy which had driven the queen into herself, to frantic labors.

Thramane brought warm mead to them. Iona drank with Prasutag as Thramane, still scolding, braided her queen's long dark hair.

The firelight caused Iona to become thoughtful. "I wanted to go across the seas once. When I was younger—do you remember? To see what there is beyond our land."

"You still may sail away, Iona," Prasutag said with a warm smile. "Soon we will be through with this battle. Perhaps we could acquire a Regni ship. They are fine builders, fine sailors. Why, they say some of the Regni have sailed to lands where there is no earth at all, but only ice, and to lands far across the western sea where there are forgotten peoples."

"It would be a prize—a Regni ship," Iona said.

"Oh, quit that, Thramane," she said, affectionately slapping the servant's hand. "I'm sure I am presentable enough for Prasutag."

Iona watched the firelight a while longer, seeing in the golden, twisting flames strange lands, exotic peoples, sailing ships. Then she glanced seriously at Prasutag's dark eyes, his affable, eternally concerned face.

"I shall never sail away, Prasutag," Iona said. "I was a child who wished to find a new world. Thrueldan has told me since then what lies beyond the waters. A world where the Romans are lords over all of our people, over all people. They have built great cities on the bones of Celts, of other peoples whose names I do not even know and who will one day be forgotten . . . as we will be unless every thought, every action is dedicated to our survival. This I know now, and the realization is more compelling than a child's daydream.

"I am tired, Prasutag," she said, rising abruptly. "Please make up my bed, Thramane."

Puzzled, Prasutag stood and nodded to Lania, then he turned and went out.

Iona undressed slowly. The fire had died to dully glowing golden embers. Lania slept in the corner, under a pile of rich furs. Thramane had gone to her quarters; all the camp was quiet. Iona stepped to the doorway and watched the silent, floating stars for a moment.

Here they twinkled, there shone with a steady light. Some were red, large, others blue, brilliant as tiny jewels. To Thrueldan, the Druid, they each meant something, revealed secret worlds. To her they were baubles to be admired; mysteries to be in awe of.

With a start she realized the sky was incredibly clear, affording a crisp view of the stars. She searched the horizon. There were no bulky clouds as there had been for week upon endless weeks. Shuddering, she closed the door.

She felt a chill in her bones as she walked to her own bed. Iona drew her furs over her, eyes watching the ceiling for a long minute before they closed and her head filled with dreams of star ships sailing endless skies, leaving blood-red wakes in their passing.

The days passed in peaceful progression. Clear, high skies dominated the far countryside. Beltaine, the first day of the Celtic summer, arrived. Great bonfires were lighted to celebrate the warm season, the season of growth and birthing, of renewal on the first of May.

The spring calves took wobbly legs and bawled at the clear skies, suckling vigorously beneath budding dogwood trees.

The people feasted, drank, and danced riotously, even Dwan Karnash whose figure had swollen to a ripe maternity.

Werken, the bard, played lively tunes on his lyre and sang of distant exploits through the long day until his fingers became numb, his voice hoarse.

Iona walked among them, happy for their joy, yet unable to share in it. Rule had set her apart from them, the burdens of it depriving her of even a moment's recreation.

The fires fountained into the air in the night,

golden sparks raining down. The merrymaking continued unabated. Thrueldan found Iona watching the firelit dancers.

"A happy holiday, is it not?"

"Yes. Will we celebrate Beltaine ever again?" Iona asked.

"Perhaps not," the Druid replied. "So why do you not enjoy this one, Iona? You are still a young woman."

"And you, Thrueldan?"

"My rank prohibits such antics," the Druid said, not ruefully, but with a touch of pride. "Fun—one can grow weary of fun! I have my separate, quiet peace. I do not long for strong drink, spectacles." Thrueldan hesitated. "But you, Iona . . ."

"I am your student, Thrueldan," she replied. Yet a part of her longed for the freedom of the dance, as a part of everyone longs for a moment of childhood—of touching—of impossible hopes.

Breyton whirled past with Dwan Karnash, his laughter drifting toward them. He seemed hardly to notice his queen. Perhaps he had forgotten. He had a woman to be with him on the hunt, in the night. And a child within her.

"It is best," Thrueldan said as if reading her thoughts.

A child's dream . . . a momentary lapse.

Iona turned and walked toward a gathering of warriors, holding her skirts high. Throg was roaring with laughter—an uncommon expression for him. Prasutag grinned broadly at a joke, holding a cup of mead.

"Iona, Queen Boudicca!" Nertomorus hailed, but she waved and walked past them with a faint bow. She was not as her father. Athair could have stood with them, sharing their drink, their laughter; she could not.

She did not belong among these warriors except at times of conflict. She did not belong with them, nor did she belong among the dancers, the youth, the women her age who whispered of lovers, boasted of their husbands' prowess, of the secret, coming life within them, or showed their bright garments, sharing small jealousies, small hopes.

Her larger concerns blocked out all such interests. The Celtic tribes still had not massed; they still delayed as the muddy roads over which the Roman armies would march dried beneath the warm spring sun.

Iona walked slowly through the night, the voices of her people fading behind her. Without planning her direction, she found herself at that secret place which had been her girlhood refuge. The same great gnarled oak spread against the starlit sky, the jumbled white boulders poised against the outcropping of earth as if they might tumble at any moment. Yet they had never tumbled, they had withstood the years of wind and rain, frost and the merciless, irresistible force of gravity.

There she rested, watching an owl preen in the low branches of the oak. Surely not the same owl, yet it might have been. Thrueldan said they lived long lives and were wise beyond any other bird.

Whether or not it was the same round-eyed owl, it lent authenticity to the impression that in this place alone on all the earth nothing would ever change, all would remain firm, immutable.

Behind her the haze of the Beltaine fires colored

the black skies. And to the south, as she sat gazing toward the far sea, other fires showed against the black earth.

Chapter Twelve

They came with the crimson dawn. At first a hundred or so, a thousand in scarlet ranks, armor glistening in the copper rays of the coming sun. Far across the gray-green valleys they were visible through the soft morning mist. Eyes along the walls of fortress Viron watched as a thousand more appeared from the deep, bluish evergreen woods across the silver of Killdeer Stream. They came like a red, spreading fungus bleeding across the fields. There were tens of thousands. Unreal in their numbers, inconceivable. Hundreds of thousands, they had sprouted like blood-red mushrooms from the earth.

Why?

Why had they come to this land far from their own, laying siege to a foreign citadel, calling loudly for blood or obeisance?

No matter—they were here, and they set about their work, pitching tents, drawing machinery forward, digging trenches as if the Iceni were of no consequence. Against such numbers, perhaps they weren't.

Iona, awakened by the insistent pounding on her door, rushed out into the morning. The people mingled excitedly near the open gates of Viron. Open!

She pushed through them, their excited voices raised in terror, in frustrated anger, in curses.

Leun, not yet dressed, came at a run with a hastily snatched shield and sword. Sighting Iona he slowed, then stopped, realizing that the battle had not yet been ignited. Sleepily he stood in the center of the stockyard, shaking his head.

Thrueldan was at the gates when Iona arrived and he wagged his head. "What do they want?" the Druid asked in tense sorrow. He threw his head back and bellowed to Cernunnos. "What do they want, Almighty God!"

"How many there are ... how many ..." Dwan Karnash said. She was holding Breyton's arm tightly, unable to walk easily on her own. The child was due in a matter of days, and her legs were often swollen in the mornings.

"I spit on them!" Arawn was astride an unsaddled horse, angry eyes flashing, a lance in his hand.

"Arawn!" Iona snapped, running a harried hand through her disheveled hair. "Would you stop them yourself? Get down!"

These men. Leun and Arawn and a thousand like them. Their instincts must be controlled if there were to be any concerted defense and not a mass death caused by chivalric fervor.

Yet she shared their anger; she understood their fury. If by riding down among the hordes of vermillion insects, if by striking right and left until she herself were slain, the Iceni nation could be saved, she would not have hesitated a moment. Yet she had learned that it would mean only suicide.

Nertomorus hobbled up, Barra with him. They stood without speaking, Nertomorus biting his lip until he brought blood to it. Barra cursed horribly and clenched his sword's hilt. Throg ambled to the open gates, took one look and walked away without saying a word. What was there to say?

Behind Iona a woman fainted, a man began to dance crazily, losing control of his emotions— emotions he was unused to checking. He was called Freka, and he was a good soldier. Yet all of his thinking went no further than to retaliate when attacked, to brook no affront. Any man Freka met in combat was certain to be gravely tested. He had no fear of any man. Yet how to fight a thousand? A wave of frustration, mingled with terror and savage anger swept over the Celts. While some pressed forward, ready to rush down the hillside, others withdrew, shrieked, or simply complained.

"Close the gates!" Iona ordered. The guards hesitated a moment, and she repeated her command more sternly.

"Some people are outside, my queen."

"Then let them go down and satisfy their curiosity!" she said. The guards closed the gates, those outside rushing back before they slammed shut. "When the gates of Viron open next, we shall have direction and purpose."

The weeks rolled past, the hours spent in the forging of weapons, formulating new battle plans;

of retreat there was no discussion. Viron would stand or fall; the Iceni fate would be written on this spot.

"It's Dagda," Nertomorus said worriedly when Iona questioned the concern on his face. "Our chariot commander is still drinking. More. And more. I think his senses are leaving him. He speaks of taking his forces against the Romans . . . but he does not call them Romans. Dagda has named them the Black Precursors."

"Black Precursors? What does he mean by that?"

"I have no idea, besides the obvious. Yet to Dagda it is no term of infamy, but a real image. He says they rise up from the earth and must be pressed back into the ground—mowed down, I believe he says—if we are to live."

"Perhaps he extends his imagery," Iona suggested hopefully.

"No. Dagda has retreated to the inner wards of the mind, drawn there by a collapsing mentality. He should be . . . watched closely at least."

"Or relieved of command, Nertomorus?"

"I did not wish to suggest that," the graybeard said slowly. "Yet . . . he should be under close observation, Iona."

The warriors were on pins and needles. Breyton walked the compound, his eyes vacant, grinding his teeth. He hardly spoke—even to Iona. When she did encounter him he could only lament, "My son shall not be a slave! My beautiful baby will be born and live freely as we have. He shall hunt stag in the morning mist."

Iona's eyes grew damp as she listened to the god

of the Iceni warriors; but even that seemed outside of Breyton's perception. He thought only of his child, unborn future of the Iceni nation.

Iona watched the smith working. Swords by the dozen lay in the shop as the man beat against a fresh, red blade with a demonic energy, sparks flying, his hammer falling in magical rhythm.

"Do they advance, Queen Boudicca?" the smith asked.

"Not yet. There is still time."

Werken walked past. The slender bard wore a sword, his lyre across his back. Iona had to smile at this soft man, so willing to sacrifice his blood. Werken had never struck a blow at any living creature, and indeed would not know how. Yet he was ready. All of them were ready—herdsmen, old women, youths, weavers, the elite fighting men like Leun and Arawn who stalked the wall impatiently.

Yet it was not time.

Days passed. Word was sent to Kowlter, to the tribes of Regni, Atrebates, Belgae, Cornovii; yet they delayed as the last hope of Celtic independence prepared for Armageddon.

Marcus Atreus surveyed the fortifications. A ring had been constructed around this last Celtic redoubt. Nine miles of Roman fortifications enclosed the trapped barbarians.

The pits had been dug, long stretches of defensive weapons lay across the open spaces where a charge could be expected. Under the direction of Rhoetus who had the experience of three Gallic sieges, terrible refinements were added. Iron hooks anchored in logs were concealed under litter and brush, capable of ripping and breaking legs of men and horses.

Brush covered fire-hardened stakes capable of gutting a horse were concealed in the least likely places. Log and earth ramparts were thrown up along the northern face where Viron's gates opened onto the broad plains. Protective ditches ringed the entire circumference.

The catapults were ready, well stocked. Thousands of half-ton boulders had been dragged from the far hillsides on massive drays and coated with incendiary pitch.

Simonedes, somewhat subdued of late, strolled among the laboring legionnaires. Catching sight of Marcus and Rhoetus, he came up to them.

"And how do these defense works look to you, Marcus Atreus?" Simonedes asked jovially.

"They are enough," Marcus said solemnly. "We will shred them to strips if they do not surrender."

"But you do not appear happy about the state of affairs, dear Marcus."

"Happy?" He shook his head, gazing toward Viron. "It is death, that is all."

"Happily not ours."

"Happily," Marcus answered, watching the little man's face which still boiled with ambition despite the recent catastrophe.

Marcus Atreus continued to watch the bulk of the massive fortress called Viron against the wild skies now frothing with gray clouds. It was only death. A man gets tired of death, however; even a soldier, a warrior by profession. There were times he could not sleep for seeing the faces of men he had killed, and he wished only for his own death at moments, so that there might be an end to it.

"Marcus," Simonedes said, interrupting his thoughts, "you wax pensive. Come," he added cheerfully, throwing an arm around the general's shoulder. "Let us drink a toast to the victory you formulate. Soon the overseas reinforcements will arrive. Perhaps then our vast superiority will induce bloodless surrender."

"Perhaps," Marcus answered with a sigh; yet he knew it would be otherwise. He had been among the Celts too much. There would be blood, more blood. Eternally.

He even dreamed of it now. Eternal rivers of crimson running from the mouth of the she-wolf, while the twins, swords in tiny fists, suckled at her dangling teats.

It was always the same, this dream. An eagle gliding lazily in the April skies. A song, a thunder, a death. A woman's face falling to corruption.

When he dreamed like that he awoke in a sweat and would not sleep again the reminder of the long night, but would sit watching the stars, wondering at man's fate . . . a fate which seemed to be woven by arms and soldiers.

When it was full dark, Iona, the Queen Boudicca, slipped from the fortress Viron, with runners darting through the shadows before her, finding safe passage through the ranks behind the stronghold.

It took half an hour to maneuver the first hundred yards, an hour to travel the next ten miles. She raced free on the grasslands, northward riding as Throg had ridden to the west and Nertomorus to the south, each carrying the same message.

Iona found the camp of Kowlter well guarded and she stopped her white stallion before the two men who came to challenge her in the torchlight.

Kowlter was at his evening meal when Queen Boudicca was taken into him. The Coritani chief was barechested, wearing a gold and coral necklace. Two maidens fed him. Their faces came up, studying the young woman with impudent interest before a snap of Kowlter's fingers sent them scurrying into another chamber.

"So—you have come playing the beggar," Kowlter said coldly, drinking from a goblet of gold. "I have long awaited this day. The mighty Iceni chief suing my succor."

"Should I be angered?" she asked mildly. Without being asked she sat across from Kowlter and poured wine for herself.

"Yes, I ask your aid, Kowlter. The Romans have massed at Viron. And when Viron falls, it will be the turn of the Coritani to feel the Roman sting."

"So what do you propose, my child-queen?" Kowlter asked belligerently.

"Just what I proposed before. Come to Viron. Burn what you have here. Let us gather to combat the Romans. In unity we have a chance. In disunity, none."

"And still you would lead! Still it is we who must burn crops and buildings, poison waters, slaughter cattle while Viron stands!" Kowlter stood, raging, his pent-up fury bursting free. The bitter years of war, of losing battles, had poisoned his mind.

"It is only logical . . ."

"Logic be damned! *Queen* Boudicca. The Iceni

be damned! I will come to the Iceni aid when my horse walks around on hind legs and speaks in your behalf. No," he waved his hands with finality. "It will not be done."

"Then *you* are damned, Kowlter." She rose. On her face was genuine sorrow. "You are damned by your bitterness, by your petty motives, your jealousy."

"So be it!" Kowlter shouted, his face crimson. "I accept that risk. I am damned. So be the Iceni!"

It was cold, black, and still moonless when Iona reentered Viron. A baby cried in the huts to the east. A horse stirred, whinnied and then was silent. Iona released her white stallion into the pen, her cloak around her as she walked toward her home.

The man appeared suddenly out of the darkness.

"How did it go?"

"Not well. Kowlter will never join us, I fear."

"How does that leave us?"

"Painfully weak, Breyton."

He nodded, walking with her. Neither said a word until they passed the monument to Sequana where many wreathes beseeching bodily well-being were stacked. Then Breyton took her roughly by the shoulders, more roughly than he had intended.

"If we must die . . ."

"We must. Let go of me, Breyton. Please!" Iona's commands were breathy, weak against this mightily muscled warrior.

"I do not wish to hurt you," Breyton said, as a child might. Yet he had not let go of her. His thumbs moved restlessly against her arms. "I only meant to say . . ."

"Nothing must be said. Nothing need be."

"It must!" His hands tightened on her and he drew her to him, his mouth locking on hers. She fought the kiss only for a moment. Then she felt him against her, heard a humming in her brain, felt her heart leap.

"I love you, Iona. I never quit loving you. If I must die, then let me repeat it now. Before I can no longer speak."

"Dwan Karnash . . ."

"I would not hurt her," Breyton said. He held Iona at arm's length. Stars danced in the black heavens behind him. Breath fogged from his lips as he spoke. His arms trembled, possibly with the cold, perhaps not. "Yet I have had but one love in my life. Know that. Know that we shall meet again in the darker life—know it, Iona!" Then again he kissed her throat, gently, and he was gone, leaving her trembling, lips tingling in the night.

"What is it?" Lania asked as Iona came into the warm hut.

"Nothing. It is cold out."

"You seem upset." Lania took her daughter's cloak, kissing her lightly on the cheek. "You tremble."

"Kowlter refuses to join us."

"You expected as much," she heard her mother's cracked voice answer.

"Yes." Iona's eyes looked at nothing, studying a dark corner of the room.

"What is it, Iona?" Lania came forward and sank to her knees, her eyes studying her queen's taut face.

"We must fight. We must bleed again, Mother. I

was thinking ... thinking of things which might have been if these Romans had not come to our land. That is all," she smiled. "Come," Iona said, rising. "Let's think of it no longer. Let us go to bed, to sleep, to dream."

It was a time then before Lania heard her daughter slip into bed, the fire low, the night cool, and begin weeping. It was another time, quite a longer while, before Iona slept.

Chapter Thirteen

The days were still, clear, long summer days when the pale remnants of sheer clouds drifted slowly past; a fawn dipped a curious muzzle into the brook; there were brilliant flushes of gold and crimson at sundown, long starlit nights—yet it could not last forever.

On the first day of the third week following Beltaine, the Roman forces under Marcus Atreus began the assault.

A four-cornered front was formed and they began to move forward in even ranks. They approached to within a hundred meters without signal or response from the fortress Viron. There, the Roman archers drew to one side and the assault forces, bearing ladders, rushed for the fortress walls.

It was an eerie charge; the Romans made no sound. No war cries filled the air, no challenges to those within; and Viron might as well have been deserted for the response the charge brought.

"Let them come," Iona said softly. The soldiers were poised behind her, yet she did not signal counterattack. "Let them come."

Nertomorus felt his palms grow damp. He fingered the haft of his sword constantly. The Roman foot soldiers were at the outer defenses and they charged up the steep hillside, silent still but for the grunting, the sounds of leather creaking, of armor rattling.

"Do not open the gate," Iona said sharply. Barra had moved his men closer yet to the massive gates.

"She's lost her senses," Leun said frantically. Breyton silenced him with a cold glance.

"No. I understand her. The archers are in range. To go out would be to fall to them. The infantry cannot breach our defenses, not effectively. They will straggle, fall, be impaled on our stakes. They will reach the walls, yes, but they will die there."

Arawn stalked furiously in front of his division of infantry, his teeth grinding. To restrain a man like this war-lover was not an easy task.

Iona watched them come. Red beetles, crawling up the earthen mounds. Falling into pits. Curses filled the air now from below, foreign curses. Their ranks had been broken on the terrain. A cry of pain filled the air, and another as a man tumbled onto a trap.

Iona still hesitated. She could see them now. Only a dozen or so Romans, yet so near she could see the perspiration on a whiskered face, hear a man grunting with exertion as he breached the ninety-foot wall.

"To the ramparts," Iona said in a conversational

tone. "But do not shout, do not fight back, not just yet."

Disgustedly, Barra led his men onto the stockade platforms, their heads below the palings.

The Romans now seemed indecisive. They were far from their command post. They stood in confusion. For half the morning they had struggled over dikes and through barricaded passes to fight their way toward the massive Celtic redoubt. Now their breath was gone, their comrades bleeding or broken below them. Yet no arm had been raised against them. The impassive citadel stood high above them, with no face showing. Were they fighting ghosts then?

The wind flattened the grass, turning it silver; a lone crow swung lazily through the skies, its cawing breaking the silence. The wind chilled their flesh. They were under command to move silently, and so they did not speak. Armor seemed to weigh a thousand pounds, hearts rattled in their rib cages. Eyes, swollen with peering into the sun, raw from dust, studied the redoubt, Viron.

A sword grew heavy, a halberd trembled in a usually firm hand. Nothing. No one. Perhaps the Celts had withdrawn in the night. They marched forward, struggling up the critical slope. Far beneath them the archers, now hopelessly out of range, watched in neat files.

"Now."

Iona spoke and then turned her back, walking from the parapet, with no doubt in her mind as to the outcome of this first skirmish.

Barra's men raised up and unleashed a hail of sling stones, lances, and arrows. The Romans first advanced and tried valiantly for the walls, the sounds of battle filling the day before they realized they had no ladders, no archers to support them.

Then in confused retreat they fled the hills. The walls, lined with Celtic soldiers, rained death upon them. In their haste to withdraw, as many Romans were torn apart by the hidden defenses as were chopped down by weaponry.

Battered, broken, they stumbled down the earthworks, some falling dangerously, some carrying Celtic steel in their flesh.

Marcus Atreus watched it all and swore solemnly. "They are entrenched," he announced to Catilus who could make no response. The broken infantry straggled across the open fields.

"Archers?"

"No! They would fare no better. The Celts offer no targets." Marcus let his eyes search the earthworks where some of his men still writhed, and others lay still in death. "They mean to stay rooted," Marcus said slowly. "Yet we will break this siege. We will break it."

For every grim expression in the Roman camp, for every painful curse, there was a smile or shout of joy inside Viron. Even Barra exchanged his habitual scowl for a faint smile of relief.

All but Dagda. Drunken, apoplectic at the failure of Iona to summon him from his stupor, he stumbled into the yard, cursing his queen, the Romans, the day with equal virulence.

"Attack!" he screamed, sword dangling in his hand. He walked aimlessly in circles. "Attack, we must attack!"

"Barra, it must be you to speak to him," Breyton said.

"He's lost his sense," Arawn said flatly.

"We are old friends," Barra hedged. He had unslung his shield and taken off his boar's head helmet.

"So it should be you," Arawn insisted. "You know he will not listen to any of us. He has felt cheated since Thrueldan named Iona queen. He has not borne it well."

"His madness could cause deaths," Nertomorus added softly. Barra lifted his dark eyebrows and sighed. He watched Dagda, naked, drunken, wandering around the compound, calling for attack.

"I will speak to him," Barra agreed.

"And what now?" Throg asked his queen in her hut. "They will batter us down, in time. They shall burn our homes, Iona, slaughter us."

"We will delay them and hope the Coritani, the Belgae, will join us," Iona replied. Her only hope was for a second front. Throg growled disparagingly.

"And we will wait for the sun to come up in the western sky?" Throg shook his head heavily. "We must mount some sort of offensive. Enough to unsettle them. Enough to let them know we will not always be found on our nest."

"And you propose to lead this offensive?"

"I do."

Iona studied the massive man's scarred face, looked deeply into his dark, fierce eyes. Throg was right—yet it would mean death for many to attempt a counterattack. Every move now meant death somewhere.

"All right."

She said it softly, reluctantly, her eyes turned down. And when she lifted her head, Throg was gone, Iona left to her own thoughts. Lania rested in the corner near the fire. Iona held her hands out to her, and the woman smiled, tried to get to her feet and failed, collapsing.

"Mother!" Iona was to her in a moment, gently raising her head.

"Iona," Lania nodded feebly, her eyes filmed.

"You are ill. You said nothing."

"Now is no time to busy your thoughts with an old woman," Lania said. She put a hand to her fluttering, thin breast as Iona helped her lie back.

"There is always time for you," Iona scolded. Lania's hand reached up and clumsily stroked her daughter's dark hair.

"Still pretty. You are so pretty, Iona."

"How long have you been ill?"

"How long?" Lania smiled again, faintly. "Since your father went his way. Since I became alone."

"You have me. And Thramane . . . where is she?"

"Out for a while. She's been bothering herself with me. She grew pale herself, faithful old thing."

"I'll call her."

"You won't!" Lania said sternly, eyes flashing once. "She can do nothing for me. Let her have an hour away from us. It has not been easy on her either."

"But you shall get well," Iona said cheerfully, taking both of her mother's hands. "You shall."

"No. I do not even wish it. Don't look so startled, Iona. I do not wish to survive into the times that are coming. I shall miss all of our young men and women coming back with their boar from the hunt, their broad, smiling faces. The strong children we have produced—you, pretty one...." Lania's voice trailed off, her eyes becoming damp again.

"It is not over! They have not beaten us yet! You speak nonsense."

"I do not, my Iona. And you know it above all others. Our way will pass. And it grieves me. I would go to my husband on the dark side."

"They will not pass the gates of Viron!" Iona swore. She moved around the room in agitation.

"Let us hope not," Lania said.

"We will fight to the last Iceni. Blood will run, yet not all of it will be ours."

"And what will that profit us, Iona?"

"Athair would have...." She paused. What would her father have done?

The people, Iona, he had told her. *The tribe must come first. We must survive as a people.*

Yet had he known that there would come a time when the choice would have to be made to live as slaves or die free?

"Iona!"

Arawn had burst in the door, bowing in quick apology. "It's Dagda—he's leading a party of warriors out! Youths, old men, anyone who would go."

"He's insane! Can we stop him?"

They burst out the door and her question was answered by what she saw. The gates of Viron were open to a column of soldiers. Most of them were boys, whipped to a fighting frenzy by the old general's speeches.

"Close the gates! Close the gates!"

They ran across the intervening space, Iona and Arawn calling. Breyton had climbed the walls, shoving the gatekeeper aside to catch the winch himself.

Still all but a dozen of Dagda's ragged troupe had squeezed through the gates. These frustrated warriors-to-be began cursing, pleading to be let out.

"My queen!" one girl pleaded.

"Go home to your mother," Iona replied harshly.

Arawn waded among the armed youths, applying kicks and shoves to keep them away from the gates as Iona climbed the ladder to survey the expeditionary force.

"He can hardly stay on his horse," Breyton snarled. "Look!"

Dagda was hanging onto his horse's withers, a sword waving wildly. Lustily cheering young soldiers followed.

"Werken!" a breathless Arawn pointed out.

The slender bard was indeed there, bearing a sword and not a lyre. Around him many others of scant years, ill-equipped, ill-trained, marched proudly.

"We can attempt to drive them back," Breyton suggested. The Roman camp had spotted the excursion and there was a flurry of activity already.

"Not without warring among ourselves," Arawn guessed. Dagda was determined. Arawn glanced at Iona who agreed with him. They stood, transfixed at the sight of their people being led to certain slaughter.

Already Roman cavalry were racing across the field, splendidly mounted, splendidly disciplined.

Throg arrived at the ramparts, his chest quivering with anger.

"The fool. The drunken idiot!"

He clenched the stockade walls with white, massive hands. "He will kill them all."

Iona knew what Throg's thoughts were. Not only was Dagda leading the youth of Viron to the slaughter, he was also negating the surprise of Throg's planned offensive. Now the Romans would be wary of a frontal attack, not believing that Viron would hold in a state of siege.

Across the lines Marcus Atreus rushed from his tent, half-dressed, eyes red. He had just lain down for a rest when the summons reached him. Rhoetus was at the command post atop the dais when he arrived with Simonedes and Catilus.

"What is it?" Marcus demanded, climbing the dais ladder rapidly.

"An offensive," Rhoetus replied, yet he was smiling grimly.

"What is this ragged force?" Marcus peered into the sunlight. "Do they send their youth to die first?"

"Girls—no more than twelve or thirteen years old," Rhoetus spat in disgust.

"It makes no difference," Simonedes countered.

"No," Marcus agreed reluctantly. "It makes no difference." They were coming with their weapons in hand. Peach-faced youths, old men, a drunken general. Yet they were coming with a single purpose—to war.

"Send out the archers!" Marcus ordered.

"Prisoners?" Rhoetus asked, but Marcus Atreus only shook his head and turned his back. There was no place to house prisoners, nothing to feed them. Besides, as he well knew, these Celts would not surrender. None ever did.

Iona could only watch. The battle sounds echoed from the fields. Roman precision against wild-eyed impetuousness. It was not a battle, but a mass execution. Trembling, she turned from the wall. One voice far below was raised in painful prayers to Cernunnos. Then that prayer was silenced, the fields growing cold, stained with wretched maroon.

"Iona . . ." Breyton stretched out a hand, but she pushed it aside. She stumbled down the ladder, her stomach turning, her head spinning.

"Iona!"

She ignored Breyton's call. Dagda! He had ignored her. Perhaps it was her fault that these people had died. Dagda would never have dared disobey Athair. Yet the general had always felt contempt for the woman he called the child-queen.

She was running now, without realizing it, toward the spring. Finally, breathless, she stopped in the oak grove, her head still reeling. She was at her father's grave where he stood buried, lance aimed southward toward the Roman assault.

She bent her head nearly to her lap and sat for a long minute, composing herself. All right! It was not her fault. Yet she might have foreseen it, and had Dagda put where he could do no harm. She had been remiss in that.

It was not her fault. Yet how many more would die through events which were not her fault? She had accepted leadership; she must carry its weight.

It was nearly dark before she wove her way home through the massive dark trunks of the oaks. The camp was silent. No lyre or flute was raised in song. Werken would be missed.

Lania was deathly ill; Iona was sure now that her mother would not survive the siege. She sat up through the long night holding her hand as she slept. Morning's light etched a rectangle on the packed earth floor of the hut when Thramane came in, concern flooding her compassionate features.

"Go out to your people," Thramane said. "They need you."

"My mother . . ."

"Where would your mother tell you your duty lies?" Thramane asked gently.

Iona nodded, stood, stretching the sleep from her muscles. Then she brushed her hair and slipped gold bracelets onto her arms. Outside Throg sat waiting; by the tracks cut into the earth, he had been there for some time.

"Iona!" the giant's head came up.

"If you are going to ask about the offensive . . ."

"I am. The offensive can still weight the battle's balance in our favor."

"No," Iona said brusquely. "I will not allow it."

"Iona, my queen," Throg pleaded, "I beg you not to let your sorrow over yesterday's travesty cloud your judgment. This will be a planned offensive with our vanguard troops."

"No, Throg." She touched his hand briefly then began walking away.

"Let them know we still have teeth!" Throg called after her, but she did not even shake her head. Disgustedly Throg kicked at the dirt.

"Nertomorus!" Iona called into the general's darkened hut. Sleepily her father's old friend came forward, sheepishly pulling on his cloak.

"I sleep late . . . age, Iona. Age is upon me."

"Nonsense." She studied the tired lines in Nertomorus's face, the gray hair, those powerful hands which were now crooked.

"What is it you wish, Queen Boudicca?" Nertomorus asked.

"Four riders. Men with our fastest horses."

"The alliance?"

"Yes. We must try once more. The others must be made to see that with the fall of Viron, they are doomed."

"I will see that it is done."

"Perhaps Macha should be sent to the Belgae. His wife is of Belgae stock. As for the Coritani . . ."

"I will ride to see Kowlter," Nertomorus announced.

"I do not want valuable men riding out just now."

"Valuable!" Nertomorus laughed. "Look at me, my Iona. My eyes are dim . . . my strength gone. I cannot lead, I cannot fight. Besides, what service could be more valuable than convincing Kowlter to bring the Coritani into the fold?"

The old man stood straight, shoulders thrown back, eyes unblinking. "All right," she said finally, "if you believe it is best."

In an hour the four riders were gone. Nertomorus crossed Troth while the sun still lazed behind the oaks; the horse moved easily under him and he framed his arguments to Kowlter as he rode.

He knew Kowlter well, he believed. For twenty summers they had fought one another, at twenty festivals they had spoken and drunk from the same cup.

Kowlter was fierce, slightly devious, and immensely proud. Foremost in his code, however, was a concern for his people. He must be made to see the threat to the Coritani was not hysterical imagination.

Nertomorus smiled at the image of Iona before Kowlter. Kowlter had many faults, among them a disdain for the young. Iona's words could have carried no weight at all with the savage Kowlter.

Nertomorus dipped into the vale where the slow-running rill, icy yet at this late time of year, wove among the ferns and wild roses.

He urged his horse up onto the far bank, the gray gelding slipping as it climbed. Then they were around him. Six men in red cloaks. Six legionnaires.

Nertomorus reached for his sword, yet too slowly. Too slowly. The sun swirled in the silver branches of the trees, the gray horse spun on its hind legs. Something hard came up to meet Nertomorus, slapping him in the face; a burning pain erupted in his side. The horse shied and threw him. Nertomorus fell on his back, the wind driven from him. He watched a lark dart through the sky, saw a face leaning over a lance shaft, watched a tunnel of red and black open and then constrict, enveloping him in blackness.

Nothing . . . .

Not one of the riders had returned. Anguish tore at Iona's breast. Three days it had been, three nights. They were alone at Viron and they would remain alone.

"Nertomorus is dead," she told Leun. "You will take command of his division."

Was this the way a people died? Man by man.

Piece by piece, blood slowly trickling from them?

Thramane was in the dimly lighted doorway when Iona found her way back to the hut. The nurse said nothing. It was inscribed on her face. Her red, pouched eyes spoke it. Lania was resting, arms folded across her unmoving breast.

"We will bury her in the morning. Beside Athair," Iona heard herself saying through a gray mist. Calmly then she strode from the room. Thramane heard something crash against the wall of the queen's chamber, then for hours later, soft sounds of mourning.

Throg was sleeping heavily, wine having loosened the intensity he felt, the knots in his muscles. It was utterly black, yet his instincts told him that someone was in the room. With a start he sat up, reaching for his dagger.

"Take them out in the morning. At first light."

Throg nodded, scratched his head, and swung to his feet as Iona pulled back the door and stepped out of her general's house.

Chapter Fourteen

At the moment of golden dawn they rode forward, challenging the might of the Roman Empire. The finest of Viron's warriors were among them. Leun, Arawn the war-lover, Breyton, Throg and his first-line infantry, Prasutag, Barra.

Iona blinked her eyes and turned away. Distant sounds of the Roman camp stirring to hectic life rolled to her ears across the mist-shrouded fields. She turned and walked toward the cattle pens as the forces of the Iceni nation streamed past.

In the pens three sickly-looking beef were all that remained after twelve weeks of siege. They rolled melancholy eyes at her and lowed.

Children looked up with hollow, admiring eyes as their queen strode past, dressed in white and gold, long dark hair tumbling free in the slight morning breeze. The sun blinked through the oaks; a mighty roar rose from the plains, like the summoning chimes of Hades. Iona walked on even faster.

A cry of travail met her as she walked the long street past the empty huts. A cry of pain, proud pain. Swinging open the door Iona stepped in as the cry sounded again.

"Easy . . . easy." Women rushed helter-skelter about the interior of the dimly lighted hut. In the corner on a pile of furs was a woman in pain, her face glistening with perspiration, hands and teeth clenched. She was in hard labor.

"Dwan Karnash!"

Dwan Karnash's face flashed with triumph, with contempt. She lay panting for the moment, hands opening. She had cut her palms with her nails.

Iona turned to go, but Dwan Karnash called out.

"Stay my queen! Stay and see what could have been yours. Stay and watch my beautiful Breyton come into this world!"

Then again a contraction took hold of her, and she threw her head back, throat muscles bulging, eyes closed.

"It is a difficult birth, Queen Boudicca," one of the midwives whispered. "This young warrior wishes to land on his feet to begin his life."

Iona nodded, understanding. Dwan Karnash relaxed again, again flashed a look of pride at Iona and tensed once more.

"Now, my darling," the midwife said. "Now my beautiful Dwan Karnash. Once more. Once more."

Dwan Karnash's face was utterly pallid, the pain overpowering, yet she would not cry out again now that Iona had come.

"Once more . . ."

Dwan Karnash pushed and sudden exultation colored her fair features. The baby had begun its passage. Again she pushed, tiny jewels of perspiration on her downy upper lip.

"Not so hard . . . yes, once more."

Dwan Karnash's face glowed. The pain must have been excruciating, yet she smiled, closing her eyes except when assuring herself that Iona still watched.

"At last. All right. We have him!"

"A man-child? Is it a man?" Dwan Karnash demanded, craning her neck, eyes awaiting the answer.

"There is every indication that he will be a man one day," the midwife said. As she took the baby a sudden powerful bawl filled the room. Dwan Karnash lay back, breast heaving, her face going suddenly soft, angelic.

"A boy. My Breyton," she murmured. "His first food shall be given to him on the tip of his father's sword. He shall be an Iceni warrior, by the gods!"

Then the baby was handed to her and she caressed his dark hair, immediately suckling him, wrapping him in a soft yellow blanket as Iona turned and slipped silently from the hut.

She walked the long dusty alleyway. An old man wove past her, his face a death mask. "They're dying," was all he said.

"Who? Who's dying?" she demanded, grabbing his birdlike shoulders.

"All of them. All of us. We're all dying, my queen." Then he pulled himself away and wandered off. Iona began to run for the wall, but she stopped, falling to a rigid, shuffling gait. There was nothing more to be done, nothing to hurry for.

Faces turned to her, saying nothing. It had nearly ended. So quickly. Everywhere chariots were upturned and broken, horses running in confusion, men sprawled on the grass.

Within the hour they straggled back. Those who could. Arms dangled uselessly, blood clotted ears and hair. Men shouted out, cursing the gods. Women stumbled across the yard, conscious of nothing.

Throg arrived, riding a chariot horse which had broken free. Prasutag was close behind him, crimson spilled across his breastplate.

"Prasutag!"

He turned to Iona, dark eyes expressionless. "We have been defeated," he said blankly.

"How many did we lose?" she pressed him.

"Half. More than half. Two-thirds," he guessed.

"And Leun?"

"Leun was beheaded, Iona."

"But Arawn . . . surely Arawn—he is charmed, our war-lover."

"Not charmed today. There were no charms today. Arawn took many men with him. He is dead, Iona."

Prasutag turned to walk away. Then he stopped, his back to her, arms hanging limply. He realized she had not asked the last question.

"Breyton . . .?" Iona waited, but he did not answer. She took Prasutag by the arm angrily and spun him around, her eyes hot, lips nearly venomous. "What of Breyton!"

"Dead, my queen. Breyton is dead."

Chapter Fifteen

Prasutag had been chosen. Under a flag of truce he rode into the valley through the early morning fog. Milk white, it reduced the world to a phantom sphere. Yet here and there Prasutag came upon up-jutting arms, stained armor, gaudy cloaks trampled into the earth.

They rose up and fell away. He gingerly crossed a series of earthworks, guided now by a centurion who had appeared from nowhere, dew glossing his armor.

Prasutag's hair was damp with the fog, his bones chilled when he finally stepped down before the massive tent hung with pennants, and met the enemy.

Prasutag waited, stoop-shouldered, in the doorway, his face slightly bewildered. These were the enemy? The red horde? Why, they appeared ordinary men, many darker-skinned than the Celts, shorter, yet only men.

The man in armor sat behind a table, his hair

curled. A noble warrior by his features, he also had the look of compassion as if he were intimate with suffering. An interpreter stood by his side.

"Come in," Marcus Atreus said, beckoning.

"I am Prasutag, of the Iceni. I have come to speak for my queen."

"Queen? So the tactician was a woman." Marcus nodded to himself, sparing a short smile. "And what does she wish to say to me?" the Roman asked, spreading his stubby fingers on the table.

"She wishes to sue for peace," Prasutag said, hardly able to force the words out.

"Peace?" It was not the first time, yet it was rare that a Celtic tribe did not battle to the last able body. "She is intelligent as well as clever," Marcus commented. He scooted aside a roll of parchment he had been studying and gestured with a hand. "Sit."

Prasutag perched nervously on the chair, back stiff. A guard's face appeared at the tent flap, then disappeared. A time later a large, red-haired man with the mark of rank on him peered in.

Marcus sighed heavily and stood, hands clasped behind his back. "What sort of peace? Unconditional?" the Roman asked.

"No, certainly not!" Prasutag answered quickly. "Queen Boudicca wishes to ascertain certain guarantees . . ."

"I need grant you none, you recognize?"

"You need not depart with the numbers of men you have now. We are not so crushed that we cannot fight. Old women would take up the sword. Many Romans would be lost attempting Viron's fortifications." Prasutag did not boast or grow angry; he spoke what he believed to be the truth without embellishment.

"You have a point, certainly." Marcus admired the candid manner of this Celtic spokesman. "Tell me then," he demanded, leaning nearer to Prasutag, "what are the conditions of surrender?"

"A guarantee of the survival of the Iceni nation as an individual state. It would, of course, be in vassalage to Rome. Yet she is adamant on this point: the Iceni must survive as an entity."

"This might be done," Marcus hesitated. It had been done, of course, yet Simonedes must be consulted. "If the reigning Celtic nobility swears allegiance to Rome alone. If weapons of war are destroyed, if the fortified cities are reduced ... yet those who led this war must be transported."

"Transported?" For a moment Prasutag did not understand. "Transported to Rome? My Queen Boudicca?"

"Your queen, as well as any other warriors or lords who might have followings. There is a giant who leads a cunning infantry—"

Throg.

"—he must go to Rome. There is a general called Barra, I believe ... and a man named Breyton."

"Breyton is dead," Prasutag told him.

"Men like these—others whose names escape me just now—cannot be allowed to remain in Britannia where their influence might be misused against the Roman Empire."

Prasutag blinked at Marcus Atreus, not yet understanding that the interview was at an end, the truce concluded. He only understood that Iona would be chained and thrown aboard a ship bound for Rome if this peace were finalized.

"Was there something else?" Marcus Atreus asked.

"Something . . . no. I shall inform my queen of your counterdemands."

"Thank you." Marcus stood, nodded, and watched as the Iceni pulled the tent flap aside and walked into the sunlight, seemingly stunned.

Yet the terms had been relatively soft. Simonedes would have demanded much more. Marcus stepped to the doorway himself and watched the man swing onto his horse's back and stiffly ride away toward the fortress these barbarians called Viron which jutted through the low fog across the battlefield.

Iona . . . Prasutag rode with his mind in fragments. Bitter passion rose in his breast. He felt suddenly compelled to urge Iona to continue the war, to wait for Kowlter . . . anything but lose her.

To lose her at last, now when it seemed . . . he put aside that forlorn hope. Tangled thoughts rode with him to Viron's somber gates.

When he told Iona of the Roman proposals she was not dismayed; she seemed rather pleased, in fact, her face cheerful. "So it will be then. The people must not bleed, must not fade from the earth. Our nation will survive the Roman occupation—you will see, my dear Prasutag. It will survive each wave of conquering peoples. If we cannot win through arms, we will outwait them. Let them stay their hour; we will stay our eternity."

"It means you must go." His voice was steady, but he did not know how it could be so. Crazily it came into his mind to reach for her, to cling to her, yet she buzzed away, calling for Thramane.

"See that Throg and Barra are informed," she told Prasutag, regaining her tone of command.

"Is that all, Iona?"

"All?" She turned to him, eyes wide. "Yes, of course."

Thramane entered in time to see Prasutag sweep angrily out the front door. She glanced from the door to Iona who stood smiling.

It was then that Iona lost her composure and control; she sagged at the older woman's feet, her eyes filling, her fingers clutching the fabric of Thramane's dress.

Thramane stroked her head gently, murmuring soft sounds.

"What else could I have done? The children must survive, Thramane," she said, her head still bowed. A tear fell to the floor. "The people must not bleed anymore."

"You have done what your father would have willed, Iona."

"Athair would never have surrendered."

"He was bound by the tradition of years, the old ways, the pride of a warrior king. No, Iona, Athair would not have done it, yet he would have wished for it. Above all Athair loved his people."

Iona stood shakily and moved aimlessly from trunk to trunk, examining her clothes, her jewelry. The sea—she had always been destined to cross it, it seemed.

Yet she could not have guessed how it would come to pass that she would finally traverse the great ocean and come to know the foreign lands. As a queen; as a slave.

At the appointed hour Iona emerged from her

hut. She wore purple embroidered with gold. On her head was a golden crown, a simple ring. Around her throat was the jade-eyed torque. On her upper arms she wore the coral and gold bracelets Athair had brought from a Belgae excursion one summer, lifetimes ago. Her horse was ready, the white stallion claimed from the Romans, caparisoned in gold, tail woven with purple and gold ribbon, wearing gold horseshoes.

The people stood like wooden images. Eyes hardly lifted to their queen as the white horse pranced past. Thrueldan was there and he handed her Athair's massive sword, her own battle lance, and a gold-handled dirk.

"I await your final victory," Thrueldan said.

Then the Druid, dressed in a cowled robe, withdrew, turning his back to all of them. Thrueldan went to his knees and uttered a strange sound. It was a moment before they realized what was happening. Thrueldan's back went rigid and he toppled forward dead, the sacrificial knife still clenched in his hands.

Throg was beside Iona, his massive chest hung with golden chains, his hair bleached and stiffened with lime, wearing red-checked trousers, carrying the sword which it was said no two other men could wield. His mustache was curled wildly.

"We journey together my queen."

"Where is Barra?"

"Barra is hanging from his ceiling, my queen."

Prasutag led Iona's horse forward, the chinking of the weapons, the gold chain, the only sounds.

Suddenly there was a high-pitched cry and Iona turned to see Dwan Karnash rushing from her hut, blond hair flying. She carried a small bundle.

"Iona . . . my queen, Boudicca," she said breathlessly, catching the bridle of Iona's horse. "Kiss your Breyton good-bye."

Shyly, uncertainly, she lifted the baby to Iona. The baby, naked in the sunlight, kicked but did not cry. His hair was turning light now. He was deep in the chest, well-formed. Iona held him a moment, tightly. Then she kissed his rosebud mouth and gave Breyton back to his mother.

Dwan Karnash's face was streaked with tears now and she ran alongside, saying words which Iona could not hear through the humming in her ears.

Throg signaled the gate and it opened. Prasutag held the reins a moment too long, opened his mouth to speak, but could find no words. For only a moment his eyes locked with those of Iona, and then the gates swung wide and Iona spurred her great white horse into a run, racing down the long grassy hillside. Throg looked back, just once, then followed.

After another second a fragile figure appeared, carrying a small trunk. Thramane trudged dutifully after her queen.

Marcus Atreus asked the hour once more. He sat his dais impatiently, wearing his golden laurel on his silver hair. Then across the fields he saw the gates open and two horses emerge.

The first was the Celtic queen, he had no doubt. In brilliant purple, riding a horse which Marcus recognized immediately as his own Placidus.

There was no movement for a stark, wavering moment; then she spurred the horse downhill at a wild pace, her lance poised aloft.

She raised a battle cry, a loud mournful sound which sent chills up Marcus Atreus's spine. Still she charged onward. There was no movement in the Roman ranks as she raced across the long grass, the horse moving in magnificent rhythm, mane flowing.

She was young. So young it surprised Marcus. She was also beautiful, he could not help but notice. She slowed the horse with one hand and put it into a tight circle, neck arched, riding in a ritual sunrise-to-sunset ring around the dais as Marcus Atreus watched, surrounded by his legions.

She held her head high, dark eyes defiant, lance still poised; and he had no doubt she could deliver that lance with accuracy.

Abruptly she stopped before the Roman general. Then with utter disdain this Celtic queen threw down her weapons, and with eyes haughtily on the Roman, she walked the steps of the dais, sitting stonily in silent submission at the feet of Marcus Atreus.

Iona's head came up as the flap of her darkened prison tent was thrown back. A woman stood there, hands clasped.

"Thramane!"

"I have come with you, mistress."

"You shouldn't have. We don't know where we will be going."

"No. But I know what remains behind. I have no one else, my queen." Thramane came forward. "I was wet nurse to you, Iona. I will not leave your side simply because you travel a winding road into darkness."

* * *

They came in the early morning. They were not rough, but only coldly efficient, and Iona did not protest at all. Together with Thramane she walked to a rough cart where they were seated. The women caught a glimpse of Throg, driven in chains with several Belgae and Regni warriors.

For a day and a night they bumped along in the cart until at last they arrived at a small harbor set in the low bluffs near Cold Ring. The wind off the broad green sea was chilly, smelling of salt, the clouds painted crimson and purple in the late hour.

Three Roman ships, one a trireme, lay at anchor along a stone jetty. Iona and Thramane were immediately taken on board one of the smaller vessels and locked into a small cabin belowdecks. Behind them and below they could hear the wretched cursing and moaning of others.

They spent the night in silent darkness, and when first light fringed the eastern clouds with a thread of beaten, brilliant gold, the slave fleet weighed anchor for the southern oceans.

Chapter Sixteen

They sailed a straight, unvarying course for endless days beneath the flat, unvarying skies. The slate gray seas stretched out toward all horizons, showing not a promise of landfall.

The skies were the constant blue of cornflowers, the breeze soft off the western seas; yet within the hull of the Roman ship it was dank, gray with the absence of all light, without a breath of saving wind.

The timbers creaked as the faceless men below struggled against the weight of the massive oars. Above, a nameless pilot rested against the tiller, guiding the slave ship toward a land which conjured no pictures, no images of color, nor musical sounds.

Iona lay belowdecks, fighting the nausea which was constant. Opening her eyes she could see Thramane patiently sitting on the trunk she had carried along, and the others—nameless, rootless

Celts from tribes unknown to her.

They had eaten nothing but a thin gruel and a sort of salted meat which was nearly unpalatable and which only increased the demanding, constant thirst which coated Iona's throat and mouth with dry longing.

She had known that this Rome was very far away—but they had been on the sea for days, long rolling days with the smell of bilgewater and the scurrying shadows of bold rats.

That they would come so far to destroy a single people, to dismantle their way of life and crush their hopes for a future seemed incredible. Yet what was not incredible this last year?

Athair dead; Lania. Breyton—dead. Viron, the impregnable, crushed. Thrueldan—dead. What had not died, had not passed to the darker side? As she stared at the hunched figures around her, inhaled the fetid air, listened to the creaking of the planks, she wondered with sharp suddenness why she had not taken her own life as well.

She lived; passed through; continued. To what end?

Thrueldan had told her one dark night when the moon coasted high through veils of cloud that life was not read completely by men—that there were ways subtle, quite fantastic through which a destiny is reached.

Yet Athair had said that life ended for a ruler when his people died.

Thramane was behind her. She felt the old woman's bony hands fussing with her hair and she slapped them with irritation.

"What does it matter? Leave me alone," Iona said.

"It matters. You are a queen!" Thramane said with the stern tone she had used with Iona, the child.

"Yes." Iona gripped Thramane's hand tightly a moment. "And we shall return to Viron. Soon."

"Soon," Thramane said. She hummed a broken tune as she worked, yet her voice broke off and she could not continue.

The guards were only stern, helmeted men who appeared twice a day to deliver the gruel and to have the dead removed. After a time they would hear the sound of a soul splashing into the sea.

Such a long swim home, Iona thought each time. Yet it was a wonder so many survived with such a diet, such conditions.

The days and nights had begun to blur—time whirled past meaninglessly. The only light filtered in through the cracks around the hatch, a chink in the bow planking.

"It's so far, so far!" a woman's voice cried out of the darkness. "Where can they be taking us?"

"To the end of the earth," a grumpy voice answered. "To shove us over."

"It's not where they're taking us," a calmer mind insisted. "They wouldn't care if we all gave up the ghost here and now. They're only taking us away— away from Britain."

Iona nodded agreement, yet for that one moment she had heard the voice say: "They're taking us away from *Breyton.*" Her mind was instantly flooded with images. A cool September day, a flight of geese against the indigo of the late sky. She felt warm breathing in her ear, the soft touch of lips running down her throat, saw the fire in the sunset clouds . . . . Thramane touched her shoulder.

"Are you all right?"

"All right." Iona touched her forehead, swung the hair from her eyes, smiled. "Yes—just dizzy. It's the lack of proper food. Only that."

Thramane nodded, leaning back, making herself as comfortable as possible. She too was weary, glum to despondency. Yet it was not the cold, the damp, the emptiness which gnawed at Thramane's stomach.

It was the absent light.

The light which did not blaze in Iona's dark eyes, flaring up with intensity, intelligence, bold challenge. The light of humor had also dimmed, the necessary light of love.

Thramane studied her queen. Still very young, beautiful in face and figure, glossy dark hair, her mouth tempting to men. Iona sat with her back straight, her chin lifted, yet there was a woodenness to her carriage, a sad drooping at the corners of that wide mouth.

Thramane, perhaps better than anyone, knew Iona. A spoiled baby, headstrong youth, she had been brought in a single summer's evening to full blossom, the moment of challenge summoning the full strength of her womanhood.

The moment had produced a queen. Yet that moment, the moment which Iona had answered with all of her resources and with those of her heritage, had passed.

In these long moments, days, years to come, Iona would perhaps need more strength than ever before. War is not the only setting for heroic acts;

it is far braver to suffer dark, silent solitude and keep the light of the soul alive.

The oars on the port side were drawn into the ship's bowels with a single, crackling sound and their heads snapped up expectantly. The ship seemed dead in the water, the rolling of the last days slowed to a faint swaying.

"We're docking," a low voice said. "That's the only reason for taking up the oars."

Yet hours passed and nothing happened. Below, with the absence of any breeze, the temperature soared and tempers grew short. "Why don't they open up?" a slight Belgae demanded angrily.

Iona let her head rest on her arms as she sat crouched, waiting. It seemed that the man had been wrong—they had not docked at all.

Yet suddenly the hatches were thrown open, piercing blue-white light flooding the hold with a brilliance which stung their eyes. Blinking into the sky which was crystalline, Iona watched the dark, bulky silhouettes of sailors with long poles shoving the hatch fully open, the wash of fresh air thrilling her as she filled her lungs with it.

All around faces were turned toward the sun, necks arched back, drinking the air in deeply, and for the first time Iona saw the faces of her fellow passengers clearly.

Pale faces, streaked with dirt, their cheeks were sunken from lack of nourishment, eyes unnaturally bright in the sunlight. The Belgae, a man of thirty, slight of build with a hooked nose, glanced at Iona.

"It won't be long now," he confided. "We'll be ashore. I know."

"How do you know?" a huge Cornoviian chieftain growled.

"How? It's not my first time," the Belgae answered. He lifted his dark hair and showed them the cropped ear of a Roman slave.

The Cornoviian shrugged but Iona winced.

"Don't you worry, my queen, they'll not do such a thing to you."

"Then you have been captured before?" Iona asked, her voice low.

"Captured, yes. My horse broke a leg on the rocks at Danelaw. Six years I spent in the Roman prisons before I saw the full light of day."

"But they released you?" Iona asked hopefully.

"Released!" the Belgae spat. "I was sold to a farmer who used me like an ox for two more long years. Then they found out old Dado—that's me—could work jewelry. I was sold to an artisan named Flavius. He dressed me like a fine, trained dog, pampered me as I taught him what I know of enameling. I was fed, bathed, petted by his concubines..."

"What happened?" Iona asked. On deck the ship was being winched to the wharf, the creaking of the heavy windlass merging with the labored curses of the sailors.

"We returned to Britain," Dado told her, "to trade with the Belgae. My master built a fine house there. We profited."

"And?"

"And then I killed him. At the first opportunity I slit his Roman dog throat," Dado said, his deep eyes expressionless. "They had not erased the barbarian from my soul."

A file of Roman soldiers entered the ship's hold, their heavy footfalls echoing in the dark chamber. They lined the lowered staircase and a command was issued.

Dark men, helmeted, they stood woodenly as the command was translated by a faltering tongue.

"All prisoners on deck!"

Iona walked swiftly forward in the press of prisoners eagerly moving toward captivity. So long as there was fresh air; no prison could be worse than the wretched ship. Or so it seemed then.

The sunlight hurt her eyes, yet she was pushed roughly forward. The town beyond the docks was white in the brilliant sun. Far off a child screamed with joy, a dog barked. A gull wheeled shrieking through the clear sky.

The houses sat on the hillsides, all of the same white stone. Groves of unfamiliar trees filled the empty spaces between the houses. People in carts and on foot bustled up and down narrow, cobblestoned streets. The first paved streets Iona had ever seen. It was incredible.

The town was not fortified. There were no huts. No forests beyond. All was white, orderly, bright beneath the Mediterranean sun.

"Rome . . ." Iona said, not able to fathom it.

"No. It's not Rome," Dado said. "Only a small town. Sometimes the slave ships go right up the Tiber. We have to dock here!" he griped. "That means ox-wagons for us."

Iona, befuddled, turned to ask a question of Dado who seemed to know everything about Rome, but she was pushed away by a strong, guiding hand and herded along a wooden planked ramp to a waiting area.

Dado had been pushed off in the other direction, but Thramane was there, shoving through the crowd of prisoners to be beside her.

"Dado says this is not Rome," Iona told the older woman. "We'll have to travel on."

"Why?" Thramane snapped. "Let them kill us here." She waved a hand about her. "Wherever we are."

There was a Roman in a plain white toga standing on a platform. A harried man with only fringes of hair above his ears, he waved his arms excitedly.

"Prisoners—slaves!" he yelled in faulty Celtic. Then he turned to the centurion in charge, a tall man with a single eye. "We need more soldiers, sir! Nearer the wharf!

"Slaves! Citizens of Britain. . . ." No one paid any attention to this hectic bureaucrat. Instead the Celts wandered morosely about, studying the Roman town, the fishers along the sea, the ships, with open interest. When they wandered too far they were prodded back by legionnaires, most of whom were the old or disabled.

"What are they waiting for?" Thramane asked impatiently.

Iona shrugged, then suddenly she caught her maid's arm and pointed toward the trireme where a last few prisoners were being led, in chains, to the wharf.

A bulky, threatening figure appeared, weighted down with the black iron links of his shackles. A massive man, he threw his head back and laughed beautifully, a tremendous roar which astonished those who were guiding him.

"Throg!"

Iona's hand tightened on Thramane's wrist. The

giant, bearded Iceni chieftan was being led by four Roman soldiers armed with short swords. Moving through the throng, Throg's head was clearly visible above them.

He snapped and joked and growled at those around him as he moved heavily toward an unseen goal. Iona waved and Thramane called out his name.

"Throg!"

The giant's eyes flickered toward them only for a moment, but they could not tell if he had seen them, and after a minute he had disappeared beyond the press of humanity which crowded the wharf.

"Here they come," the Cornoviian warrior grunted.

Iona's eyes followed those of the Cornoviian and she saw the long string of carts drawn by oxen winding through the town. One by one the teams were driven up to the wharves, the soldiers forming ranks around them.

"Ox carts," the Cornoviian sniffed.

"Worse." They were only ox carts, but the carts were fitted with oaken bars and padlocked doors.

Quickly, quietly, without protest they were organized into groups and nudged forward by halberd-bearing soldiers to the slave wagons.

Iona looked once more toward the spot where Throg in chains had disappeared, but she could not see him. Moving on legs stiffened by the weeks at sea, she followed the gestures of the guards and clambered into the cart, receiving a last, rough shove forward.

"Animal," Thramane muttered behind her.

Iona stared at the sea, the road to Britain. Yet it was wide, empty. The skies silent as she glanced to them. People were pushed forward into her cart, filling the wagon with tired, hot flesh.

There was no place to sit, and Iona clung to the bars at the back of the cart, watching a moment longer. Then the ox driver lashed the lumbering animals into motion, and the cart jerked forward.

The sea became a faint blue ribbon, seen between gaps in the low, green-gray hills, the ship a distant, dark dot. Iona leaned her head against the bars of her cage and watched miserably.

There was a time when the children of the town came out to throw stones and jab at the strangers from across the sea with sticks, calling out childish, foreign curses. And then the town was gone, the children having fallen away, the road only an empty line winding back to nothing—nothing at all.

And ahead—what lay ahead Iona did not wish to think about. As a child might, she refused the moment, refused to accept it all for just that little span of time. Soon enough it would all be brought back harshly.

It was a peaceful twilight across the hillsides. Olive groves, silver in the vanishing sunlight, turned to melancholy black clusters of trees silhouetted against the orange of the darkening skies.

Here and there a farmer striding home from the fields could be seen, hoe across his shoulder. Yet they were faceless men. Nameless as the town had been nameless, the seas, the rivers. All nameless but for that single name which strangled the heart with sharp fear.

Rome.

It lay ahead. It—the place where these world conquerors were bred, where plague sprang from the earth. Iona turned her eyes eastward, toward the great city which lay somewhere in the darkness beyond.

Her hands closed tightly around the bars which surrounded them and she closed her eyes as tightly as possible. She would not think of it, she vowed. Would not!

Yet as the cart bumped and pitched along the road, unable to sleep, she did nothing else but fill her weary mind with terrible images, and for a single, terrible and grand moment as the cooling night closed in around her, she was able to imagine herself emerging from the ox cart not as a slave, but as a conquering queen, glittering sword in hand, and it buoyed her spirits.

Thramane stood near her in the darkness, but the old woman said nothing. Iona's face was suddenly placid, stronger in the brittle starlight, and Thramane read the dream, at least a portion of it on her queen's face.

She was careful not to disturb Iona—such dreams, even those we know are but fantasy, at times may sustain us.

Thramane crossed her arms and stared at the dark countryside, happy that Iona, at least, could lose herself for one moment. Not that Thramane was too old to dream; she was simply too weary to be sustained by them.

Only Iona could sustain her. Only that dark-haired girl. For the rest, for herself, Thramane cared nothing. She would have died easily on the day Lania was buried. But for the girl.

Iona was a queen! Her queen. And she would rule again—Thramane would live to see the day. And with that dream, the old handmaid sustained *her* self.

Chapter Seventeen

The chamber was cavernous, dark. Light seeped in through narrow chinks high above them. The stone dripped water, the loamy soil underfoot had an unhealthy odor. And around Iona hundreds of people milled, of all manner of dress, from nations incredibly distant. Men burned black by a fierce sun, others of a golden tone who wore their straight black hair in series of knots topped with brilliant combs of mother-of-pearl.

They had traveled the night through in the ox cart, reaching a long, incredibly smooth road of stone which ran straight into the heart of the city. Dawn rose and Iona caught her breath. Rome was immense beyond the city of the gods!

Great roads led out to all corners of the globe. They passed beneath tremendous arches emblazoned with the exploits of the Roman warriors, and everywhere were horses although it was still early morning. Enough to mount every Celt in Britain.

Arched causeways carried water to the city, enormous marble-fronted buildings lined cold, empty streets. Water gushed from fountains where still more warriors, statesmen, and lawmakers were honored with their forms immortalized in stone.

Then, after a short winding course through the heart of the city, they clattered across a bridge toward a mammoth building beyond. There had been no time to examine it, to discover its use. They had been shuttled inside and herded below where hundreds of other unfortunates scarcely glanced up at them.

"What is this place?" Iona asked, but the man shook his head, not understanding. Everyone spoke in a different tongue, the babel filling the gigantic chamber.

"Ask him," Thramane said, lifting her head.

Dado was standing not far from them, his sharp face unmarked by concern. Iona walked to him, stepping around a man in purple silks wearing a turban.

"Dado," Iona said. The Belgae bowed low, although his arms remained crossed on his chest and he carried a faintly mocking smile on his lips.

"My queen," he replied.

"What is this?" she asked, waving a wondering hand around the chamber.

"The sorting house, my queen."

"Call me Iona," she begged him. "To hear a Belgae call me 'queen' is unbearable." She laughed as the absurdity of old distinctions in this place occurred to her. Here there were no queens, no Iceni and Belgae—only barbarians, as they called them. Slaves.

"Iona," Dado nodded.

"What kind of house did you call this? A sorting house?"

"Yes, my . . . Iona. The Romans must decide which of us they make use of, which has this or that talent to make him a profitable slave. And which—alas—must be killed."

"Killed?"

"Yes—some perhaps at once. Some may be taken and fattened and armed to be killed later in the Games." Dado shrugged again, his eyebrows lifting in a heavy sigh.

"What will they do with you?" Iona asked.

"Me?" Dado laughed out loud. "I am a runaway slave who has killed his master. I assure you they will not trouble to fatten me up."

"These Games—" Iona fell silent as a centurion of stature strode through the slaves, a scribe at his side scribbling something down. "What are they?" she asked in a lower tone.

"Butchery."

She stood looking at Dado whose dark eyes did not reflect any hope.

"Butchery," she repeated, nodding with understanding.

"Savage games," Dado went on. "They amuse themselves with them."

"I see." So for such things were men and women transported thousands of miles.

"Do not look so glum, my queen, Iona," Dado said, flashing a sudden, toothy smile. "They will not hurt you. I do not think so. You are too fair—far too fair."

Thramane frowned deeply, and Iona felt a cold chill crawl the length of her spine. Yet there was little time to reflect upon what Dado had left unsaid. Suddenly the room was filled with Roman soldiers and several strong-looking women dressed in red.

They moved through the throng, sorting them in ways unintelligible to Iona as they shouted in their Roman tongue. A woman was dragged off screaming by a burly soldier, and several Celtic men were lined against one wall to be guarded by a soldier with a pike.

"You." Iona glanced up at the figure in breastplate and plumed helmet before her and for a moment bitter anger flared up in her, the wish for a sword of her own. Thramane's hand fell gently on her shoulder.

"You," the soldier said, waving his sword toward a narrow corridor to the left. "You go there, woman," he grunted in what Iona was barely able to recognize as her own language.

Iona turned to follow his instructions and Thramane picked up Iona's trunk.

"Not you," the soldier said rudely.

"I'm her maid," Thramane shot back. "I have to come."

The soldier glanced around for a superior. Seeing none he shrugged and motioned angrily.

"Come on."

He spun and marched toward a heavy door which was swung open for them. Iona glanced about her, hoping for a glimpse of Throg. But the giant seemed to have dropped out of sight since leaving the docks.

They walked a long dark corridor which eventually wound to their left and met a long, steep flight of stone steps. Iona heard low sounds beyond the wall, but they were so muffled she could make nothing of them. Above, the doorway at the end of the steps showed as an arched, pale gold opening.

The black, plodding silhouette of the soldier led the way toward it. The man was breathing heavily now, his huge fist fixed to the hasp of his short sword.

They arrived finally at the landing and the soldier, still panting, pointed toward an open door with a broken knuckled finger.

"In there."

Iona and Thramane exchanged glances, but there was nothing to do now but go on. From a narrow window beyond, a bluish patch of light marked a rectangle on the stone wall. From beyond the doorway they suddenly heard the sound of a feminine voice raised in pleasant laughter.

It was so incongruous—that laughter in this gloomy prison—that Iona stood a moment, transfixed by it.

"Go on," the soldier grumbled. Iona nodded and walked into the room.

The scents of powders, perfumes, of new silk, met them as they entered the chamber. The room was airy, light, with a high, vaulted ceiling. The walls were blue, a long window was cut into the southern wall, and from there Iona could see the bustling, white sweep of the city.

"Oh, my dear." A woman who appeared to be Roman, yet spoke faultless Celtic, greeted her. "You just have to be our Queen Boudicca."

"I am." Iona stood hesitantly near the doorway as the woman, perhaps forty with an abundant figure and a perfectly dressed head of pale hair, approached.

The woman smiled and bowed superficially. Over her shoulder, Iona could see the others. Perhaps fifty women filled the long room. And everywhere servants bustled, carrying reams of silk and trays of jewelry, perfumes, and cosmetics Iona had never seen and could not dream of a use for.

An ebony-skinned woman of Iona's age sat imperially in a wooden chair while servants fussed with her hair and slid golden bracelets onto her slender, dark wrists. A statuesque blonde, perhaps a Gallic Celt, strolled across the room as a servant tried desperately to pin a crimson silk toga around her tall frame.

"You come along with me now," the matron said kindly. She had blue-gray eyes which did not match the smile she wore. Harsh, they were, calculating—or so it seemed to Iona. Perhaps all Roman eyes would seem so to her. There were tight little lines around her small mouth, yet Iona nodded submissively and stepped forward as did Thramane.

"You can't remain here, old thing," the Roman said to Thramane.

"I will remain," Thramane insisted. Her mouth was set. She still clutched the trunk tightly. "This girl is a *queen!* My queen!"

"My dear," the matron said with strained patience, "every woman in this room is a queen or a princess."

Iona looked up, overwhelmed by it. There were fifty women there, and now that she took notice, they all did seem marked by the regal stamp. A haughty group, of all ages, some proud, some simply enduring. So many nations! That seemed incredible. Fifty rulers represented fifty separate nations the Roman machine had crushed into submission.

So that was Rome's true strength!

"I have all of Queen Boudicca's clothing in here," Thramane argued. "I see she is to be dressed—*I* shall dress her. No other."

"I won't argue it. Do what you will for now."

So saying, the woman turned and beckoned them into a second chamber where the captured royalty was being bathed in individual bronze tubs while maidservants rushed here and there with soap, perfumes, and towels.

The water was heated in that very room using a bronze heater which held perhaps fifty gallons and was profusely decorated with swans, lions, and forest scenes.

Thramane unpinned Iona's gown as the Roman matron watched. When the cloth fell free, revealing Iona's perfect figure, full breasts, long, lithe legs, firm hips, the woman nodded with satisfaction.

"Beautiful, a beautiful creature," she said in a hissing voice, walking in a circle around Iona. "Step into this tub, dear."

Thramane's mouth was pursed in unhappy compliance as she took Iona's hand, helping her to settle into the steaming hot bathwater which was rose-scented, bringing soothing relaxation instantly to Iona's travel-weary muscles. Luxuriously she stretched out her long legs and smiled up at Thramane who still frowned bitterly.

"That some hag like that should command you!" Thramane complained, watching as the matron scurried away.

"It is their world," Iona reminded her. "We are the defeated, and for now we are not being treated so badly as Kowlter might treat a vanquished Queen Boudicca."

"For now," Thramane grumbled. "For now—"

"For now let me take my ease. The water is soothing, and there is nothing else to be done."

Thramane nodded and began folding Iona's travel-stained clothes, selecting another, deep purple dress for her from the trunk. Hesitating, she also selected Iona's finest jewelry—golden bracelets, the lion head torque and an enameled brooch.

The matron had returned, bringing another young woman to the bath room. She was a short girl, a Celt by her features, with reddish hair and a figure softer, fuller than Iona's. She searched the room with eager eyes, a smile revealing her wide teeth.

She was undressed and placed in the tub next to Iona. Sliding down into the hot water, she lifted her hair with both hands and fairly purred with the sensual comfort.

"I've never had a bath so warm, so luxurious," she told Iona, beaming. "I am Princess Trixcia of the Epidii."

"Iona," she replied. The Epidii she had heard of, but never encountered. From the far north of the Island Britannia, they were said to be a solitary, brooding tribe. Yet Trixcia hardly fit that mold. Ebullient, chatty, she appeared near Iona's own age, yet one would have guessed her own life had not been as turbulent as Iona's.

"I was taken in my sleep," Trixcia giggled. "I didn't know what they were doing." She laughed again. "It was a small hunting party—just my uncle and three others were with me. I think they would have killed us," she said, eyes opening wide, but she added with a smile, "I told them I was a princess, though, and they took us alive. I was very afraid of the Romans before that, do you know? I was silly."

"Silly," Iona answered. Probably Trixcia's family and town were now nothing but a memory perpetuated by mounds of cold ash in that far north-country. The girl was unaware of such occurrences. She had never lived, apparently, in the real world, but only in the sheltered bosom of her family, her rank. Perhaps Trixcia, in her happy ignorance, was far luckier.

"It's a terrible land I come from," Trixcia went on. "We lived on the north coast where icy gales sweep across the barren bluffs all winter long. And winter lasts eight months." Trixcia rolled over in the bath, her smooth buttocks showing above the opaque water. She rested her chin on her hand as she talked to Iona.

"Nothing keeps us warm but the furs. And after a winter the furs are stinking vermin refuges. Filled with lice!" Trixcia made a disgusted face and then laughed out loud, sitting up once more.

"That's why I don't mind so much being a prisoner. Although I didn't like the sea." She was thoughtful a moment. "My father wanted me to marry a warrior named Curdge—he had black hairs in his nose, and wide pores. He was dull and ugly as a mole. Do you know where we're going?" Trixcia asked with sudden eagerness.

"No."

Iona's head came around sharply. Thramane who had been fussing over Iona's clothing looked around as well.

"We're so lucky," Trixcia went on gleefully. "Today," she said, emphasizing each word, "we are going before the emperor! That's after the parade, of course. Or maybe before—I'm not sure."

"The parade?" Thramane's forehead tightened with a wary frown. She had seen too much in her time to be converted easily to spontaneous joy such as Trixcia displayed.

"We are prisoners," Iona said. "I fear we would only be paraded in chains."

"Look around you," Trixcia exclaimed. "Where are the manacles? No! I have it straight from Flavia herself."

"Flavia?"

"The matron," Trixcia said in exasperation. She stacked her reddish hair on top of her small head and pinned it up with the ivory hairpins on the dressing table beside the tub.

"What sort of parade is this?" Iona wanted to know. She stood from the tub, drying herself with a soft, thick towel such as she had never seen before. Thramane did her back as Trixcia explained.

"We are so lucky. I feel that suddenly the luck I have not had has come to me all at once." Trixcia, too, stood and, holding a towel against her full breasts, she stepped daintily from the tub, leaving damp patches on the polished marble of the floor.

"In what way?"

"It's time for one of the great Roman festivals," Trixcia explained. "The festival to Venus—their goddess of love." Trixcia gurgled. "We are all paraded through the streets. The Roman citizens do it too. There will be garlands and priests, statues of the goddess herself—they say that sometimes she appears carnate! The emperor, of course, will be viewing it all. And we in our finery, beneath this lovely warm sun, the flowers all around, we will parade."

"As trophies," Thramane remarked sourly, brushing Iona's fine dark hair.

"Yes," Trixcia agreed. "Prizes of war. But not treated so badly, do you think?" she asked hotly. "In Epidii right now, where would I be?" she demanded, hands on her naked hips, leaning slightly forward. "In bed with that filthy Curdge under a filthy heap of stinking winter furs with an icy wind blowing through the chinks in his hut!"

"But free," Iona reminded her.

"Free. Yes. Free to be miserable, to freeze, to go hungry, to run across the countryside in fear of the enemy. Free to be Curdge's slave. A slavery far less endurable than *this* slavery."

They dined then, these foreign queens, at a long table set with sweetmeats, roast lamb and oxen, carp and duck, nuts and honey-glazed fruits—orange sections, sweet, purple plums and enormous platters stacked with red and white grapes. There were cheeses of all varieties, sharp and pungent, and hot bread spread with butter and honey, sprinkled with nuts. And wine—the wine which was a Roman passion as much as it was a Celtic love. Deep, dark, ruby-colored wines, tart and dry, white wines which followed the fowl and carp with a crisp, settling polish.

Iona's eyes swept the table as she sipped at her wine, studying their faces, these royal faces. Each had lost a home, a family, a nation to the Romans. Yet now they were content, most of them. Contentment purchased with a bath, a new dress of silk, a plate of green figs. Trixcia sucked at the pulpy center of an apricot and stretched out a slender hand for another bloody slice of steaming Roman ox.

At the head of the table sat a stoic, blue-eyed giantess of a woman. Blond hair in braids, back rigid, she refused to touch a drop of wine, to take a morsel of roast pork.

She was not a Celt; her people were called Northmen, and Iona read no surrender in her pale eyes. The matron called her Drusilla as she begged her to eat, that professional smile on her dry lips.

But Drusilla turned hot eyes on Flavia, and the matron shrunk away from this woman of the north, reading correctly in those eyes a temper and a will which would tear the throat from Flavia at any provocation.

The meat courses were swept away by silent eunuchs, and cakes and honey rolls were brought out, with still another variety of wine—sweet, syrupy. The eyes of the blond woman, Drusilla, met those of Iona briefly and Iona, who had eaten only lightly, found she had no taste for these Roman dainties.

They were led out into a sunny courtyard, Iona, at the insistence of Flavia, wearing the thrice-stolen crown of the Iceni. Ox carts waited there, perhaps the very same ones which had transported them from the coast. Yet now there were no bars, and the carts as well as the stoic oxen were brightly garlanded with white and red flowers, their bridles festooned with more blooms. The driver appeared to be a priest; certainly he was not a soldier. He wore a white toga, his narrow skull shaved completely.

Around the courtyard ancient olive trees bent in the slight breeze which pressed the filmy fabric of Iona's skirt to her legs.

"So you see," Trixcia said, passing her with airy steps, "it is a fine enslavement."

Iona stepped into the cart, taking from one of the silent eunuchs a garland of camellias which she held. Thramane had been ushered away after the bath and vainly Iona searched the upper ramparts, the narrow windows of the massive stone building for her handmaid—her last contact with the Iceni past.

From somewhere unseen a signal was given and the massive gates to the courtyard were opened. The long line of carts moved out, passing through the grove of citrus trees which filled the air with lemon scent, then under the high, porticoed gate into the streets beyond.

The streets were filled with people of all sorts. Enough, Iona decided, to populate the globe. They wore all complexions, features, marks of rank. Bald-headed priests moved together, hoisting an image of Venus high above them.

Behind them moved a phalanx of women devoted to the goddess, wearing sheer white robes, several with their own heads shaven. People crowded the balconies above them; some jeered the passing foreign royalty, a few threw flowers.

As the ox carts swung into line, the procession was joined by a regiment of Roman infantry carrying the man-sized rectangular shields so effective against archery. Most of them seemed veterans of some war or another, and generally they were of the lower ranks.

"Look there," Trixcia said, clutching Iona's arm. There was a Roman centurion riding a glossy black charger of enormous size leading his cavalry in parade, a haughty set to his finely chiseled features, steel gray eyes staring forward. "*That*, now, is a man. Perhaps I shall take a Roman husband," the girl said petulantly.

Iona nodded, studying the man who had fine strong shoulders, and a battle scar creasing his broad forehead. A man. He was only a man to Trixcia—to Iona he was still the enemy. A Roman. Perhaps this man had killed Arawn, struck down Leun . . . who knew? He rode on proudly, following these prizes of war.

The long boulevard was filled with laughing children, carts where honey rolls could be purchased, with the music of lyres and drums, the long blankets woven of flowers. The city was a brilliant white in the clear daylight. On the hill to their left stood the ancient temple to Jupiter. On the Capitoline Hill behind her the column of Marcus Aurelius was visible, towering some ninety-five feet into the air. The ancient stone had discolored some, bleeding moisture, yet Iona had never seen such things, nor imagined that the skills for their making existed anywhere—even in Rome.

The procession, with the accompanying tinkling of bells, the chanting, the dancing, flowed through the Forum where most of the craftsmen and merchants had closed up business for the day, and on toward a huge dark structure to the south.

Everywhere the people sang, danced in mad circles, drank enormous quantities of wine, freeing all inhibitions. Iona watched it silently, though

Trixcia seemed intoxicated herself at the sight.

"I want to be a Roman," she said out loud, passionately.

Iona could not answer, could think of no answer. She rode on as if in a dream. There was the texture of rough wood under one hand as she gripped the ox cart for balance, the fragility of the flowers in her other, the soft caress of wind-shifted silk across her thighs and abdomen. The sky was a quiet, shimmering veil above the glare of the city. The women around her were silent; yet just beyond them, in the streets, men and women, children and the aged scurried like sun-warmed ants in every direction shouting, singing, whirling in mad pirouettes.

For every light there was a deep shadow between buildings where piles of garbage sat rotting. For every smile, a frown in the cart. For each song a dirge answering in the hearts of the vanquished who rode silently.

I want to be a Roman.

Iona still saw an embattled Throg, a wounded, dying Leun, an Iceni god, Breyton, who had passed Viron's gates with a smile never to return. She still saw the gaunt-sided oxen, the helpless infants, the scorched earth of Britain.

Yet, it could be said—and by a Celt!—*I want to be a Roman.*

The Druid, Thrueldan, had his magic. The gods their own. Yet power has its magic—it summons those who fear defeat, poverty, anonymity. Power lures those who would share its magic. And Trixcia was captured in the web of that magical spell.

Far from being captured by it, the woman of the north, Drusilla, sat insolently in the front of the cart. The garland they had handed her lay torn and trampled at her feet. Again she looked at Iona, again flashed that glance which told her that the spirit of this warrior of the north could not be trampled under. There was no magic in this southern land that strong.

The shadow of the great amphitheater blacked out the sky, falling across them as they wove up the slight incline to its cavernous entrance. The carts flowed quickly through, and—Iona noticed—the gates were quickly made fast.

The cart driver turned to the right, making his way through a labyrinth of stone corridors until they came to an arched entry cut into the gray stone which was too narrow for the carts.

Flavia walked from one cart to the next, instructing them.

"Out of the cart. To your left inside," the matron said.

"But the emperor!" Trixcia wailed. "You promised we would have an audience before Claudius."

"My dear," Flavia smiled, "it is here that the audience is to be held."

Trixcia glanced around dubiously at the mossy, rough stone of the walls, but the sight of the other, gaily-clad women dispelled any doubts.

She took Iona's hand as she stepped from the cart. "Come in with me, Iona," she invited her. "But Iona—you've dropped your garland."

"So I have," Iona said, but she made no move to recover it.

None of the brightness of their clothing, of the procession could dispel the doubts which now crept into Iona's heart. She knew nothing of the Romans, nothing of their ways, yet she doubted royalty was introduced in such a fashion anywhere in the world.

They passed into a narrow corridor where the windows were high, narrow, and blocked by bars. The entrance behind them had slammed shut and had been locked. Now as Iona moved along, following the proud Drusilla, she trod other garlands dropped absently to the floor.

They stopped for a long moment for no apparent reason, a royal parade deep in this tomblike vault, then moved on into an interior chamber where soldiers lined the walls.

"No!" It was Trixcia who cried out. The others stood silently, proudly. Iona watched as Trixcia's hand slowly opened, allowing her battered garland to drop to the earth.

Chapter Eighteen

Trixcia cried out again. Drusilla spat angrily on the floor. Iona let her eyes run over the immobile, helmeted soldiers. Flavia had stepped back to be nearer the guards and she instructed them now, her words still calm, friendly.

"Strip off your gowns, ladies. Your new costumes will arrive shortly."

Sullenly they began undressing before the eyes of the soldiers. Standing there, naked, Iona crossed her arms in front of her. Trixcia, in tears, demanded to see the emperor.

"You shall see him, dear," Flavia said. "Soon. But you must change."

"Do as she says, Trixcia," Iona advised her softly.

"But, Iona . . ."

"Do as she tells you," Iona said with firmness. She did not know what lay before them, but she could read the deep hatred which lay in Flavia's eyes, and she knew that not to obey was perhaps to die.

"Fine," Flavia said with glassy approval.

There was a rapping at an inner door and Flavia's eyes flickered that way. "Here are your costumes," she said.

Two dark-eyed girls appeared, carrying a heavy trunk. They looked apologetically at the roomful of women, then set the trunk down and disappeared as quickly as they had entered.

"Here." Flavia opened the trunks and removed a short white skirt. She tossed it to Drusilla who wrapped it around herself, her eyes burning coals.

Iona dressed in turn and they waited, bare-breasted, each in an identical half-skirt, many still wearing jewelry and crowns.

Trixcia stood apart, eyes still filled with hot tears. She looked pathetically to Iona for help, yet there was nothing to be done. Iona stood regally, the thrice-stolen crown encircling her raven hair, her bracelets winding up her forearms.

I want to be a Roman.

The words returned to her suddenly and Iona laughed out loud. Flavia glanced sharply at her, but said nothing.

"I don't see . . ." Trixcia pled with Flavia. The matron smiled back, a smile which seemed would split her face.

"It is the festival of Venus, my queens. You are all children of Venus."

"And so?" Iona asked. Flavia blinked at her, startled at the change in Iona's manner. Her face was set, eyes as cold as those of Drusilla so that the matron took an involuntary step backward as their eyes met.

"Why, it is the day of the Games. After the procession the Games are always held. And today, you daughters of Venus are the special attraction. Fifty queens! Conquered maidens before the emperor of all the world. Celebrating the day of the goddess."

Trixcia shook her head, not understanding. Quietly she asked Iona as a child might, "Are we not going before the emperor, then?"

"We are," Iona answered, and it seemed to placate the girl. Still shaking her head, Trixcia wiped the tears from her eyes, turning away from the guards who stood woodenly, watching. She still had no idea what would happen. Drusilla must have known from the first, yet the woman from the north could not speak their tongue, and could do nothing but watch, holding her bitter contempt silently.

The others, it seemed, were becoming slowly aware. Step by step, moment by moment, the icy knowledge had crept into their hearts.

Iona knew. Perhaps she had suspected it from the first moments, yet had been afraid to acknowledge it as a certainty.

The Games. So that was where this lead. And what was it Dado had called these games? *Butchery.* She offered a smile she did not feel to Trixcia who, in her childishness, was only concerned with keeping the Roman eyes from her full breasts.

Suddenly, from beyond the walls, a thrilling, deeply muffled, electric roar went up. Many hundreds of thousands of voices raised in excitement. The sound, distant as it was, chilled Iona.

Butchery.

They waited. An interminable wait filled only with the silent thoughts, the ragged breathing. Some prayed, others carried blank expressions. Iona's thoughts ran back to her childhood when she was free to roam the forests, bow in hand, to sit beside that narrow waterfall above Hartscliffe and let her own thoughts, her own life, mingle with the rush of water, the flight of the heron, the warmth the sun spread across the earth. . . .

From beyond the walls that chilling, incredible roar sounded again and Iona's head snapped up. A grating, metallic sound followed as the roar died away and the guards began herding them forward. Down a narrow ramp they went toward a huge iron portcullis which was being raised. Beyond that was brilliant sunlight and the roaring which continued, building to an incredible crescendo as they emerged onto the floor of the colosseum.

Iona stood, transfixed by it. Tiers of people, stacked one upon the other reaching toward the very skies, stood yelling, cursing, drinking wine, throwing things down onto the sandy floor of the stadium. To her left Iona saw a huge cat, of a kind she had never seen, with stripes on its orange coat lying mutilated, dead.

The women were led forward past the wreckage of a chariot, a dead horse and driver. A broken sword blade was thrust into the earth nearby. And surrounding it all was the color, the blur, the ceaseless bloody roar of the throng—faceless, nameless.

They walked in a double file once around the arena floor, the sun warm on their naked breasts, the blood pounding in their temples, the bloody roar ever increasing, demanding.

"There," Iona said with a harshness born out of anger to Trixcia who walked unsteadily beside her. "There is your emperor!"

High above them in a box curtained with purple silk sat the emperor of all the Romans, of all the world. They could see nothing of him but a languid, white hand draped casually over the side of the box. That was the hand that ordered nations crushed, towns set afire, people killed.

"There is your emperor; here are your Romans!"

They paused before the box a long moment. A young woman, her hair intricately arranged, leaned far forward, pointing down at them, making some comment which could not be heard, but only guessed at.

Then the hand of the emperor was raised and the soldiers surrounding the women below withdrew. They stood another long minute beneath the hot sun. No breeze reached them on the floor of the arena. The sand was hot beneath their feet. Slowly an ox cart drew forward, driven by a youth of no more than twelve.

He hopped from the cart and let down the back gate, spilling weapons out onto the hot sand. Twenty short swords glittered in the sunlight, twenty lances. A dozen halberds.

"What is this?" Iona demanded, but the boy, after one pathetic glance, leaped into his cart seat and drove hurriedly away, the weapons lying in a gleaming, menacing pile.

She asked, but she need not have asked. Iona knew what the weapons meant, and before any of the others she stepped to the pile and hefted a lance. The Viking woman picked up a sword and the others followed suit, even a trembling Trixcia.

She had come this far. No farther would she go, Iona knew. The final battle had not been won nor lost at Viron. The Romans had simply delayed the moment of final defeat so that it might be symbolically enacted on this bloody playing field, so that all of her citizens might share in the triumph of the state.

A terrible roar from the crowd brought Iona's head around toward the southern gate and she saw them enter. Long files of men on chariots, afoot, carrying swords and lances, shields and axes.

"They're not Romans," Trixcia said.

"No." Not Romans, these warriors they must battle. "Why risk their own in this entertainment?"

Other prisoners, slaves trapped within the framework of this sprawling, bloody play, came forward. Iona stood ready to meet them. They were not Romans, but Roman tools—men of Asia, Africa, the barbarian Teutonic tribes. They had come prepared for battle, but apparently not prepared to fight against women.

One of them, a massive German barbarian, leaped from his chariot, threw back his head in amazement and laughed loudly. He pointed at the enslaved queens and shook his head, waving a hand in disgust, yet from behind Iona a panicked hand unleashed a lance and the barbarian caught it deeply in his chest.

In angered frustration he turned toward his chariot, toppled forward and died, the lance cracking beneath his weight as he fell.

Then the roar of the crowd mingled with the sudden, thrilling roar of the warriors as they charged forward, knowing that they must kill one another or die. Men she had never seen, whose tribal names she could not guess, who had never stolen an Iceni ox nor crossed Killdeer Stream, bore down on her with wild expressions on their faces. Expressions of shame, fear, anger.

Yet they meant to kill her.

Iona saw a wild-haired blond man in a chariot driving at her, a lance lifted high, his blue eyes almost apologetic. Yet he was apologizing only for trying to kill her. He meant to survive.

Iona stood motionless, yet she read the death on the man's face. She forced herself to see him as a Roman, sweeping across the plains of Viron, and her own well-honed skills enabled her to meet him in full combat.

She leaped aside as the charging horses bore down on her, nostrils flaring wildly, mouths bleeding from the hard bit.

The chariot wheels barely missed crushing her and she slipped, momentarily going to one knee as the barbarian spun the chariot around and poised his lance for the kill.

Iona had come to her feet and regained her balance. She saw the man's eyes, his face, even the small scar in his eyebrow, then she flung her lance and watched as the head buried itself deeply in his chest and the face went suddenly expressionless, the muscles loose.

He dropped the reins and the chariot horses turned frantically aside, dodging the woman before them. The chariot cartwheeled crazily through the air, and beyond Iona a man screamed in pain as the falling war machine crushed him unexpectedly.

Drusilla was in single combat with a shorter, dark-skinned man. He lunged and she parried. As he lunged again, the Viking princess swung out with her sword, lopping his arm off.

Iona stood dazed but had the presence of mind to snatch up the barbarian's lance and fend off another horseman who was already bleeding profusely from the face. His crimson mask was broken by the anguish of an open-mouthed scream as he collapsed across the bulwark of the chariot, tossed free seconds later by the rumbling horses.

Iona grasped for the bridle of the chariot horse and with an arm-wrenching jolt, managed it. She took one running stride and was to the horse's back. Slowing them, she got to the chariot, her hair in wild confusion, a trickle of blood running across her breast.

Trixcia was near her, pinned to the earth by a tall barbarian, and Iona swung toward her, cutting down with her lance which took the man in the neck at the base of the skull.

Trixcia, she saw, had scooted to one side, sitting immobile amidst the carnage and clashing of arms.

The day twisted and inverted into a crazy blur of color, sound, horrible screams, death. Iona fought one man, then another, and she saw her sister queens lying dead, saw the blood stain the sands of the arena, and from the corner of her eye, saw the cheering throng of Romans above and beyond them, cheering death as they sat in their fat, pompous safety.

Her arms were leaden now, her legs wooden. The horses foundered and stood trembling, exhausted to the point of death, their white flanks streaked with crimson.

Iona saw a dark-bearded face before her and she cut at it. Hands grabbed at her breasts, her legs, and she fought back in a fever of animal combat. The Viking woman was crumpled against the earth, dead. A horse with a lance in its chest struggled past, fell once and scrambled to its feet once more, wandering in crazy circles.

Then there was nothing but the high sun, the empty sky, the smell of death, the frantic kicking of a horse in its death run. Iona wandered in an aimless circle. Trixcia was there still, sitting with her hands across her face in the center of the field. No others.

Iona walked toward the emperor's box. In her hand was the lance; her hair hung across her face, flowed across her breast. She looked into the sun, seeing a white hand in the box, a shadowed face.

She tried to lift the lance, to fling it against that face, but her muscles were knotted, the nerves dead, and she could only stand there, head hanging limply, watching as the pale hand formed a fist and turned a thumb up toward the sky.

The roar sounded again, infinitely distant, echoing loudly.

The Romans cheered as Iona stood before the emperor. Cheered! If she only had the strength to lift that lance, to hurl it against Rome! But her hand loosened from exhaustion and the bloody lance dropped to the earth.

She was cast into a dark, damp underground chamber. The door slammed shut behind her, and Iona scooted toward the wall where she rested, head flung back, the tenseness draining from her.

She could see nothing in the dim light, hear nothing. At that moment it did not matter.

A trembling began in her legs and spread to her arms, a trembling she could not stop as the muscles, tense with combat, now loosened. Nor could she stop the tears which began, the sobbing which racked her breast. In the darkness of this dungeon she cried unashamedly.

Suddenly she stopped, aware of some other presence in the darkness. She sensed another person, one she could not see or hear.

"Go on. Have your cry," the voice said from deep within the dungeon. "Maybe it will help for a time. Cry."

The voice was that of an older woman, cracked by time and the harsh conditions of the cell. The dampness which crept into the throat and lingered there as a rasping, which in time settled into the lungs, in such places, and brought death.

"Who are you?" Iona asked.

"One like you. But another like you," the old woman answered.

"Like me?" Iona laughed. Were there others so tortured?

"Like you. I have survived a time. A time. Like you I came from another world and watched as it was destroyed, pulled down around me." Now in the dim light Iona could make out a dark form which might have been a bundle of rags tossed negligently in the corner. It was from there the voice came.

"Who are you? What are you doing here?" Iona demanded.

"What am I doing here?" the old woman laughed, a cracked laugh, little practiced. "Like you I wait."

"Await what?"

"Ah—that is the question which has no answer. Not for us. The answer is inscribed on the winds of whim, shifting winds which answer no questioner. Have your cry," the woman said with sudden sharpness. "I have no tears left . . . otherwise, I would gladly join your unhappy ritual."

Iona fell silent. Her teeth now began to chatter

and she crossed her arms, trying to warm herself. It was still and cold in this chamber far underground. The tears which had gushed forth hotly now cooled her smooth cheeks.

"Here." The old woman had scooted beside Iona and she wrapped a tattered, colorless blanket around her trembling shoulders. "I am more used to this—I do not need another blanket."

"Thank you." Iona clutched the blanket tightly, eyes following the dark, shambling form of the woman as she scuttled back toward the far corner.

"What was your crime?" the old woman asked Iona.

"Crime?" Iona asked, perplexed. "Not being a Roman," she supposed.

"Yes. Yes—that is all it takes. That is enough of a crime."

"May I ask what your crime was?" Iona ventured. Slowly, in the vague light, the features of the woman came into focus. Rather long-faced with an equally long nose, still she must have been handsome in earlier days.

"My husband grew weary of me," she said flatly. "He wished to put me away for a younger girl, and I would not allow it! Would not!" she snapped. "I had my life invested in Simonedes's career, in his home, his children. While he was off across the seas, it was I who advanced his career. I had the ear of the Emperor Claudius."

"The devil's own ear," Iona said angrily.

"No," the woman answered. "Do not judge Claudius too harshly. He is a progressive emperor. Yet the people, the Senate, the nobility, struggle against him. The Games must be held—yet Claudius has tried to condemn them."

"He watched a hundred die today," Iona said, her temper flaring.

"Yet he allowed you to live," the old woman said. "He is a good man, weighed down by tradition and influence. It is Claudius who has allowed freedmen into the civil service—former slaves who in other times would have remained slaves until they died.

"In earlier days," she went on, "slaves grown old or crippled by misuse were simply abandoned to die. Claudius has made this a crime, and such an act can be termed murder."

"That seems only proper, and not progressive to any impressive degree," Iona said dryly.

"Yes. But you must understand that slaves are not only despised, but feared since the time of Spartacus. The spectre of another revolt haunts the Roman mind. Claudius flies in the face of this prejudice."

"Spartacus?"

"An escaped slave. With a few score gladiators he hid in the crater of Vesuvius—a great volcano south of Rome—until his forces increased. They say his fold eventually numbered hundreds of thousands. They rampaged across the countryside like an avenging cloud of death until finally the flame was extinguished."

Iona nodded silently. Despite the cold, the hunger she now felt, she found herself growing sleepy. So he—who had commanded the death of the foreign queens—was considered an enlightened ruler!

"There was a girl I met," Iona said drowsily, "who would be a Roman above all else. Trixcia, they called her."

"But she was not so foolish," the woman told

her. "Rome is the world. A Roman citizen is a human being, all else half-alive, animals. A slave is dealt with as the master sees fit; a Roman citizen, no matter his rank, has the emperor's protection and that of the courts.

"She was not so foolish, this Trixcia. To be Roman is to live; to be a slave is to die. Perhaps your chance will come, my beautiful young queen. Perhaps you shall have your chance to become Roman. Do not scorn it, but leap upon it. Your life will continue in Rome, will end here. Live it as well as possible—for one thing is certain, you will never see your homeland again."

What would there be left to see of it? Iona asked herself. Viron was a part of Rome now, as was all in between. A city which covered the earth, this Rome forbade all resistance, smothered all hope. To return to Viron, even if possible, would lead to her execution—she had already been told that.

The past, without mother, father, tribe, seemed irretrievably lost. In that way the old woman was right; if Iona were to go on at all, to continue to live for any reason, the reason must be found in Rome.

No longer able to stay awake, Iona huddled inside the worn blanket and closed her eyes, dreaming a peaceful, quiet dream of no content which she could not remember upon awakening except that there was no Rome in that dream. She was certain of that: there was no longer a Rome.

With a start she awakened; there was a hand on her shoulder, the faintest beam of light falling from somewhere high above.

"Eat, dear. They've brought us our daily meal."

Iona scratched her eyes open and stretched the

battle-knotted, night-tightened muscles of her arms and legs. She was sore everywhere as she walked to the door to find a poor earthen pot filled with pickled fish and a goblet of sour wine.

"That's all there ever is," the old woman told her. "Better eat, though I hate to imagine what it does to the stomach."

The days were empty, dark. Iona asked the woman, whose name was Sophia, how long she had been imprisoned. Sophia could only shrug.

"A year. Two? Three . . . who can say? Time has no meaning left."

"When will you be released?" Iona inquired, but Sophia's face, without expression, spelled out the answer.

"Never?" Iona asked, her voice a whisper.

"No," Sophia replied. "My life ends here."

"How . . ."—Iona scooted closer to her—"how is this possible? You are a Roman citizen, aren't you?"

"I am," Sophia affirmed.

"Then—"

"Because there was no trial, no sentence, no judge but my husband. You see," Sophia went on, "Simonedes is highly placed, a nephew of the emperor. He needed ask no one's permission to have me caged. He commanded and the cell doors opened. He commanded and they closed. The guards are paid to know nothing. I have been forgotten, Iona—no one searches for me."

"And your husband—"

"Simonedes plays the fool with his young trollop," Sophia remarked. "One day, when it pleases him, perhaps she shall share my cell."

The days passed and it seemed that Iona, too, had been forgotten, that she, too, would end her life in this dank cell. She exercised for the sake of her health, and also to combat the boredom, stretching for hours at a time while Sophia watched. Then it was time for her lessons. Sophia coached her in Latin and in Roman history, and Iona assimilated both readily.

After learning about the mad Emperor Caligula whose reign had preceded that of Claudius, she was able better to understand how the present emperor could be called progressive, enlightened, moral. This wretched man, this Emperor Caligula, enjoyed watching his slaves tortured and murdered as he dined. Crazed, he deified himself and had his favorite horse named consul. The officers of his personal guard had assassinated him.

Iona studied diligently, and Sophia was a tireless teacher. For each of them it was entertainment, the only communication possible. Many weeks passed in this way, and one day Sophia complimented Iona:

"I've known slaves and freed men who have spent five years in Rome who did not have your mastery of the language. True, the accent is strong, but now when they curse you for a slave, you'll know it. But then," Sophia recalled, "we haven't taught you our Roman curses, have we?"

"No." Iona was thoughtful. "Is there magic in these curses? Thrueldan, our Druid, used to say that knowing the magic in mystical words neutralized them. In that case, I should know the curses. If they are only vile words people hurl at each other thoughtlessly, I do not want to know when they are cursing me."

"There is no magic in the curses, Iona," Sophia admitted.

She watched this British queen with thoughtful

fondness. The girl was possessed of a quick mind, a ready wit, and an ingeniously analytical intelligence.

Beautiful, even in that ragged dress they had fashioned from the blanket, she carried herself with a regal bearing, and at no time since Sophia had met her had she given in to self-pity, nor displayed the arrogance of rank.

A child, a queen, a woman—if any could survive this slavery with strength, it would be such a woman as Iona, the Queen Boudicca.

Iona made one promise to Sophia.

"If I am released, I shall see that your imprisonment is made known. It may take a long time before this slave can be heard, Sophia, but justice shall be done. I swear it," she added softly, in her own tongue.

The breakfast trays arrived. Eating silently as usual, they replaced the serving dishes at the door, and it was then that the door, long closed and barred, opened, flooding the cell with a terrible, brilliantly overpowering light from beyond.

"Queen Boudicca," the guard grunted. "You come with me, woman."

"Certainly . . . just as soon as I have—"

"Now!" he commanded and Iona nodded, turning back once toward Sophia.

"I will not forget you," Iona said. "Do not forget my promise, Sophia."

Then she was whisked from the cell and the door closed heavily, leaving Sophia alone in the darkness as she had been for so long. She treasured the vow Iona had made to her; yet Sophia knew well, too well, that whatever future lay before Iona, it would not be a future which afforded her the ears of the important people, the influential.

Sophia settled into her corner, once more covering herself with her tattered blankets, once more trying to sleep, to pass time in that way.

"Iona," she thought briefly, before sleep did, mercifully close her eyes, "I only pray that your slavery is as tolerable as this cell. I would wish you more, yet to wish for more is vain hope."

Chapter Nineteen

Iona was half dragged, half pushed up the long ramp to where a wagon awaited. Drawn by two horses, one white, one deep gray, the wagon had curtains on the side, hiding the interior from prying eyes.

"Here she is," the soldier said. A second man, perhaps a low-ranking civil servant, glanced up at her and made a mark on the parchment roll he carried.

"Get her inside. She's the last."

Iona started to protest, but before a word could be said she was shoved and manhandled into the wagon and the horses snapped into motion so that Iona lost her footing and slammed to the floor of the darkened interior, bumping roughly into a leg, a shoulder.

A woman grunted, but no one spoke. Iona clawed her way forward and found a place to sit on the rough plank floor. They traveled in silence although Iona asked several times in Celtic and in Latin.

"Where are we going?"

The horses were being driven furiously, as if the wagon were racing time or another wagon. The wheels jolted and rocked over rough stone, the passengers being thrown against the walls on each rough, sudden bend.

There was a man of some age next to Iona. She could read his profile against the light filtering through the side curtains. She asked him again, "Where are we going?"

He barely turned his head toward her, making the slightest of shrugs with his birdlike shoulders. He apparently spoke neither Latin nor the British tongue.

Iona sat passively with the rest of them. She could not get out of the cart; no one could say where they were going. As with all else since coming to Rome, she was a complete captive of whim and circumstance.

Restless after a time, she decided to try to peek beneath the curtain at her back, but no sooner had she turned to do so then the wagon ground to a screeching, brake-assisted halt, throwing Iona against the old man. He blinked and shrugged again as if none of this were unsettling or in any way unexpected.

The door was let down with a tremendous crash which scattered light dust into the bright sky. The light filling the wagon revealed the faces of all her fellow travelers. They were young and old, women and men, seeming to have nothing in common. Three at least wore leg irons—one of these a nasty-looking black-bearded man with the cut of the sea about him and a single good eye.

"Come on, come on!" a voice outside urged

them, and Iona fought with memory to find a face which matched that voice. It was familiar: a woman's voice. Ducking, she stepped out into the day and saw Flavia, arms crossed, urging the soldiers to hurry the slaves.

"My good Queen Boudicca," Flavia greeted her, mockery stretching her mouth into a humorless smile.

"Shall *we* do combat this day, Flavia? You and I with lances?"

"Your warring days are over, my queen," Flavia said. "And if you were to strike out at me with bare hands at this moment ... I would gladly see you executed. Now move along! Guard—take this woman!"

Iona was pushed along with the others. The black-bearded man, moving too slowly to suit them, was cudgeled and kicked. They were, Iona judged, adjacent to the Forum itself, though they were being kept far away from the marketplace where hawkers worked beside orators and the business of the nation, small and large, from clay statues of Venus or Bacchus to ten hundred amphorae of wine or a fleetload of grain were exchanged.

They moved dutifully forward now, and Iona saw the crowd of spectators below and to the left of the raised platforms.

"It's the slave mart!" she said out loud. She had been brought here to be sold to the highest bidder.

"I'd rather they cut my throat than send me back to the chain gangs," the blackbeard muttered.

"You'll have your wish if you don't move along," he was warned. The soldier lifted his cudgel again and blackbeard flinched and moved forward onto the long ramp.

"The chain gangs," Iona asked, "is that bad?"

"The worst. Building roads in the rain, digging ditches with shackles weighing you down. Me—I expect it. Look at me!" he spread his arms. "I frighten them out of chains. They think I'd tear their gullets out—and I would, pretty Celt."

Iona must have looked concerned, for blackbeard added, "You don't have to worry about hard labor, pretty Celt. They'll not waste your charms."

"Shut up!" the soldier shouted. It was warm, and his red face streamed perspiration. The slaves were marched onto the platforms to join hundreds of others—some obviously just ashore from some foreign land, others who to all appearances might have been respectable Romans themselves.

They stood rigidly in the narrow ribbon of shade cast by the restraining wall behind them as a stout, nearly bald auctioneer strode slowly up and down the platform. At an unseen signal he nodded and stepped forward.

"Friends, Romans, the market is open. We have what you have come seeking. Strong bulls of men, docile enough for family gardens. Road builders, stone masons, carpenters, a scholar or two—a scribe, a wheelwright." He waved his hands as he spoke, jabbing at this man, then that with his short quirt.

"And women who cook, weave, wet nurse...." His glittering eyes settled on Iona. "Women for all purposes!"

"Let it begin!" a hoarse voice shouted from the crowd.

The auctioneer nodded and pointing at a Gallic

woman of fifty years or so, he began the bidding.

Time dragged slowly. The sun which had been warm, turned hotter; there was not a breeze to offer relief. The auctioneer's voice droned on, extolling the virtues, the skills, the beauty of each item, yet Iona doubted half of it was true.

Finally it was blackbeard's time and he ambled forward, prodded by the guards, his chains dragging on the platform.

"This sturdy workman—" the auctioneer began, but he was cut off angrily.

"That's Graculus! The thug belongs in prison—or on a cross."

"This sturdy specimen—" the auctioneer continued without the slightest hesitation.

"Is a butcher," the same, taunting voice cried out. Other accusations were hurled against the auctioneer. "Graculus isn't worth a drachma! Another slave is needed just to watch him so that he doesn't kill you."

Graculus—Jackdaw—stood smiling on the platform, his good eye surveying the mob of citizens. Iona smiled faintly at the sudden furor. Whatever Graculus had done, it had been widely publicized, for the Jackdaw was notorious.

"Gentlemen. Ladies!" The auctioneer held up his hands for silence. "You say he is not worth a drachma." Then the man's hand stretched out and ripped off the shirt from Graculus's back. The man was massively muscled, his abdomen hard, his back criss-crossed by jagged scars.

"Look at this ox!" the auctioneer shouted. "Not worth a drachma? For field work, heavy labor? The man is an ox!"

"He's strong enough," someone shouted. "But who could sleep with Graculus on his estate?"

"You have said, sir, that Graculus belongs in prison. Sir," the auctioneer said, lifting the heavy leg chains Graculus wore, "he carries his prison with him. As for the nights—if ships can be anchored, an ox can be tethered."

"Forty sesterces!" a voice boomed.

"Forty-five," a second citizen offered, "though I must be crazy to let you charm me into such a bid, Calumnus!"

The bidding stopped at eighty, and the Jackdaw was led away by a dour soldier. Iona's eyes swept the platform. She let her gaze linger for a while on a young blond woman who sat peacefully nursing her child. A sudden, sharp jab in her ribs brought her attention back to the auctioneer.

"A queen of the Celts!" he shouted, leaning far forward, his quirt describing tight circles in the air as he begged for their attention.

Yet he had it already.

Their eyes were on Iona as she strode forward, tossing her hair back haughtily. She carried herself erect, proudly, as she stepped beside the auctioneer who blinked at the woman, a head taller than he, who stood beside him.

"A Celtic queen called Boudicca," he said and he nodded to the soldier as he did so. The soldier who was stationed behind Iona pulled the blanket up over her head, leaving her standing only in the short skirt she had worn to the arena.

"Exquisitely formed," the auctioneer said, "as is most obvious." He stretched out a hand as if to touch Iona's breasts, but his hand froze midway as her icy, defiant glare met his eyes. "Turn around, my dear," he said.

She did so, slowly, her eyes watching the far hills, blue at this late hour, studying the shadows which formed in the vales where beautiful homes perched among thriving groves.

"Need I say more?" the auctioneer asked. As he said that, he lifted the rear of Iona's skirt with his quirt, hoisting it past her thighs. The breeze was cooler now off the western sea, a distant flight of seabirds winged homeward.

I am being sold.

The idea flitted through her consciousness. It was vaguely amusing to her, yet also infuriating. She watched the distant hills a while longer. Then Iona was turned to face the mob once more. Voices rose out of the crowd; the white city lay behind them, itself bluing as the shadows lengthened.

A deep, male voice shouted a number, a second voice on the heels of that called out another.

They are buying me. Deciding how they will use the flesh of my body.

"Two hundred sesterces!"

Iona felt strangely drained, apart from her body. It—that body—stood before a demanding, shouting crowd. It would be purchased, selected, used, dressed, bathed, or punished.

"Three hundred and fifty!"

Yet where was Iona? Was there an Iona the huntress with no forest, no hart or boar to hunt? A daughter, Iona, with no mother or father? A queen without a nation? Rome had destroyed that Iona; Rome would define the new one.

"Eight hundred sesterces," a woman's voice, somewhat shrill offered.

"You're mad, Andrea," someone grumbled, waving a hand.

"Mad!" she laughed. "It's only because your purse is empty that you say so. Mad? She'll bring back a hundred times eight hundred. You'll be one of them begging to help repay me, Barnabus."

"No more?" the auctioneer asked. "Shall Andrea have her, you men? For a paltry eight hundred sesterces?"

But the auctioneer was well satisfied. Eight hundred was the best price of the day, double what he had hoped for. As the woman, Andrea, counted out the gold, the platform was emptied of those slaves not sold this day.

Dusk spread rosy hues across the city. A last golden ray of sun gilded the dome of Jupiter's temple. The trees receded into dark anonymity, the crowd drifting away in two and threes.

"Come, girl," the woman called Andrea said. "You have much to learn, much to repay."

Iona stood dumbly a while longer, then, submissively, she followed the woman into the streets where a man with two white horses waited.

Andrea was forty or so, plump in the face, with tiny blue eyes which revealed a certain hardness. She had small hands and an equally small mouth—a child's face which her womanly form had outgrown.

"You shall have a good life," she told Iona. "An easy life. We shall pamper you, school you, feed you with delicacies and provide you warm, secure beds. That is the way I want it to be. That is the way to pass your life: pleasantly, without hardship of any sort. You will want for nothing."

She stroked Iona's hand, nodding as she did so.

"You are a fine, beautiful young woman. Life is kind to such as you. I will be kind."

Andrea's hand suddenly tightened on Iona's wrist and she squeezed with incredible strength. Iona's arm shot through with pain, yet she did not move as Andrea stepped nearer to her in the soft darkness of the street, her fingernails digging into Iona's flesh.

"You need only be obedient, dear. Obedient," she said again, her tiny eyes sparkling. "Or you will find life is not so kind, not always so pleasant. You will discover that terrible things can happen to young, beautiful women. Things that may leave them no longer so young. No longer so beautiful."

Suddenly Andrea's hand dropped from her wrist and she stepped away, smiling as if nothing had been said. "Now then, Pusio," she instructed the young man, "let us be off for home."

Iona was helped onto the back of the horse and Andrea led the way through the narrow streets with Pusio dog-trotting along behind, holding a tether to Iona's horse.

The night was a welcome, concealing blanket. Iona enjoyed the solid movement of the horse beneath her, the cooling relief of the evening. Yet her mind turned with turmoil, splintered with vague fear, indistinct anxiety.

A new life was beginning—yet what sort of life was it introduced, as it was, by Andrea?

They traveled half a mile through winding streets and up broad boulevards where drunkards sagged against the walls, soldiers in lockstep marched, people held what seemed to be secretive meetings, their eyes flashing to the passing traffic, eyes wide, mouths grim.

Suddenly they were there. The horses halted

before a broad, two-story building of white marble, fronted by sixteen Doric columns, guarded by two sober, dark-jowled men who stood with arms crossed, bowing to Andrea who stepped from the horse like a returning heroine.

Iona followed, her head filled with fleeting impressions, the coldness of the marble, the stern guards, the cold, black sky.

Then they were inside, enveloped by warmth. A lyre and flute intertwined in tune from somewhere deep within the great house.

They entered through a high foyer, walking over a mosaic of tile depicting an eagle with a viper in its talons. On the walls tapestries hung, richly woven with arabesques of gold thread. Odd wooden figures posed against velvet backgrounds, their dress ancient or foreign.

Andrea's slippers whispered against the deeply grained marble of the floor. Silver and gold urns and chalices were ensconced in niches carved into the blue marble of the walls. A marble Venus posed coyly near a small basin decorated with a relief of shells where water trickled from a bronze spigot in the shape of a lion's head.

Beyond that room a second, larger room stood empty but for red velvet cushions strewn about the floor. Laughter reached Iona's ears from still deeper in the interior of the mansion. A woman's voice raised in shrill amusement.

"I have a surprise for you," Andrea said, that puffy child's face of hers puckered into delight. The expression somehow made Iona aware once again of her arm where the woman had scratched her. She glanced at the drying blood there, then back at Andrea who still smiled.

They walked a narrow corridor flanked by many

identical doors. The smell of cooking now reached Iona—pork and sweet fruit mingled in her nostrils.

Triumphantly Andrea turned sharply left and escorted Iona into a mammoth chamber which was filled with the sounds of splashing, of laughter.

Iona halted, spellbound. A dozen young women, all naked, with startling figures, played in a broad pool filled with water so warm it steamed into the air. Two girls near her splashed each other playfully. Another lay languidly near the pool, dangling a long hand into the warmth of the water.

"Let me welcome you to paradise," Andrea said. At the sound of her voice heads turned toward Iona, curious, haughty eyes examining her minutely. Suddenly there was a shrill, excited shout.

"Iona!"

Startled, Iona's head swiveled toward the sound. A plump, completely naked girl with reddish hair came bounding toward her, water streaming from her body as she crossed the room.

"Trixcia!" It seemed impossible, but it was Trixcia. Her face was a portrait of pure delight. Childish glee accented her every movement, her expressive eyes and petulant rosebud mouth.

"Iona! It's true, it's you!" Trixcia embraced her tightly, her body slippery with oil and water. She hugged Iona tightly, then stepped back to arm's length. "Andrea promised me that you would come, but I hardly dared believe it. You're so good, Andrea!" Trixcia gurgled.

"I will always fulfill my promise, dear," Andrea answered. "And aren't we happy to have Iona with us? I am as overjoyed as you—she will be a welcome addition. Now why don't you let her bathe and take off that filthy rag? Then you may show her around, Trixcia."

"I will, Andrea," Trixcia replied, holding Iona's hand tightly. "I will never let you regret this—you'll be so happy here, Iona. It is paradise, as Andrea said."

Andrea turned away, the smile fading from her face as she did so. Taking a doorway to one side, the woman disappeared, leaving Iona alone with the others. Trixcia still clung to her.

"Is this the British queen?" one of the women asked. Tall, with ringlets of auburn and exquisite facial bones, she sniffed derisively, let her gaze sweep Iona's body once and then dove into the pool, her long legs perfectly straight.

"That's Deidra—you've made her jealous."

Deidra emerged from the water at the far end of the pool. She swept back her hair and, resting her elbows on the edge of the pool, sat staring at Iona.

"She's like that," Trixcia said. "Don't let it bother you."

"No, I won't," Iona answered.

"But Andrea is right," the other girl said. "We must bathe you!"

Iona let Trixcia call for perfumes and soap. A eunuch scuttled off for these as Iona stepped from the skirt she wore and slid into the water so warm that she hesitated before completely immersing herself.

"We'll be such good friends," Trixcia effused. "And everything will be perfect. No more cold winters or hunger for us at all, Iona. We'll be perfectly taken care of."

Yet Iona could not help recalling vividly the last

time the Romans had bathed and perfumed them, fed them . . . then led them off into the arena to die.

Yet the water was warm, and she scrubbed away at the dirt which seemed to have crept into her pores during those months in the cell with Sophia, losing her concern in the sensual enjoyment.

A shadow moved above her and she caught the motion from the corner of her eye as she stood, waist-deep in the water.

Above them, on the arched balcony which ran along three of the four walls, Iona caught sight of a man of middle years, heavily jowled, sipping wine from a golden cup.

She sank into the water until only her head was visible and watched as the man, now smiling thinly, beckoned to Andrea who appeared beside him on the balcony.

He nodded with what seemed approval and disappeared again, Andrea following after a short, searching glance at Iona.

"He's pleased," Trixcia said, handing a thick, luxurious towel to Iona as she stepped from the pool. "Lucius Burrus is pleased. Now I know everything will be fine. Forever. But, Iona," she said, taking her hands, her eyes pleading, moving with intensity, "you must be very good, too. You must do whatever Lucius Burrus asks of you. You must!"

Iona finished her bath and was led to her bedroom by Trixcia. A spacious chamber, it was furnished sparingly. A glass mirror, the first Iona had seen, hung from one wall. There was a balcony which opened onto the garden. From there she could study the city below, the sweet scent of lemon blossoms filling the warm summer's evening.

"Isn't it lovely?" Trixcia asked, leaning beside Iona on the balcony rail.

"It is," Iona agreed. The city sprawled across the hills, now silent but for the occasional clatter of a horse's hoofs on the streets. A brilliant star hung pendant above the western horizon; thousands of others glittered overhead. "A city where no one wants for anything. They have food, warm houses, comfort—yet they must slaughter and roam the planet looking for others to conquer. How can this be? Let them be content, let the world be peaceful."

Iona whispered the last of this, and Trixcia stood looking oddly at her, not hearing, or perhaps not understanding what it was that bothered Iona.

"But you must tell me about this house, this Lucius Burrus, Trixcia. Tell me how it has gone for you."

"I will!" Trixcia said excitedly. "It has gone so well for me, Iona. And will for you."

"What sort of place is this then?" Iona asked, although she knew full well.

"What sort? A place where men—and sometimes the ladies—come to take their pleasure. They settle their weary minds, ease tired bodies. Bathe, are anointed and . . . pampered."

"A brothel."

"Yes." Trixcia shook her head, annoyed at the term. "A brothel, but you must not call it that. It is a private bath. Commonly it is known as Andrea's Garden though Lucius Burrus owns the house. Andrea was once a girl as we are—and now look at the power she wields."

Iona nodded, surprised again at the awe in Trixcia's eyes, the ease with which this Celt had made the transition to Roman slave. Would she do the same?

"And none of this bothers you, Trixcia? To entertain men for money? To be bartered for, used, then pushed aside at evening's end? To be slave and serving girl?"

"No!" Trixcia snapped defiantly. "And why should it?" She settled onto the blue bed in Iona's sleeping quarters, chin uplifted. "I have told you before, Iona, how it was with me. Icy winters. Little food. The fear of soldiers or Northmen. Curdge was dirty, ignorant, stinking of furs. The Roman men I meet are clean, educated. They give me baubles and do not demand that I cook or bear children, scrape their furs or hoe their corn! I am warm. Safe. I need only do as they wish."

"And you do it—whatever it is?"

"I do. As you will, Iona. I do whatever pleases them. Is it wrong to make them happy—it costs me nothing, hurts not at all. It is a service, that is all. A service I am paid for, and one which causes me no suffering, no pain."

A thought echoed in Iona's mind as she studied Trixcia. Words the girl had spoken and lived to regret. Yet time—and such a short span of time—seemed to have erased the regret from Trixcia's mind:

I want to be a Roman.

"I see no older women here," Iona said thoughtfully.

"No, of course not," Trixcia laughed, but then Iona's point came home to her. What happened to those women skilled only in pleasing men when the time came? Trixcia did not want to think about it, refused to. Were they the hags one saw walking the streets? She pushed that sudden, vivid thought aside.

"Andrea has done well," she replied sharply.

"Yes. She is a wealthy slaveowner. But we, Trixcia, are only the slaves, and likely to remain so until we die." Iona was silent a moment, then she added, "I do not think older slaves are kept and pampered as we are. I do not think they have value. Rome will keep us as long as we are young; then Rome will cast us aside."

"You are the proud Celt, aren't you, Iona?" Trixcia asked. She stood from the bed, her eyes brimming with tears—of shame, of anger, of realization; Iona could not tell which. "I will tell you this: Andrea's Garden is warm—a cell is cold. The baths are safe—the streets deadly. I am fed here—how would I be fed in prison? With sour wine and bread. I see the sun rise in the morning, and I am happy. I greet Gaius Rhoetus at the door in the evening; I am happy to see him, and he pleased with me. Or perhaps it would make you happy, my *queen*, to see me suffering under sheaves of wheat on some estate, growing old and more hungry each day under the hot sun, under the heavy burdens.

"Or perhaps you would have me attempt to walk the many thousand miles home to suffer under the drunken weight of the filthy Curdge, the Epidiian?"

"I meant nothing like that," Iona said softly. "You *are* my friend, Trixcia, no matter what you believe. I would like for your life to be full, happy.

But I cannot forget that I am a slave. Transported, purchased, imprisoned, and sold—as it pleases them. Nor should you, Trixcia. You *must* not forget it. You must not forget that you are a free Celt as long as you breathe."

Chapter Twenty

The soft light of dawn startled Iona awake. She sat abruptly, eyes searching the room where she lay. Where was she . . . ? It took several long moments for the memory to come to her. In a brothel, Andrea's Garden, where—she supposed—she was to work today.

Angrily she stood from the low bed and walked across the room to the balcony. Flinging open the iron gate she stepped out. Below her a man with broad shoulders and a cruel little mouth watched back.

Iona slammed shut the gate and returned to the bed where she sagged to a sitting position, her head searching for some answer, some way out. There was none. Below, the guard watched her balcony; inside, dozens of eyes would be watching. There was no way out; nothing to do but obey as a slave must. Obey or be disposed of.

Iona's life had been fiercely independent, however; it is not only galling but sacrilegious to such a person to accept tyranny. And this was absolute tyranny.

Again she paced the room, her heart constricting in her breast as she realized with finality that there was no way to escape the Garden. Not alive—and so perhaps it would be that way.

To be able to accept it as Trixcia had, to even bless her good fortune! Yet Iona had never learned to accept such domination. She was loyal, fiercely so, to those who deserved such loyalty—like Athair, her father. That is not submission, but respect.

Yet to accept it . . . perhaps it would come down to living with her honor shattered or dying in support of her convictions.

The door opened and Trixcia, dressed in sheer lavender, popped in, her face bright, her eyes dancing.

"It's the big day, Iona! Good morning."

"Good morning, Trixcia."

"But you haven't started to dress. Let me fix your hair."

"I'll only brush it out," Iona said.

"Oh no, Iona! Let me dress it with pearls, pin it back for you. You'll be so lovely. You'll please the men so! And that is the thing to do. If they like you, Andrea and Lucius Burrus are happy. And if they are happy with you they'll give you anything. I'll show you the gifts I've gotten from Lucius Burrus sometime."

As she babbled, Trixcia pinned Iona's hair in the Roman fashion, drawing it back and pinning it. Iona stared at herself in the mirror. The same woman lived behind those painted eyes. The same memories. . . .

"What happens to those who do not please the men, Trixcia?" Iona asked, and Trixcia, looking at her in the mirror, was so startled that she dropped a handful of pins.

"But you must, Iona! I've told you that."

"And those who don't?"

"I've never known it to happen," Trixcia said, "although Deidra once told me a story of a girl who wouldn't behave." Trixcia shuddered. "It was terrible, Iona. I can't repeat it."

"Perhaps I shall learn for myself," Iona said.

"Don't say that! To be so prideful, Iona. Pride will lead to your destruction. I know you were a queen. . ."

"I *am* a queen," Iona said quietly. "But more importantly, I am not a slave. I am a free Celt. The enemy has captured me, but he has not broken my will to resist."

Iona turned on her chair and stood, holding her head up, her hair perfectly arranged, her lithe body elegantly draped in blue silk.

"Perfect. Beautiful!" Iona's eyes turned toward the doorway. The short, bulky Lucius Burrus stood watching. He studied Iona with puffy, slightly drunken eyes. His heavy jowls barely moved as he attempted a smile.

"It shall go well for you here," Lucius Burrus said. "I will personally guide you, teach you."

Iona stood stiffly, staring back at Lucius Burrus, the whoremonger. He scowled, his eyebrows arching with annoyance.

"She does not speak Latin well, sir," Trixcia interceded. "I will tell her how welcome you have made her."

Lucius Burrus nodded, again attempting that heavy smile. "Do that, Trixcia. Make sure she understands what I have told her."

Then with another, last glance at Iona, he turned and walked from the door, his heavy shoulders rolling. When Iona looked back at Trixcia, the girl was petrified.

"You must not do that, Iona! I beg you. You belong to Lucius Burrus—do not forget it."

"I will not forget," Iona answered.

Lucius Burrus walked the marble hallway of Andrea's Garden sullenly. Deidra ran up to him and threw her arms around his neck, kissing him eagerly. But Lucius Burrus had no thoughts for Deidra now, and in annoyance he simply shoved her away, leaving her pouting, hands on hips.

He turned into Andrea's apartment and found the woman at her bath. Sighing, Lucius Burrus poured a goblet of wine and sat on her bed, watching.

"The new girl," he complained, "she is recalcitrant."

Andrea looked around at Lucius Burrus, the sponge in her hand halting. He was drunk again. So early in the morning.

"There is always a period of adjustment," she reminded him.

"Yes. But I don't like the fire in her eyes. Usually after a few months in those damp prisons, they embrace the warmth, the food, like adopted puppies."

"She will come around," Andrea said. She stepped from her tub, flesh quivering slightly. Lucius Burrus studied her plump body, that child's face, and it caused him to wonder why he let Andrea continue here. Yet without her he would have to handle those petty jealousies, those women's complaints, himself.

"Julius Decanus will be arriving this evening. He would set the Celt straight quickly," Andrea suggested.

"No." The general was a brute, a lout. "Decanus has ruined prime slaves before. Let her have the towel and oil duties for now. I will break this one in myself," he announced.

Andrea stopped her toweling and her lips tightened in annoyance. Odd, that she could still feel jealousy after these long years. She nodded.

"All right."

"Let no one molest her for now," Lucius Burrus said, rising. "I will mold her into the woman we want."

Iona's days settled into a colorless ritual. Lucius Burrus approached her occasionally, yet he seemed easily handled. The men came and went from Andrea's Garden. Soldiers, statesmen, merchants. They bathed and sat naked in the sun on Andrea's patio garden, sleeping or sipping wine as the girls pampered them.

Iona delivered towels to the girls' rooms and cleaned up after them. Also, she was required to massage both men and women with the warm, scented oils after their baths, before their visits to the rooms of Trixcia, Deidra, and the others.

Deidra was openly hostile, the others resentful.

"Are you too good for a Roman nobleman, you barbarian slave?" Deidra taunted her. But Iona never replied to their acidic taunts—they knew as well as she where their bitterness had its origins.

Iona slowly massaged a corpulent, white-bodied merchant as he lay flat on his great stomach, sleeping. She worked the oil into his calves which seemed to have no muscle in them, then rubbed his back which was only rolls of sedentary fat.

She leaned forward to grasp the oil bottle and instantly the merchant came to life. He tore off the top of her dress as he clawed at her, dragging her to him. Laughing, he pressed his fat, oiled body to her, biting at her throat, her ears.

Frantically Iona pushed him away, raising the heavy oil bottle menacingly as she backed away. He followed her, panting.

"I'm ready now, dear," he puffed. Iona backed up farther until her back was against the wall. The merchant laughed and pressed her against it, his stubby fingers clenching her wrist.

"No." It was Trixcia who spoke. She had come in the side door and she smiled, holding out a hand. "Eputus—don't you care for me any longer?" she asked, smiling, undoing her dress as she stepped nearer. "This one doesn't know how to have fun," she said, nodding at Iona. "Let me make you smile. Let me make you happy."

"But I like her," the man answered, fairly slavering.

"She belongs to Lucius Burrus," Trixcia replied. "She is his alone."

"The greedy whoremonger!" Eputus muttered. He let his eyes roam over Iona, let his fat hand cup her breast. Eputus still held her wrist; now, angrily he threw Iona's hand aside and turned, embracing Trixcia. "Then come, my barbarian," he told the red-haired girl. "Show me the delights of your savagery."

They turned, arm in arm, to walk away, but the merchant halted and turned back to Iona.

"I shall see you again, dark eyes. Eputus will see you again, and it will be soon."

Trixcia excused herself for a moment as she led Eputus toward her room. Running back to Iona, she told her, and harshly—"This cannot go on for long, Iona. Not for long. Burrus will not tolerate it."

Trixcia looked toward the balcony and then scurried away as Iona too looked up. Lucius Burrus himself stood leaning against the archway, drinking from a golden goblet, his eyes heavily hooded, flinty.

Then he was gone and Iona was left alone. Alone for the moment only in her prison. Let them send her back to prison! She preferred it, she suddenly decided. Preferred to rot away.

"This cannot go on!" Andrea said. She breathed into Lucius Burrus's ear as they watched the woman below. "There is too much of an investment in our young queen's appealing flesh."

"You are right," Lucius Burrus said. Yet he was not thinking of his investment as his heavy eyes watched Iona's naked breasts, the tantalizing broad hips of this tall Celtic queen. He emptied his goblet and stumbled back toward his room.

"It will not go on," he vowed to himself, falling onto his bed.

* * *

It was long after dark before Iona went to bed. The house had fallen silent, finally, the last of the guests departed. The shrieking laughter of the women had faded to whispered conversation—and in at least one case, muffled sobbing.

Iona undressed and put out the lamp which sat on her bureau. The bedclothes were cool, the breeze off the garden warm. She fell asleep within minutes and scrambled briefly through a dream in which she hunted an elusive, great hart.

Then she blinked her eyes open. Awakened by some subconscious warning, she lay instantly alert, eyes searching the darkened room, heart palpitating. Yet she saw nothing; heard nothing.

Again she closed her eyes and rolled over, throwing her blanket irritably aside.

Then she *did* hear it.

A soft wheezing, a ragged breathing. Rolling abruptly over she saw him standing there naked, bulky in the backlight of the moon.

"Lucius Burrus!"

"It is time," the man answered. Before Iona could answer he was on top of her. She struggled frantically against his weight, his unsuspected strength. He ran his hand up her thigh, and she lay utterly still a moment, the sour smells of wine, of his body, repelling her senses.

"Get out of here," she warned him.

"Get out!" he laughed. "You are mine, my queen. Bought and paid for. The bitch does not send her master away!"

Lucius Burrus clawed at her body, his panting growing louder in her ear, his huge torso pressing her to the bed though she rolled and kicked out, scratching at his back.

"Fight! Fight, I love it," he roared.

Then she felt him against her and in frantic revulsion she stretched out her hand, finding the heavy bronze lamp. Lucius grunted pleasurably, then with astonished pain as Iona hefted the lamp and brought it crashing down against his skull.

Roaring with fury he clawed at Iona's face, his other hand forming a fist. Then she struck him again, harder yet. And again and again until Lucius Burrus stiffened and lay still, his weight pressing the breath from her. Once more she raised the lamp and drove it against his skull.

Still. She lay still a long minute. Was he breathing? She did not think so. The rest of the house was quiet—why hadn't they been awakened by the sounds? Perhaps they had, but they might have been conditioned to ignore such sounds.

Panting, shoving with her knee and arms, Iona rolled the man from her, and he crashed to the floor with a dull thud.

She sat looking at him in the moonlight a long moment. A great white fish, dead. His eyes rolled back, a trickle of blood dripping from the corner of his slack mouth.

There was still no sound in the house. Only the panicked breathing of Iona as she stepped rapidly to her closet and drew out a plain dark cotton dress which she slipped on.

She crossed to the balcony and peered out. The guard was there, whistling a tune as he pondered the starry sky. Iona backed away.

There was no thought of remaining, only of flight. But how? Where?

Obviously the front door could not be used. The guard below negated any attempt at the garden grounds from that exit. Trixcia! Her room also opened onto the garden, yet toward the far corner of the olive grove where the guard might not see her.

Taking a deep breath, Iona opened the door onto the hallway where only a single, low burning oil lamp glimmered. Stealthily, heart pounding in her throat, she slipped to Trixcia's room. Praying that she was alone, Iona opened the door and quickly stepped inside.

Trixcia lay asleep, the breeze fluttering the light curtains. She sat suddenly up.

"Who is it?" she asked, hiding herself behind her bedclothes.

"Iona."

"Iona?" Trixcia stepped nearer and started to light her lamp. Iona's hand fell on hers.

"Don't."

"But . . . why?" Trixcia's eyes, frightened now, locked on those of Iona. "What has happened?"

"Lucius Burrus is dead. I killed him."

Trixcia tittered hysterically, not accepting it as fact. "Dead? No."

"Yes. Yes, Trixcia—he is dead. He came into my room and attacked me. I fought back and he is dead."

"Oh!" Trixcia moaned and wiped her forehead in confusion. "Oh, Iona. No. Whatever will you do now? Whatever will happen. . . ?" Suddenly she stopped, mouth open soundlessly for a moment. "And to me—what will happen to me, Iona?"

"Nothing. Nothing at all will happen to you, Trixcia. But I must leave here. Quickly."

"Leave? You cannot."

"I must and you know it."

"But why did you come here?"

"I must use your window, Trixcia. My own is watched."

"I see . . . but," she exclaimed, "they will know, Iona! They will know you used my window. That I allowed it."

"You could not stop me," Iona argued.

"You cannot, Iona! They will hurt me."

"They will not," Iona snapped. "I have no time to talk now, Trixcia. I will never see you again. All I wish to do is say good-bye," she said. "Don't you recall that I saved your life? In the arena when you lay like a lamb awaiting the sacrificial knife? I stood over you, protecting you. All I ask from you is silence. That will be repayment. Good-bye, Trixcia," she said.

"Iona—"

"Good-bye. I wish you happiness."

Then Iona was to the window and she stepped over the balcony railing. With one quick glance around she dropped to the garden grounds below, squatting low for a moment as she searched the darkness for the guards.

It was still. Silently she moved toward the garden gate. At that moment from Trixcia's room a shrill scream split the night. Trixcia's face appeared momentarily at the window and she screamed again.

Iona heard the sudden rush of footsteps, someone crashing through the garden and she raced to the garden gate, hair flying. Locked!

It was locked and she turned back toward the house where lamps were being lit, a crowd of faces appearing at Trixcia's window. Trixcia pointed out.

She tried the gate latch again, but it was useless. Leaping up, Iona grasped the top of the wall, and with a desperate push threw her leg up and slid over the wall with a lunging leap, crashing to the street below.

Chapter Twenty-One

She ran until she could run no more, the stones of the streets tearing her feet, the breath in her lungs cutting like jagged glass. Then she ran again until her legs turned to rubber and she could only stumble blindly through the night. Away from the center of Rome, away from it. The moon was a dying globe above a long line of poplars; a faint rosy glow in the east promised the accusing finger of dawn.

Runaway slave. And how were they treated? Death, torture. She had killed a Roman citizen, and like Dado, she would not be fattened for the Games again. She would be executed if caught. And how could she not be caught? There was nothing to do but run on through the dawn, the torpid day which would follow. But run where? Rome extended to the corners of the earth. Dado had been captured by the tentacles of Roman justice even in Britain. She had no hope of running so far.

Now she began to pass carts heaped with vegetables, fruits bound for the marketplaces and the eyes of the farmers searched her. Even they knew. Runaway slave. Running only to her death.

For a fleeting moment she even thought that Trixcia had been right—accept it; it cannot be changed or struggled against. But it was only the weariness which caused Iona to think that, the fear which stormed through her heart.

Dawn approached. A long line of beaten gold lay along the eastern horizon, lighting the tips of the trees with golden candles.

Her head snapped up. Along the road came a cavalry corps. The Roman soldiers, their armor glittering in the sunlight, their faces reddened by the coming sun, came directly toward her.

She could not turn and dart into the woods. Nothing would be surer to cause her capture. Steeling herself she marched directly past them, returning the wave of one of them, smiling lightly.

When they had passed she stood in the center of the roadway, the dust from their horses sifting over her. Her head ached, her legs were wooden.

Iona moved off through the trees, oak and poplar, bright in the new sunlight. If only she could find a place to lie down. A hidden thicket. Sleep would bring her new strength; perhaps the dream spirits would bring her an inspiration.

There must be a way out! Isn't there always some way?

She stumbled over an unseen snag and tumbled headlong down a rocky embankment. On the road beyond, a heavy wagon rolled past, loaded with blocks of salt. Iona rose, moving on, her knee tender, scraped where she had fallen. The day was growing warm already.

She forded a small, dry creekbed and suddenly heard a shout from upstream. Whether they pursued her, a wolf, a lost cow, she never would know. The shout spurred her on, and she ran into the thickest part of the forest where undergrowth clotted the seldom used pathway and thorns tore at her legs, face, and arms as she pushed through.

"Here."

Iona's head came around in disbelief. A man stood there; a raggedly dressed, scrawny man with a narrow beard. "Here, slave," he said. "It's safety —you have no chance out here."

She hesitated but only briefly. The man turned, beckoning her with his arm and she followed him up a concealed trail.

She nearly fell into the mouth of the small tunnel before she saw it. Screened by stunted trees and rocks, it appeared only a cleft in the reddish earth.

"Down there," he said. "You'll be safe."

She started to ask if he wasn't coming, but he was already gone, filtering through the trees. Iona paused, trying to decide, weariness fogging her intelligence. *What choice is there for me?*

Then she clambered into the tunnel which went straight down for some eight feet then bent to a gradual downward angle, descending into murky darkness.

Iona felt her way downward, wondering if she had made a mistake. Who was that man, anyway? Yet there was no escape above ground, she knew that.

The stone of the walls was rough beneath her searching hands. Ahead there was a faint light, yet it did not help her avoid a sharp drop-off. Falling, she clawed her way forward. The candle was perched on an outcropping of gray stone, and the tunnel forked at that point.

Without knowing why, she chose the tunnel to her right and proceeded into the interior of the earth. A cold breeze wafted up from somewhere below, a musty, damp breeze.

Iona moved more slowly than ever through the darkness, her hand feeling its way along the guiding wall. That hand sunk abruptly into a depression and Iona withdrew it hurriedly as it contacted something which was definitely not stone.

Yielding, somewhat stiff—perhaps cloth. She stretched out her hand cautiously and felt the form which rested there.

It was a corpse. She withdrew her hand slowly, eyes searching the darkness, finding nothing. In the now complete blackness she inched forward, finding another cubicle. In that recess too, a corpse lay. By bending forward she found that another niche was carved below that, and another above.

Tiers of bodies lay hidden in this dark burial chamber.

The empty darkness prompted her to think: *Perhaps I've descended to the house of the dead.* Vague, tangled Druidic superstitions rose into her consciousness and died away as she crept forward.

She stopped. Something lay ahead. Iona crept forward, listening to what at first seemed wind sound, or that of an underground river. But it was neither. Deep, wavering voices murmured within this cavern of death. Chanting, far distant at times, at other moments seeming just beyond the walls.

Legions of the dead, were they? Or perhaps only worshipers of the dead like those devotees of Isis who populated Rome, with their strange rituals and secret symbols.

Iona rounded a sharp corner and found a faint, leading light before her. A light which also illuminated the walls where row upon row of the dead lay, where strange symbols had been painted.

Shivering, she moved ahead. She rounded another corner, went up a steeply sloping ramp where the footing was soft, sandy.

Then she saw them.

Rows of them, dark, kneeling figures lighted weirdly by rows of candles set along the walls. Their voices were raised in chants which Iona could not understand; motionless before them stood a dark-cowled priest.

She stood stock still. The celebrants—perhaps a hundred of them—continued their ululations, moving not a muscle, turning not a head toward the opening where she stood.

Abruptly the chanting stopped, and at the same instant a hand fell on Iona's shoulder and she was spun around.

"Iona! My queen! I had given you up for lost!"

The old woman stood trembling before her and Iona lifted her hand, touching the woman's hair gently, a question, a smile forming on her lips.

"Thramane. Old thing!"

"It is I, Iona. I, your Thramane."

Iona folded her arms around Thramane's narrow shoulders, squeezing her tightly, kissing her forehead. A lazy, warm tear streaked her cheek.

"But how have you come here?" Iona asked. "Where are we? Are these all slaves, and this a refuge?"

"And you, Iona," Thramane said excitedly. "What has happened to you? I will explain it all—and you will tell me how Rome has received you. For now, I see you need rest and food. Oh, Father!" Thramane exclaimed, startled by the tall, dark-eyed man who appeared at her shoulder. "This is my Queen Boudicca."

"I welcome you," he said. He was not a Roman, Iona saw immediately. Bearded, he wore a cowl, but from under the shadows formed by it, black, deeply disturbing eyes peered out. Iona could hardly look at the man. He wanted something—what?

"Is she one of us, Thramane? Has she adopted the Lamb as her savior?"

"No, not yet."

"Very well," he nodded. "Feed her, Thramane. Take care of her."

"I will, Father," Thramane promised.

Nodding slowly the man walked away, speaking in low tones to another man.

"Who is that?" Iona asked. "What have you gotten involved with, Thramane? The lamb—what did he mean?"

"We are Christians, Iona. Christ is the Lamb. That is Paul of Tarsus."

"Paul! The man has a price on his head. You must knock all of this out of your head, Thramane. Christianity is outlawed. Is that why you meet here?"

"That is why we meet in the catacombs," Thramane answered. "But I cannot knock all of this from my mind. Until I can free my heart, my soul, which tells me Christianity is right."

"It seems a dangerous pastime," Iona said.

"More dangerous not to accept Christ,"

Thramane said, but Iona only shook her head.

Iona had heard, briefly, about these Christians from Sophia. They believed themselves immortal and followed charlatans like this Paul—a man who had once slaughtered Christians. Yet it gave the slaves hope; a belief in a better life after death to counterbalance the drudgery, the hopelessness of slavery.

"You will tell me about it sometime," she told Thramane.

"Yes. Yes, Iona! I will tell you—such an opportunity for you to arrive when Paul himself is in Rome."

"Yes. Such an opportunity," Iona said, closing the subject. She wondered how Thramane had come to trust that dark-eyed man so. She, who had even mocked Thrueldan!

She was shown to a small chamber where three other women slept. Thramane went out to bring soup, but before the maidservant returned, Iona was sleeping soundly, curled into a ball.

Thramane smoothed a blanket over her and bent forward, kissing her queen lightly.

"You will see," Thramane whispered. "You will come to understand."

Iona awakened and sat up suddenly. It was impossible to judge how long she had been asleep. The room was empty, a short candle burning in the corner. Stiffly she stood, stretching her legs. A hunger now gnawed at her stomach and she walked into the anteroom beyond. No one seemed to be around although the candles were lighted.

Exploring, she found a plank table in a large, now empty room. There was bread on the table, on a crude ceramic platter, and cheese. She sat at the table and ate ravenously, tearing the bread from the loaf in large chunks. Sweet water filled a stone pitcher and she drank deeply from that.

"May I have some of that?" a feminine voice behind Iona asked weakly. She turned to see a pale young woman, no more than twenty, leaning against the wall. Dressed in rags, she came forward at Iona's nod, and trembling, drank water.

"You're feverish," Iona commented. She stood and placed a hand to the girl's forehead.

"Yes." She smiled weakly. Her mouse-brown hair hung in strands. Her face was flushed, pale beneath that. She had widely spaced teeth and a generous mouth.

"Where is Thramane?" Iona wanted to know.

"Thramane?" the girl replied, surprised that Iona knew Thramane. "Back at her master's house, I imagine."

"And Paul?"

"Paul has sailed for Ephesus," she answered.

"Ephesus—where is that? Never mind. They surely didn't leave you alone, these good Christian friends of yours?"

"No, not alone." The girl's knees wobbled and she sagged to the bench, smiling apologetically. "John has gone to get milk."

"Milk?" Iona questioned the girl, but then she heard the squalling. An infant in a chamber nearby cried out desperately for food.

The girl clutched her breasts and told Iona, "I have nothing for him to drink. Longinus—his Christian name is John—is my husband. He has gone to try to find milk."

Iona followed the girl to her room and tenderly

she unwrapped the baby who was pathetically small and weak. He was slowly starving, this one.

"How long has he been gone? Your husband?"

"All night," she answered. She picked up the baby and held it to her. The infant swiveled his head from breast to breast, desperately trying to find food.

"Perhaps they have captured him—is he an escaped slave?"

"No. John is a freedman. But he is a Christian," the girl added softly. "And that is much worse."

"Where has he gone?" Iona asked.

"There is a farm near here. The man has given us goat's milk before. Perhaps this time—"

"Where is this farm? Where *exactly*?"

"You cannot go out!"

"How can I *not* go?" Iona asked. "Now, quickly. Tell me!"

The girl gave her exact instructions, and Iona threw a blanket over her shoulders, preparing to go out. She looked at the sick girl again, her starving baby.

"They won't come for you here, will they?"

"No. I am safe in the catacombs. All of us are. Burial places are inviolate under Roman law. So far Claudius has respected that law."

Iona nodded, took a deep breath and smiled— a smile she did not feel. "I will be back soon, with John and some milk for the baby."

"You are a Christian woman, Iona. Bless you."

"I'm not—" But there was no sense in explaining it at that point. Christian was it? A baby was hungry. That baby, with its unfulfilled promise worth more than any of them who had grown to their mature uselessness. If that was Christianity, then perhaps Thramane had not fallen in with a bunch of erratics and dreamers.

It did not matter at that point. The baby mattered. Iona slipped through the tunnels, finding the entrance she had used, and with the blanket over her head, she emerged into the full sunlight, walking the narrow path toward the farmer's house.

It was foolish. She told herself that. *Foolish.* If she were captured she would be executed. Yet was she to sit in safety listening to the life run out of a baby whose only crime was hunger?

She found a road which led down onto the fields below where men and women worked at their crops of grain, and she took it, eyes alert for the red tile roof of the small white house the girl had described.

The barley waved in the soft breeze, and the laborers busy at their work did not look up as she passed, head shrouded in the light blanket.

Below, beyond the grove of almond trees, she saw the house of the farmer. The courtyard was empty but for three white chickens which pecked at the dusty earth. Iona glanced left and then right, yet there seemed to be no one there.

A cow lowed in the meadow, answered by the goats' bleating.

She rapped at the door, but there was no answer. Circling the house, she walked toward the goat pens, determined to milk them herself.

She found a dilapidated barn and in the corner near the loft, a milk jar. Iona picked it up and walked out of the barn door.

"There she is!"

Instantly hands were on her. A great bearded man looped an arm around her throat and another grabbed her hands, tying them with stout rope as she struggled, kicking and scratching against them.

"I told you," the red-headed man said triumphantly. "I told you his wife would be along."

"Wife? Whose wife?" Iona demanded.

"Longinus's—or are you going to deny your husband, woman? What did you want the milk for, anyway?"

"I was thirsty."

"Come on, bring her along," the red-haired man growled. "The sooner we round them all up, the better. Why wait for Claudius to act? These Christians are saboteurs, all of them, intent on burning Rome."

"Would you deny that, woman?"

"I can't deny it. I don't know. I'm not a Christian," Iona told them.

"Lies! Ask the farmer!" the big man insisted. The farmer, in rough work clothes, stood nearby, slightly perplexed by all of it. "Have you seen this woman around here before? Can you vouch for her?"

"Never saw her," the farmer shrugged.

"Then what are you doing here, woman? Who are you?"

She could not answer that so she stood silently, and they took her silence for an admission of guilt.

A breathless, red-faced man rushed around the corner of the barn. He panted out his message: "Longinus has escaped!"

"Escaped! You idiot, can't you watch him for a minute?"

"Never mind. We'll find him again—he'll come looking for her." The big man nodded at Iona, who stood tied hand and foot.

She was dragged to a cart and thrown in. The cart horse was startled into motion by the snapping reins and the cart turned—back to Rome.

She laughed out loud. Laughed! What did it matter if these people didn't crucify her for being a Christian? By now all of Rome would be looking for an escaped slave matching her description.

"She's crazy," the red-headed man said, glancing at Iona.

"They all are," his friend agreed.

"Tell me," she asked. "What is it you fear from the Christians?"

"Fear? We don't fear them. We hate them."

"But why?"

"Why—they would destroy the empire. That Christ of theirs, he said as much himself. Said he would erect his own empire. Christians deny the laws; they would destroy Rome!"

They? That ragged bunch of Thramane's? Iona smiled at the thought. Yet maybe there were other Christians—like Paul—who would destroy Rome.

In that case, she thought venomously, *maybe I am a Christian.*

The city loomed over them, majestic, white, powerful. The cart did not enter the city gates, but skirted the walls, traveling until they had come to a small marketplace near the Pontine Marshes.

There Iona was roughly unloaded and thrown to the ground. Her feet were cut free and she was led through the market, a rope around her neck, and taken to a platform where a man of many years with a craggy, seamed face and a gigantic nose sat tribunal.

If he was her only judge, then Iona could guess

the sentence readily. There was no compassion on his compressed lips, no soft light in his eyes. He worked his teeth against each other as if chewing some leathery intangible.

"The wife of Longinus, known as Mary," the red-haired man said crisply. The eyes of the tribune fell on her coldly, and he asked her:

"Are you this Mary?"

"No."

"Are you a Christian?" he demanded, slapping his palms against the bench before him.

"No."

"Then who are you, woman? You speak with a foreign accent. Are you a Roman citizen?"

"No."

A small crowd had gathered around the platform. Tight faces peered into the sun at her. Several of the women held sticks, the children stones. They would make a holiday of it.

"You offer no explanation," the judge, who by his dress was a priest of Jupiter's temple, said. "I will ask only once more: Who are you?"

Iona did not answer. She stood, bound, watching as the hatred below gathered in the faces of those who watched. A hatred for something they did not understand, against a woman they did not know.

"She is obviously guilty," the judge snapped.

"No." The voice was stern, ringing with authority. Iona looked up to see the man on a white charger. A general by his uniform. He was familiar somehow. He had steel gray hair, white at the temples, and a piercing gaze.

"She is not guilty, Sextus. This woman is my slave. Sent to do my errands."

"Marcus Atreus . . . I assure you."

"Do not assure me. Only set her free. She is my property!"

"She would not answer the charges," the judge insisted.

"Her Latin is only halting," Marcus Atreus said. "I doubt she understood your questions. Now set her free. Instantly!"

"Yes. Yes, Marcus Atreus."

Hands freed the ropes on Iona's wrists. In astonishment she stood looking at the Roman general. Marcus Atreus—her adversary had become her savior. Then what kind of Roman was he? What sort would he be if he knew her for a murderess?

"Don't stand there, girl!" he commanded her. "Get up behind me!"

Iona, dazed, stepped from the platform and took the strong hand of Marcus Atreus who pulled her up onto the horse.

"Watch who you crucify, Sextus," Marcus Atreus said in parting. "Who you abuse. You are outside of the law even now. A wrong step could mean your own death."

Then he wheeled the big white stallion and rode from the market at a furious pace, slowing as they crossed into marshland beyond.

"You see, Placidus is still well, my queen," Marcus Atreus said without turning his head. "The horse," he added at her silence. "I don't know what you called him when he was yours."

"Placidus." Only then did she recognize the white stallion. The very one Arawn had taken prize from the Roman camp. The horse she had ridden to her surrender. "I did not know his name."

They rode silently for a while, through forest and over grassy meadows. Once Marcus Atreus kneed Placidus to a long, driving run and Iona closed her eyes, absorbing the sensation of speed, the air racing past them as the heavily muscled horse beneath them glided across the ground, guided by a sure-handed rider.

Marcus Atreus slowed the horse gradually, sensing that it had had enough. The stallion, like Marcus Atreus himself was no longer young. Tried in battle, he needed his exercise, but deserved a light hand.

Finally Placidus broke his gait to a walk and they moved through a scattered forest of oak, the sunlight streaming through the trees.

"How did you recongize me?" Iona asked.

"At first I didn't," the general admitted. "Or perhaps I would not have come to your aid."

Startled, Iona looked questioningly into the blue-gray eyes of the Roman. He smiled faintly, wistfully, his finely chiseled face set.

"Why not—because you and I have fought a battle?" she wanted to know.

"No." Marcus Atreus shook his head. Halting Placidus near a thin rill, allowing him to drink deeply, he answered, "Because I have heard rumors of a slave queen who three evenings ago killed a whoremonger named Lucius Burrus."

"Is that so?" Iona asked.

"It is."

"There must be quite a story behind that," she commented innocently. She slid from the back of Placidus and cooled her neck and face with the water from the stream.

"There are always stories behind such occurrences," Marcus Atreus agreed. He knelt down and scooped a handful of water to his mouth. He stood, watching Iona, the wind tousling his curled, silver hair. His eyes were deep gray in that light, slightly amused. "Perhaps someday I shall hear it."

"I doubt she will return to Rome," Iona said, smoothing back her long dark hair.

"I doubt she would willingly. It would mean death. And death for any who shielded her."

"Yes—then the story is lost to us," Iona said. She turned a quarter away from Marcus Atreus, her beautiful face coming into profile.

"And you, my queen," Marcus Atreus said, taking an unexpected step toward her. "You must have your own stories to tell. How is it that you still live—a free woman?"

"A Celtic woman is free until she dies," Iona sparked.

Marcus Atreus smiled faintly, understanding the emotion. He admired her spirit, unbroken by what must have been harsh treatment, long imprisonment. Could he endure so much?

Yet he had admired her spirit long ago, far away. A great queen she had been, a great warrior.

"It is growing dark," Marcus Atreus said finally. Long shadows wedded beneath the oaks, forming dark lace. The sun reddened his ruddy face still more, gleaming on his breastplate. *This man*. This one had destroyed Viron. Yet he seemed decent, totally noble. He had rescued a girl he did not know from death, perhaps tarnishing his own image in front of his fellow Romans.

He moved with the sureness of men of rank, the strength of a warrior. She wanted to dislike him; finding it impossible, she answered softly.

"It grows dark. The time of day when slaves slip away, running from Rome."

"They may run, but not escape. Rome does not allow it—and I know her far better than you, my Queen Boudicca."

"But you may run!" she said angrily.

"No." He replied softly, a small shake of his head following. "No Roman may escape her, either. Mother Rome is a stern parent."

Iona stood by the slowly running rill, watching the dying sun beyond the oaks. She was astonished by the words of the general. She did not understand their implications, yet the sincerity behind them was unmistakable.

Marcus Atreus stepped into his saddle, watching Iona from the back of his great white stallion. She stepped nearer to him, placing a hand on the shoulder of Placidus.

"If there is no escape . . . for Romans. How then do they live?" she asked.

"In silence, in shadows. From moment to moment. Secretly as Christians in their catacombs. That is how life is lived in the imperial city."

"With blind eyes."

"Just so. Men of dignity, of strength, lock themselves away, keep silent, look the other way." Marcus Atreus allowed himself a bitter smile, perhaps believing the closing night kept the expression from Iona's eyes.

"And so—Rome exists as pretense." Iona thought vividly of Trixcia. Poor Trixcia so eager for her ease that she accepted any degradation. Keep silent, lock yourself away. Rome will protect you.

"And so Rome exists. We exist with her or cease

to exist," Marcus Atreus said. "And you, Iona?" Hesitantly his hand stretched out toward her in the darkness. Hesitantly she accepted it and slid up behind him. They rode silently through the night, toward the great city. Only once did Iona break the silence to ask:

"This act is a compassionate one for one who lives in silence, in obedience."

"Rebellion," Marcus Atreus said strongly. "It is rebellion! Yet perhaps the only sort of rebellion a general might be forgiven, might dare."

They were into the city itself now, the thousands of lanterns glaring, the throngs crowding the streets. Yet Iona closed her eyes and placed her head against the strong back of this man, this general, this rebel, and all else was shut out but the movement of the war horse beneath her, the strength of the man who guided him.

Chapter Twenty-Two

The house of Marcus Atreus sat alone on a low knoll near the Via Lata. Two-storied, of white marble, it was in the heart of the city, yet isolated by the rambling grounds where meticulously pruned poplars and cypresses grew. A great bronze lamp burned outside, lighting the park. Near this Marcus Atreus halted Placidus.

"You must follow that hedgerow to the back entrance," he told her. "The door with the small iron grate set in it. Avidus will meet you there—tell him I have sent you. He is my servant, and a good man."

"All right." Iona nodded, sliding from the horse's back, memorizing the instructions carefully.

"But even to him," Marcus Atreus cautioned Iona, "say nothing of who you are, where you come from. The fewer who know, the safer you will be."

"Sir," Iona said, touching the broad hand of

Marcus Atreus. "I cannot thank you enough for doing this. I know your own reputation must be risked to do so."

"It is nothing," Marcus Atreus answered, removing his hand from under hers slowly. "I would ride with you up to my front door and show you my hospitality . . . but such things do not set well with a man's wife."

In the faint, moving light of the lamp, Iona again saw that bitter smile form, briefly, on Marcus Atreus's lips. She stepped away quickly as he turned his horse toward the entrance to his house, shouting a greeting to the servant who had come for Placidus.

"You rode long today, Marcus Atreus."

Marcus Atreus answered shortly, his words indistinct across the garden. Iona turned and slipped through the shadows, finding the side door. She tapped lightly, twice.

A narrow face appeared in the grate set into the door.

"Yes?"

"Are you Avidus?" Iona asked.

"I am."

"Marcus Atreus has sent me."

There was a hesitation, then the door clicked open. "Come in."

Avidus was along in years, hunched slightly, but spry, with quick eyes. He motioned Iona along after him, turning into a narrow, cedar-paneled corridor. He unlocked a room and showed Iona in.

"You will sleep here."

He left her for a moment, returning with a wooden platter filled with bread, beef, and cheese.

"Eat," Avidus urged her. "Then sleep." He

glanced at the dark-eyed woman before him, her tattered dress, the set of her proud mouth. Then he handed Iona the heavy key. "That is the only key to this door."

Then he gave her a candle and backed from the room, closing the door behind him.

The door opened with a creak and a thud, and Marcus Atreus strode in. She was asleep, or nearly so on the silk-upholstered bed, a wine goblet fallen from her long-fingered white hand, on its side against the mottled blue marble of the floor.

He slung off his cloak and walked to the sideboard, pouring wine for himself. Slowly Amelia's eyes opened and she struggled to a sitting posture, her eyes clouded with wine.

"How did you find Brindisium?" Amelia asked.

"Brindisium?"

"Or was it Antioch?" she said caustically. "You were gone long enough to have ridden there!"

"Placidus needed the workout," Marcus Atreus said. He walked to his chair and sat, arms draped heavily across his knees.

"Yes—the needs of a *horse* concern you. I had forgotten," Amelia replied. Shakily she got to her feet and wobbled to the wine.

"You have had enough."

"You won't command me as if I were a soldier!" she shouted. Her concave cheeks flushed and the tendons on her throat stood visible. Marcus Atreus said nothing, watching silently as she filled a goblet to the brim, and hoisting it with both hands, drank deeply.

"It is my comfort—my only comfort," Amelia said, pacing the floor before him. "More comfort than a husband who goes away for three years at a time then returns wanting to be my master."

"I was a soldier when we wed," Marcus Atreus said quietly. He rose and unbuckled his breastplate, removing his sandals as Amelia watched. It was an old argument. One well practiced, dragged out from time to time to fill the empty space between them. Yet it was a game which wearied Marcus Atreus, and he refused to rise to the bait.

Amelia was not so easily wearied—the wine pushed her forward. She stopped before her husband, one hand on her hip, the other precariously juggling her goblet.

"This is hardly your house, hardly home to you, Marcus. How strange it must be to return here, finding your wife older, more wrinkled. Your son nothing like you remember him—and he scarcely able to remember you."

"It is necessary . . ." Marcus Atreus began laboriously.

"No!" Amelia was livid with her denial. "Not for your career. Not any longer. You have proven your generalship. The Senate is the place for you. I"—Amelia touched her breast with her fingertips—"I work for that—and you against it. You crave the blood, the foreign soil. You care nothing for me or for Augustus—"

"I love my son dearly," Marcus interrupted hotly.

"Then stay in Rome, Marcus. I know you—you will make a statesman. There are those who would support you. Powerful people."

"You speak of Simonedes," Marcus said sourly.

"Yes, of Simonedes. And why not! He is the emperor's nephew."

"He is an ass. He cost me troops in Britain, and nearly cost the war."

"You are not in Britain now!" Amelia shouted, hands outspread. "Now you are in Rome! Now you must think of Augustus. Already your son is nine years old . . . and how many days of his life have you spent with him, Marcus? Simonedes can help you. Let him!

"The gods only know," Amelia went on hopefully. "Claudius is no longer vigorous, and Simonedes's claim to the throne is stronger than many others. Simonedes may be your emperor one day."

I will curse that day, Marcus Atreus thought grimly. Yet, in order to end the argument, he told Amelia, "I will consider it."

"Seriously?"

"I will consider it quite seriously, I promise. Now, I am tired. If you will excuse me, Amelia, I will retire."

"I too am tired. . . ." Amelia's voice was broken. Unsteadily she put her goblet down. "The house is too much for me some days. We need more help."

"I will have Avidus find a slave girl for us tomorrow," Marcus Atreus said. Amelia only nodded with faint appreciation before moving off toward her own chambers.

Marcus Atreus did not go to bed immediately. He stood at his balcony window, watching the coming moon gild the soft, distant hills.

It was a stroke of luck, Amelia mentioning that she needed help. Yet by tomorrow she might well have changed her mind—especially upon seeing Queen Boudicca . . . or Iona, as she called herself.

Iona. He turned the name over in his mind, not quite deciding if he liked it or not. Yet he liked the woman. She had the characteristics of greatness. To toss such greatness to a dog like Burrus was despicable.

Burrus—the man was dead, but he had had friends. Undoubtedly they wished to find the girl. Rome would not be safe for long. Momentarily Marcus Atreus questioned the wisdom of his acts. Yet he knew he was right, knew that he would do it again.

It was a bad time for it, however. With Amelia plaguing him with these suggestions of a Senate career. With a sigh Marcus turned back toward his empty bed.

Undressing, he slipped into it, arms folded behind his head. He watched the ceiling of the room for long minutes.

Perhaps his place was at home. He missed the boy terribly, missed watching him learn, grow . . . yet in his heart he was only a soldier, always a soldier.

Marcus could not even say with certainty why he loved it so. Certainly it was not the bloodshed, the damnable food and hard weather, the foreign lands.

But life there moved according to his plans. He controlled his fate. It was the generalship, he supposed, which he loved. The test of wits.

Perhaps inside he was just as raw and savage as any barbarian he had faced, needing the contest of arms as all people written in history seemed to have needed it.

That need to conquer, to dominate the elements, the savage animals, other men, which was both the salvation and the curse of the race.

Finally, fitfully he slept.

The house was already filled with noise when he awoke just after dawn. Rising slowly, bathing, he dressed in a simple white toga held together by a golden lion's head clasp at the shoulder.

Brushing the silver curls on his head forward, Marcus Atreus went down. They were there, all of them.

Shoemakers, soapmakers, pillow vendors, candlemakers. The gardener, orchard keeper, wheelwright, cheerful tailor and glum mason.

They each had wares, or bills to present, claims to make. Hangers-on whom he scarcely remembered—the sharecropper, the pudgy secretary. All of whom he owed, or who hoped for some favor, like the mother of the schoolboy from Pontus who depended on Marcus Atreus for book money. She pressed immediately upon Marcus Atreus.

"Sir, good general," she said loudly, above the din, "Trophimus is here. See how he has grown." She yanked a scrubbed, frightened-looking boy Marcus barely recognized from behind the cobbler. "He is studying oratory—you yourself told him that it is important to study speech if one is to succeed. Trophimus!" she nudged the boy, "recite for the general."

"The essence of logic . . ." he began in an adolescent monotone.

"That's all very fine," the cobbler said impatiently, pulling the woman aside, "but I beg you, sir, my accounts show an imbalance. Since you left for Britain, Marcus Atreus, it has been difficult to collect for work already done..."

Marcus Atreus placed a hand on the man's shoulder and tilted his head toward him, studying the ledger the cobbler had gripped tightly in his hand.

This was the way business was commonly conducted in the city, and Marcus Atreus had no recourse but to tend to them. It might take until noon, and after getting rid of them all—merchants, beggars, favor seekers—the afternoon might bring a new crush of them into his house.

He lost his patience only once, with the whining secretary who insisted on being heard out of turn, yet there were a dozen moments when he wished for a stave to chase them all out of there, longed for the silence of a bivouac.

Amelia did not come down until they were all gone. Marcus Atreus looked up at her wearily.

"So now you see what I must go through without a man around to settle these matters."

"It can't be easy," he agreed. "Yet they are only trying to make their livings as well."

"Did you pay the cobbler?" she asked, pouring herself a glass of wine. Marcus Atreus started to comment on her drinking, but restrained himself, nodding.

"His sandals fall apart! I believe he uses harness leather for his shoes. They are not supple." She sat down and rubbed her ankle. "They hurt my feet," she pouted.

"Nevertheless, you should have paid him. Then found a new cobbler."

"You defend him?" Amelia asked sharply, but Marcus Atreus would not answer, seeing that she was only priming herself for a new argument.

Amelia glared at Marcus, nervously moving her crossed feet. She drank deeply from her wine cup, eyes dark.

She was fresh from her bath, hair arranged in a braid atop her head. She was still an attractive woman, Marcus decided, although gray streaked her hair more with each day. She moved her mouth in a way he did not like, making tight, bitter expressions. There were dark circles around her eyes, however, from the wine.

Had he destroyed the woman he had married? The exuberant child who had laughed frequently and cried as intensely had become a woman who did neither.

It hurt him now to look upon her. The bitterness was etched into her face, the eyes revealed only a hostility he did not fully understand.

"Have you seen the girl Avidus brought from the slave market?" she asked suddenly.

"No."

"I don't want her, Marcus. She is too pretty—perhaps Avidus thought he would please you by bringing her."

"I doubt that," Marcus said quietly. "We both only wanted to please you, Amelia. You said you needed more help."

"I don't want this slave!" she said, angrily throwing her goblet down. Then she stood, and arms crossed, glared at him for a moment before stalking away.

Marcus Atreus watched her go, saying nothing. What was there to say? He picked up the goblet, turning it around by the stem. Startled, he looked up to see the girl standing there.

"Yes?" he asked.

"I will clean that up," Iona said. She was dressed as a household servant now, raven hair drawn tightly back, accentuating the prominent cheekbones beneath obsidian eyes.

"Thank you. I don't know your name," Marcus said.

"Iona." She stood before him a moment, their eyes meeting, holding for a fraction longer than they should have. "My name is Iona, sir."

Marcus Atreus nodded, half-smiled, and handed her the goblet, his fingers barely touching hers.

Amelia stood in the doorway, watching, and with a start Marcus Atreus walked past Iona to his wife.

"I do not want that slave girl here," Amelia said, and she stretched out a trembling finger toward Iona. Spinning on her heel, she said across her shoulder, "I only came back to tell you that I have invited Simonedes here this evening."

Marcus Atreus only nodded, but Iona's head came around sharply, and she nearly dropped the goblet she now held. Amelia, shoulders set, back rigid, had gone into the garden.

"Simonedes?" Iona asked.

"Yes." Marcus Atreus studied her inquiringly.

"Had this Simonedes a wife named Sophia?" Iona asked.

"What do you know of Sophia?"

"A little. This Simonedes," she asked, turning her eyes up to Marcus Atreus, "is he a friend of yours?"

"Not of mine," Marcus answered. "He is Claudius's nephew, the man who once ordered pursuit into a collapsing pincer of British Celts."

"And his wife is a prisoner," Iona told him.

"Sophia is dead," Marcus replied. "You are mistaken."

"No, not mistaken. It is she who taught me Latin, and a little of history, of geography. It was she who gave me a ragged blanket to wear when she herself was trembling from the cold of a cell we shared. I tell you, whoever else this Simonedes is, he is his wife's jailer."

Despite himself Marcus Atreus put his hands on her shoulders. Searching her deep eyes, he asked, "Are you sure of this, Iona? Sure!"

"I am certain. The woman has not seen the light of day for years. Yet she lives. Locked away by her husband."

Marcus Atreus let his hands drop. It seemed like Simonedes, yet even for him it seemed callous.

Iona stood watching him, the question in her eyes.

"I don't know what I can do," he said, wiping back his hair with a harried hand. "But if I *can* do anything, I promise you I will, Iona."

Marcus Atreus lingered in the room after Iona had gone. Slowly he walked toward the garden, mulling it all. If it were true that Simonedes had locked Sophia away, and Marcus did not doubt it, then all had suddenly become dangerously complicated.

Amelia's dream for a political career for Marcus obviously would be shattered by the mention of Sophia. That was not so important. More important was the certainty that Simonedes could be a dangerous, vindictive enemy. His power was deeply rooted in his family. Marcus Atreus could be destroyed utterly.

Obviously there would be no hope for Iona if her

part in such a divulgence were learned.

The house, his life, that of Iona would be risked. The position of Amelia ... and that of Augustus. ...

The boy was there, in the garden, beside the pond. Marcus Atreus smiled as he watched the boy who lay face down, a finger tracing patterns in the water. His sturdy legs wound and unwound in preoccupied movement.

"Augustus!"

Slowly the boy turned back his face. Pale, he was, blue-eyed, his small mouth pursed in childish annoyance. Augustus looked at his father a moment, then turned back to his daydreaming.

"Augustus!" Marcus called again, moving nearer to the boy who would not turn his head back again. "Would you like to go riding with me?"

Marcus watched the round, dark-haired head shake negatively. It caused his heart to sag, a pang of sorrow to cut him.

"We could take Placidus. I'll let you ride him alone," Marcus Atreus coaxed.

"I don't want to."

"We could talk—I'll have Avidus pack us a lunch!" Marcus said spiritedly.

"I don't want to talk."

"Not with me?" Marcus asked, smiling a smile which the boy could not see. His legs had stopped their motion. The finger lay inert in the pond. Marcus crouched down and placed a hand on the fine, dark hair of his son. The boy had no answer for him.

Standing, Marcus Atreus turned away and strode back toward the house. He saw Avidus standing there, hands folded and he shouted:

"Saddle Placidus!"

"And shall I pack a lunch?" the servant asked.

"Saddle him," Marcus said angrily.

Amelia's head came up groggily. A strand of hair crossed her eye and she wiped it back, tossing her head. Marcus Atreus stood before her rigidly, wearing his uniform and helmet.

"Riding again?"

"I am going riding. I need to feel the wind in my face! Amelia," he said in a softer tone, "let's go to the country house. Take Augustus. We will hunt, ride—"

"It is filthy out there. The mosquitoes are a plague," she complained. "Who would we talk to? What is there to do?"

"I need to make a friend of Augustus. I need to get away from the city—these hangers-on, the merchants, politics."

"Then go. I will not!"

"Augustus?" he asked.

"He is your son. Take him if you want. Yet I doubt he will be happy there."

"Is he happy *here*?"

"How can you ask that? Is that an accusation, Marcus? Of course he is happy. He is with his mother. We have done well—without you."

"He seems . . . alone."

"If he is, you know where the blame lies," she answered shortly.

"Perhaps," Marcus Atreus answered honestly. "Perhaps it is so. Yet it is that I wish to amend."

"Then do so!" she answered, flippantly waving a hand. "Yet I am sure he prefers his home, his mother to a wild country estate." She turned her head toward the doorway.

Marcus's eyes followed hers. The boy stood there, pale, frightened. As his father's eyes met his, he turned and bolted. Amelia smiled insufferably.

"It is only that he does not know me," Marcus Atreus said in a low voice.

"*I* know you, Marcus." Amelia sat stiffly, watching her husband. She smiled faintly, triumphantly. "And do not forget about that slave girl! I want her gone—immediately."

"I shall see to it," Marcus Atreus promised. Then, mechanically, he turned to leave, slapping his quirt against his leg.

"And don't forget that Simonedes is coming this evening!" Amelia shouted after him.

Simonedes. No, it would be difficult to forget him. Marcus Atreus strode through the great room of his house to the doorway. Avidus held the reins to Placidus. The great war horse stamped and blew, tossing its neck as the general walked down the marble steps.

Marcus Atreus stepped into the saddle, taking the reins from Avidus without saying a word to the old servant. He nudged Placidus into a run immediately, racing through the garden grounds.

He wanted only to ride, to let the speed, the wind in his face push aside Amelia, Simonedes, all of life. Yet it would be only temporary respite. All of those problems must be met. Iona . . . and she was the one thought he was not able to resist.

Yet it was nonsense—the way he found himself thinking of her. He caught himself in brief, fragmentary, quite loving thoughts. It was only the loneliness which brought these on, Marcus Atreus convinced himself. His lack of love for Amelia.

Yet she continued to fill his thoughts—this barbarian queen, and she rode with him wherever he went that afternoon, like some winged enchantment.

Late in the afternoon when the shadows had already lengthened, fleeing the reddening sun, Marcus Atreus stood on a low hillrise, watching the white city, his Rome, suffer coming dusk. He spoke in a low voice:

"Rome, I have offered you my life. Can you not spare me one woman?"

Chapter Twenty-Three

Simonedes lounged on his chair, picking grapes from the full, wine-red bunches with white, ringed fingers. Beside him sat his wife, a girl not yet twenty with a broad mouth, open green eyes and milk-white complexion. Amelia poured wine for Simonedes who smiled, accepting it.

"You are the supreme hostess, Amelia. But why is our general so taciturn this evening? Marcus Atreus—is your mind on the coming battle?" Simonedes asked crookedly.

"I have not yet adjusted to the quiet home life," Marcus answered.

"You find Rome quiet!" Simonedes laughed. "My God! She crawls and slithers, roars on hind legs, paws and purrs, her citizens prowling the night, filling the daylit streets with activity. You don't dare blink or you'll find a familiar section of the city torn down, a new one thrown up overnight. You can hardly walk down the streets, so clogged are they with workmen, traders, architects scrambling madly about."

"There are always the Games," Amelia put in, "and the theaters, the baths, the gambling halls. Yet Marcus Atreus will not venture out, my dear Simonedes. What am I to do with such a man?"

"There are delights to be had at home," Simonedes smirked. He rubbed the thigh of his wife lecherously for a brief moment, watching Marcus who stared back stonily. "If one is imaginative. But we have not come to discuss that. It is time to ask, Marcus Atreus," Simonedes said, leaning far forward, "what your future holds. You are popular among the citizens of Rome. You must consider such popularity a tool to achieve greatness."

"I have promised Amelia I would think of the Senate," Marcus answered. "Yet I have not made my decision yet."

"No?" Simonedes exchanged glances with Amelia.

"Not yet," Marcus repeated.

"There is little time to delay," Simonedes urged. "Presitonus is old. He will retire his seat, I believe. It is the time for you to move ahead, Marcus. The people need you, a warrior, just now. The northern barbarians are encroaching once more. Someone must stand up and press for war. Claudius seems unable to decide a thing these days. My uncle is not well."

"And we need someone to speak against these Christians," Amelia added. "I understand they are still among us, mostly unmolested."

"What do you know of the Christians, Amelia?" Marcus Atreus asked.

"More than you, I dare say. I have been living in Rome. People talk. They say the Christians want to burn Rome. They say they steal infant children to raise as Christians, killing their mothers."

"I understood it to be a religious sect," Marcus replied. "Rome tolerates many religions."

"I will not tolerate this religion!" Simonedes said emphatically. He shook his head. "No! They oppose the empire! Taking that stance they become my enemies . . . and I would hope yours, Marcus Atreus."

"We have not yet lost any infants," Marcus said wryly.

"You scoff!" Simonedes said in amazement. "You have not a full understanding of these people, Marcus. I beg you not to make any tolerant statements in public. Such a position could ruin you."

"I only say that I do not know," Marcus Atreus said. "How can I support the persecution of a people I do not understand—most of them are Roman citizens, are they not? And entitled to legal process?"

"I will not argue it," Simonedes said, dismissing the subject with a wave of the hand.

The emperor's nephew glanced up at the passing figure. A young, dark-haired servant was removing the empty plates from the table. Beautiful, she was, somehow familiar. Yet Simonedes was so habitually involved with only himself that he had no memory for faces, for people.

If he had he would have been astonished to glance up and see the queen of the Iceni Celts working as a servant in the house of Marcus

Atreus. And if he had looked up a moment longer, he would have been startled by the single, searing glance Iona aimed at him.

"I can only repeat that I will consider it," Marcus Atreus said. "I am not sure it is the life for me."

"Consider what is best for Rome," Simonedes counseled.

"I have for all of my life; now I must consider myself."

"Very well," Simonedes replied angrily. He was wasting his time, trying to convince a man to do what was best for him. What did Marcus Atreus want if not power? There was no understanding these soldiers.

He stood abruptly, bowing to Amelia who was apologetic.

"He will decide for the best," Marcus Atreus's wife said.

"Decide soon," Simonedes advised sternly.

"I will walk you to the door," Marcus said. Together they walked into the warm evening, and as they found themselves alone, Marcus told Simonedes:

"I have heard rumors, disturbing rumors, Simonedes."

"Rumors?" Simonedes asked impatiently. "Of what sort?"

"Rumors which concern you. It is said that Sophia is alive in prison."

Simonedes fell back as if slapped across the face. His crooked face twisted violently into shocked amazement. He stuttered a gurgling denial. How could Atreus know that?

"I see it is true," Marcus said calmly.

"Perhaps she is dead," Simonedes answered hotly.

"If she dies now . . . it will be known who ordered it."

That was true enough. Someone among his guards, some confidant had broken a vow of silence. Yet how had the information come to Marcus Atreus? He realized that he hated this tall, handsome general. That he had always hated, perhaps envied Marcus Atreus.

"What is it you want?" Simonedes whispered.

"That she be released."

"Impossible!"

"It was not impossible for her to be imprisoned; it cannot be impossible for her to be released."

"Do you know what that would cost me if it becomes known?"

"I do," Marcus said quietly, firmly. "And it will become known."

"You are finished, Marcus Atreus. I will find the time to deal with you."

It was no idle threat, Marcus Atreus knew. Simonedes was furious, and dangerous. He had the ear of the emperor.

"I think, perhaps, I shall not run for the Senate," Marcus said, with a smile which infuriated Simonedes still more.

"You will be lucky if you are not quartered and thrown to the dogs," Simonedes hissed. "In time, Atreus. In time."

Simonedes whirled around and strode to his waiting horse. He brushed his wife aside and rode away, leaving her perplexed in the garden.

Simonedes rode at a breakneck pace for a few minutes, then slowed the horse. He should have killed Sophia initially. All he had wanted was a new wife—plus the money of the old. Under Roman law a wife could be divorced, yet her property—which had been considerably more than that of Simonedes—would have to be returned.

Simonedes gambled heavily, lived high. He had managed to convince himself that it was right to have Sophia locked away.

Three years had passed. Three contented years. Now it was discovered, and by a man who hated him for a coward, a fool.

There was no way out that Simonedes could imagine. Perhaps Sophia would swear not to accuse him if she were released. . . .

Simonedes reined his horse roughly to a halt, and he turned back toward the house of Marcus Atreus. *But you, my general, you have written your fate with your defiance; and I shall see it fulfilled in blood!*

Iona was awakened by a tap on the heavy door. She sat up, looking around. The room was still dark, a faint gray light seeping through the shuttered, high window. Throwing a blanket around her shoulders, she went to the door.

It was Avidus.

"Get dressed," he told her. "You are traveling."

"Traveling where?"

"I was told only that you should get dressed. Hurry now."

Iona slipped into her sandals and dress, her mind flitting from conjecture to vague apprehension. She swept back her hair and went into the dawn-grayed hallway. Avidus had a basket of food which he pressed on her.

"Good-bye. Good luck," the old man said. There was a finality to his words. Iona took his rough hand briefly, then followed his directing finger to the courtyard.

Marcus Atreus waited there, standing beside a cart drawn by two horses. Augustus sat in the cart, his little back rigid, his eyes blank.

"Where . . .?"

"Get up beside the boy," Marcus Atreus said. He was fresh in his white toga, scented with faint lavender, his hair curled neatly. She took his wide hand and stepped onto the seat beside Augustus who inched away.

"What of your wife?" Iona asked quietly.

"She never rises at this hour," Marcus answered. "She has not been able to for some time," he added in an undertone.

He took the reins himself, and with a jerk the cart started into motion, passing through a side gate which was quickly closed behind them.

Iona took one last backward glance, but she saw no one. Amelia's window was empty.

They sped through the narrow alleyways of Rome in the early light. Augustus had removed himself to the tailgate of the wagon and he sat there, gloomily watching the city blur past.

"Where are you taking us?" Iona asked. The wind was shuffling her long hair, and she had to draw it back from her face to watch Marcus. He drove masterfully, his face intent.

"I have a country house," he told her. "I wanted

to leave Rome for a time. I believe Augustus needs to. You must."

"Must I?"

"Amelia ordered it—it is for the best. How else could I have gotten you to come with me?"

"Won't I be in the way? Between you and Augustus, that is," Iona asked.

"No, not at all."

"He seems to resent me."

"He resents much; he has little reason behind it."

They broke into the open countryside and Marcus slowed the horses to a trot as they gained the highway. After a mile or so he turned off onto a rutted, long dirt road which rambled for miles into the hills where orchards and vineyards grew.

"How far is this country house?" Iona inquired.

"Quite far. We won't make it until after dark." Marcus added after a moment, "You cannot even see the city from there."

It seemed a dream to be able to ride through open country, the breeze cooling, playful in her hair. The people they passed were farmers, herdsmen who lifted hands in friendly salutation.

Marcus had fallen silent, and Iona guessed that there was something he had not told her. Augustus had wearied of the ride already and had curled up in the wagon bed, atop a pile of luggage.

"He is a fine-looking boy," Iona said.

"Augustus? Yes he is," Marcus agreed with a touch of fatherly pride. "Yet it is the coming man in him I worry about."

"You want to form him?"

"I want to guide him, yes. Is it not a debt we owe the next generation? Not to discipline, but to inform."

"To love?" Iona suggested.

"That goes without saying."

They had come to a river crossing, slowing to dip through the hollow filled with trees and vines, then they made a sharp bend and began a steep climb. Abruptly Marcus halted.

"Soldiers," he whispered.

Marcus slowed the wagon and Iona sat petrified as two armed soldiers blocked the roadway. Marcus Atreus drew slowly abreast of the men. One of them recognized Marcus Atreus instantly and saluted.

"General Atreus!"

"Good day. Is there trouble ahead?"

"No trouble, sir." His eyes flickered to Iona and to the sleeping boy. "It is only road work."

Along the roadway now they could see the slaves in chains, the road crew moving heavy rocks to form the road bed.

"This road has needed it for some time," Marcus Atreus said.

"Allow us to escort you through the slaves, General. They are the scum of the earth. One never knows what fills their minds."

"All right."

The soldiers clung to the sides of the wagon as Marcus guided the wagon through the chain gang. Vicious, hulking men they were, dirty and scarred. Iona sat tensely on the seat beside Marcus, and the soldier, believing she was frightened of the workers, spoke up.

"They will not harm you, ma'am. If they knew who your husband was they would scatter like dogs."

"I assure you," Marcus Atreus bantered, "if they knew my wife's temper they would be scattering now!"

Iona smiled briefly, still tightly clenching the rail beside her seat. She wanted only to be gone from there, to be away from soldiers, free across the countryside.

Yet just then she saw him and her heart leaped, her eyes flooding instantly with tears.

He was a giant of a man, with one blind eye, snarled graying hair to his waist, huge bare shoulders gleaming in the sun. He held a massive rock in his thick, crippled hands.

Throg.

Astonished, she could not help gawking at the giant, and he, glancing up, saw her. His face fell with puzzled disbelief and then, astonishingly, he laughed, roared with pleasure.

He raised his hands above his head and bellowed a single Celtic word. At that the soldier nearest Throg leaped from the wagon and beat him with the flat of his sword. Throg turned back to his work, yet still he laughed.

"I apologize," the second soldier said to Marcus Atreus. "These animals!"

"It is nothing," Marcus Atreus answered. "It is fortunate we do not understand his language, aren't we?"

"Yes. There is no telling what he shouted."

They had come to the end of the construction and the soldier dropped from the wagon. Augustus, sleepy-eyed, frightened, clung to the railing, watching him go.

"What was it?" he asked his father.

"Nothing, Augustus."

"But that savage shouted something—what was it?"

"I do not know," Marcus answered. "I do not speak their language." He looked at Iona who was still shaken, a last errant tear running across her cheek.

They drove silently after that, Iona longing to look back, daring not to. What was there to be done? Charge down upon them with a cavalry corps? *Nothing.* Nothing could be done. She rode woodenly, eyes fixed to the road.

She had seen one other familiar face among that crew. A man she had known only briefly, but who had recognized her as well. The man named Graculus—the Jackdaw. But where she had seen joy on the face of Throg, she had seen only bitterness, hatred in the eyes of Graculus. It had sent a shiver up her spine.

Night came slowly over the countryside. The deep vales filled with purple shadow. A single star —the one the Romans had named for their goddess Venus—peered through a frail pennant of rose-colored cloud.

"What was it he said?" Marcus asked.

"Who?"

"The giant. Your general."

"It means *I salute you.* It is the greeting for a sovereign."

"I can do nothing for him," Marcus said. "Nor can you."

"No." *Nothing.* She nodded slowly, admitting it was so. And in the darkness she felt a reassuring hand stretch out and rest on her shoulder, squeezing it briefly, lightly, rubbing the back of her knotted neck. She glanced at Marcus who withdrew his hand quickly.

"Thank you. Thank you, Marcus Atreus," Iona said.

It was full dark when they reached the country house. Stars glittered across a far-reaching empty sky. A low light burned in the window of the house which was larger than she had expected, sprawling.

"It is Colonus, the caretaker. He and his wife live here," Marcus said, indicating the lantern. The front door opened a crack and then swung open. A man of middle years, quite heavy with long dark hair, rushed out joyously.

"Sir! General Atreus. Welcome, sir! Welcome home."

"Greetings, Colonus. How is Eugenia?"

"Both my wife and I are healthy and happy, sir." Colonus clambered onto the wagon to remove the luggage and stopped, the lantern held high over the sleeping boy.

"Can this be Augustus?" he asked. The boy pawed at his eyes and sat up.

"So it is," Marcus answered.

"It hardly seems possible. Come, my young man, Eugenia will have dinner for you, and your bed made up." He paused, looking at Iona, not able to decide who she was. "And the young lady, General?"

"She will eat as well, Colonus."

"Yes, sir. And shall I find her quarters?"

"She shall have the guest's room, Colonus."

"Yes, General Atreus," Colonus replied.

"She shall be the mistress of this house as long as she stays," Marcus Atreus told him. Iona looked at Marcus, her eyebrows knitting.

"Yes, sir. I understand." He stretched out his hands and helped Augustus down. They walked into the house together, Colonus holding an arm around Augustus. Iona and Marcus were left alone; he helped her down from the wagon.

"He thought I was a servant," Iona guessed, nodding toward the house. "Colonus has a quick eye."

"You were. Now you are not," Marcus Atreus said.

"Then what am I?" she asked. He was close to her in the night, so close she could feel the warmth from his body.

"A guest. Why? What would you wish to be?" he wanted to know.

"Mistress of your house," she said, and she was more astonished than Marcus that she had admitted it. "For as long as I shall stay here."

He stood there, this brave warrior, this conqueror, not knowing what to say. Deep within him he had prayed for such a response, yet he had hardly dared believe it could happen.

They ate quietly, the only conversation between Marcus and Colonus concerning estate conditions. Eugenia, a cheerful pale-eyed woman, served them eagerly. Augustus had barely eaten when the weariness of the long day overcame him again.

"I will carry him to his bed, sir," Colonus said, nodding at the sleeping boy.

"No, let me," Marcus insisted. "It is a pleasure I have done without."

He hefted the lanky boy as if he weighed nothing, and patting his back gently, walked down the dimly lighted corridor. Iona finished eating, thanked Eugenia, and rose. She was weary now herself.

Iona's room faced the south. A window opened onto a small garden and after bathing, she stood there, naked, watching the distances. A single light burned miles away, a wolf farther away howled and his mournful baying echoed across the dark hills. The stars were plentiful—handfuls of glittering jewels flung against the velvet of night. The soft scent of jasmine reached her from the garden. The door opened quietly behind her.

Marcus stood there, still dressed as he had been. He was startled by her nakedness, yet she turned toward him as if it were all quite natural.

Outlined in the starlit window she was utterly beautiful, long dark hair nearly to her waist falling down across her shoulders, her breasts.

"I only wondered if you had everything you needed?" Marcus asked hesitantly.

"Everything. You have given me everything, Marcus Atreus. She went closer to him, her hand reaching out, taking his at the wrist. "Yet I have no *one*. Rome has left me empty, alone. One starves from loneliness as surely as from lack of food."

She bent her head toward him and he kissed her, his lips warm against hers. With his other hand he closed the door behind him.

He stripped off his toga, and for a moment she looked at him. His figure was that of a mature lion.

Heavily muscled in the chest and shoulders, his abdomen was still flat, his thighs were large, hard. He was a beautiful man, this Marcus Atreus. She closed her eyes as he slipped into the bed beside her.

He made love as she had never experienced it. He moved gently to her, almost shyly. He found her breast beneath the veil of her soft dark hair and kissed it tenderly, his hand lingering on her abdomen before finding her thigh which he stroked with gentle fingers.

Iona's pulse had begun to race, and she drew him nearer, letting his lips find her throat, her ears, her eyes, and her mouth. His heart pounded against her and she took his hand and placed it between her thighs, her arms encircling him, her lips touching his temples, ears.

He moved cautiously, as if afraid he might not please her, that he would disappoint her. Iona bent his head to her and whispered, "You please me, Marcus. You give me pleasure."

She opened her eyes slightly, watching the stars across his shoulder. Softly she rubbed his hair, his trembling shoulder. A warm breeze filled the room, a hot flooding wind. Iona's ears began to ring, then she felt all sensation focus on Marcus where he touched her—so slowly, lovingly. Then again all sensation drifted away and she fell into some deep void which began spinning crazily, in a maelstrom of brilliant color, voiceless sounds, until it collapsed in a crushing explosion of pleasure which throbbed violently, died away and returned, like drumming not only in her ears, but throughout her body. For a moment she seemed to be inside of

Marcus, inside of herself, and she turned inside out, trying to draw him inside to share the overwhelming ecstasy which shook her again, shaking her until the life seemed to flow out of her, leaving her drained, with only the echoes of the drumming, the lingering, intermittent flashes of color . . . or was it sound? She could not be sure.

They lay together, trembling. Iona felt the tension, the rigidity flow out of the muscles of Marcus Atreus. He lay utterly still, and they kissed deeply, breathing each other's breath, touching each other's exhaustion.

"I love you, Iona," he said, his head resting against her breast. She did not answer him, but stroked his hair, his ears, his lips. "I love you," he repeated.

"Only tell me that tomorrow, Marcus Atreus," Iona said.

"I do not need to wait until tomorrow," he argued. "I tell you I love you . . . tonight, tomorrow, forever."

Iona did not answer. They shifted positions and Marcus lay flat on his back, her head on his arm. He caressed her back and suddenly squeezed her so tightly it took her breath.

She opened her eyes and looked at him. He was watching back, his eyes deep in the starlight. He clung to her a moment longer before his grip slowly loosened. Iona stretched up and kissed his lips, lightly.

"I love you too, Marcus," she said, smiling.

He nodded then and closed his eyes, the tension going out of his face. She watched him a minute longer, then curled up against his strong chest, letting sleep take her. A deep, untroubled sleep such as she had not had for lifetimes, it seemed. Not since childhood, before Athair had died, before Rome ... it no longer seemed important. Not at that moment.

Only Marcus Atreus. He was her only reality, and she slept like a child in his arms.

Chapter Twenty-Four

The days passed in peaceful progression. They walked the peaceful valleys, sat near the quiet stream among the oak woods. In the evenings they sat in the garden before dinner, and after it was dark they shared their common love. Only the misunderstanding in a small boy's eyes dimmed the brightness of their lives. Augustus continued taciturn, unhappy amidst the happiness his father and Iona shared.

They rode with him, cajoled him into singing, to playing games; yet he was one of those children who never seemed to have touched happiness, to have never shared, knowingly, the love of a parent.

He seemed not to truly resent Iona who was kind and patient with him; what he did seem to resent—or not understand—was all of life, his roots, his destiny.

"He will grow out of it," Marcus suggested hopefully.

They sat on a low, grassy knoll, watching the

boy walk the riverbanks, searching for fish in the silver water, crawlers and worms along the banks.

Iona clasped her knees to her breast; she recognized in the boy, Augustus, the common sadness of all mankind—and she had participated in the empty communion deeply. She understood; but how to bring him out of it, out of himself?

"Here," Marcus said, waving a hand around him, "is where he shall be raised, where he shall find himself."

"Here? But how?" Iona asked.

"Amelia will want the townhouse. After I divorce her . . ."

Their eyes met. Iona's heart raced—was he then saying . . . ?

"We will marry, Iona. Who else would I live out my years with? You and I—together—will overwhelm the melancholy in this boy with our love."

"Amelia will allow it?"

"Amelia will welcome it. Now," Marcus added wryly. "She sees that my public career is over. Since I spoke to Simonedes of Sophia."

"I hope she is free now," Iona said. She vividly recalled the acts of kindness Sophia had offered her. It had been only yesterday.

"I do not think Amelia will oppose my having Augustus," Marcus Atreus said meditatively. "She is a night creature, a lover of excitement—gambling halls, places where a boy may not go. She will cavil, of course, but in her heart she does not want Augustus badly enough to oppose it."

"But," Iona wanted to know, "is any of this legal, Marcus. I, an escaped slave, a foreigner? To marry you—it seems impossible."

"No. All that must be done is to obtain Roman citizenship for you. For the rest of it—no one knows who you are, where you have come from, what you might have done."

She leaned her head against his shoulder. Augustus turned to look at them one moment, then returned to his solitary, childish wanderings. All that need be done was that she become a Roman!

It was an astonishing, incongruous notion; yet it was that Iona wanted above anything now. To live out their days in this peaceful place, shut away from the world. Augustus would come around, in time, enveloped as he was by love.

Had it then finally come to an end? It seemed settled the way Marcus explained it. She glanced lovingly at him. His curled, silver hair, his fine straight nose, rugged jawline. He was watching his son fondly; feeling her gaze, he looked at Iona and kissed her hair.

I want to be a Roman, she thought, the irony not escaping her. She held her man, her Marcus Atreus, more tightly and thought again: *I want to be a Roman.*

The following day Marcus awakened her while the sky was still gray. He kissed her lightly then sat beside her on the bed as she slowly blinked her eyes open.

"Today?" she asked unhappily.

"Yes. I must take Augustus back to his mother. The legal matters must be settled. But I will not be gone long. Not so long, dear Iona."

He kissed her then and she felt herself quiver, tasted the salt of her tears mingled with their kiss. "It will be only for a little while."

"I wish I could accompany you," Iona said.

"You cannot. It is too risky by far. After we are married we shall travel where we will together. Yet why would we leave this house?"

"Why, indeed? Travel carefully, Marcus. Return safely—soon."

"You are the mistress of this house," he reminded Iona as she dressed, hurriedly pinning up her hair. "Colonus and Eugenia know that. Whatever you require, tell them."

They walked together to the front garden where Augustus waited soberly, his eyes downcast.

Colonus stood by as well, and he and Marcus spoke together for a moment; a moment in which Marcus seemed concerned. Then he came back to her and held her tightly. She clung to him, afraid to let him go. Finally he drew back.

"I won't be gone long. Nothing can keep me from you. Nothing!"

He stepped into the wagon and Augustus followed, sitting rigidly beside his father. The wagon turned and with a plume of following dust, they drove from the garden, Iona waving a hand. Suddenly the wagon stopped and the boy leaped from it.

Running frantically back he came directly to Iona and he fell into her arms, hugging her boyishly for a long minute.

"You were kind to me; I unkind to you. Goodbye, Iona," he said simply. "I love you."

Then he ran away, waving over his shoulder, to where the wagon waited and Iona waved back, her heart bursting, standing with her arm raised until long after the wagon had dipped into the hollow beyond and disappeared from view.

Colonus still stood on the steps, and as Iona walked slowly to the house, she asked him, "What was it you and Marcus Atreus spoke of?"

"That?" Colonus asked with surprise. "Why nothing. Marcus Atreus has a surprise for you; he only reminded me. Now if you will excuse me, please." He bowed quickly and scurried away.

Eugenia found Iona still standing there and she enlightened Iona.

"It is probably nothing—a soldier came in the middle of the night to inform Marcus Atreus that several prisoners had escaped from the road gang. The general warned Colonus to be watchful. They did not want to worry you, but I think a woman needs to be informed."

Prisoners.

"But they are quite far from here," Eugenia remarked. "And the soldiers will be right after them. In chains they will not run far or fast."

"I see." A series of thoughts, hopeful and frightening swept through her mind. "Colonus made up some story about a surprise for me," Iona explained.

"Oh, he did not make that up!" Eugenia insisted, her honest face conspiratorial. "The general has planned a surprise for you."

"Tell me, Eugenia. Tell me what it is—I do not like to be surprised."

"No!" Eugenia laughed. "I told you what I thought you *needed* to know; but I would not spoil the general's surprise."

Iona was suddenly alone. She found that she had no idea how to fill her time. She took a long walk in the woods, yet her thoughts were filled with Marcus. There they had sat watching Augustus;

there played an impromptu, wild game of tag. . . .

The house itself was even emptier. Eugenia and Colonus kept to themselves, regarding her as mistress, not as friend. Iona spent some time before the mirror, arranging her hair—arranging it for whom?

She watched the road, knowing he could not come back now, hoping that some circumstance might return him to her.

The nights were far too lonely, nearly beyond endurance. She slept only by imagining him near her, awakening to find he was not.

She began doing yard work, chores reluctantly given up by Colonus who insisted they were his duties. She fed the chickens, caring for a newly incubated brood of fuzzy yellow chicks, pitched hay for the work horses and exercised them when Colonus did not need them, taking long, slowly rambling rides through the countryside, always studying the distant road which wound toward Rome.

She thought too of Throg, tearing at her brain for an answer to his release, knowing there was none. At times she prayed that he had been one of the escapees. Yet she knew that they could not have run far in chains; it had been a week and no one had word of the slaves. Probably they had been captured, executed on the spot.

She refused now to let Eugenia prepare large dinners for her, and she ate with them. On this evening they had a green dinner, as Eugenia called their simple fare: cabbage dipped in vinegar, spinach and sorrel, a few green figs and a small portion of chicken. It was enough for Iona who ate absently, leaving the chicken.

"Starving yourself won't bring him back sooner," Eugenia said to her. "Eat, preserve that bloom you wore while he was here."

But she had no stomach for food. Instead Iona walked out into the cool night, a shawl wrapped around her. The sky was sheeted over with thin clouds. The horses nickered in the barn, and remembering she had not fed them that evening, Iona walked across the empty yard, her feet kicking up tiny puffs of dust.

It was dark in the barn as she swung open the door, but a lantern hung inside and she reached for it.

"Don't touch that!" a voice in her ear hissed and Iona gasped as the door was slammed shut behind her. The dark bearded man hovered over her. He was bleeding from many scratches on his face and chest, his hair was a tangled mat.

"Graculus!" she breathed, suddenly recognizing him. He cocked his head curiously, studying her more closely. Then he laughed, briefly.

"You! And you remember me, little slave girl! Look whose house we have found, friend," he called to the man in the corner. Seriously injured, he struggled to his feet, staggering toward them. A head taller than even the huge Graculus, he had recognized Iona already and he thrust out his chained arms.

"My queen."

"Throg!"

He embraced her, tears running from his battle-scarred face, his tangled hair all around her. His hands were crippled now and he held her lightly. This giant, this general, still lived!

"If I had known," Throg said, still holding her

arms, "I would never have come here. It can only mean trouble for you."

"We have often endured trouble together, Throg," she reminded him.

"Yes, Iona, but this is different. You have found a new life.... I, as you may see, am still locked into the old—and I would drag you back into it for nothing."

"Is there anything to remove these manacles?" Graculus demanded impatiently. "Have you food, water?"

"Yes, yes," Iona answered in a whisper. "But you must be quiet. Where will you go?" she asked, turning back to Throg. "How will you live?"

"I only long to live in freedom for another day, one last day," Throg answered, "unchained, unfettered. They will never take me alive again."

"Nor me," Graculus vowed. "Hurry, woman, find a chisel and hammer—if you are his friend."

She nodded and stepped out into the yard once again. The house lights were still on, but she saw no one. Hurriedly she walked to the tool shed and felt around for the tools Graculus needed.

"None too soon," Graculus greeted her. He snatched the tools from Iona and began hammering the pins holding the leg manacles together.

"So far to have come," Iona told Throg. His eye had been put out in the arena, he told her, his hands crippled by an angry master. There was so much to say to this gentle giant, yet no time now. The soldiers would be sure to sweep through the area of the house.

"Throg, my general . . ." she began once.

"Say nothing. I only care that you, in your youth, are surviving well. For old Throg it matters little any longer. I only want that single day of freedom."

He was no longer well, that was obvious. His hands trembled, his face twitched as he spoke. The wound in his side was a nasty gash.

"Get food, woman. Water," Graculus ordered her.

Iona nodded and slipped out into the night again. She had no plan on how to explain the provisions which would be missing from the larder; she simple packed all that would fit into a sack, even adding a bottle of wine.

When she again saw Graculus and Throg, they were free of their irons. Red, bleeding bands encircled their wrists and ankles. She gave the sack to Graculus who told her, "The chains are buried in the back of the stall, covered with earth and straw."

"There must be some way . . ." Iona started to say to Throg, but he shook his head wearily.

"There is no way you can help me, my queen. Not any longer. I cannot be saved by your valor any more than Viron could have been. The world has changed, transmuted, and now it will swallow old Throg up . . ."

"Come on!" Graculus hissed.

"Yes," Iona agreed. "Go hurriedly. Into the hills. Hide. So that they may never find you."

Throg touched her hand and then was pulled away by Graculus and the giant hobbled off into the darkness, leaving Iona alone.

A light rain had begun to fall. She realized with relief that it would wash away their tracks, perhaps helping them for a little while. Throg ran. A bold warrior, a nobleman in his own country, his own

time. He was a fugitive, a slave, a criminal. This
night he would sleep upon the hard ground, hunted
and cursed. *He would die.*

She knew it suddenly, intensely. Throg would
die, if not on this rainswept night, soon, in a foreign land, hated, struck down like a savage animal,
buried as a dog might be, not as a warrior deserved.

Iona stood there, the shawl around her shoulders, the rain drenching her hair, soaking her dress,
watching the night where a man had vanished.

Iona sat at the breakfast table, watching Colonus and Eugenia who ate heartily. She refused an
egg, a slice of bread and honey.

"She has no appetite, poor thing," Eugenia
whispered to her husband. "Not since the general
has gone away."

"No." Colonus, who had been in the cupboard,
shook his head. "Not in the daylight hours—but
she must be eating like a horse in the night. The
cupboard is nearly bare."

That was the morning the anticipated surprise
Marcus Atreus had promised arrived. Iona was in
the yard with Eugenia who happened to glance up
the road. Iona, deep in her own thoughts, was
startled by the nudge Eugenia gave her.

"Here it is, Mistress," Eugenia said happily.
"The surprise the general promised. You look unhappy now, but I promise you this will be a happy
morning."

Iona stood, hands on hips, watching the horse
come toward the house. It was Placidus. The great
white stallion held his tail high as he side-stepped
down the road, his knees lifting in graceful, long
strides.

"You see," Eugenia asked triumphantly.

"Yes. It is wonderful," Iona said with a weak smile. It was kind of Marcus to send Placidus to her. He would be a pleasure to ride. But it would have taken more than a horse to transform this morning into a joyous one.

Then Iona looked again at Placidus. At the rider, and she took a step forward, hardly believing her eyes. She took another quick step and then broke into a run.

Rushing toward Placidus, her hair flying, she kept her unbelieving eyes riveted to the rider. It was a woman. An older woman. One she knew well.

"Thramane!"

Thramane's hair was completely white now, and she had difficulty dismounting from the stallion, but she smiled widely, her old eyes flashing.

"I can still ride a war horse," she said proudly.

"Thramane." Iona took her into her arms, and the old woman held her tightly. "How is it possible."

"I am your servant once again," Thramane told her. "Marcus Atreus purchased me from my former master . . . he was anxious to be rid of me anyway, after finding out I was a Christian."

"But how. . . ?" She had mentioned Thramane to Marcus, yet to receive her old maidservant was too much to be hoped for, too much to be believed. "If only you had arrived yesterday," she whispered. "Throg was here!"

"Here?" Thramane had difficulty understanding that possibility.

"I will tell you later," Iona told her. "We shall have much time to talk now. Eugenia was right—nothing could have made me happier on this morning."

"Nothing but seeing your general return," Thramane suggested.

"He will return, Thramane. Soon. I have only to be patient. And with you here," she said cheerily, "there will be much to fill the hours with. Colonus! See to Placidus, will you?"

Thramane insisted on working although she was obviously in failing health and there was little to do. Yet there was time for the long talks, the reminiscing, in the old tongue.

"But you hardly seem to miss it, Iona, our Britain. Not with your general."

"I miss it. I long for the old soil, yet I know that there is nothing left for me there. Only here does my life have a purpose. But you, old thing, you seem hardly to miss it either."

"I have you. I may end my days happily. And I have the Lord Jesus in my heart."

"Must you speak of that?" Iona asked.

"I must—but words cannot express the comfort I have found. My people—my new people, these Christians—they are a loving race, not believing in lying, stealing, hurting. And we know, Iona," she winked, "know that the darker side of life as we used to call it, is not the darker side at all, but an eternal and brilliant continuation of this. For those who accept the Lord."

"I cannot understand it," Iona said impatiently.

"But a time will come when you will. When the brutality of man governed by man comes home to you. Then you shall reach for divine order, Iona."

"Perhaps." Iona was thoughtful a moment. Perhaps she simply did not hear what Thramane was trying to tell her. It seemed to make no sense; but then Thramane said she must listen with her heart, not her mind. "But when you pray, Thramane, pray for Throg. And pray for my Marcus Atreus."

"I will, dear Iona, and I will pray for you."

Thramane slept on a bed in Iona's own room. Usually after her prayers, the older woman fell quickly to sleep. But Iona was seldom so lucky. She stood at the window, night after night. Winter had settled in—twice they had had snow—and still there was no word. No word at all.

Where are you Marcus, she asked the silent, dark night. *What could have happened to you?*

Marcus Atreus stood on the balcony of his small apartment. The cold wind washed over him. He was lost in deep thought. Thoughts of Iona, of her and her alone. His petitions to Claudius came back unanswered, unopened. The emperor was old, quite ill, he knew. Yet he asked of Rome only this one favor—one favor from the Rome he had served all his adult life in war and in peace: that Iona be granted citizenship.

No answer came. He determined then that he would walk to the palace personally in the morning, although it was not proper form to do so.

Surely Claudius could not deny him face to face!

With that hopeful thought in his mind, Marcus turned back to his bed, flinging himself down. Iona —her dark eyes, silky hair, her laughing mouth, filled his thoughts as he tried to sleep. But sleep would not come, not for hours as the stars rolled slowly past.

And when he did sleep it was a nightmare filled with the old dream, that which had tormented him for years.

Blood. Eternal rivers of scarlet blood running

from the mouth of the she-wolf, Romulus and Remus suckling at her dangling teats, swords in their chubby hands.

Again the eagle soared through the empty April skies. The echoing, toneless song thundered. A death attached itself to Marcus Atreus who tried to fight back and found he had no arms. A woman's face smiled, beckoned, then fell away to corruption. . . .

He awoke, dripping wet, the bedsheets soaked, and he dared not to sleep again that night.

With the first light Marcus Atreus was up, dressed in full armor, even wearing the golden laurels he usually disdained. He re-read his petition, deciding at the last moment that he may have omitted too much, justified too little. It was only the anxiety, he decided, which caused it to read that way. He had spent many hours drafting the petition which modestly, but fully, recounted his exploits in the field, his service to the emperor. He explained little about Iona, saying that she was a free woman he wished to marry after long consideration. He ended with a personal plea to Claudius.

The imperial apartments were quiet, unusually so when Marcus Atreus arrived. Most of the routine business of state was being conducted at the proconsul's office due to the emperor's illness.

Marcus stood nearly at attention for almost an hour. The emperor's personal secretary had announced him, yet the man now sat at his desk, hardly glancing at Marcus.

Abruptly the door to the inner chambers opened

and the secretary was summoned within. He returned immediately.

"The Emperor Claudius will accept your petition now, Marcus Atreus," the secretary said.

Marcus started toward the door, but the secretary stopped him.

"Your petition only, sir. The Emperor Claudius is seeing no one personally."

"You are certain he knows it is I?" Marcus asked.

"I am certain, General."

"Very well." Marcus handed the man the document and walked to the window, hands behind his back. He watched the city spread out before him. *It makes no difference,* he told himself. Claudius could not refuse him. Yet he did not like it—not at all.

"Sir." The secretary handed the petition to Claudius's aide. The emperor lay on his couch, his breath coming raggedly. There was an unabated pain in his chest. His face was sunken, the flesh on his throat sagging sadly. He opened his eyes, blinking them rapidly, fighting the pain of coming death.

"What is it?" he asked his aide.

"A petition from Marcus Atreus."

"Marcus ... yes," the emperor smiled weakly. "A fine officer. What is it he wishes?"

"He is weary of Rome. He longs for the frontiers, my uncle. Marcus Atreus requests assignment."

"Yes, I understand that. He is a vigorous man," Claudius replied, forming his words with difficulty. "What would you suggest?"

"Alexandria—if he will accept it. The Egyptian corps could use such a leader, Uncle," Simonedes said.

"Alexandria . . . yes, certainly. If it is suitable to Marcus Atreus. Of course."

"I will see to it, Uncle," Simonedes assured him. The petition he crumpled in his hand, throwing it into the pile of scrap nearby. "I am sure Alexandria will please our General Atreus."

Chapter Twenty-Five

He returned on the coldest day of that winter, the wind shrieking in the trees, the rain running off his head, across his set, chiseled features. Iona ran to meet him and Marcus leaped from his horse, holding her close as the rain beat down upon them. He kissed her through the rain, through the tears, and together they walked to the house.

Marcus stopped suddenly, holding Iona to him. When he drew back his face was grave.

"I cannot stay," he said. The rain made crazy patterns of hair across his forehead, his gray eyes were sober.

"Not stay!" she laughed. But through the laugh she realized that he was serious.

"I have been ordered to Egypt. Iona...." He dropped his hands miserably. "What have I done to you? Where can you go now?"

"I will stay here, of course. Why would I leave? After we are married—"

"No." He said it solemnly, and her heart fell.

"We cannot be now. My petitions were rejected."

"But why?"

"I cannot say. I can only promise to continue to try. I did not mean for this to happen, Iona . . . I will be gone . . . for some time."

"Years?" she clenched his arms, studying his eyes.

"Yes." His face brightened. "But there is hope I can reverse the orders. Only the emperor is gravely ill. All state affairs move slowly. I can plead with him . . ."

"Yes," Iona said, her voice muted. She wiped the rain from his face although it returned instantly. "There has been some error. Surely they can't ask you to go—you've just returned. Is there war in Egypt?" she asked, suddenly realizing she had not an idea where Egypt was.

"No. Libya has been subdued. All is quiet."

"Then why?" she asked, not understanding.

"I don't know. I don't know why I have been ordered there; cannot fathom why my petitions were denied. It is all a mistake which will be straightened out. We must stiffen to it and fight back."

"Yes." Iona smiled. "We *will*. We will fight back."

She made a clenched fist and waved it and Marcus laughed. For only a moment, then he was sober again.

"Then how soon must you go?" she asked inevitably.

"I must ride in the morning."

Iona stood immobile, the sounds of the rain the only sounds. She reached up and took his face between her hands, smiling bittersweetly.

"Then we have tonight, my Marcus Atreus."

The rain continued to fall, drumming on the roof. The winds twisted out of the hills, clawing at the trees. Iona slept fitfully, holding on to a man who was there, yet not there. Strong, loyal, he slept like a child.

She awakened once to the rattling of shutters. Rising, she secured them and then stood long minutes watching the peaceful, sleeping face of Marcus Atreus.

Again she slipped in beside him, listening to his deep, easy breathing, watching the rise and fall of his chest. Then she slept, soundly.

When she awoke again it was morning and for an instant she could not remember if she had dreamed it all, if he really had returned. She sat bolt upright—he was gone!

Running to the door she saw nothing, nothing but the eternal, damnable rain.

"He's gone, Iona," Thramane said. She stood beside her queen on the porch, a cloak wrapped around her. "I do not think he could bear telling you good-bye."

Iona turned to Thramane, her eyes blank. The old maidservant held her tightly a moment, feeling the trembling which racked Iona's shoulders.

"He will be back soon," Iona said, lifting her head, tossing her hair back. She stood, arms crossed, staring at the road where not a track remained under the pelting of the rain. "Very soon, I know."

The days passed with a painful sameness. Spring warmed the land, the countryside came to bud, burst forth in blossom. There was no letter from

Marcus; perhaps he had not yet even reached Egypt—a distant land, he told her, where much of the earth was sand, where the searing sun beat down eternally and where ancient civilizations had carved out strange memorials to their race. *Egypt* —she tried to imagine it, believed she could; yet what did it matter? That would not bring him back, make his memory more vivid. At any moment he may ride back, she told herself constantly. If Claudius were understanding. . . .

It was at that moment that she thought of Simonedes. Simonedes!

She wondered if Marcus had had the same suspicions?

She tried to shake it from her mind, returning to her garden where she startled a mother hare with its brood among the fennel.

It could have been Simonedes—he was the nephew of Claudius, and some said he would be the next emperor. What that would mean to Marcus, she knew. His next petition would be rejected, and the next, the next. . . .

She tried to push the thought aside, yet it lingered there. Without knowing why she did it, Iona stood still suddenly and lifted her eyes to the blue, cloudless skies.

"Thramane's God! If you are there, hear me. My name is Iona. I pray you do not let Simonedes ascend the Roman throne. He is an evil man."

Then, partly ashamed, she returned quickly to her work, wondering what had caused her to offer prayers to a strange god.

The soldiers arrived the following week. A dozen armed men.

"Iona! Soldiers!" Thramane called and Iona

rushed to the house, hoping against hope . . . but he was not there.

A ruddy-faced sergeant told her, "We're searching for the criminal Graculus."

"Graculus?"

"The Jackdaw," he said in a gravelly voice. "He's loose in the area. Now he's got a band of men with him and they're sworn to die fighting the emperor. Not two days ago a farmer was found murdered. You'd best sit up nights," he told Colonus.

"He certainly hasn't been here," Iona objected as the soldiers stepped down from their horses and began searching the house.

"You never know where he is," the sergeant said. He helped himself to an apple and took a huge bite, talking around it. "He's like a cat, this one. You'd never know he was here unless he *wanted* you to know." He looked more closely at Iona then, a filthy thought crossing his mind.

"But we'll get them. We caught one last week. Giant of a man. Dangerous."

"Oh?" Iona wanted to ask, to know, but she dared not.

"Man called Throg."

"Then at least one has been recaptured," she said in a faint voice, turning her back to the soldier.

"Recaptured? I told you, ma'am. None of the Jackdaw's men will surrender. He cut up a couple of my men pretty good first, but we finally killed him."

"Sergeant!" A voice rang out from the yard and the man turned, leaving a rigid, waxen Iona standing there. After a second, taking a deep, slow breath, she followed the soldier.

They were gathered around the door to the barn and after a moment a soldier came out, holding the rusted chains aloft.

"Buried in the corner," he said.

"You see," the sergeant told Iona. "Graculus was here. Last year sometime, when he made his escape. The man is a shadow."

"Chains!" Colonus stepped forward, glancing from Iona to the chains, to the soldiers who watched him now.

"What about it?" the sergeant asked.

"Why, last year," Colonus said, "after the escape—our larder was raided. That villain was in our house and we never knew it!"

The sergeant turned his eyes on Iona triumphantly, yet she was ashen, shaken, it seemed to him, and he decided to say nothing more—the woman was frightened sick. He couldn't know that it was the news of Throg's death which had caused the color to bleed from her face, her eyes to go vacant. She scarcely heard the men speaking. Finally he offered, "I'll leave two men here if you like."

"No." She waved a weak hand. "We'll be wary. We'll be all right—you must have other uses for your soldiers."

"I do," he nodded. "It's quite understanding of you, but do be careful. The man is as wild now, as vengeful as Spartacus ever was."

Then they mounted and rode out, a fine plume of dust following them, sifting slowly to the warm earth.

Another. Iona stood silently. Another Celt, another death. Throg. One of the finest, strongest men the Iceni had to offer. Cut down because he wished freedom—his only crime.

Thramane stood just behind her, as silent as Iona herself, the light breeze moving her white hair. Together they turned without a word being said and returned to the house which had seemed empty enough before, and now seemed utterly barren, death-filled.

The days dragged like iron chains. Hours passed during which the sun refused to move. The nights were each an eternity, each colder than the last, more empty. Stars beckoned from the womb of heaven but beckoned to whom? Not to Iona, she was sure. Nor did the rising moon offer a lover's light, the breaking dawn quicken her heart with gladness.

She rose early every morning, brushing her hair, rushing to the door as if he would be there. He would be! One morning. Yet that morning hid in reluctance, tantalizing and incredibly tormenting.

A messenger's arrival punctuated a sullen summer day. Iona received the letter from Colonus. Hoping for word from Marcus, she was disappointed to find it was not his hand. Nevertheless, it was gratifying to read:

Dear Iona,

It is thanks to your noble dedication that I may sit at my apartment window, in the clear light of a summer day and write. (Forgive my hand, it trembles still from the cold.)

Yet it hardly matters—I live each day with joy, a realization of life's worth which I could not have had before. I paid a terrible price, yet even such a terrible episode has its rewards.

I do not know if I shall survive tomorrow.

But today is grand, glorious, wonderful in small ways—all thanks to you, my Iona.

Whatever I have is yours; whatever you may need I will do. With the grateful heart of one returned from death to brilliant life, I remain

Your Indebted,
Sophia

The leaves on the trees had curled and gone to brown. The winds of coming winter swirled them skyward, then let them drop to the cold earth where they were trampled underfoot or left sodden by the rains, frozen by frost; but finally the letter did come. A letter from a god, all hope and life on a rough page of parchment.

Iona ran with it to her room and she read it. Not once, but a dozen times, then again, touching the strokes of the pen as if that could bring back the man whose hand had scribed them—Marcus Atreus.

My Dearest Iona,

I write—yet where can I begin? My heart is so filled with thoughts of you, with love for you, that my mind crowds with words, emotions, pleas, and plans all at once. You have become my world.

I stood last night and watched the sea—it is a Roman sea, grand and broad, a majestic product of nature. Only not now, not now—white water rushes up out of the blackness slamming suddenly against this foreign shore. It growls and rages like some caged, mammoth beast. Now it is only a barrier.

Nights here are long, much longer than our Roman nights. I turn the night long, reaching out for you.

Yet I have good news—I dare not raise your hopes too high, nor my own. Yet I feel there is a great chance I may return soon, that we may be married, my Iona.

Isolated as you are, you may or may not know that our Emperor Claudius has died. The word has come to us that his replacement has been chosen.

A young man, talented in the arts, with a fresh open mind, I have heard nothing but good about him. His tutor was the great Stoic, the philosopher, Seneca. He seems a man of even temperament, objective and open.

Simonedes can have no influence on him, I think, and I mean to petition the new emperor immediately—tonight.

His crowning can only augur good for Rome, Iona, and augur hope for long, joyous years for us.

May the gods watch over us and reunite us; may the gods preserve our new emperor, Nero.

Soon—I may return soon. Iona blocked out the rest of the letter. It said only one thing: soon he would be home.

She did ask Colonus if he knew anything of Nero. He looked up from the harness he was mending.

"No," he could only shake his head, "I recall nothing of the new emperor. Yet we are hardly in the mainstream," the old man smiled. "Marcus seems to think well of him—and he is bound to be better informed than we."

Iona's spirits were lifted by that letter and she found herself singing one of the old songs as she worked in the garden.

Yet the winter dragged by, finally breaking into new spring. Time and again she re-read the letter until it was separating at the folds, until it yellowed.

The summer was long and hot. The chickens had trouble surviving, and there were several fires in the dry foothills; some said they had been started intentionally by Graculus and his band.

Soon. She sat at her table, reading the lines as if she had never read them before, as if some secret meaning lay hidden there. No, she had not misunderstood. *Soon.*

Each morning she would saddle Placidus and ride the aging war horse down the road, hoping to intercept a messenger. Hoping, although she would not admit it to herself, to see that beautiful man himself riding toward her, his smile brilliant as they came together, his strong arms enfolding her.

The dry wind swept across the low knoll. Iona sat Placidus, studying the distances.

She stepped down, holding the reins to the white stallion who tugged disinterestedly at a clump of dry grass. Iona leaned against Placidus, holding tightly to his neck, and the war horse rolled melancholy eyes to her.

The wind swirled her skirt, uncombed her hair, dried the tears on her cheek.

"Will he never come, old Placidus? Will he never come back to us?"

* * *

The ship's captain walked forward and leaned across the rail beside the soldier. A long and placid sea it was, following days of dark, rolling squall. The headlands lifted from the deep green sea.

"It's a beautiful sight, eh, General?"

"Most beautiful," Marcus Atreus answered. "Can that really be Italia? It seemed magical, so distant that I can hardly accept that it is so, we are home."

"Aye," the captain replied. "I know the feeling. Many's the time I've come home, overwhelmed by her. Yet," he laughed, "in a month the feeling's gone and I long again for planking beneath my feet." He glanced at the tall, iron-haired general and asked, "Do you know what I mean?"

"I do," Marcus answered, his eyes fixed to the horizon where the bulk of Italy still rose from the sea, taking on form and substance. "Yet it will not be so this time. I have sailed my last sea."

Chapter Twenty-Six

"I cannot understand these architects," the emperor complained, his voice a shrill protest. "My circus should have been completed in two years. Two years," he said, turning suddenly. "I wrote down two years. It's right here!"

"Yes, Most Excellent," Simonedes agreed.

"I'm sure I wrote down 'two years' and showed it personally to Caligula. I am so weary!" Nero said, sitting heavily. He patted his own flushed, plump cheeks and sighed, smiling at Simonedes. "The crown *is* heavy."

"I am sure it is; yet you bear it regally, as if it weighed nothing."

"You flatter me," Nero replied, waving a limp hand. "Have you read my newest poem?" he demanded, leaning far forward, his pudgy hands fixed to the gold arms of the chair.

"I read it still," Simonedes hedged. "I want to fully appreciate it, not rush madly through it like a bull through a field of lilac."

"You should," Nero said, his voice falling from menace to soft faintness. "I have much to say. Much. And this Marcus Atreus?" he asked, his voice suddenly alive once more, his deeply set eyes electric.

"The condemnation," Simonedes said, "was brought to you—"

"I have not read it."

"His petitions—" Simonedes began again, his narrow face impatient.

"I have not read them either. Does a general concern me?" He paused, but Simonedes could not answer before Nero went on. "Why cannot our warships sail beneath my window?"

"There is no water," Simonedes replied vaguely, shuffling through the stacks of petitions.

"Why! I will have a channel cut," Nero decided.

"You will see," Simonedes said, finding the lost papers, "that Marcus Atreus is a traitor to the throne."

"To me?" Nero touched the fingertips of both hands to his chest incredulously.

"Yes. You will see here—" He tried to hand the documents to Nero, but was refused.

"Tell me briefly, Simonedes, before I tire of you," he said.

"Marcus Atreus freed a Christian from the docket of Sextus, the priest of Jupiter . . ."

"Why could the canal not be canopied?" Nero asked.

"No reason, Most Excellent Nero."

"Call me Imperial Nero," the emperor said.

"Yes, Imperial Nero. You will see," Simonedes went on hastily, "that Marcus Atreus now wishes to marry a Celtic queen named Boudicca who opposed the Roman State. This woman has been hidden away in a farmhouse where other Christians Marcus Atreus has tried to free now live."

"The Christians may no longer move about as they have—let that be written!" Nero shouted to the scribe who jumped and wrote down the commandment.

"As you may see, Marcus Atreus befriended the enemy, sheltered Christians, affronted the church of Jupiter, and succored the brigand, Graculus."

"Graculus!" Nero was suddenly enraged. "One of my own generals. That is treason! I suppose," Nero said ominously, "that this can be proven."

"Certainly," Simonedes replied, smiling smugly. He handed Nero another report, but the emperor withdrew in horror.

"I don't want to touch any of those filthy reports!"

"It is a letter from a sergeant attached to the Graculus expedition, reporting a strange occurrence to his commander."

"On with it."

"These . . ." Simonedes said dramatically. He reached into the heavy sack he had carried in with him and withdrew a set of rusted shackles which he dropped rattling onto the scribe's desk.

"Those?" Nero asked, pointing at them with repugnance.

"They belonged to Graculus and were found secreted in the country house of Marcus Atreus."

"They are filthy—remove them."

Nero turned and went to his window, hands clasped behind his back, humming softly.

"Most Excellent . . . Imperial Nero," Simonedes began.

"Of course we would have to remove a dozen city blocks," Nero said, pointing below. "The channel could be cut in . . . two years?" he asked. He turned, surprised to Simonedes. "You are still here!"

"I did not realize I was excused," Simonedes explained.

"Yes. Go, go." He waved a dismissal.

"But the matter of Marcus Atreus—"

"That matter is settled. I leave it to your disposition."

Marcus Atreus had been shown his quarters at the general officers billet, had eaten and bathed. The rap at the door, he assumed, concerned his luggage or some such trifle. The man handed him instead a royal command.

The blood surged in his brain—Nero wanted to see him immediately. Hot anticipation caused Marcus Atreus to tremble slightly, momentarily, then he examined his toga—hardly suitable for the emperor, this plain white garment, yet it was clean and he had no other.

It was already growing dark when he stepped onto the street, the summons rolled in his hand. The traffic rushed by in the street, a drunken charioteer, a scurrying band of dirty orphans chasing a bread wagon.

He longed for the country where those milky, haze-screened stars would be clear, diamondlike, where she would be waiting. *Iona.*

To see the starlight in her eyes, to feel the rise

and fall of her breast against him, to touch those lips with his own once more....

Let the gods roam their Elysian fields! His paradise was beside her.

He walked swiftly through the night, clenching the summons as if it held all promise—and indeed it did. All life, all hope. He had served Rome, even going to Britain and Egypt, on her whims. He asked but that single favor: citizenship for Iona.

The palace was dark, unusually so, it seemed. Marcus turned without hesitation up the marble steps before the great, columned entranceway. The usual knots of beggars waiting to approach the noblemen clustered on the steps, and he was not surprised when they tried to halt him.

"Not this evening, citizens. Nero waits."

"Let him wait a while longer," one of them said, and Marcus saw the flash of silver in his fist. The man's eyes gleamed in the starlight and the knife he held was driven into Marcus Atreus's abdomen to the hilt.

Marcus spun, struck out, but a second dagger was plunged into his back, just above the liver and he stumbled forward, blood filling his mouth, pain tearing at his chest, abdomen, back.

There were five of them, and each had a knife. A blade ripped up beneath the ribcage and found the heart. Marcus Atreus, strangling on the blood which filled his throat, his lungs, slumped forward, clawing out at the steps. Beneath his hand he felt the warmth of his own blood. His head filled with whirling images, brilliant waves of color.

To die now! No—he would not allow it! He got to his knees, fell forward once again, then dragged himself a little way, the summons still clenched tightly in his fist.

He found it difficult to breathe, to recall his own name. The stars above him spun in pinwheels of blue-white light. Shadowy figures hovered over him, muttering in distant voices....

To die now.

Who dies? He could not say. He saw only the rivers of blood. The twins at the teats of the she-wolf, the lone eagle soaring through a crystalline sky. And then he felt himself in the eagle's body, understanding the dream at last.

But I must not die. The pain drove him toward death, harmonious, distant songs called him ... yet he could not! *Iona!*

Iona!

"Come on. He's dead. Simonedes will have silver for us."

Iona.

"Iona!"

Iona awoke with a start, sitting upright, a chill washing over her. Thramane was there, holding a lantern overhead.

"What is it?"

"You cried out in your sleep, Iona. You had a nightmare."

"No," she shook her head, but then she remembered. "It was nothing." A face had been bent over her, a mask with a painted grin, hollow eyes. Through the mask a voice hissed: *It's me, darling.* And the voice had seemed to be that of Marcus, but when she reached out to remove the mask, there was a horrible, mummified death face behind it and the face had begun to cackle insanely.

"That was when I must have screamed," Iona told Thramane.

"What a terrible dream," Thramane said. She sat the lamp on the table beside the bed and held Iona, rocking her as if she were a child.

"Was it an omen?" Iona asked, her eyes searching Thramane's face.

"There are no such things," Thramane said softly. "Will you pray to the Lord Jesus with me?"

"No. Not now. Not now, Thramane," Iona said impatiently.

"All right," Thramane said, smiling gently. "I'll leave you to yourself, Iona."

"No. Don't go," Iona begged, holding Thramane's hand. "Stay with me."

Thramane nodded and she lay down beside Iona, silently praying.

The moon was screened over by sheets of cloud, the night air cold. Iona lay awake long hours, recalling the dream, trying to put it down to foolishness. Still she could not sleep—that face! That dream must not come again.

Thramane slept peacefully beside her, her long white hair spread out across the pillow. The moon which had shown faintly through the thin layer of clouds had now been swallowed up by gathering gray thunderheads. Iona rose and went out into the garden, unable to sleep.

She stood alone, arms crossed against the cold, watching the dark forms of the trees torn by the rising wind. Clouds slipped past and the first few drops of rain spattered Iona's face.

A horse nickered in the stables and she turned

her head that way. Then again it nickered, more unhappily. Placidus, probably. The horse was old, no longer entirely sound.

She walked the winding garden path, picking her way through the deep night. Again the horse whinnied—but loudly, followed by a muffled thud.

Iona clutched her nightdress to her and hurried toward the stable, circling the house. The wind was much stronger now, black tumultuous clouds twisted past. A sheet of rain curtained the far hills, moving swiftly toward her.

She splashed across the already muddy yard and swung open the stable door. Placidus!

The big horse was down flat on the stable floor, unmoving. Iona moved to him and put a hand to his warm shoulder, withdrawing it quickly.

Blood. His shoulder was smeared with warm blood, the floor of the stable pooled with it. She reached for the lantern hanging near the door, realized she had no way to light it, and squatted down next to Placidus who was still, dead.

"What could have ... ?" A terrible scream pierced the night.

Her head swung around, her heart pounding.

Someone was at the house. *Graculus*. She thought first of him. Shaken, blood coating her hands, Iona opened the door and slipped out into the terrible night. Lightning arced overhead, the cannonading thunder rolled down the long valleys.

There was no light in the house, no movement. Hesitantly she moved across the yard, her bare feet churning up the oozing mud.

She heard then a clattering, a thud, a scraping sound, and she pressed herself against the cold wall of the house, the rain in her face, dress soaked through.

She stood a moment longer, eyes searching the yard for shadows, movement. There was nothing at all but the black night, the driving rain, an occasional, heart-stopping peal of thunder.

Iona found her way to the door. The latch had been slipped and she moved inside cautiously.

Colonus. She must wake Colonus.

Carefully she opened the door to his room, then withdrew, horror-struck. It was black in the house, ominously so, yet she could see the two figures well enough. Colonus and Eugenia intertwined in death lay on the floor, bedclothes wrapped crazily around them. A dark puddle ran out across the marble of the floor.

Thramane! She ran back toward her own room, heart in her throat, lungs dry, tight. The door to her room was open.

She lay on the bed, peacefully sleeping. Yet as Iona moved toward her, she knew Thramane would sleep a long while, hopefully in the arms of her God. The faithful woman was dead, stabbed unmercifully by many blades.

Did they think it was Iona they killed? Thramane lying on her bed, features masked by the black night, may have been mistaken for Iona . . . yet who wished to kill Iona herself now?

Again Graculus entered her thoughts; yet he owed her a favor and had never seemed hostile toward her. There was no reason. None at all.

Slowly Iona got to her knees, slowly clasped her hands as she had seen Thramane do. She bowed her head.

"If there is a God whose son is named Christ, take this good woman into your home in heaven. She harmed no one her life long, and was filled with love."

Unsteadily she stood, dazed for the moment. It occurred to her starkly, abruptly, that they might still be in the house, or encircling it, looking for her. She snatched up her cloak, and with one last, terrified, loving glance at Thramane, Iona darted from the room, entering the garden again where the sounds and swirling opacity of the night covered all movement.

She ran. She could not say how long, how far. She ran until her feet were torn by stone and bramble, her legs leaden. Then she found a tiny hollow at the base of a mammoth oak tree where the roots had spread over a boulder, and dragging herself into it, exhausted, Iona slept.

It had rained for three days and it rained still. There was a knock at the side door and the old woman stood, grasping her cane in her crippled hand. The only servant was off for the night, tending the birth of a grandchild.

Sophia opened the door and the girl tumbled in. Soaked through, hair tangled, she seemed a storm-swept sparrow blown into her apartment. She blinked twice and then recognition came, suddenly.

"Iona!" she gasped.

Iona had struggled to her knees and with Sophia's ringed hand around her arm, she came to her unsteady feet. "It is so cold out. Cold," Iona murmured.

"But, child . . . !" Sophia swung the door shut

and locked it tight, stripping off Iona's tattered, sodden dress, bundling her in towels.

"I'm so tired, so tired," Iona said, her eyes closed, lips barely parting.

Sophia forced her to drink warm goat's milk as she dried the girl's long, matted hair, and her feet which were torn, marked with ugly bruises.

"Someone came to the country house . . . they murdered everyone. Even Placidus . . . even a noble, harmless animal." Iona sat up, her eyes suddenly wide, startled. "I must find Marcus Atreus! He will know what to do." She sagged back once more. "He will take care of me."

Sophia could not look at Iona. Her eyes must have revealed the secret, however, for Iona, who had been studying Sophia's long face, suddenly blanched and stiffened. A terrible shiver ran through her body. The cold she thought had been left behind, outdoors, clambered up her spine and pummeled her brain with certain knowledge.

The dream.

"Marcus Atreus!" she demanded of Sophia who could not lie, could not speak. "Marcus Atreus?"

Then Iona closed her eyes and leaned back, the cup of milk spilling from her hand. She felt the world suddenly going dim, collapsing upon itself. She had run to him, her last hope in life. Yet she had feared it, known it, refused to accept it.

The dream had not lied. The attack on the country house was only a final extinguishing, the smothering of all that had belonged to Marcus Atreus—the end of the battle, the mopping-up, not its climax.

He could not be dead; she would not allow it! She would not accept it. They could not make her accept it, and if she would not, then he was *not* dead!

Sophia's eyes were soft and kind as Iona's met them. Iona started to speak but could not. She tasted a single tear as it spilled down her cheek and trickled across her lips. Her lips tried not to tremble, a trembling which she fought, to which she would not surrender. But it engulfed her mouth, then her shoulders and she cried, the strength going out of her entirely.

She felt Sophia's arms around her, tasted more tears, felt her heart go stale, shrivel and convulse. Then, suddenly, there were no tears. No convulsions. She sat rigidly, eyes fixed on the wall opposite. She cried no more, felt neither cold nor pain. Only the tiny seed of knowledge which grew within, growing stronger with each moment. He was dead.

She believed it.

How could it be different? How could life's grand sweep alter so much? Fate's pen had so dictated. There may be moments of joy, days of respite. Days the sun shined through the trees, mottling the streams, the fragrance of new grass drifting through the summer hours. Yet joy would ultimately be snatched from her, death parting her from it. It could be no different. Not in this life, this world.

He was dead; she believed it.

Iona's hands slowly clasped and she spoke, aloud, "My lord, Jesus. Take Marcus Atreus to you. He was just, honest, strong, loving. He did not know Christian ways, yet he persecuted no one, helped many . . ."

Her voice fell off and Sophia stood wonderingly,

watching the tall, dark-eyed girl whose face had suddenly gone immobile, whose heart had faltered, lost its will. There was no fire in those eyes, no will to continue.

"Iona?"

She only sat, hair in damp disarray, eyes fixed, mouth set. He was dead; she believed it.

Outside the wind continued to rage, the rain closing around Rome, darkening it like a veil drawn before the world.

Chapter Twenty-Seven

She stood alone at the bow as the merchant ship cut through the cold fog, dipping and rolling on the sea. The mate nudged the helmsman and asked, "Who is that?"

The helmsman blinked, stroked his short white beard and looked toward the dark-haired woman forward. He shrugged.

"She came on board in the middle of the night. The captain himself escorted her. I heard she was the heir of one Marcus Atreus."

"She dresses well, like an aristocrat," the mate said in a low voice. "But she doesn't look Roman —I heard her speak once. She has a British accent."

"Then she's headed home," the helmsman commented. Then he offered some advice. "Don't be so curious. There's many people going into Rome silently now, many leaving under guard or behind the cloak of night. Our responsibility's this vessel. Whatever that woman's business is, it's none of ours."

They made first landfall at a small port called Troews, in the land of the Belgae on the south coast of Britain. Even there, in this tiny coastal village, there was a Roman garrison quartered and soldiers patrolling the streets at night.

"Can a horse be purchased here?" Iona asked the surprised, heavily-bearded captain.

"A horse, ma'am? We've only stopped for fresh water and provisions. Tomorrow will find us up the Tamesis to Londinium."

"I have gold," Iona said.

"Yes. I know you have, and I have been instructed to give you what you wish, yet I do not think it wise." He calculated Iona's determination. Her dark eyes were vaguely weary, sure. "When the men go to bring water, I'll see that they hire a good riding horse," he agreed hesitantly.

She waited, not moving from the rail, watching the sun rise, flushing the sea incarnadine, bringing the emerald green hills above and beyond the rising sea bluffs to life. Gulls wheeled across the sky, creating words of freedom which only secret, lonely watchers could read.

Before the day was an hour old Iona was away from Troews, riding free toward home. Home. Viron. Was there a home, an Iceni nation? She avoided the villages and towns, riding the long vales and wooded hills.

When she did happen on a village the scene was always similar—poverty, inactivity. She never saw a weapon, seldom a horse. Where were the wild free Celts she recalled? They stood facing the southern oceans, lances in hands, dead and buried as Athair had been.

She walked frequently, keeping the horse fresh.

A long-legged, intelligent-looking sorrel with a white splash on its forehead, it would hardly have made a war horse, yet he was a swift runner, smoothly gaited.

Her breath caught. From the knoll where she had ridden at sunset she saw a river winding sinuously through the deep oaks below. It was Killdeer Stream, the ancient boundary, and beyond Killdeer she could see the smoke of scattered fires rising into the deepening blue of the evening sky. Viron.

Suddenly she balked. To go there! It was an idea which frightened her. Who, after all, was there? There would be a few old faces, weary faces like those in the other villages she had passed.

And she who had failed them as queen, as their war leader. Perhaps she had not failed them—they lived still, Roman vassals. She could turn, ride away, run . . . run where? To Rome where she was wanted as a murderess, where nothing was left, or onward to Viron where the dead past, an empty future lay?

She rode on, now crossing the empty fields where men had died valiantly for a losing cause. She sat in the alder woods, recreating the last battles morbidly. There had Throg's infantry been placed, there Dagda's men. There Breyton . . . .

Her eyes misted at the distant memory.

There the dais of Marcus Atreus. She broke into tears. She had loved them both, Celt and Roman. Equally, in different ways. Breyton had been a man for her youth, Marcus the man of her adulthood, both strong, both loving her greatly in return, she had no doubt.

Now dead. All of them.

She rode on through the gathering darkness, finding the road to Viron. There were no bulwarks, no traps or fortifications. All of that had been pulled down, buried, pushed aside. A single, wide road rose off the plains and wound to what had been the high gate and was now only a break in a low fence which could hardly keep a goat in.

She rode into the village, the village of her fathers, surveying it closely. Only a scattered gathering of small, dirty huts. The cattle pen had been moved—in it were a few sickly cows, no more than there had been in the last days of siege.

Iona stopped an old woman and asked her, "Who is your king?"

The old woman shrank from the rider who appeared to be a Roman noblewoman.

"The Emperor Nero, my lady," the old crone said with a bow.

"The Iceni king!"

"Prasutag, my lady. King Prasutag." She leveled a gnarled finger. "That is his hut, my lady."

Iona turned her horse toward the poor hut and the old woman watched after her a moment, dim recognition working in her mind.

Prasutag sat wearily at his table, studying the documents before him by the firelight: quotas assigned by the Roman governor. There were to few cattle, too little bread, as always. They had not bothered to mention iron, as expected. They needed iron for the wheel rims, the hubs, the smelter, but the Romans denied them iron as a matter of course, as they denied bronze. All implements were to be made of wood and only wood, yet even oak broke, splintering under light use. The people had been forced to dig the new well with wooden paddles. But, Prasutag reflected hopefully, Governor Suetonius Paulinus had not denied the request, only failed to respond to it. Perhaps it was undergoing further consideration. . . .

The fire caught a gust of breeze and flared up slightly, and the eyes of Prasutag flickered to the open door of his hut. A woman stood there, a Roman—

"No! It cannot be."

"It can be," Iona replied. "It is I, Prasutag. I apologize for—"

"You will apologize to me for nothing," Prasutag said, rising. "Ever. This seems a dream." He ran a hand across his short, curly hair, smiling. His features were still soft, perhaps heavier now; there was an incredible weariness in his eyes. "You must tell me how you've come to be here . . . what has happened?"

"No, let us not speak of it," Iona replied. "I walked a winding road, met friends and enemies alike. I am only happy to see you now, to be home. I want to stay here, in Viron, finish my life where it was begun—if that is possible, if the Romans will allow it."

"And that is why you have come to see me this evening?" Prasutag asked. "So that I may inquire for you?"

"Yes, certainly."

"I see." She was still lovely in the firelight. Her eyes sparkled. All humor had not been extinguished there, nor all love. Prasutag stepped forward a pace, then caught himself. He longed only to embrace her, had always longed for only that.

"I will immediately make inquiries, Iona," he told her, returning to his desk. She smiled, nodded and turned away, her back straight, her hips fluid. A sudden desperation overcame the shyness of Prasutag and he blurted out, "I love you, Iona. I have always loved you."

"Yes," she replied, turning back her glance for only a moment. "I know that, dear Prasutag."

She knew it. Prasutag watched the door close, then he stood himself and went to the door. The air was cool; Iona was nowhere to be seen.

She knew that he loved her—he asked himself if that meant there was hope yet for him, after all this time! His heart beat rapidly, like a young boy's. Perhaps, he reflected more soberly, it meant there was no hope. If she had always known it, yet discouraged him. . . . He was perpetually shy, perhaps that was why he had never married. Yet there was only one way now to discover the truth, to have her, if it were possible. Shyness must be beat down to dust, reticence overcome.

"I love you still, Iona," he said to the darkness. Then, he turned and hastened to his desk, drawing a fresh page of parchment from the bin at hand, composing his letter to Suetonius Paulinus.

Iona arose early, walking from the unmarried women's hut while the sun still lay dormant behind a cold bank of eastern fog. She walked through the compound, recognizing here and there a face, older, marked with time and concern. She spoke with no one.

Beyond, the woods were silent, dew still glazed the grass beneath the oaks, the stream rushed past as if it were an immortal thing, appearing for all of time's slow unreeling to be exactly the same. Yet the waters of her youth had flowed into the sea years ago, being swallowed up by its vastness.

She came suddenly upon it, the old burial ground of kings where Athair, his grave unmarked, still stood watching the southern coast.

"Put down your lance, Father," Iona whispered. "Let your bones rest—it is all done. All done."

The shrine to the god Cernunnos had been toppled and the head of this horned god, protector of her nation, was pocked by time's torment. A single, withered wreath lay there.

She followed the silver river to the low bluffs beyond. Almost without thinking, she found the old path which she took to the summit. The ancient oak was there, but it had seen its time and the branches were dead wood; it tilted heavily toward the sea. She searched minutely for the owl which seemed forever perched there, but could not find it.

It too had flown. The river flowed still into the sea, far distant. And near it Londinium sprawled, a mammoth reminder of the Roman domination.

And now she knew where the seas led, as Thrueldan had. She knew that the Romans would not be stopped or slowed. She knew; and it was a desperate knowledge which could not be gainsaid or suppressed.

The people survived. The nation, the land. Yet never again would they flourish. The glory of the Celts, the love, the happiness, would not again be encountered on this earth. Now, when one met a Celt one found a dour face, a deeply sorrowful soul. On this earth. . . .

Iona went to her knees and prayed. She prayed against war, domination by one people of another, blood which ran to no end, to no purpose, but passed into time like the waters of the river; all swallowed by the sea, an eternal, unknowable sea which rolled endlessly on.

Chapter Twenty-Eight

They rode together to Londinium, to the mansion of Suetonius Paulinus, the governor of all Brittania. The dark-eyed woman and this sad-faced king of the Iceni.

Londinium was a replica, in miniature, of Rome. One saw beggars in the streets, yet they were all Celts. Raggedly dressed people—Iona's people—surviving only by the whim of the empire.

"It is a poor nation," Iona commented. She had hardly spoken since leaving Viron and Prasutag turned toward her.

"It is worst in the cities," he told her. "The governor assures me that this poverty will be alleviated."

"Promises from Rome," she commented dryly.

"Suetonius Paulinus is an honest man, Iona. Surely you must have met some honest Romans."

He was a young man still, this governor, and he

nodded politely to Iona, taking Prasutag's hand firmly. "What is it you need, Prasutag? Your letter was vague enough to make one believe it had been contrived so."

"Probably it is only my poor Latin that caused it to seem so, Excellency."

"It concerned . . ." Paulinus began, picking up the letter which lay on his table, "a man who wishes to marry—but this is in your province, King Prasutag. We do not have a vested interest in marriages or the like."

"It may concern you," Prasutag clarified, "concerning as it does the line of succession."

"Line of . . . you, Prasutag!" Paulinus laughed and nodded approval, looking from Iona to Prasutag and back. "I see. You have chosen your queen at last."

"At last."

"There are a few matters, as you have divined," the governor agreed. "The oath of loyalty must be administered. The same oath you took, I dare say. Do you object?" he asked Iona.

"I will swear loyalty to the Roman Empire," Iona said softly.

"Of course that is only a matter of formality," Paulinus smiled. "What else can you be but loyal—though I am sure your allegiance is as true as Prasutag's own," he added hastily.

"Of course," Iona answered.

"Then—that is that," Paulinus answered.

"There is also the matter of iron, sir," Prasutag added. "Without it—"

"That I can do nothing about," Paulinus said, waving his hands. "There is still fear in Rome that iron may be forged into weapons."

"Yet without it—"

"I am sorry, King Prasutag," Paulinus said, closing the subject.

"Also, it pains me to mention," Prasutag went on, "we are still having occasions when high-ranking officers of your own staff demand and at times extort the personal possessions of our chiefs."

"Nonsense."

"Sir," Prasutag began again, "I beg you—"

"I will look into it," Paulinus said, cutting off the unpleasant subject. "For now," he added, rising, "let us administer the oath to your future wife. Are you ready?"

"I am ready," Iona said without inflection.

The oath was laborious, involved, yet Iona swore to each clause and paragraph, vowing never to raise insurrection, or oppose direct orders from the Roman Emperor, the governor of Britannia, his magistrates and officers.

Finally it had been done and Paulinus, smiling, shook the hand of Prasutag again. Turning to Iona, he said, "I understand that a queen among the Celts chooses her own name—have you yet decided what you shall be called?"

"Yes, I have. I shall be called Boudicca."

Prasutag blanched and turned startled eyes to Paulinus, yet the governor seemed calm. He rolled the name around on his tongue, pursing his lips in thought.

"There was a Queen Boudicca of the Iceni."

"Yes, sir."

"She was a warrior, that one. I pray that you will not be such a queen," Paulinus joked.

"I will not," Iona answered. "Those were earlier times, an earlier queen."

They rode silently, hurriedly from Londinium, their business completed. Prasutag drew up his horse suddenly as they reached the outskirts of town.

"That was a dangerous move, Iona," he said seriously.

"I have chosen my name," she told him. "Now when Queen Boudicca is mentioned, it shall not raise war spectres, but only vague memories of your new wife."

"Yes, you may be right," he agreed. Yet his eyes were worried, deeply so. "I love you, my Iona. I want only to protect you—you must promise me that you will do nothing so foolhardy again."

"I do promise it, Prasutag," she told him. Promise it and repromise. What did he fear? That she would take up arms? Perhaps wooden spears and wooden swords against the ever increasing might of British Rome? And to what end? War's only end was blood, war's cost the homeland, the youth of the nation . . . one does not attempt such a valorous enterprise twice in a lifetime. Not having once seen the result.

"I do promise."

They were passing through a small village on the perimeter of Londinium when Prasutag slowed his horse and then deliberately changed directions. Iona glanced up and saw why.

A group of Roman boys were gathered around a small, dirty, tow-headed Celt. They spat upon him, taunted him and yet he smiled back, following after them until finally they chased him off. He sat alone in the gutter until, eyes flashing he saw Prasutag and Iona.

"Get out, get away!" he shouted, scooping up a handful of mud from the gutter. He ran after them, throwing mud, stones, and sticks at them. In terrible Latin he shouted, "I am not a Celt! I am not a Celt!"

Prasutag's face was a mask. Iona put her hand on his arm and looked at him. He nodded slowly.

"That is Breyton—Dwan Karnash's son."

"And Dwan Karnash?"

"Dead two years. The boy suffered her loss."

She turned back to watch him. Bony, dirty, it wrung her heart to see the boy. When she thought of his father—proud, robust, fiercely independent.

He is ashamed, she thought. *He wishes to be a Roman.*

"There will never again be a Celtic nation," Iona said bleakly.

"Of course there will," Prasutag answered with conviction. "It is guaranteed in our truce—the very truce you negotiated. There will always be an Iceni nation. And as you yourself once said, one day the Romans will be gone, and Britain shall again be ours. We have simply to wait."

He is ashamed of being Celtic: a son of Breyton!

To watch the world alter in a rapid and inexorable way; to watch the youth turn sour, their hearts empty of hope and promise. . . . She turned to see Londinium once again, the highways built for the Roman war machines, the Tamesis crowded with Roman ships, the streets with lost, homeless Celts. Nothing was constant, certain. Nothing, except perhaps this smooth-faced, steady man beside her. Prasutag who could endure it, and therefore survive it.

She reached out a hand and gripped his arm tightly for a moment. He smiled back, touched, surprised by the display of affection.

He could endure. He could build upon ashes. He was not given to despair, but to endurance. There was much to be learned from a man like Prasutag. None of the past could be altered. Perhaps she, too, could learn to build upon ashes. To go on—to simply continue.

Axim was born in the spring of the year. A darkhaired, healthy girl with fine lashes and strong lungs which echoed across the compound when she was wet or needed the nourishment of her mother's breasts.

She was her father's pride and the smile on her mother's lips. She babbled like a magpie, studying all that surrounded her with clear, intelligent eyes. Iona taught her Celtic for her first tongue.

"She would be better served learning her Latin," Prasutag commented as they sat on the steps to their hut, watching the child play. "Our language is dying out—it is forbidden in the cities."

"The more reason to teach it," Iona said. She had her arms wrapped around her knees, watching with the wonder of a child herself as Axim discovered tiny miracles everywhere she probed.

"To have waited so long," Prasutag said meditatively. "For you, for Axim. You have no idea what happiness you have brought me, Iona." He took her hand pensively, kissing it lightly.

"Have I made you happy?" Iona asked.

"More than I can tell you."

"And Axim?"

"She is my life," Prasutag said.

"Is there room for still more happiness in your world?" she asked him.

"I do not understand. . . ." He studied her eyes, then caught the restrained smile in them, on her lips, and he understood. He held her closely, stroking her hair, and after a moment Axim came up to them, throwing her tiny arms around them both.

Her sister was born in the fall, and Iona called her Lania, after her grandmother.

For Iona it was a happy time of life, as it was for Prasutag. Yet on many evenings—far too many—she found her husband, the king of her nation, sitting up by the firelight, writing petitions to Nero, to Suetonius Paulinus. Prasutag, who had never appeared vigorous, was now exhausted, his eyes hollow, appearing shrunken in the firelight.

She stepped up behind him, kissed his neck lightly, and rubbed his shoulders.

"Are the babies asleep?" he asked.

"Asleep. Happy. At peace."

"Do I not appear at peace?" he asked, turning a quarter toward his wife, pretending a smile.

"No."

"To rule with absolute power must be awesome in the responsibility it carries," Prasutag supposed. "Yet to govern without authority, without the ability to lead, to supply even bread for their mouths without a nod of approval from Rome. . . . It is insufferable at times, Iona."

"Yet you suffer it."

"Yes. I suffer it—what else can I do?"

"There has been another incident," Iona guessed.

"Another. And another. A cattle herder burned out of his home by garrisoned Roman troops. The property of Fereguard taken upon his death—his wife left with nothing. It goes on."

"We have the protection of the treaties!" Iona said hotly, her anger flaring briefly. She watched the fire, feeling the same frustration Prasutag now did, the same sense of failure. It was her own hand which had signed those treaties. "Our vows have been kept."

"And what can we do, Iona?" Prasutag asked. He crumpled a petition and threw it into the fire. Standing, his arm around Iona, they watched it burn to embers.

She slept uneasily. A tormenting dream had troubled her. Athair, naked before the fire, stood accusingly. He spoke, yet the voice was not his. "The people, Iona," her father had said. "The people must survive."

"Your time is gone," she had whispered back, and the fire had consumed him as rapidly as it had the petition. Briefly Breyton appeared—swaggering, laughing wildly, head thrown back, the wind in his long blond hair, a sword singing over his head—and behind him came the armies of Iona, each of them appearing like young Breyton and all armed with identical wooden swords which they beat futilely against the towering iron-taloned eagle.

Iona awoke suddenly, her heart pounding, and she went to the girls' room. They slept quietly, Axim's now long hair curled back over her bare back. The baby gnawed contentedly on her fist. Iona covered them and walked to the door, studying the distant stars spread out across the silky night. She wished to frame a question, but could not find the words. What had once seemed a promise, however mysterious, written across the night sky, now seemed only a banner of mockery.

They endured. The Celtic nation endured.

"Is it enough?" she asked silently. Then, frightened by her own words, she rushed into her hut and slipped into Prasutag's bed.

Chapter Twenty-Nine

Beltaine came and passed without being noted or celebrated. The long winter was hard, the crops suffered, yet they passed the year as they had the many lean years before.

It was the year that Lania got her first horse to ride, the year of her sixth birthday that Kowlter returned.

He appeared suddenly in the door of Prasutag's hut, and it was Iona who first saw him. She was shocked at the appearance of her old adversary, astonished that he should arrive at their door, at Viron for any reason.

"Kowlter," she said, greeting him with the esteem she reserved for a Celtic king, enemy or not.

He stood perplexed, studying this tall woman with eyes which watered and seemed at times unfocused. He was hunched forward, leaning heavily on a stave. Finally it came to him, and he laughed

in a crackling voice. This woman, Prasutag's wife
—the silver in her dark hair had put him off at first,
yet now he knew her.

"Iona! The Queen Boudicca!"

"It is I—the child-queen," she said, recalling
that he had called her that. "Prasutag is riding with
his daughters."

"Ah," Kowlter waved a weary hand and sagged
to a seat. "I will wait. Yet you—" he said, his eyes
brightening, "perhaps it is you I should be speaking to." He rose, dragging a foot as he drew nearer,
his jaw slack, breath heavy.

"Not me," Iona turned her back, waving her
hand. "I do not rule, or decide, or grant. I am the
wife of Prasutag. Whatever it is, you must speak to
him."

"Prasutag is a soft man."

"He rules well."

"He rules well; he does not snap at his master's
hand."

"He who snaps at the Roman hand will be throttled by it."

"You speak from experience."

"I do," Iona answered. The old warlord had fire
in him still, yet it was foolish to speak the way he
did now. "What is it you wish to talk to my husband about?" she asked.

He bent even nearer and smiled, nearly toothlessly. "I wish to speak of war," Kowlter growled.
"Of a Celtic League."

"To Prasutag?" she laughed. "To us?"

"It was you who proposed it, Iona."

"I proposed it when it was necessary; now it is
folly. There is a difference."

"Yes, and there is a difference between dying in

battle and being starved to death, between honor and disgrace."

"That is the way the Coritani feel; it is not the way the Iceni feel. We will endure—the Romans will leave one day."

"When we are all dead!" Kowlter shouted. "I will wait and speak to the *king*," he said sourly.

"You may as well go out and speak to the trees, Kowlter. There will never be another Iceni war. We have signed our treaties."

"And the Romans theirs—they mean nothing to Paulinus!"

"I have seen my land bathed in blood," Iona said, more loudly than she intended. "I will not see it again!"

"But you will," Kowlter said, hobbling toward the door. "You will see it. It is inevitable. But first you will watch your people starve, struggle, suffer —then you will take up arms again, Queen Boudicca! But it will be too late."

She told Prasutag what Kowlter had suggested and he laughed, yet there was a hollow ring to it. She knew what was worrying Prasutag; it had worried her as well. If one Celtic nation were to take up arms, it could bring destruction to all.

"He is old," Iona told her husband, "but I do not think him mad. Kowlter knows that there is no chance at all without an alliance. He was bitter, only testing the waters."

"Yes," Prasutag agreed. He ran his fingers through his thinning, gray hair. "That is all. There is nothing to it. Come, Iona," he said, "let us go to bed."

Arms around each other they walked to their

bedroom. Iona suddenly felt Prasutag stiffen, sag so that she had to hold him up. He clutched his chest, then smiled weakly.

"It is nothing."

"No," she replied, smiling in return. Kowlter meant nothing, the stabbing pain in Prasutag's chest meant nothing.

Iona slept near to him, listening to the hesitant rise and fall of Prasutag's chest. She closed her eyes, surprised that she had to blink away a tear. Then Iona slept, next to this good man, allowing no dream to interrupt the solitude of night.

Prasutag continued to live vigorously, yet his body, more insistently with each passing year, commanded that he slow himself. He no longer could ride with the girls, or hunt boar. He knew himself that his time was short.

He was a Celtic king, and he did not fear dying. He feared only for his family's well-being. It preyed constantly on his mind.

"Their fortune must be preserved," Prasutag told Iona. They lay together in the darkness.

"You do not trust Paulinus entirely?"

"I trust him—yet there are constant incidents. The villages are looted ... it must not happen."

"It will not happen," Iona said, touching his hand. Yet she knew no words of hers could erase the worry. Without their family wealth the girls might be forced one day to serve the Romans themselves as maids or laundresses, or worse, being mocked and abused.

"Should we hold a celebration at Samhain this year?" Prasutag asked. "Perhaps the girls would like it. They are older now, they should meet boys of their own ages—Celtic boys."

"Samhain is a long time away," Iona said, yawning slightly.

"We must plan ahead . . . we haven't celebrated it properly for so many years. Not since before the Romans came," he said, turning to her in the darkness. "Remember the last Samhain before you left?"

"Yes—the songs, the contests—"

"Breyton won the chariot race."

"Yes." Iona smiled and put her arm around Prasutag, rumpling his hair as they lay close together in the darkness. "But what would the Romans think of a gathering of the tribes, Prasutag?"

"That it was a conspiracy. A Celtic League forming—they are aware of Kowlter's rabblerousing."

"There can be no Samhain."

"No." Prasutag was silent in the night for a long while. "Yet it would be—"

"Be what?"

Iona waited, but he did not answer. He had fallen asleep. She removed her arm slowly, surprised at his weight. Then she saw the starlight in his open eyes.

"Prasutag?"

He did not answer, and she lay her head on his bare chest, her tears dampening his unmoving flesh.

Prasutag was buried in the grove of kings in the early morning when the sun lit the deep copse with golden highlights.

Lania was brave, or tried to be, but she was just fourteen, and as the earth was heaped over the grave, she burst into shuddering tears, leaning her head against Iona's shoulder. Axim looked around helplessly, then walked swiftly away, afraid that she too would cry.

Iona did not cry, not then, but she stood silently watching the burial, recalling that of Athair, those of so many others. Kings recalled only in myth lay buried there, a long line of queens going back to antiquity, to the roots of the Celtic people. All dust.... She held Lania tightly and guided her back to the house where they shared a breakfast and their happy memories of the good man, the king who had been husband and father.

Later, when she went through Prasutag's effects she found everything perfectly ordered, divided, accounted for. He was not a man to leave matters to chance, not Prasutag. He had never fallen into the trap of believing himself immortal.

His horses, oxen, gold and silver were accounted to the last tick. And neatly prepared was a last will which Iona read carefully. Fearful of being plundered, he had left his estate divided evenly in two. One half would go to his daughters; the other half to Nero.

The will was addressed to Suetonius Paulinus, and Iona planned to deliver it herself.

It was already going to dusk as she walked toward the door of the hut. Axim sat silently near the well, plucking the petals from a flower. Iona went to sit beside her, yet neither of them could find words.

It was a good plan, she thought. Whoever would loot Prasutag's wealth would be stealing also from Nero.

The sun died slowly. The cooking fires were lighted all across Viron. Below, the long valleys were flooded with reddish light. The shadows stretched out toward them and nightbirds took to silent flight. Iona put her arm around Axim. The girl looked up with damp, dark eyes and managed a dim smile.

Then she nodded and Iona held her closely for a moment. Together they walked back to the hut which was a little more empty now, a little colder.

Chapter Thirty

When they came it was far from expected. Yet one day Iona looked up to see a column of Roman soldiers in full armor riding the road through Viron's gates. Dogs yapped and the Iceni women gathered their children and scurried away. They came directly for Iona's hut where she, Axim, and Lania had been planting a spring garden.

Iona stepped forward, soiled hands on her hips, a strand of graying hair loose across her eyes.

They had a Celtic interpreter with them, a spare, blond young man who dressed in a gold embroidered toga and wore rings on nearly every finger of his narrow hands. His teeth were widely gapped, his manner surly.

"Ask them, Brittanius!"

The man who spoke was a Roman field grade officer. The Celt addressed as Brittanius nodded and turned haughtily toward Iona—and it was only then, as the light profiled his face, tugging a memory, that Iona knew who this Brittanius was.

Breyton was his rightful name! The son of a Celtic warlord, a tormented boy who would be . . . who had become, a Roman.

"Woman—we are looking for the Iceni queen, Boudicca," Brittanius said.

"Boudicca." Iona stood silently a moment, transfixed by this man, this sycophant, this son of the greatest of the warriors her tribe had produced. He, too, had wanted to become a Roman. . . .

"Woman!" Brittanius snapped.

"I am Boudicca," she answered in Celtic.

"This is Boudicca, sir," Brittanius translated.

The Roman's eyes arced with amusement. He smiled and turned to a lieutenant. "The old one is Boudicca. A queen!"

He looked at her dress, soiled with the garden work, her gray-streaked dark hair which was tied loosely back, and shook his head.

"Tell her why we have come," he said.

"Boudicca—" Brittanius began.

"*Queen* Boudicca," Iona interrupted. "I am the queen of the Iceni nation. Of your nation. I am your queen, young man."

"Hardly," Brittanius muttered. His eyes had shifted to Axim and to Lania who stood apart a little ways, their heads held proudly.

"Speak to her!" the officer, now clearly irritated, commanded.

"Yes . . . yes," Brittanius said hurriedly. "Woman, we have an order in our possession that the properties and assets of the late King Prasutag be confiscated by the Roman governor until a legal disposition of such properties can be adjudged." Iona did not respond, and after a long moment Brittanius asked hotly, "Did you hear, woman?"

"I heard. Excuse me. My thoughts were with your father, your mother. Your father was a great warrior, a strong man. Your mother a proud lioness. It is mysterious—this life. To think that a jackal could be whelped out of such a union."

Brittanius flushed deeply, the cords of his neck bulging. The Roman officer was obviously impatient and he demanded, "What did she say?"

"She claims not to understand," Brittanius lied.

"Make the old wench understand," the Roman shouted. "Make her understand that this town shall be burned, her bones broken, her worthless hide stretched on the wall. Now, see if she understands that!"

"I understand," Iona said, and her Latin was impeccable as she spoke. "Now see if this profiteer understands that Prasutag's wealth has been willed to the emperor, Nero. See if this great warrior understands that Suetonius Paulinus has been given a letter in Prasutag's hand attesting to this."

The Roman blanched, trembled with anger and began to speak, but Iona interjected, again speaking in flawless Latin, though her eyes were fixed on Brittanius, "See if this Roman officer who would have shamed Julius Caesar, and many great Roman generals after him, has the courage to face an old woman in single combat with lances."

Brittanius could not speak; the Roman laughed but there was a hollow ring to it. A wooden-faced lieutenant behind his commander broke momentarily into a grin.

"You"—the stubby finger of the Roman commander fell on Iona—"you have sealed your fate." Then, wrenching his horse's head back on the reins, he spun the animal and galloped from the yard, his column following.

Iona watched, hands on hips. The dust settled over them as the last horse swept through the gate. Brittanius remained behind, immobilized.

"His name is Tacitus, and he is a dangerous man," Brittanius said quietly. "He will make you pay. And heavily. He is angered because Paulinus will know of it. Because he must, he will silence you. Perhaps under the pretense of smothering an uprising."

"Does it matter to you, *Breyton?*"

"Does it? I do not know. My life has left me unable to make moral decisions, to assess even my own values. I only know I do not like to be cold, to go hungry, to be despised and assaulted as I was." He straightened. "Well," Brittanius went on, his momentarily meditative mood passing, "you must consider it seriously. I can tell you one thing— Suetonius Paulinus is not in Britain; he has gone to Rome and will not be back for many months."

Iona's face must have shown her surprise at learning this. If Tacitus were to confiscate Prasutag's property and then destroy Viron as he had threatened, the governor might never know of it. Not if the action were camouflaged as a reprisal against a Celtic uprising.

"It may be costly," Brittanius said somberly, "this indiscretion of yours. Better at times to swallow your tongue, my queen."

"And become as Roman as possible."

"Yes. As Roman as possible, my queen," Brittanius said. "That is the only way to survive. For the rest, those who cannot become Roman, the future is already written in stone."

Then Brittanius turned, without a farewell, and

departed, riding toward Londinium, a bitter, lonely young man.

"Who was that scoundrel, Mother?" Axim asked, stepping up beside Iona.

"The son of a great Celt," Iona responded thoughtfully.

"He is as pompous as any man I've met," Lania offered, "and very foolish."

"Pompous. And very foolish; yet he is right in one respect. It is better at times to swallow pride. I am afraid that I have challenged Rome once again. At the wrong time, in the wrong way."

They ate a silent meal that evening. Iona barely touched her own food. She watched the soft faces of her daughters, their eyes which were already burdened with worry. She felt a sudden amazement at a simple fact: she was now the mother of girls who should be preparing for their own lives. It seemed only a blink of the eye since Iona herself had been a child, unconcerned with all about her, with the larger rivers, the currents of life which flowed as entire peoples sprang up, birthed, died in war. A lifetime was gone, yet she hardly felt the wiser, or older for that matter. The gray in her hair had crept there overnight, the wrinkles around her eyes, the tiny villains, had come as rapidly. Neither made her feel older; neither had touched her vigorous heart.

She feared only for the girls, as Prasutag had. She had heard that Belgae ships sailed daily now for the far island, to the west, where the Romans had not come.

Perhaps the girls could go there, though it wrenched Iona's heart to think of having them leave her. There they might be able to live as free

Celts, to marry good strong men, to have babies who might live out of slavery. It was something to ponder. . . .

She sat suddenly upright, her heart pounding. Iona had been half asleep, half awake with worry. She looked around her in the darkness. There was nothing there, no one. Crossing to the window she saw that the village slept peacefully, the high, brittle stars hung quietly against the deep night.

Nothing. She was growing foolish, she decided. Yet it had always been in the night that trouble came to her, sneaking upon her like a cowardly thief. She lay back on the cool bed, heart still palpitating. She closed her eyes tightly, as tightly as possible, not to shut out the light alone, but to shut out the darkness.

Iona slept a while, her thoughts, in sleep's raveled confusion, going to Rome, to Londinium, to distant seas which ran a crimson tide.

When she awoke again it was to a sharp crying sound. An owl was perched on the ledge of her window, its round yellow eyes fixed on Iona.

"You—" She smiled. "Can you still be alive, old owl? But you've awakened me . . ."

The cry sounded again and the owl winged rapidly away, leaving Iona with the certainty that no owl's hoot had awakened her. She slipped from the bed without dressing, moving to the door. Star-cast shadows marked the floor of the hut. A war lance hung near the cold fireplace, and Iona took it from its iron hooks, holding it low as she moved silently across the hut.

She went to the outer door. It was ajar! She put a palm to the heavy door and opened it slightly. There, sweating shoulders glistening in the feeble starlight, stood thirty horses, Roman horses, and from the darkness a cry, miserable, human, sounded.

Panicked, Iona's eyes swung back to the corner beds. Gone!

Axim and Lania both had been dragged from their beds. Prasutag's chest stood open, papers and small items scattered across the room.

Iona slammed open the door, a hot rage flaring up in her. She lunged through the door, and a beefy arm went around her throat.

"Stay where you are!" a low voice growled. But Iona wriggled free, stepped back for leverage and drove forward with her lance, taking the soldier just below the breastplate. He bellowed a painful curse and slumped to his knees, holding his abdomen as he screamed for help.

Already Iona was rushing across the yard, toward the corncrib where a lantern burned and a hysterical cry pierced the night. Iona stumbled on, heart racing wildly, mouth dry with the fury.

She burst through the door to the corncrib and they were there. Axim was pinned in the corner by a burly naked Roman. His head swiveled toward Iona and his eyes opened, his mouth sagging with silent pain as she drove her lance into his heart.

Lania, her dress ripped to shreds, cowered in the corner, three men around her, all drunken members of Tacitus's command. One lurched for his short sword, but he was too slow in his movement and Iona's lance arced down with a savage thrust, taking the man in the throat. He lunged toward her, hands scratching at her face before he collapsed in a heap, life draining from him.

"Get back!" Iona ordered the two who remained, half undressed, unarmed. They looked at her with challenge, then studied the cold fierceness in her eyes, the lance she still held low, the blood staining its point.

"All right," one grumbled, and he staggered backward.

"Go!" Iona shouted to Lania. "Run south, into the forest. As far as you can run. Help your sister. Run. Now!" Iona shouted as Lania paused to fasten her dress. "Before it's too late."

"Mother—" Axim stood, her eyes streaming tears, face dirty, scratched. She held her arms out; her lip trembled.

"Go!" Iona said as severely as possible. She longed to take the girl in her arms, to love her, but there was no time. "Get out of here!"

There was a small loading gate on the southern wall and they slipped through it, Axim crying, shaken, dazed.

Iona stood watching. The door closed with a clack. The soldiers, wobbly from wine, stood against the wall, their weapons stacked ten feet away.

The door behind Iona slammed open and Tacitus himself appeared, ten men with him. Iona did not move. She stood facing the prisoners, lance poised.

"Put that lance down, woman!" Tacitus commanded. His small mouth was tight, cruel. He glanced at the dead soldiers who lay against the corncrib floor.

"These men are criminals," Iona said, flashing a bloody glare at this Roman general. "I want them executed."

"Executed?" Tacitus said mildly.

"They are rapists, thieves, and deserving of death under law. Unless it is the law which condones these acts of pillage," she said, her words snapping off.

"They are soldiers in an enemy camp," Tacitus said, waving an arm.

"Enemy! We have signed treaties of peace. We are guaranteed an independent state under those treaties. And guaranteed the protection of Roman law. Once we fought a bloody war; once we were strong," Iona told him. "We put our weapons aside to buy peace for our people, to ensure their lives and well-being. This," she said angrily, eyes sparking, "this is treachery—it is criminal."

"Those treaties were signed very long ago," Tacitus said. He smiled, cocked his head and shrugged, taking a half-step forward. As he did his hand shot out and he tore the lance from Iona, breaking it over his knee.

"You have murdered my men. Now you shall learn about the law!" Tacitus shouted. His face was contorted terribly, his fists clenched tightly.

"Bring a rope," he ordered. He stepped forward again and tore the dress away from Iona's back. She stood proudly, eyes filled with contempt as the soldier returned with a rope which was thrown over a beam in the corncrib roof.

Her hands were tied roughly to the rope and the slack taken up so that she stood on tiptoes, her back exposed.

"This is the law, woman," Tacitus said. In his hand was a short-handled scourge. There were nine leather thongs attached to the handle, and knotted into each thong, balls of lead.

The lash fell and Iona's head exploded with painful color, the breath going out from her lungs in a hot gasp. The lash fell again, flaying her flesh. Rivulets of blood ran from her back down into her waistband. Again it fell. Again, and it seemed he would not stop until her back was broken, her flesh a lacerated, formless mass.

Again the scourge crackled through the air, followed by the tragic splitting sound. Iona kept her head up, and from the corner of her eye she saw a Roman soldier, his face pallid, sickened by it. It had gone beyond pain. Her body was a thought, a fiery empty expression of her mind.

The whip snapped again, and now she could hear Tacitus panting with the exertion as he put all of his strength into the savage beating.

Night swung into day. Iona was suspended by her wrists for a sad eternity. The sun collided with the moon, and beyond the cosmic explosion, the brilliant light, the heat of the collision, voices called softly, in chanting unison. Christians, Iceni, Roman voices—perhaps the voices of the gods. She could not understand their voices above the crackling of flame, yet it was cool in the forest, blue, silent and soft as he ran to meet her, fresh from the river where he had bathed. . . . He fell back in horror, studying her face, touching her back where small, crimson plumaged birds devoured her flesh.

It was cold. The night was purple and black. Clouds filled the interior of the corncrib. Eyes watched her. Iceni eyes.

Two children stood staring, wide-eyed. When she tried to speak a small gurgle emerged, and the children fled. Iona sank into darkness once again: a swimming, terrible black river where she drifted endlessly, eyes open to the night stars above her.

It was growing to golden dawn when the man came—a nameless, nearly faceless hulk of an Iceni who cut the ropes with an ancient two-handed sword. Then she was taken away, placed face down on a bed where she slept with a single dream.

Again and again her rescuer appeared in her mind's eye—that bulky Iceni with the great sword catching the light of dawn, his face set with angry purpose.

Chapter Thirty-One

Iona rested for three days in the house of the smith, Taws. She could not be rolled over, but the wife of Taws, a slender, black-eyed woman called Frawna treated her back with a cooling salve, and Iona, her arm draped to the floor, was able to write her letters.

There were many of them to be delivered by trusted hands; the two most important were to Lambar, the ancient Belgae king, requesting a ship be prepared for the youth and aged of the Iceni, with which to sail to the far island of Eire; the second letter was to Kowlter.

Taws lifted his heavy black eyebrows curiously as this second letter was sealed and handed to him. "Now we are, finally, to be allies of the Coritani?"

"Now," Iona answered. "Now that it is too late. Now when it makes no difference, Taws. We will die. Yet we will die as warriors, not as slaves. We will not be extinguished like vermin at the whim of Rome, crushed beneath their boots. Our fate, it has been said, is already written in stone.

"If the nation must perish, let us ensure that our personal fates be valorous."

"I still have my sword," the smith said. "Hidden all these years beneath the floor of my hut. But the others . . ."

"Fire your forge. Gather the plows and iron tools. Tear the rims from the wagon wheels, melt down the torques, the household iron. Beat our pots, axles, and jewelry into swords, Taws. Work your bellows with a vengeance, temper your steel well—it will be well tested."

"Yet without these implements," Taws commented, "there will be no life possible in Viron."

"There will be no Viron," Iona said slowly. "Time will destroy it. Those who wish to sail to the far island—let them go, let them live. Those who wish to follow me, let them follow. But Viron will never survive. It will lie buried in the mud and ash of time. And we with it," she added. Taws nodded, understanding that the time had now come—the end of Celtic time, the end of the nation.

"Yewen!" he shouted. "Where is that lazy apprentice of mine! Yewen, fire the forge!"

They massed at Tamden Knoll on the Ouse River. The pre-dawn mist shifted and rolled slowly past. Ranks of Celts, multitudes waited in the chill of morning, low fires dotting the rolling green of the velvet countryside.

"Now we are many," Kowlter said. Iona nodded. The old Coritani king wore an expression she did not recall—passive, exultant, a memory of the past mingled with a knowledge of the future. In a bronze-studded leather vest, helmet fixed, he seemed somehow younger, somehow ancient.

"My child-queen," he said, and without forewarning, he knelt and kissed her hand. "I apologize for my stubbornness, my rancor. Perhaps without my recalcitrance, my petty jealousy—"

"It could have ended no differently," Iona said. "It seems at times that history is well-ordered, decreed beforehand. We are pawns only, Kowlter, moving before the winds of eternity. Stand now. Let us begin the ending."

The vast Celtic armies swept southward, and before the Ninth Legion could be organized, the torch had been set to Camelot, or Camulodunum as the Romans called it. The fighting outside of Verulamium, the second city to be razed, was bloody, but brief, the Roman Ninth being crushed utterly beneath the unsuspected weight of the Celtic army, their tacticians outwitted at every turn by a Celtic commander who was well experienced in combat.

A force under the command of General Tacitus of the Ninth Legion was destroyed to the last man at Battersea Crossing as the combined Celtic forces pushed across the Tamesis toward the Roman capital at Londinium.

The inhabitants had fled before the approaching army, and it lay a ghost town as the torch was set. Londinium burned, and not an arch remained standing. Imperial Rome swayed, toppled, and was consumed by rising waves of fire.

It had gone dark across the land. The woman sat alone beneath a great, wide-spreading oak and watched as the golden sea of fire swept through the great city, as rising tongues of reddish flame sparked up hotly, filling the night-starred skies with showers of golden spark. As Londinium burned. As Rome burned.

Author's Note

The burning of London in 60 A.D. by the Iceni under Queen Boudicca was the last serious uprising against the Roman Empire in Britain.

Ireland was never occupied by the Roman forces, and Celtic life flourished there for many more centuries.

Boudicca, our Iona, rather than again suffer Roman capture, took poison and was buried secretly, perhaps in the grove of kings beside her father, where presumably she still stands, lance in hand, guarding her country against invasion from across the southern ocean.

E.W.

There are a lot more where this one came from!

ORDER your FREE catalog of ACE paperbacks here. We have hundreds of inexpensive books where this one came from priced from 75¢ to $2.50. Now you can read all the books you have always wanted to at tremendous savings. Order your *free* catalog of ACE paperbacks now.

ACE BOOKS • P.O. Box 690, Rockville Centre, N.Y. 11570

Don't Miss these Ace Romance Bestsellers!

☐ AGRIPPA'S DAUGHTER	Fast	#01175-6	$1.95

Haunting story of divided lands and divided passions.

☐ DANGEROUS OBSESSION	Peters	#75158-X	$2.25

Passionate novel by the bestselling author of SAVAGE SURRENDER.

☐ FALLON BLOOD	O'Neal	#22665-5	$2.50

A novel of history, adventure and passion in the New World.

☐ THE MASQUERS	Peters	#52102-9	$2.50

A love triangle sizzles with the heat of passion in the beautiful city of Venice.

☐ TENDER TORMENT		#80040	$1.95

A sweeping romantic saga in the Dangerous Obsession tradition.

☐ TO DISTANT SHORES	Gregory	#81465-4	$2.50

A compelling novel of exotic lands and dangerous romance.

☐ WILD VALLEY	Paul	#88965-4	$1.95

A sprawling novel of heartache and love in the northwestern frontier.

Available wherever paperbacks are sold or use this coupon.

---

ace books, Book Mailing Service
P.O. Box 690, Rockville Centre, N.Y. 11571

Please send me the titles checked above. I enclose $_____. Include 75¢ for postage and handling if one book is ordered; $1.00 if two to five are ordered. If six or more are ordered, postage is free.

NAME _____

ADDRESS _____

CITY_____ STATE_____ ZIP _____

More Fiction Bestsellers From Ace Books!

☐ **Mark Coffin, U.S.S.** Drury 51965-2 $2.75
Political fiction by the author of ADVISE AND CONSENT.

☐ **Quiet As A Nun** Fraser 69885-9 $1.95
Spine-tingling mystery by the bestselling author of MARY QUEEN OF SCOTS.

☐ **Reap The Harvest** Briggs 70850-1 $1.95
Saga of family pride and passions in 19th century England.

☐ **The Sweetman Curve** Masterton 79132-8 $2.25
Brilliant thriller in which a senator, a young man, an aging movie star and a scientist all are marked for death.

☐ **The Widow Of Ratchets** Brookes 88769-4 $2.75
A sensual, supernatural thriller of ancient rituals and primitive incestuous taboos.

Available wherever paperbacks are sold or use this coupon.

---

ace books, Book Mailing Service
P.O. Box 690, Rockville Centre, N.Y. 11571

Please send me the titles checked above. I enclose $_____. Include 75¢ for postage and handling if one book is ordered; $1.00 if two to five are ordered. If six or more are ordered, postage is free.

NAME _____

ADDRESS _____

CITY _____ STATE _____ ZIP _____

DON'T MISS THESE OTHER FICTION BESTSELLERS FROM ACE!

☐ **Borderline** Keener 07080-9 $2.50
A fast-paced novel of hijacks and hijinks!

☐ **Casino** Lynch 09229-2 $2.50
Blockbuster in the bestselling tradition of AIRPORT and HOTEL!

☐ **Charades** Kelrich 10261-1 $2.50
A yacht-filled marina is a private pleasure oasis for the rich and beautiful, where survival depends on how well they play the game.

☐ **Plague** Masterton 66761-9 $2.25
Millions succumb—others must wait to die.

☐ **Diary of a Nazi Lady** Freeman 14740-2 $2.50
Riveting confessions of a young woman's rise and fall in Nazi society.

Available wherever paperbacks are sold or use this coupon.

----

ace books, Book Mailing Service
P.O. Box 690, Rockville Centre, N.Y. 11571

Please send me the titles checked above. I enclose $_____. Include 75¢ for postage and handling if one book is ordered; $1.00 if two to five are ordered. If six or more are ordered, postage is free.

NAME _____

ADDRESS _____

CITY_____ STATE_____ ZIP _____

78E

HALL OF FAME SERIES
Historical Novels
Produced by LYLE KENYON ENGEL
Creator of THE KENT FAMILY CHRONICLES

☐ 13890-X	Daughter Of Eve	$1.95
☐ 20555-0	The Emperor's Ladies	1.95
☐ 24685-0	The Forest Lord	2.25
☐ 44520-9	The King's Messenger	2.25
☐ 18000-0	Each Bright River	2.25
☐ 53505-4	The Mohawk Ladder	2.25
☐ 10270-0	The Charlatan	2.25
☐ 73112-0	Roanoke Warrior	2.25
☐ 07810-9	Branded Bride	2.25
☐ 29732-3	The Golden Lyre	2.50
☐ 75885-1	Seneca Hostage	2.25

Available wherever paperbacks are sold or use this coupon.

---

 ace books, Book Mailing Service
P.O. Box 690, Rockville Centre, N.Y. 11571

Please send me the titles checked above. I enclose $_____. Include 75¢ for postage and handling if one book is ordered; $1.00 if two to five are ordered. If six or more are ordered, postage is free.

NAME _____

ADDRESS _____

CITY_____ STATE_____ ZIP _____

78F

Sure-Fire Entertainment From Ace Westerns

☐ 13907	The Day The Cowboys Quit	Kelton	$1.95
☐ 24907	Four From Gila Bend	Constiner	1.75
☐ 43721	The Keystone Kid	Roderus	1.95
☐ 51639	The Man From Colorado	Trimble	1.75
☐ 76065	Shadow Of A Star	Kelton	1.95
☐ 76901	The Skull Riders	Owen	1.95
☐ 88565	The White Man's Road	Capps	1.95
☐ 88851	The Wild Quarry	Lutz	1.95

Available wherever paperbacks are sold or use this coupon.

---

ace books, Book Mailing Service
P.O. Box 690, Rockville Centre, N.Y. 11571

Please send me the titles checked above. I enclose $_____. Include 75¢ for postage and handling if one book is ordered; $1.00 if two to five are ordered. If six or more are ordered, postage is free.

NAME _____

ADDRESS _____

CITY_____ STATE_____ ZIP _____

Romantic Suspense

Discover ACE's exciting new line of exotic romantic suspense novels by award-winning authors:

☐ **Call Of Glengarron** Buckingham 09102-4 $1.95
A frightened young woman stands between a devious killer and an innocent child.

☐ **Cloud Over Malverton** Buckingham 11222-6 $1.95
Drawn to two men by deadly desires, could Dulcie Royle distinguish between love and evil?

☐ **The House In The Woods** Lance 34382-1 $1.95
A much-needed home—or a mansion where sudden death becomes an ever-darkening plague?

☐ **The Lion Of Delos** Worboys 48425-5 $1.95
A search for her twin sister involves Virginia in a sinister plot of smuggling and murder.

☐ **Memory Of Megan** Lovell 52437-0 $1.95
In a picturesque Welsh village, Sheila Griffith encounters the ghost of a little girl.

☐ **Summerstorm** Cleaver 79088-7 $2.25
A spine-tingling chiller of murder, revenge—and madness.

☐ **The Wild Island** Fraser 88819-4 $2.25
Jemima Shore investigates the death of the man who was to be her host on a vacation.

Available wherever paperbacks are sold or use this coupon.

---

ace books, Book Mailing Service
P.O. Box 690, Rockville Centre, N.Y. 11571

Please send me the titles checked above. I enclose $_____. Include 75¢ for postage and handling if one book is ordered; $1.00 if two to five are ordered. If six or more are ordered, postage is free.

NAME _____

ADDRESS _____

CITY_____STATE_____ZIP _____

Anne Maybury Gothics

☐ **Falcon's Shadow** 22583-7 $2.25
The search for her true parents leads a young woman into a dangerous past.

☐ **Green Fire** 30284-X $2.25
The mysterious Orient held the terrifying secret of the "Green Fire."

☐ **The House Of Fand** 34408-9 $2.25
A young bride finds herself on a terrifying honeymoon of danger and deceit!

☐ **I Am Gabriella!** 35834-9 $2.25
Karen meets her long-lost cousin, only to have her vanish again—and reappear with a new identity!

☐ **Shadow Of A Stranger** 76024-4 $2.25
Tess senses that her husband is becoming a stranger to her. Then one day she overhears the words that are to change her life . . . if she lives long enough!

☐ **Someone Waiting** 77474-1 $2.25
A joyous reunion turns into a terrifying nightmare of evil —and murder.

Available wherever paperbacks are sold or use this coupon.

---

ace books, Book Mailing Service
P.O. Box 690, Rockville Centre, N.Y. 11571

Please send me the titles checked above. I enclose $_____. Include 75¢ for postage and handling if one book is ordered; $1.00 if two to five are ordered. If six or more are ordered, postage is free.

NAME _____

ADDRESS _____

CITY_____STATE_____ZIP _____

D. E. STEVENSON ROMANCES

"Finding a re-issued novel by D. E. Stevenson is like coming upon a Tiffany lamp in Woolworth's. It is not 'nostalgia'; it is the real thing."
—THE NEW YORK TIMES BOOK REVIEW

ENTER THE WORLD OF D. E. STEVENSON IN THESE DELIGHTFUL ROMANTIC NOVELS:

01965	**Amberwell**	$1.95
24088	**Fletchers End**	$1.95
48470	**Listening Valley**	$1.95
54725	**Music in the Hills**	$1.95
73325	**Rochester's Wife**	$1.95
76180	**Shoulder the Sky**	$1.95
86560	**Vittoria Cottage**	$1.95
95048	**Young Clementina**	$1.95

Available wherever paperbacks are sold or use this coupon

ACE BOOKS, Book Mailing Service
P.O. Box 690, Rockville Centre, N.Y. 11571

Please send me the titles checked above. I enclose $_____.
Include 75¢ for postage and handling if one book is ordered; $1.00 if two to five are ordered. If six or more are ordered, postage is free.

NAME_____

ADDRESS_____

CITY_____ STATE_____ ZIP_____